Henry Benjamin Wheatley, William Edward Mead, David William Nash, John Stuart Stuart Glennie

Merlin, the Early History of King Arthur

Vol. 2

Henry Benjamin Wheatley, William Edward Mead, David William Nash, John Stuart Stuart Glennie

Merlin, the Early History of King Arthur
Vol. 2

ISBN/EAN: 9783337348304

Printed in Europe, USA, Canada, Australia, Japan

Cover: Foto ©Andreas Hilbeck / pixelio.de

More available books at **www.hansebooks.com**

Merlin

or

The Early History of King Arthur

A PROSE ROMANCE

(ABOUT 1450–1460 A.D.).

EDITED FROM THE UNIQUE MS. IN THE UNIVERSITY LIBRARY, CA[...]

BY

HENRY B. WHEATLEY, F.S.A.

WITH AN INTRODUCTION CONTAINING

OUTLINES OF THE HISTORY OF THE L[...] OF MERLIN.

BY

WILLIAM EDWARD MEAD, Ph.D. (LIP[...]

ALSO,

ESSAYS ON MERLIN THE ENCHANTER AND MERLIN [...]
by D. W. NASH, F.S.A.; and ARTHURIAN LOCAL[...]
by J. S. STUART GLENNIE.

VOL. II.

LONDON:

PUBLISHT FOR THE EARLY ENGLISH [...]
BY KEGAN PAUL, TRENCH, TRÜBNER [...]

MDCCCXCIX.

I.

INTRODUCTION.

Of the great cycles of mediaeval romance none was more popular throughout Europe than the Arthurian cycle. From the first introduction of the Arthurian legends into French literature they caught the popular favour, and stimulated writers to an unwonted activity for a period embracing a well-rounded century, beginning toward the middle of the twelfth century and ending before the close of the thirteenth.[1]

In the history of the cycle we may distinguish with more or less accuracy three periods[2]—a period of preparation, a period of production, a period of translation and imitation. To the first period belongs the work of the Welsh bards and the pseudo-historic Latin chroniclers, Nennius and Geoffrey of Monmouth. To the second period belongs the work of the French romancers. To the third period belongs the work of translators and imitators in England and in the north and south of Europe.

In each of the romances the interest centres in a very small group of characters; so that what the story lacks in breadth it makes up in minuteness of detail. The earlier forms of the romances contain two figures that stand out most clearly—Arthur the King and Merlin the Enchanter. So great an interest attaches to these two names that we learn

---

[1] G. Paris, *Hist. Litt. de la France*, xxx. p. 1.

[2] We need scarcely remark that these periods overlap one another to some extent.

with some surprise that there is no adequate treatment in any language of the origin and development of the romances dealing with Arthur and Merlin. But there are two facts that have especially hindered the solution of the numerous problems involved in a history of the Arthurian romances: first, the vagueness and paucity of the earlier sources; and, secondly, the wide range of the later materials, which demand if they are to be satisfactorily treated an extensive and critical acquaintance with the French and Celtic literatures. Such an equipment is possessed by scarcely anyone who has thus far discussed the subject, and is expressly disclaimed by some of the most eminent investigators of portions of the Arthurian cycle.

Especial difficulties in the way of a demonstrable conclusion with regard both to the origin of the legend of Merlin and the development of the prose romance from earlier sources, meet the student at the beginning of his investigation and attend every step of his way. An initial difficulty appears in the chronology of the possible sources. We do not really know how much older any of the extant Welsh literature is than Geoffrey of Monmouth's *Historia Regum Britanniae* (1135–47), to say nothing of the ninth-century Nennius.[1] As Mr. Nutt well observes: " The study of Celtic tradition is only beginning to be placed upon a firm basis, and the stores of Celtic myth and legend are only beginning to be thrown open to the non-Celtic scholar." A little further on he adds that " as a whole Welsh literature is late, meagre, and has kept little that is archaic."[2] If this be true of Welsh literature as a whole, still more is it true of the portions available for our purpose. Even after including all the poems, spurious and genuine alike, that assume the existence of Myrddin, we have only a few lines with which to construct a portrait. But when we are

---

[1] But see pp. lxxxiv–cxii.   [2] *Studies on the Legend of the Holy Grail*, p. xiii.

compelled to reject much of this material as late and un-
trustworthy, we can with difficulty resist the feeling that it
is hardly worth while to thresh the old straw until we have
some new data upon which to base an opinion, or until Celtic
scholars agree somewhat more generally as to the meaning of
the scattered fragments that we do possess.

There is now a very general agreement with regard to the
chronological order and authorship of most of the Latin sources;
but their origin is still obscure, and the interpretation of them
by no means harmonious.

In the French romances we find more abundant material,
but we are left in almost hopeless confusion as to the exact
order in which the several French versions of the prose
romance were produced. The partial copying of the romance
by those who were at once copyists and authors, and the
retention of allusions to passages of the original romance—
passages afterwards dropped from most of the versions—would
be quite enough to throw us off the track. Then, too, romances
that in all probability were written later than the original
prose *Merlin* are by the aid of interpolated passages made to
seem earlier works than the *Merlin*. As to the authors of the
various prose versions of the *Merlin*, nothing is known and probably nothing ever will be known. We are obliged, therefore,
to content ourselves with a *perhaps* where certainty would be
most desirable. If we possessed all the Celtic literature that
ever existed, Welsh poems, Breton *lais*, all the Latin sources,
and all the French romances in prose and verse, with authentic
dates and the names of the authors, we should still have an
almost interminable task in attempting to follow out the
tangled threads of the romances. But, as already remarked,
these favourable conditions are lacking. The Welsh literature
—the only Celtic source that we can seriously consider—is
scanty and of not too convincing antiquity. The origin of

the Latin sources is doubtful; and even the Latin sources at most provide an explanation for only a portion of the romance. The French versions (with two or three exceptions) bear no date, and afford scarcely any guide to the chronology. The manuscripts are numerous and still unclassified as to age and generic relations. Only two manuscripts of the *Merlin*[1] have been published, unless we include the early printed editions of the fifteenth and sixteenth centuries. These old printed versions, it is needless to say, are exceedingly rare as well as uncritical, presenting a later, modernized text, and taking numerous liberties with the earlier versions.

These difficulties might be dwelt upon at greater length, but enough has been advanced to show the necessity of extreme caution in our assertions. Nothing final can be established with regard to the development of the romance until we possess a critical text, not only of the *Merlin*, but of all the other prose romances of the Arthurian cycle with which it is interwoven, and until a number of special researches have been made concerning the age of the manuscripts, the extent of the interpolated passages, and the meaning of the allusions to other romances. And even then we may seriously question whether a thoroughly consistent history of this or of any of the other romances of the Arthurian cycle can ever be written.

In taking leave of the questions that have occupied me so long, I regret to be obliged to confess that I have been able to add so little to what was already known. The account of the French manuscripts is new, and I trust will prove not altogether valueless. New also is a considerable part of the history of the legend in English literature, as well as other portions that need not be specified. Throughout the whole work I have

---

[1] The Huth MS. (*Soc. des Anc. Textes*) has been edited by G. Paris and J. Ulrich. Only pp. 1–107 of the English romance are here represented. Brit. Mus. MS., Add. 10,292 (cf. pp. cxl, clxvii, ccl), has been printed by H. Oskar Sommer, but without any investigation of the questions discussed in the following pages.

tried to be useful rather than original, and to present no theories unsupported by a large basis of facts. If once we can get a firm foundation of fact for the history of the romances, there will be abundant time for constructing theoretical explanations of the missing links.

I had originally intended to discuss the dialect and the grammatical forms of the *Merlin*, and to point out in detail the extent to which the structure of the sentences has been modified by the French original. But the fact that the entire romance as printed by the Early English Text Society had to be collated once more with the English manuscript, compelled me to defer that portion of the work, and to confine my attention almost wholly to literary questions. After the collations arrived I found that an adequate treatment of the language of the romance would unduly delay the publication of the other portion of the work. I have, therefore, attempted nothing more than to cite a few of the countless instances where French words have been transferred almost without change to the English translation.

It is perhaps unnecessary to remark that without the aid of the researches of Francisque Michel, Paulin Paris, Gaston Paris, H. L. D. Ward, Alfred Nutt, and others, a considerable part of this outline could not have been written. So much, too, remains yet to be done in the way of special investigation of the Arthurian romances, that I can at most regard this account as a mere passing contribution to the history of the *Merlin* legend. If this sketch can in any way serve to incite other scholars to a more careful study of French romance in its relations to our older English literature, I shall welcome the day when my own work is superseded.

It remains for me sincerely to thank those who have in any way aided in these researches. I owe much to the Director of the Bibliothèque de Ste. Geneviève, and the keepers of the MSS.

in the Bibliothèque de l'Arsenal and the Bibliothèque Nationale in Paris; to M. Paul Meyer, Director of the École des Chartes, who made several suggestions about the French MSS.; to Mr. H. L. D. Ward, of the Department of MSS. in the British Museum, who discussed with me the earlier forms of the legend and read some of the proof; to my colleague Professor L. Oscar Kuhns, who read a portion of the proof, and translated Professor Novati's note on Arthur's fight with the great cat of Lausanne; to Mr. E. G. B. Phillimore, who read the proofs of the chapter on the early forms of the legend, and supplied several valuable notes; and most of all to Dr. F. J. Furnivall, who furnished me while in Paris with several much needed books, and has since attended to numerous details that could not easily be superintended at a distance of three thousand miles.

I may add that the proofs of all the extracts from the French manuscripts have been read in Paris while I have been in America, so that the accuracy of the specimens is to be credited to the MS. reader rather than to me.

The greater portion of the present investigation was completed in 1892, and placed in the hands of the printers. Numerous delays, which need not be explained here, have hindered the appearance of the book until now. The supplementary notes on pp. ccl-ccliv take account of later work on various matters connected with the Merlin legend. But the most important part of the following discussion—the account of the MSS.—is quite independent of any work that has recently appeared.—W. E. M.

WESLEYAN UNIVERSITY,
 MIDDLETOWN, CONNECTICUT, U.S.A.
  July 2, 1897.

II.

BIBLIOGRAPHY.

1836–38. Wace.—Le Roman de Brut. Éd. par Le Roux de Lincy. 2 vols. Rouen. The same reprinted, Paris, 1838.

1836–48. Paris, P.—Les Manuscrits françois de la Bibliothèque du Roi. 7 vols. Paris.

1837. Galfridi de Monumenta Vita Merlini.—Vie de Merlin attribuée à Geoffroy de Monmouth. Ed. by Francisque Michel and Thomas Wright. Paris and London.

1838. Arthour and Merlin : A Metrical Romance. Now first edited from the Auchinleck MS., by William B. D. D. Turnbull. Edinburgh. Printed for the Abbotsford Club. (*Cf.* 1890.)

1838. Nennii Historia Britonum ad fidem codicum Manuscriptorum recensuit Josephus Stevenson. Lond.(Eng. Hist. Soc.). Contains critical Preface, pp. v-xxxii; *fac-similes* of four MSS.; text; index.

1841. Schulz, A.—An essay on the influence of Welsh tradition upon the literature of Germany, France, and Scandinavia. Translated from the German of Albert Schulz by W. Rees. Llandovery.

1841. Michel, F.—Le Roman du St. Graal.—Bordeaux. Printed from B. N. MS. 20,047. The concluding lines (3515–4018) contain the fragment of Robert de Borron's poem of Merlin.

1842. Grässe, J. G. Th.—Die grossen Sagenkreise des Mittelalters (2 Bd., 3 Abth., 1 Hälfte, of Lehrbuch einer allgem. Literär- geschichte, 1837–59). Leipzig und Dresden.

1842. San-Marte (Albert Schulz).—Die Arthussage und die Märchen des rothen Buchs von Hergest. Quedlinburg und Leipzig. [Bibl. d. gesammten deutschen Nationallit., Bd. II. Abth. II.]

1844. Galfredi Monumetensis Historia Britonum. Ed. by J. A. Giles. London.

1848. Six Old English Chronicles. Translated by J. A. Giles. Nennius, Geoffrey of Monmouth, etc. (Bohn's Antiq. Libr.) London.

1848. Ellis, G.—Specimens of Early English Metrical Romances, etc. New ed. Revised by J. O. Halliwell, London (Bohn's Antiq. Libr.). Contains an Analysis of *Arthour and Merlin*, etc. (Orig. ed. 3 vols., London, 1805).

1849. Guest, Lady Charlotte.—The *Mabinogion*, from the *Llyfr Coch o Hergest* and other ancient Welsh Manuscripts, with an English Translation and Notes. 3 vols. London.

1849. STEPHENS, Thos.—The Literature of the Kymry; being a critical Essay on the History of the Language and Literature of Wales. Llandovery.

1853. SAN-MARTE (A. Schulz).—Die Sagen von Merlin, etc. Halle.

1854. SAN-MARTE (A. Schulz).—Gottfried's von Monmouth Historia Regum Britanniæ, und Brut Tyssylio, altwälsche Chronik in deutscher Übersetzung. Halle. San-Marte reprinted Giles's text (cf. 1844), and added many notes.

1860. VILLEMARQUÉ, H. de la.—Les Romans de la Table Ronde et les contes des anciens Bretons, 3ème éd., considérablement modifiée. Paris (1st ed., 1842).

1862. VILLEMARQUÉ, H. de la.—Myrdhinn ou l'Enchanteur Merlin, son histoire, ses œuvres, son influence. Paris. [The Bibl. Nat. in Paris has corrected 1862 to 1861 by using a red stamp.]

1865-69. Merlin; or, The Early History of King Arthur: a Prose Romance (about 1450–1460), edited from the unique MS. in the University Library, Cambridge, by Henry B. Wheatley. With an Introduction [*Merlin the Enchanter and Merlin the Bard*], by D. W. Nash, Esq., F.S.A. Part I. London, 1865, E.E.T.S. Part II., 1867. Part III., 1869 (with an Essay by J. S. Stuart-Glennie, on *Arthurian Localities*).

1867. HALES, J. W., and Furnivall, F. J.—Bishop Percy's Folio MS., Vol. I. London.

1868-77. PARIS, P.—Les Romans de la Table Ronde, mis en nouveau langage, etc. Paris, 5 vols.: I. and II. 1868; III. 1872; IV. 1875; V. 1877.

1868. SKENE, W. F.—The Four Ancient Books of Wales, containing the Cymric poems attributed to the Bards of the Sixth Century. Edinburgh. 2 vols.

1871. SURTEES, S. F.—Merlin and Arthur [an essay printed privately for the E.E.T.S., Hertford].

1874. HUCHER, E.—Le Saint-Graal, ou le Joseph d'Arimathie, première branche des Romans de la Table Ronde, etc. 3 vols. Le Mans.

1879. The story of Merlin and Vivien, gathered from the British and Breton Chronicles and Poems, by E. G. R. (Of this book I know nothing. The place of publication is not given.)

1883. BORDERIE, A. de la.—L'Historia Britonum attribuée à Nennius et L'Historia Britannica avant Geoffroi de Monmouth. Paris and London.

1883. BORDERIE, A. de la.—L'Historien et le Prophète des Bretons, Gildas et Merlin. (Containing, *inter alia*, 'Les Véritables

Prophéties de Merlin,' a work also printed separately in the same year, and reviewed by Gaston Paris in *Romania*, Vol. XII.) [Études historiques bretonnes. Première série.] Paris. (Reprinted, 1884.)

1883. WARD, H. L. D.—Catalogue of Romances in the Department of MSS. in the British Museum. Vol. I. London.

1886. Merlin: Roman en prose du xiiie siècle, publié avec la mise en prose du poème de Merlin de Robert de Boron d'après le manuscrit appartenant à M. Alfred H. Huth, par Gaston Paris et Jacob Ulrich. 2 vols. Paris. (With Introduction by G. P.)

1888. DUNLOP, J. C.—History of Prose Fiction. Revised by Henry Wilson. New ed. London. 2 vols. Original ed.: "The History of Fiction, being a critical Account of the most celebrated Prose works of Fiction from the earliest Greek Romances to the Novels of the present Age." 3 vols. 1814; 2nd ed., London, 3 vols. 1816; 3rd ed., London 1845. Translated into German by F. Liebrecht. Berlin, 1851.

1888. PARIS, G.—La Littérature française au moyen-âge. Paris.

1888. PARIS, G.—Histoire Littéraire de la France; les versions en vers et l'origine des Romans de la Table Ronde. Vol. xxx. pp. 1–270. Paris. .

1888. NUTT, A.—Studies on the Legend of the Holy Grail, with especial reference to the hypothesis of its Celtic origin. London.

1889-91. SOMMER, H. O.—Le Morte Darthur, by Sir Thomas Malory. Vol. I. Text; Vol. II. Introduction, 1890; Vol. III. Studies on the Sources, 1891. London.

1890. Arthour and Merlin nach der Auchinleck-HS. Nebst zwei beilagen herausgegeben von Eugen Kölbing. Leipzig. [Altenglische Bibliothek. Bd. IV.]

1891. RHŶS, J.—Studies in the Arthurian Legend. Oxford, Clar. Press.

This list aims merely to indicate some of the more important books to be consulted by students wishing to test the conclusions reached in this investigation. The attempts to treat in detail the history of the Merlin legend are few, and, so far as English is concerned, are confined to a few essays and incidental discussions. Nor can all the books on the subject be used with entire confidence. Wright and Michel's introduction to the *Vita Merlini* contains much valuable matter, but some of the critical conclusions, notably those relating to the authorship of the *Vita Merlini*, are now almost universally abandoned. A similar criticism applies to much of San-Marte's work. Celtic scholarship has made great advances since his day, and rendered obsolete much of the Celtic discussion in his books. His Welsh texts are hopelessly corrupt, and the translations inaccurate. Villemarqué's work is marred by fantastic speculation, and the endeavour to make facts square with a preconceived theory. His *Myrddhin* may be safely recommended to anyone who prefers not to see the facts as they are. Mr. Nash's essay leaves untouched a large number of important questions, and settles the rest dogmatically. In the work of M. Paulin Paris we must recognize what is on the whole the best general account that we possess. He devoted many years of a long life to the study of the Arthurian romances and the MSS. in which they are contained. In treating the *Merlin*, he could not within his limits answer all the questions suggested, but he showed in a multitude of instances in what relation the *Merlin* stands to the other romances of the Arthurian cycle, and put all future investigators under lasting obligations. M. de la Borderie's work shows care and scholarship, but several of his conclusions are not convincing. Mr. H. L. D. Ward's *Catalogue of Romances* is critical and cautious. He discusses the Merlin legend only incidentally in enumerating the MSS. in the British Museum, but his remarks on Geoffrey of Monmouth are perhaps the best that have yet appeared. The introduction to the Huth *Merlin* by M. Gaston Paris—the foremost authority in France on the Arthurian romances—is avowedly a mere sketch, but no student of the Merlin legends can afford to leave it unread. Kölbing's introduction to the *Arthour and Merlin* aims chiefly at showing the relation of the verse romance to the other Merlin romances. Dr. Sommer points out in detail the relation of Malory's *Morte Darthur* to the prose *Merlin*. The slight inaccuracies in his account are chiefly due to insufficient study of the French MSS. of *Merlin*, and are pardonable enough in view of the vast field to be covered. Prof. Rhŷs transfers to cloud-land and to myth most of the characters of the Arthurian romances. His *Studies* are learned and ingenious, if not always convincing, and of great value in throwing light upon the Celtic side of the Arthurian cycle, but they touch only a few of the questions that most concern us here.[1]

---

[1] For additional bibliographical notes on the Arthurian romances, see the list of works prefixed to G. Paris's *Hist. Litt. de la France*, vol. xxx. ; the articles on *Celtic Lit.* and *Romance* in the *Encyc. Brit.*, 9th ed. ; Ward's *Catal. of Romances*, vol. i. ; Sommer's *Morte Darthur*, vol. iii. pp. 2-7 ; Gödeke's *Grundriss zur Geschichte der deutschen Dichtung*, 4 Bde., Dresden, 1859-81 ; and the works by Dunlop, Grässe, etc.

III.

THE STORY OF MERLIN.

CHAPTER I.

COUNCIL OF DEVILS AND BIRTH OF MERLIN.[1]

AFTER our Lord saved the world from hell (1) the fiends in wrath hold a great council to get back what they have lost (2), and resolve to cause the birth of a man who shall do their will. The fiend who suggests the plan hastens at once to the evil wife of a rich man with three daughters and a son (3), kills by her advice the cattle and horses, strangles the son, makes the woman hang herself, and so causes the rich man to die of grief (4). Of the three daughters, one is seduced and condemned to be buried alive (5), another becomes a common woman (7), while the eldest, after resisting various temptations for two years, is finally deceived one night by the devil in her sleep (10).

In her distress she goes to her spiritual adviser (10), who at first gives no great credence to her story (11), but afterwards saves her from being burned alive (13). The maiden is then shut up in a strong tower till her child is born (14), whom she calls Merlin (15). The boy frightens the women by his ugliness, and astonishes them with his knowledge (16). When the mother with her child is brought to trial (17), Merlin confounds the judge and delivers his mother (21). Then, as the story says, they go where they please; but Merlin and the hermit Blase discourse together, till finally Merlin asks Blase to make a book of what shall be told him (22). Blase consents, and when he is ready, Merlin begins to tell of the love of Jesus Christ, and of Joseph of Arimathia, and of Pierou, and the end of Joseph and his companions (23).

---

[1] As the only purpose of this analysis is to aid in following the text, I have borrowed the headings of the chapters given in the text, and in some cases the running analysis of the margin. Details that do not aid in the development of the story have been omitted. The numerals inclosed in parentheses refer to the page. The variety of forms of the names causes some embarrassment. I am not sure that all the forms I have adopted are best. Consistency is difficult where the original is variable.

CHAPTER II.

KING VORTIGER AND HIS TOWER.

MERLIN further tells Blase of the men who are coming to put him (Merlin) to death, and says that he will go with them, but when they have heard him speak they will not want to slay him (23). Now in the land of Britain was a Christian king named Constance, who had three sons, Moyne, Pendragon, and Uter. At the death of Constance Moyne becomes king, and Vortiger, a worldly-wise man, is made his steward (24). Vortiger wins the hearts of the people, and when Moyne is defeated in battle by the heathen, and afterwards slain by his angry barons, the steward receives the crown (25). At this Moyne's two brothers, Pendragon and Uter, are prudently taken to Gaul. Vortiger hypocritically assumes his own innocence, puts to death the murderers of Moyne (26), and when warred upon by their friends gains the victory over them. Then for fear of the sons of Constance he orders his workmen to build a mighty tower as a refuge (27). The work is begun, but as soon as the walls are a few fathoms high they fall in ruins. Vortiger therefore commands his wise men to tell why the tower does not stand (28). After much delay they agree to tell Vortiger that the blood of a child, seven years old, born without a father, must be put in the foundation of the tower. Of twelve messengers sent out (29), four chance to meet, and while passing through a field near a town where children are playing, they see Merlin, who strikes another boy with his staff (30). The child cries and weeps, and calls Merlin a " misbegotten wretch, and fatherless."

At the questions of the messengers Merlin laughs and says: " I am he that ye seek, and he that ye be sworn ye should slay, and bring my blood to King Vortiger." Then the boy takes the messengers to Blase and corrects the account that they render of their errand (31). After this Merlin sends Blase to Northumberland, and promises to visit him there, bringing materials for the Book of the Saint-Graal (32). Merlin then departs with the messengers. On the way

he sees a churl with a pair of strong shoes and leather to mend them
(33). Merlin laughs, for the fellow will die before reaching home.
A little farther on he laughs again at a man weeping over his dead
son, though the child is really the son of the priest (34). On coming
to Vortiger, Merlin tells why the messengers have sought him, and
says that the clerks have not told the truth (36). Then he confronts
the clerks, who are dreading to lose their lives, and explains why the
tower cannot stand (37). Under the tower is a great water, and
under the water two dragons, one red and the other white, and above
them two great flat stones. The labourers uncover the dragons, who
at once begin to fight (38), and continue till the white dragon burns
up the red. Merlin explains that King Vortiger is the red dragon,
and that his end is nigh (40).

CHAPTER III.

THE DEFEAT OF VORTIGER BY PENDRAGON AND UTER; THEIR SEARCH
AFTER MERLIN; THE BATTLE OF SALISBURY AND THE DEATH OF
PENDRAGON; AND THE FOUNDATION OF THE ROUND TABLE AT
CARDOELL, IN WALES.

MEANWHILE Pendragon and Uter are coming in fulfilment of
the prophecy. Merlin slips away to visit Blase (41), while Vortiger
is burnt in his castle by Pendragon (42), who becomes king. While
besieging Aungier, Pendragon hears of Merlin and sends in search
of him. Merlin, as usual, knows all that is going on, and appears
at first to the messengers as a beggar. They take him for the
Devil, because he knows all their plans (43). A little later Merlin
appears under several disguises to Pendragon himself, and announces
the death of Aungier at the hands of Uter (44). At length he
assumes his real form (45), and shortly after leaves the King in
order to return to Blase (46). Eleven days later Merlin comes
to court in the form of a boy messenger from Uter's mistress (47),
and afterwards appears in his real form. The two brothers ask
Merlin to abide with them, and to assist them at all times (48).
He agrees to help them when they have need, and so takes his
leave (49). Shortly afterwards Merlin tells the King how to take

a castle he is besieging, and how to rid his land of the Sarazins (50).
The plan is successful, and the land is freed.

Notwithstanding Merlin's services there is a baron at court who
envies him and resolves to prove the falsity of his divinations (51).
The baron feigns illness, disguises himself in three different ways,
and with each disguise asks Merlin what death he is to die. Merlin
replies that he will break his neck, that he will be hanged, and
that he will be drowned (52). The baron calls Merlin a fool, but
the prophecy is fulfilled to the letter. Then Merlin goes to Blase.
But the King and all who hear thereof say there is nowhere so wise
a man as Merlin, and they resolve to write down all that he says.
In this way is begun the Book of the Prophecies of Merlin (53).[1]

When Merlin returns to court, he advises the King to make a great
feast, and to prepare for the arrival of the Sarazins (54). He does so,
and goes out to meet the enemy at Salisbury (56). All the Sarazins
are killed, but Pendragon falls as Merlin has prophesied. Uter
buries the dead Christians, and is then crowned at Logres (57).
Merlin, who has meanwhile revisited Blase, returns to the King,
constructs a golden dragon as a rallying point in battle, and brings
over from Ireland the great stones of Stonehenge (58). Then
Merlin tells the King the story of the Grail and of the tables of
our Lord and of Joseph of Arimathia, and advises him to construct
at Cardoell in Wales a third table in the name of the Trinity (59).

CHAPTER IV.

THE FEASTS AT CARDOELL; UTER-PENDRAGON'S LOVE FOR YGERNE, AND HIS
WAR WITH HER HUSBAND THE DUKE OF TINTAGEL.

THE King follows the advice of Merlin, who selects fifty knights
to sit at the table, and leaves one place void (60). Then Merlin
departs and goes to Blase (61). Three years pass before he returns
to court; and the rumour spreads that Merlin is dead (62). At
Pentecost great feasts are held at Cardoell. A doubting knight sits

---

[1] This forms the third volume of the folio edition of the *Merlin*, Paris, 1498.
It has properly nothing to do with the romance, though it may be regarded as a
sort of continuation of the *Merlin*.

in the void place and sinks down like lead (63). Then Merlin comes
to court, and advises the King to hold all high feasts at Cardoell.
Among the guests are the Duke of Tintagel and his wife Ygerne (64).
The King is struck with her beauty, and sends jewels to all the
ladies at the feast. At Easter is another feast, and the King repeats
his gifts. When all the guests have departed, the King's anguish
increases because of his hopeless love for Ygerne. Soon he ordains
another feast (65), and sends by the hand of Bretel a golden cup to
Ygerne (67). The lady reddens with shame, but the Duke, thinking no
evil, orders her to receive it, and she obeys. After the feast the Duke
finds her weeping, and learns of the designs of the King (68). Full
of wrath he summons his men, and leaves the court without ceremony.
The King is angry in his turn, and demands the return of the Duke
(69), who refuses to come. Then the King invades the Duke's
country (70). While the King is carrying on the war, Merlin appears
as an old man (72), then as a blind cripple (73), and finally assumes
his real form (74). Merlin promises to help the King to enjoy
Ygerne on condition that the King will give him anything he may
ask for (75). Then Merlin transforms the King, Ulfin, and himself
into the semblance of the Duke, Jordan, and Bretel (76). They come
to the castle of Tintagel, where the King spends the night with
Ygerne, and in the morning they depart in haste (77). Merlin
demands the child which shall be born of Ygerne, and the King
consents. Then they ride on till they come to a river, where they
wash and resume their own forms. When the King meets his men
he learns of the death of the Duke, and says he is "right sorry" (78).

CHAPTER V.

MARRIAGE OF THE KING WITH YGERNE; BIRTH OF ARTHUR AND DEATH
OF THE KING.

At a council it is decided that the King shall marry Ygerne
(85). Her friends consent with tears of joy; and the King weds the
lady twenty days after he had lain by her in her chamber (86).
Months pass by, until one night the King asks Ygerne who is the father
of the child she is bearing. She tells him that a man had lain with

her in the semblance of the Duke. The King assures her that he is
the father, and gets her to promise to dispose of the child as he shall
ordain (87). In due time the child is born (90) and delivered to Antor,
a worthy knight whom Merlin designates (91). The child is the
famous Arthur.

For a long time Uter-Pendragon rules the land, till at length he
falls in a " great sickness of the gout in hands and feet." Then the
Danes rise against him. But by Merlin's advice the King is borne into
the battle in a litter, and wins the victory (94). After this he divides
his treasure, and after long illness dies and is buried with much pomp
(95). As the land is left without heir, the barons and prelates of the
church come together to take counsel who shall be their king.

CHAPTER VI.

ARTHUR MADE KING.

In their doubt all turn to Merlin, and ask him to seek out a man that
may govern the realm (96). Says Merlin : "Let us wait till Yule,
and pray to our Lord to send a rightful governor." They agree, and
assemble in the church at Yule (97). After "making meekly their
orisons to our Lord," they come out of the church, and see a great
stone in which is fixed an anvil, and through the anvil a sword (98).
The Archbishop explains that he who draws out the sword shall be
king, and lets all the lords try in their turn for eight days (100).
Last of all the boy Arthur comes to the stone and takes out the sword
as lightly as though nothing had held it (104). The barons are not
quite satisfied, and ask that the sword be left in the stone till Easter.
When they are all assembled at Easter, they ask for a further delay
till Pentecost (105), and so they wait till the Whitsuntide (106).
Then on Whitsun even the Archbishop makes Arthur knight. On the
morrow Arthur is arrayed in the royal vestments, and all go in
procession to the stone, from which the young king draws out the
sword. After he is consecrated and anointed, and the service is
ended, they all look for the stone, but it has vanished. Thus is Arthur
chosen king, and he holds the realm of Logres long in peace (107).

CHAPTER VII.

REVOLT OF THE BARONS; AND DEFEAT OF THE SEVEN KINGS BY ARTHUR.

AFTER the middle of August Arthur holds a great court, to which come the kings of the neighbouring realms with their knights—King Loth of Orcanye, and King Urien of Gorre, a young king much praised in arms; King Ventres of Garlot, the husband of one of Arthur's sisters; King Carados Brenbras, lord of the land of Strangore and one of the knights of the Round Table; King Aguysas of Scotland, a fresh young knight; and after him King Ydiers with four hundred knights. Arthur receives them with great honour, and loads them with rich gifts, but they disdain his presents, and refuse to have him as their lord (108). Arthur escapes from their hands; and fifteen days pass without event. Then Merlin enters the town, and is at once appealed to by the barons. Merlin tells them that the new king is more highly born than they, and advises them to send for Arthur, Ulfin, the counsellor of Uter-Pendragon, and Antor, the supposed father of Arthur (109). The barons consent. When the three arrive, the Archbishop begins to speak (110), but gives place to Merlin, who tells the whole story of the birth of Arthur (111), and of his being reared by Antor (112). The people are satisfied, but the barons declare that they will never have a bastard for king, and depart in great wrath to arm themselves (113). Merlin reasons with them, but to no purpose. Then he comforts Arthur (114), and advises him to help King Leodegan, who is at war with King Rion, the king of the Land of Giants and of the Land of Pastures (115). Arthur shall marry the daughter of King Leodegan. Before his departure, Arthur fills the fortresses with men and provisions, and makes ready against the barons. Merlin constructs a flaming dragon, sets it on a spear, and gives it to Kay to bear as a standard (116). When the battle begins Merlin casts his enchantments, and sets fire to the pavilions of the enemy. Then Arthur attacks them, and, though set upon by the seven kings all at once (118), he wins the victory, for neither horse nor man can endure against Arthur's sword Calibourne (120).

CHAPTER VIII.

THE MISSION OF ULFIN AND BRETEL TO KING BAN AND KING BORS.

AFTER Arthur's victory over the seven kings he returns to Cardoell. Then he provisions his castles, towns, and cities, and afterwards holds court at Logres, his chief city, 'that is now called London' (120). After dubbing three hundred knights he listens to the counsels of Merlin, who tells of his own wonderful birth and then of Arthur's. Queen Ygerne, says Merlin, had five daughters by the Duke of Tintagel, and two more by a previous husband. Of these maidens King Loth has married one; King Ventres of Garlot, another; King Urien, the third; Briadas, the fourth—now dead. The fifth is yet at school (121). King Loth has five sons, the eldest of whom is Gawein. King Ventres has a son named Galeshyn; and King Urien, a son named Ewein the Gaunt.

In Little Britain, continues Merlin, are two kings, who are brothers—Ban of Benoyk, and Bors of Gannes (122). They are warred upon by Claudas, an evil king, and ought to be allies of Arthur. After giving this advice Merlin says he will repair to forests and wildernesses, but will be at hand in case of need (123).

Arthur therefore sends Ulfin and Bretel to ask King Ban and King Bors to come to Logres at Hallowmass (124). The messengers find the two kings in the midst of war with Claudas, but in a great battle the brothers win the victory. Ulfin and Bretel ride direct to the castle of Trebes and ask for King Ban, but he is with his brother at Benoyk (125). As the messengers ride forth they are set upon by seven knights (126), but Ulfin and Bretel overcome them, and go their way (127). On their arrival at Benoyk (128), they announce their message (129) and receive the promise of the assistance of Ban and Bors (130).

CHAPTER IX.

THE VISIT OF KING BAN AND KING BORS TO ARTHUR; THE TOURNAMENT AT LOGRES.

WHILE the messengers are still absent Merlin tells Arthur that they are returning with the two kings, and advises him to receive them with honour (131). By Arthur's command the city of Logres is hung with cloths of silk, and the streets strewed with fine grass. Incense and myrrh are burned; and in the windows are many lights (132). Then the guests enter the minster in solemn procession, and return to the palace for the banquet (133). A grand tournament follows, in which Gifflet the son of Do, Lucas the butler, and Kay the steward, perform great deeds (135). When all is over the conversation turns upon the alliance; and Merlin tells the two kings that Arthur ought to be their lord (139).

CHAPTER X.

THE BATTLE BETWEEN ARTHUR AND THE REBEL KINGS AT BREDIGAN.

King Ban and King Bors follow Merlin's advice and do homage to Arthur (140). Merlin gives them wise counsel, and tells of Gonnore, daughter of King Leodegan of Carmelide, and of King Rion who is warring against him, and urges them to spend a year or two with Leodegan (141). They agree, and begin to make great preparations.

Meanwhile, the seven kings who had been defeated at Clarion prepare to take vengeance on Arthur and his enchanter Merlin. In great force they advance, accompanied by four other kings and a duke, and engage in battle with Arthur and his allies in the forest of Bredigan. Thousands are left dead on the field, but the rebels are beaten, and forced to flee for their lives (165). Merlin then departs from Arthur and goes to Blase (166).

CHAPTER XI.

THE DOINGS OF KING ARTHUR AFTER THE BATTLE, AND HIS DEPARTURE FOR TAMELIDE (CARMELIDE).

After the battle Arthur causes all the plunder to be put together in a heap, and then the three kings divide it among their followers (167). On the morrow, after they have feasted, they see a great churl coming through the meadows by the river with a bow in his hand. The fowls which he shoots he gives to King Arthur. No one knows the churl but Ulfin and Bretel (169), and they tell the King that it is Merlin.

Then there is joy in the King's heart, for he is sure that Merlin loves
him (170).

CHAPTER XII.

THE RETURN OF THE REBEL KINGS TO THEIR CITIES, AND THEIR ENCOUNTER WITH THE SAXONS.[1]

WHILE Arthur and his followers abide at Bredigan in "joy and
solace" till the Lenten season, the rebel kings return full of "sorrow
and heaviness" to their own cities. While on their way they enter
the city of Sorhant, a town of King Urien (171). Here they learn of
the ravages of the Saxons (172). In consternation they hold a council
and agree to help one another. They learn that Arthur and Ban and
Bors have gone to the help of Leodegan, but that the fortresses are
prepared for war (175). While the kings are making ready, and the
Saxons have already arrived, we may turn for a moment to Galeshyn,
son of King Ventres, and nephew to King Arthur (177). One day
Galeshyn questions his mother about her parents and her brother
Arthur. She tells him the whole story, and then he goes to his
chamber resolved to be one of Arthur's knights, and sends a messenger
to Gawein, asking to meet him at Newerk, the third day after Easter
(178).

The rest of the chapter relates the story of Arthur's amour with his
sister, Loth's wife, the fruit of which is Mordred (180); tells of Gawein
the son of Loth, and how he questions his mother about Arthur and
says that he will be made a knight only by Arthur (181-184); and
gives a further account of the movements of the Saxons.

CHAPTER XIII.

GAWEIN and his brothers Agravayn, Gaharet, and Gaheries, meet
Galeshyn at Newerk in Brochelonde (189). They engage in repeated
battles with the Saxons, but finally arrive at Logres (201).

---

[1] I shall make no excuse for abridging as much as possible the intolerably prolix
account of the wars with the Saxons. The story is in each case essentially the same.
Each king when attacked assembles his men and delivers battle. Hosts are killed,
and there is "battle grete and stour mortell," while Saxons are "slitte to the teth,"
but there is exceedingly little in the long-winded recital that can interest a modern
reader.

CHAPTER XIV.

EXPEDITION OF ARTHUR, BAN, AND BORS TO AID LEODEGAN AT TAMELIDE (CARMELIDE).

WHEN the three kings arrive at Tamelide Leodegan receives them well, though he does not know who they are (203). He accepts their proffered aid (204), and prepares his hosts to go out against the invaders of his land (205). As may be expected, Leodegan and his allies gain the victory (223). After the battles, the kings divide the spoil (224), and Leodegan gives a great feast. Gonnore, the daughter of the King, serves at table and wins the heart of Arthur (227), for of all the ladies in the Bloy Breteyne she is the wisest and the fairest and the best beloved except Helayn, the daughter of Pelles, who had the keeping of the Saint-Graal (229).

CHAPTER XV.

EXPLOITS OF THE REBEL KINGS AGAINST THE SAXONS.

THE Saxons sweep over the country with fire and sword and slay the inhabitants without pity, but the Britons resist like brave men and inflict terrible punishment upon the invaders. The battle still rages as the tale turns to speak of Merlin and Arthur (231–257).

CHAPTER XVI.

MERLIN'S JOURNEY TO LOGRES AND VISIT TO GAWAIN. ENCOUNTER BETWEEN THE CHILDREN AND ORIENX.

GREAT is the joy in the town of Toraise, in Tamelide, where Arthur is highly honoured by Leodegan and his daughter Gonnore (257). One day Merlin tells the three kings that he must return to Logres, but that he will be with them again before they have another battle (258). After visiting Blase (259), Merlin takes the form of an old man (261), and goes to Camelot, where Gawein and his brothers are awaiting the Saxons. The old man calls him a coward for not going to the help of Seigramore, the nephew of the Emperor of Constantinople, who has come to take arms of Arthur (263). Gawein leaps at once to horse and rides forth with four thousand men. When they draw near, they find Seigramore and the children giving fierce battle to the Saxons. The fresh warriors smite the Saxons (264), and Gawein unhorses Orienx their leader (265). Then they return with joy to Camelot (268), but the old man has departed, and they believe he has been slain (270).

CHAPTER XVII.

RAVAGES OF THE SAXONS IN THE LANDS OF KING CLARION AND DUKE ESCAM.

THE Saxons make another descent, but are driven back with great loss, and Duke Escam sends half of the plunder to King Clarion (271–277).

CHAPTER XVIII.

ADVENTURES OF GAWEIN AND HIS FELLOWS AT ARONDELL IN CORNWALL.

GAWEIN, with an army of thirty thousand men, sets out for Bredigan (278). When he arrives, a churl, who of course is Merlin, gives him letters purporting to be from the sons of Urien (279), asking his aid ; and Gawein at once leads out his men in six divisions (280). Meanwhile Ydiers and the two sons of Urien are routed by the Saxons. Then Gawein's company arrives, and after repeated fierce combats drives the Saxons from the field (294). Then comes an old man on horseback and says, "Gawein, return again and bring with thee all thy fellows into Arondell, for, lo! here come Saxons in great number, and we may not endure them" (294). Gawein follows his advice, and from the city walls looks down upon the Saxons (295). While Gawein and his followers are feasting that night, a knight in torn hauberk gallops up to the castle and cries out, "Who is the squire that dares follow me on an adventure?" Gawein answers, and asks which way he will go, but the knight replies vaguely, taunting him with cowardice.

Gawein says that though he die he will hold him company (297). With seven thousand men he sallies forth, and rides all day and night till he meets a squire on horseback with a child in a cradle. The squire says that he is fleeing with the child of King Loth, and that the mother is in the hands of the Saxons (298). Gawein gallops off, rescues his mother (299) and conducts her to Arondell and then to Logres (301). Do of Cardoell receives them with great honour, and tells Gawein that all the warnings have been given by Merlin, the best diviner that ever was or will be, and that Merlin had assumed the three forms under which Gawein had seen him (302).

CHAPTER XIX.

MERLIN'S MEETING WITH LEONCES. HIS ADVENTURES WITH NIMIANE.

AFTER Gawein has rescued his mother, the knight who brings him the news, and who is none other than Merlin, goes to Blase (303), relates all these things, prophesies darkly, and says that God has given him wit to accomplish the adventures of the Saint-Graal (304). After this, Merlin departs into the realm of Benoyk, and comes to Leonces, the Lord of Paerne (305). He warns the King of the coming war, and advises him to make ready against Claudas and Frolles. Merlin then leaves Leonces, and goes to see Nimiane, a maiden of great beauty, the daughter of Dionas (307). In the form of a fair young squire he meets her at a fountain in the forest (308), asks her who she is, and tells her that for her love he will show her wonderful things (309). Then he conjures up a company of knights and ladies, singing and dancing, and a fair orchard wherein is all manner of fruit and flowers (310). Nimiane asks him to teach her some of his skill, and promises him her love (311). At this Merlin tells her much, which she writes upon parchment; and then he joins the kings at Tamelide (312).

CHAPTER XX.

MEETING OF THE PRINCES AT LEICESTER ; RETURN OF MERLIN TO THE COURT OF LEODEGAN ; BETROTHAL OF ARTHUR AND GONNORE ; AND GREAT BATTLE WITH KING RION AND THE GIANTS.

WHEN the rebel princes meet at Leicester, they agree to go out against the Saxons, and choose for their camp the banks of the Severn (313).

Meanwhile Merlin has returned to Toraise, in Tamelide, and advises the three kings—Ban, Bors, and Arthur—to go to Leodegan and bid him prepare for battle with King Rion (314). They do not fathom his dark prophecies (315), but they follow his counsel. Leodegan is greatly troubled at the invasion of his land (318); but Merlin comforts him, and tells him that his guest is King Arthur, and that the young King desires Gonnore for his queen (319). With joy Leodegan leads in his daughter, richly clad, and presents her to Arthur. After a night of feasting the King arrays his army for the battle (321). Gonnore herself helps Arthur to put on his armour, and receives a kiss for her reward (323). Then the host rides forth, surprises the army of Rion, and so begins the battle (324). Everywhere are fierce single combats, but the result of the battle is doubtful till Arthur encounters Rion, and finally puts him to flight (342-345). Then the Christians chase the giants, and so win the victory (357). With great spoil they return to Toraise, and then, after two days, Arthur takes leave of Gonnore, and, accompanied by Merlin and twenty thousand soldiers, passes into Benoyk. Ban sends a message to his brother King Bors, asking him to come to Bredigan (360).

CHAPTER XXI.

ADVENTURES OF BAN AND GUYNEBANS; BORS' FIGHT WITH AMAUNT; MEETING OF THE CHILDREN WITH KING ARTHUR.

KING Ban and his brother Guynebans enter the Forest Perilous, and there see knights and ladies in a meadow closed about with woods (361). For the love of a maiden Guynebans "makes dances to enter," and teaches her the secret of his enchantments. When Ban departs, Guynebans accompanies him, but afterwards returns to his lady, and abides with her all his life (363).

In obedience to the message of King Ban, King Bors sets out for Bredigan (364), and on the way engages in battle with King Amaunt, whom he kills in single combat (368). Accompanied by the knights of the dead king, he rides on to Bredigan, and there presents them to Arthur, to whom they do homage (369). After three days they go into the forest in search of a great treasure of which Merlin has told them. When it is found they all set out for Logres. As they are riding forth, Gawein and his company learn that Arthur and his host are near, and go to meet him. Merlin knows of their coming, and makes Arthur and the two kings "alight under a fair tree" to await them (370).

Gawein and his followers kneel before King Arthur, who commands them to rise and promises to knight them. Again they kneel and thank him (372), while Gawein tells his name, and presents his companions. Arthur makes Gawein constable of his household (373), and then all ride forth to Logres. That night the children hold vigil in the minster, and on the morrow they are dubbed by Arthur with his good sword Calibourne (374). After the great court which Arthur holds for three days, Merlin tells the King to make ready his host to move at midnight against the invaders of Benoyk. Gawein follows the King's commands, and when he enters again, he learns all that he has owed to Merlin (376). As the host makes ready the ships at Dover, Merlin departs for Northumberland, and recounts to Blase all that has happened (378).

CHAPTER XXII.

BATTLE BEFORE THE CASTLE OF TREBES.

In the month of June Arthur and the two kings take ship and come to Rochelle. On the morrow at midday, Merlin joins them (379). Meanwhile the invaders gather about the castle of Trebes and besiege it on four sides (380). When Arthur and his host arrive there is a great battle, Merlin casts his enchantments and discomfits the enemy with flames of fire in the air, while Kay bears the dragon which vomits fire. Arthur and the two kings, and Gawein and the knights of the Round Table perform marvels, and finally chase the besiegers from the field (411).

CHAPTER XXIII.

THE DREAM OF THE WIFE OF KING BAN ; THE DREAM OF JULIUS CÆSAR, EMPEROR OF ROME.

ALL the night there is feasting in the castle of Trebes (412). When the two kings Ban and Bors have gone to rest with their wives, Queen Helayne, the wife of King Ban, has a wonderful dream, which she relates to him (413). After the first mass, to which they both go, King Ban falls asleep and hears a voice speaking to him (415). He and the Queen fear greatly, but do not at once ask Merlin the meaning of the dreams. Arthur meanwhile ravages the lands of Claudas, who afterwards, however, conquers the two kings, but is finally driven out of the land by Arthur (416). One day Ban asks Merlin the meaning of the dreams. Merlin explains a part, and then goes to Nimiane his love (417). Meanwhile Gawein ravages the lands of Claudas, returns to Benoyk ; and then with Arthur and the two kings takes ship at Rochelle to return to Carmelide (419).

Merlin leaves them and goes through the forests to Rome, where Julius Cæsar is Emperor (420). The Emperor has a strange dream which he keeps to himself, but he sits at meat pensive among his barons. Suddenly Merlin in the form of a great hart dashes into the palace, and falling on his knees before the Emperor says that a savage man will explain the dream (423). In a moment he has vanished. The Emperor in wrath promises his daughter to anyone who will bring the hart or the savage man. Now, the Emperor has a steward named Grisandol, who, though a maiden, has come to the court in the disguise of a squire. To her the hart appears in the forest, and shortly afterwards the savage man (424). He allows himself to be taken in his sleep (425) and brought before the Emperor (427), to whom he explains the dream (430), showing that the vision means that the Empress has twelve youths disguised as maidens, with whom she disports at pleasure, and advising the Emperor to marry Grisandol (433), who is a maiden in disguise. The Emperor follows the advice of the savage man, who, of course, is Merlin, and lives happily with his new wife, after burning the old one (437).

CHAPTER XXIV.

BATTLE BETWEEN THE TWELVE KINGS AND THE SAXONS BEFORE THE CITY OF CLARENCE.

MERLIN now goes to Blase and relates all that has happened. By this time the twelve princes and the duke are assembled to go out against the Saxons (438). A great battle is fought before the city,

but the Saxons are too strong for the Christians, and chase them from
the field (446). Then the Saxons burn and destroy whatever they
find, and so terrify the kings that they dare not venture again to fight
the invaders (447).

CHAPTER XXV.

ARTHUR'S MEETING WITH LEODEGAN; MARRIAGE OF ARTHUR AND GONNORE.

ARTHUR and his company arrive in Great Britain (447), and ride to
Carmelide, where Leodegan and Gonnore are awaiting them. The
marriage is arranged to take place at the end of a week (449). Meanwhile the rebel kings learn of the knighting of the sons of Loth,
Urien, and the others, of the arrival of Loth's wife at Logres, and of
Arthur's victories. Then they are sorry for their rebellion, but King
Loth plots to steal away Arthur's wife, and to put in her place
Gonnore, the step-daughter of Cleodalis,[1] with whose wife Leodegan
had long lived in adultery (451). Merlin learns of the plot and
prepares to frustrate it (452). When the day of the wedding arrives,
all march in solemn procession to the minster and witness the
ceremony (453). After meat the knights ride forth to a tournament
before the city. None can stand against Gawein, who ceases only
when Merlin tells him he has done enough (461). When the
tournament is over Arthur creates Gawein a knight of the Round
Table (462). After the feast that night the conspirators who come
with the false Gonnore, seize Queen Gonnore as she goes out into
the garden (463). But Bretel and Ulfin, who are there by Merlin's
advice, rescue her from their hands (464) and deliver her to Leodegan
(465). Then Arthur goes to his wife, " and there they lead merry
life together as they that well love" (466). On the following day
Leodegan banishes the false Gonnore. Her stepfather Cleodalis
takes her away, and leaves her in an abbey that stands in a wild
place, where she remains till Bertelak finds her (468).

[1] *Cf. Merlin*, chap. xiv. p. 213.

CHAPTER XXVI.

BANISHMENT OF BERTELAK ; FIGHT AND RECONCILIATION BETWEEN
ARTHUR AND LOTH; ARTHUR'S COURT AT LOGRES; VOWS OF THE
KNIGHTS OF THE ROUND TABLE AND THE QUEEN'S KNIGHTS ; THE
TOURNAMENT.

On account of a knight that Bertelak has killed he is banished
(470). He rides forth until he comes to the abbey in which Gonnore
is staying, and there abides a long time, plotting revenge on Leodegan
and Arthur. Eight days after his marriage, Arthur, with his Queen
and five hundred men at arms, sets out for Bredigan, having sent
Gawein to Logres to make ready the city for the court of August
(471). King Loth is lying in wait for Arthur, and attacks him with
seven hundred men (473). There is a fierce fight, but in the midst
of it Gawein comes up with four-score fellows, and Kay bearing the
banner (475). Gawein unhorses his father Loth, makes known who
he is, and compels Loth to do homage to Arthur (477). So all ride
together to Logres, where Arthur gives rich gifts to his followers
(479).

In the middle of August begins Arthur's court, where all the
knights and ladies appear in their most splendid robes (480). The
knights of the Round Table take a vow to aid any maiden in distress
(481). Then Gawein and his fellows, who pray to be the knights
of the Queen, vow that one of them shall go to the help of any
man or woman who appeals for assistance, and on returning shall
relate whatever adventures may befall him (483). When the vows
are made, the knights prepare for a grand tournament with five
hundred knights on each side (484). As may be expected, they
finish with a quarrel. Gawein lays about him with an apple-tree
club (493), then draws his sword and kills more than forty. Fighting
follows, and the tournament comes to an end. Finally, King Arthur
reproves Gawein (500), and brings about a reconciliation. The
knights of the Round Table, kneeling, beg forgiveness of Gawein, and
agree not to tourney again with the Queen's knights (502).

CHAPTER XXVII.

THE MISSION OF KING LOTH AND HIS FOUR SONS TO MAKE TRUCE WITH
THE REBEL KINGS; BATTLES WITH THE SAXONS.

AFTER the tournament is a great feast, where King Arthur and
King Ban, and King Bors, and King Loth, sit in state at the high
daïs (504). When the tables are removed the four kings withdraw
to a chamber by themselves. Then Loth begins to speak of the
Saxons, and says that with the help of the other princes, Arthur
could chase the heathen out of the land (505). All agree that Loth
is the best messenger to treat with the rebel kings, and he consents
to go to them with his four sons (506). At midnight they set out,
choosing the unfrequented paths, and so ride for eight days, having a
fight on the way with seven thousand Saxons. They kill a goodly
number of the heathen, and at nightfall arrive at a forester's house,
which is strongly fortified and encircled by deep ditches full of water,
and by great oaks and thick bushes (517). They are most hospitably
received, and pass the evening in talk till bedtime (519).

While they are asleep, we may speak a moment of King Pelles
of Lytenoys (520). This king has a fair son who wishes to be squire
to Gawein at the court of King Arthur. The King consents and sends
forth his son fully armed and accompanied by a single squire (521).
The two meet with the Saxons and defend themselves as best they
can, but they are in great straits, and there we will leave them for
a time (524).

In the morning King Loth and his sons ride forth, and as they pass
by a woodside they see the squire coming down the hill (528). He
tells them that his lord is in the hands of the Saxons, and begs their
help. They at once attack the Saxons (530) and rescue the King's
son (534); but Gaheries and Agravain quarrel, and Gawein has to
interfere (537). Then the company ride on towards Roestok, not
finding shelter till after midnight, when they arrive at a hermitage
(539). Suddenly Gawein and the King's son, whose name is Elizer,
hear the cries of a lady in distress. They sally forth and rescue her
and a knight (541). The lady is sister to the lady of Roestok, and

the knight is her cousin (543).   They now join King Loth, and all go together to the Castle of Roestok, where the lord receives them with joy (545) and agrees to deliver Loth's message to the King de Cent Chevaliers, bidding him come in September to Arestuell, in Scotland (546).   As they ride forth in the morning they find Duke Escam beset by ten thousand Saxons near Cambenyk (547), and at once put themselves at his service (548).   In the great battle which follows the Saxons are routed (553).   Then Duke Escam and his guests ride to Cambenyk (555).   When he learns of Loth's mission to the princes he agrees to accompany Loth to Arestuell. Loth asks the Duke to send messengers to the other princes that they also may come to Arestuell (557).   Loth and his company await for several days the other princes at Arestuell (558).   They arrive one after another, and hold a great council. Gawein asks them to consent to a truce, so as to fight the Saxons together.   The princes turn to Loth and learn with surprise that he has already done homage to Arthur (559).   They, however, agree finally to the truce, which they say they will keep only till they have driven out the Saxons. Then they depart, gather their people, and go to the plain of Salisbury (560).

CHAPTER XXVIII.

ADVENTURES OF SEIGRAMORE, GALASHYN, AND DODINELL; MERLIN'S VISITS
TO BLASE AND TO THE PRINCES; ARTHUR'S PREPARATIONS FOR THE
WAR.

ARTHUR and his knights are glad when they learn the result of Loth's mission. On the morning of the day after the news comes, three knights of Arthur's court, Seigramore, Galashyn, and Dodinell, rise early and go into the forest in search of adventures (561).   Three knights of the Round Table, Agravandain, Mynoras, and Monevall, disguise themselves and leave the court in the hope of meeting the first three knights and trying their mettle. When they arrive at a point where three roads separate, each chooses his way and rides off alone.

Meanwhile Merlin, who left Arthur in Carmelide,[1] goes to Blase and recounts all that has happened since Arthur's marriage—the

[1] *Cf.* p. 472.

story of the false Gonnore, of Gawein's exploits and the submission of King Loth to Arthur, of the great tournament, and of the truce to which the princes have agreed at Arestuell (562). Blase writes all this in his book; and then Merlin begins to prophesy darkly (563). After taking leave of Blase he goes into Little Britain, tells Leonces and Pharien to go with much people to the plain of Salisbury (564), then visits Nimiane (565) and various princes whom he bids also go to Salisbury, and finally arrives at Logres (566). All are rejoiced to see him, and listen eagerly to his account of the allies who are gathering at Salisbury. Then Merlin asks: "When I came thus suddenly upon you right now what did ye behold so intently down the meadows?" Says the King: "We looked on three knights that we saw enter into the forest." Merlin replies: "Wit it verily, that it be three knights of the Round Table in great need of succour" (567). At this the King sends without delay Sir Ewein, Gifflet, and Kay to their rescue (568). The knights have meanwhile met and fought with one another (569). Sir Ewein, Gifflet, and Kay arrive just as the knights are in the thick of the fight, and put an end to it (571). Then all ride together to court. In the talk which follows, Ban says that Sir Gawein is the best knight, and all agree that it is true (573).

After meat the King sends forth the messengers, summoning his people to Salisbury (574), and on the morrow the King and his men ride forth, with Kay bearing the great banner. Spies of the Saxons watch the host as it assembles at Salisbury, and guard against a surprise (575).

CHAPTER XXIX.

PARLIAMENT OF THE PRINCES AT SALISBURY; THEIR HOMAGE TO ARTHUR; AND DEFEAT OF THE SAXONS.

WHEN the princes have all arrived at Salisbury, Merlin tells Arthur that so many good knights shall not be assembled again till the father slay the son and the son the father. After another dark prophecy which Arthur does not understand Merlin sends the King to the barons (579). They tell him as he thanks them for their assistance that they are not his men, but that they are come to defend holy church. "God requite you," says Arthur, "in whose honour and reverence ye do it." "Amen," say the lords, "and be it so as ye will" (580).

When the twelve princes come to Loth's tent, they hold a stormy council, and all declare that they will not make peace with Arthur; but when the King enters with Ban and Bors and the strange princes, the twelve do him reverence, for he is a king anointed (581). After Arthur has addressed them, Loth says that they must follow the counsel of Merlin, and to this they agree (582). When the assembly is dismissed Elizer comes to Gawein, and kneeling before him prays to be made a knight. Gawein grants his request (583), and Arthur bestows upon him the richest arms in his coffers. On the morrow Elizer sits at the King's table between Ban and Bors, and in the jousting which follows wins much praise (584).

Next day the host rides forth from the plain of Salisbury, Merlin leading the way to the city of Clarence (585). Before the city of Garlot they meet with the Saxons, defeat them here (597) and at Clarence, and drive them into the sea (602).

CHAPTER XXX.

DEPARTURE OF BAN AND BORS, AND THEIR VISIT TO AGRAVADAIN.

JOYFUL over the victory, Arthur and his host with Ban and Bors and Loth and Gawein return to Camelot (603). Then by Merlin's advice Ban and Bors, accompanied by the magician, set out for their own country. As they ride toward the sea, they arrive before a great castle closed round with seven walls and defended by five high towers (604). They cross the surrounding marsh by the causeway, and sound an ivory horn which is hung by a silver chain to the branch of a pine-tree (605). Three times Ban blows the horn without result. Again he blows three times. Then in wrath Agravadain, the lord of the castle, demands what they want and who they are. On learning that their lord is King Arthur, he makes them welcome (606). In the castle are three maidens of great beauty, the fairest of whom is the daughter of Agravadain. Merlin by enchant-ment causes her and Ban to fall in love (607), and transforms himself into a young knight, who comes kneeling before King Ban (608). After supper they go to bed, and by the enchantment of Merlin, all sleep soundly except Ban and the maiden. Then Merlin comes and conducts her to King Ban (609), with whom she stays till day dawns. Merlin leads the maiden again to her bed, and breaks the enchantment (610). All arise, and the two kings prepare to depart, King Ban taking a tender leave of the maiden, and telling her that the son she has conceived will bring her joy and honour (611). With that they continue their journey till they come to Benoyk. Then Merlin leaves them and visits Nimiane his love and Blase his master, to whom he recounts all that has happened (612).

CHAPTER XXXI.

ARTHUR'S GREAT FEAST AT CAMELOT ; THE BATTLE BEFORE TORAISE ; AND THE DEFEAT OF KING RION.

AFTER the departure of the two kings, Arthur remains at Camelot, and there gives a magnificent feast (613). On the second day, when Arthur and Gonnore and the twelve kings with their queens are seated at the high daïs, there enters a blind harper, clad in samite and girt with a baldric of silk, garnished with gold and precious stones. On a silver harp, with golden strings, he harps a lay of Britain so sweetly that Kay, the steward, pauses to listen (615).

Suddenly a strange knight enters, and asks Kay which is the King Arthur. Then he delivers to the King a letter with which he has been entrusted by Rion (619). Arthur gives it to the Archbishop, who breaks the ten seals and reads. Rion, the lord of all the west, announces that he has conquered nine kings, and furred with their beards a mantle of red samite. Nothing is lacking but the tassels, and to furnish these Arthur is commanded to send his beard with all the skin (620). King Arthur is wroth, and dismisses the messenger with the declaration that King Rion shall never have his beard. The knight departs ; and then the harper harps merrily, and finally asks to bear the chief banner in the first battle (621). Arthur refuses because the minstrel is blind. Ban alone suspects that the harper is Merlin, and asks the King to grant the request. As they talk together, the harper disappears, but a moment later re-enters the hall in the form of a little naked child, and again asks the King to deliver to him the banner (622). Arthur laughs, and consents. The child goes out of the palace, and reappears in the form of Merlin. Then the enchanter passes over the sea to Pharien and Leonce, and returning, visits Urien and Loth, summoning them all to the help of King Arthur (623). In a few days the two hosts stand facing each other (624), Merlin bearing the banner that cast out fire and flame (625). All perform prodigies of valour. Finally, Arthur and Rion meet in single combat (628). Arthur cuts off the giant's head (630), and so wins the victory. King Rion's barons submit to Arthur, and return with the body of the dead king into their own land. King Arthur and his host go to Toraise till he is healed of his wounds. Then they ride to Camelot, where the queens are awaiting them, and after four days separate, each man going to his own country, and King Arthur to Logres. Merlin also takes leave of the King, uttering as he goes a mysterious prophecy (631).

CHAPTER XXXII.

MERLIN'S INTERPRETATION OF THE DREAM OF FLUALIS, AND HIS VISIT TO NIMIANE; THE KNIGHTING OF THE DWARF; THE EMBASSY FROM THE EMPEROR OF ROME; ARTHUR'S FIGHT WITH THE GIANT; THE BATTLE WITH THE ROMANS.

MERLIN passes with marvellous speed over land and sea, and comes to Flualis, King of Jerusalem, who has had a wonderful dream (632). Merlin, as usual, has no difficulty in explaining (633) what has puzzled all the wise men, and, without taking the King's daughter as his reward, he goes to Nimiane, who enchants him at her will (634). Merlin teaches her still more, and then departs and goes to Arthur at Logres, visiting Blase on the way in order to make his customary report (635). To this practice of his we owe this veracious chronicle. While King Arthur is sitting at the high daïs in the hall, there alights from a mule a lovely maiden with an ugly dwarf, whom she helps down from her saddle and brings before the King. With a courteous salute she asks him to grant her a request (635). As he promises, she asks Arthur to knight her companion. Everyone laughs (636), but Arthur keeps his word, attires the dwarf in splendid armour, and makes him knight (637). As the damsel and the dwarf leave the palace, Merlin tells the King that the dwarf is a prince, and it shall soon be known who the maiden is (638).

While they are yet speaking, twelve princes arrive, with a letter from Luce, the Emperor of Rome (639), summoning Arthur before him for having withheld the service and tribute which he should pay, and for having dared to rise against Rome; threatening him in case of refusal with the loss of all Britain and the lands that do him homage, and with imprisonment. There is uproar in the palace when the letter is read; and Arthur withdraws with his princes and barons to prepare a reply (640). In his address Arthur says: "They claim Britain for theirs, and I claim Rome for mine" (642). His princes and barons agree that they must declare war upon Rome. Arthur gives his reply to the twelve messengers, and dismisses them with rich gifts (643).

When they have gone, Merlin tells Arthur to gather his people quickly, and then departs to warn the other princes. They come at once with thousands of knights (643), take ship and join Ban and Bors at Gannes (644).

In the night Arthur dreams of a bear and a dragon who fight together on a mountain, and the dragon slays the bear. Merlin explains to the King when he awakes that the bear is a giant, whom the King shall slay. As they begin their march they hear of the giant who has seized a maiden, and taken her to Mount St. Michel. Arthur at once bids Kay and Bediver make ready to set out about midnight (645). As they come to the mountain they see two great fires shining brightly. On approaching one of the fires, Bediver sees an old woman weeping beside a tomb (646). To his questions she replies: "The niece of Hoell of Nauntes lies in this tomb, a victim to the lust of the giant, who now defiles me her nurse." As Bediver tells this to Arthur, the King goes softly against the giant with sword drawn, but the monster sees him coming, and meets him with a great club (648). They have

a stubborn fight, but Arthur finally kills him, and Bediver cuts off his
head (649). They then return to the host, Bediver bearing the head
at his saddle. The barons bless themselves when they see the head,
and praise God for the King's victory. After crossing the river Aube
their forces are increased by six thousand knights led by Ban and Bors.
Then the King fortifies a castle to which he may retreat if need be
(650), and sends Gawein, Seigramore, and Ewein with a message to the
Emperor bidding him return home. Gawein delivers it defiantly
(651), and smites off the head of a knight who says, "Britons
can well menace, but at their deeds they are but easy." Then
they leap to horse, striking down all who oppose them (652),
and finally join a party of six thousand men whom Arthur has
sent to their rescue (653). A battle follows in which the Romans
are routed, and many of them taken prisoners (654). The Emperor
is wroth at his defeat (656), and makes his people leap to horse,
and comes to Logres with all his host. Arthur sends his army to
the valley of Toraise, between Oston and Logres (658). In the
battle which follows the Romans are chased from the field, and
the Emperor Luce is slain. Arthur sends the body to Rome with
the message that this is the tribute which Britain pays and is ready
to pay again if more is required (664). Merlin then tells the King of
a great cat full of the devil, which lives by the Lake of Losane (665).

CHAPTER XXXIII.

ARTHUR'S FIGHT WITH THE GREAT CAT; THE SEARCH FOR MERLIN,
AND HIS IMPRISONMENT; THE TRANSFORMATION OF GAWAIN INTO
A DWARF, AND RETURN TO HIS PROPER FORM; THE BIRTH OF
LANCELOT.

SAYS Merlin: "It befell four years ago that a fisher came to the
Lake of Losane with his nets, and promised to give our Lord the
first fish he should take. Twice he broke his vow, and the third
time he drew out a little kitten as black as a coal. This he took
home with him to kill the rats and mice, and kept it till it strangled
him and his wife and his children, and after that fled to the mountains
beyond the lake. And now it slays whomsoever it meets" (665).

Arthur at once makes ready to kill the beast, and rides off with five companions. They go up the mountain, and the King approaches the cave where the cat is. Merlin whistles; the cat rushes out and attacks the King (666). The fight is terrible (667), but the King gains the victory, and carries off the cat's feet in triumph.

The story now turns to speak of Arthur's knights who are taking to France the Roman prisoners with whom they are charged. Claudas, the old enemy of Ban and Bors, attacks the knights as they pass a castle of his (669), but Leonces and Pharien come to the rescue with seven hundred knights. The Britons win the day, and conduct their prisoners to Benoyk as Arthur has commanded (670).

The story returns to the castle of Agravadain where Ban and Bors and Merlin were so hospitably entertained.[1] Fifteen days after their visit, a rich knight named Leriador comes to the lord of the castle and asks for his daughter in marriage. She tells her father that she is too young (671), and finally confesses that she is with child by King Ban. Returning to the knight, her father asks him to wait two years, and then he shall have his will. At this the knight departs in wrath, without replying a word. Shortly after he returns with eight hundred knights and squires and yeomen, and lays siege to the castle (672). Agravadain vanquishes one after another the knights who come to joust with him (673), and finally Leriador himself, who acknowledges himself conquered and goes home into his own country again (674). In due time the maiden is delivered of a son, who afterwards wins great renown (675).

Meanwhile the direful dream which Merlin has expounded to Flualis[2] goes into effect. The King is terrified, renounces his paganism, and turns Christian, with his family (675). His four daughters marry four princes, and are blessed with fifty-four children, some of whom. become knights of Arthur (676).

The story now returns to Arthur, who has routed the Romans and killed the great cat. After eight days of delay by the River Aube the King return with his army to Benoyk, and sends Gawein to destroy the castle of the March. This done, Gawein returns to

---

[1] *Cf.* chap. xxx.
[2] Chapter xxxii.

Benoyk (677).   King Arthur then receives a message that Leodegan
is dead, and on the morrow takes leave of Ban and Bors, never to
see them again.   On coming to Logres he comforts Queen Gonnore,
and abides there long time with his knights and with Merlin (678).
One day Merlin takes leave of the King and the Queen, sore weeping
that he shall never see them again, and goes to Blase, to whom
he recounts all that has happened.   Of the dwarf that Arthur has
knighted, Merlin says that he is a great gentleman and no dwarf by
nature.   After eight days Merlin takes leave of Blase and says:
"This is the last time that I shall speak with you, for from hence-
forth I shall sojourn with my love, and never shall I have power to
leave her, neither to come nor to go" (679).

Then he goes to Nimiane his love in the forest of Broceliande, and
teaches her all his craft (680).   She makes an enchantment of nine
circles repeated nine times while Merlin is sleeping in her lap.   And
it seems to Merlin that he is in a strong fortress from which he can
never come out.   But Nimiane goes and comes as she likes, and has
Merlin ever with her (681).   After Merlin has been gone seven weeks,
Arthur sends Gawein in search of him.   The knight sets out with
thirty others in a company.   At a cross beside a forest they divide into
three parties, and continue the search (682).   Meanwhile the maiden
and her dwarf, whom Arthur has dubbed, come to a forest.   This they
pass through, and, as they emerge, the damsel sees a knight coming
armed upon a steed.   The knight claims her for his love, but the dwarf
defends her, unhorses the knight (683), and makes him promise to go
to Arthur and recount his defeat (684).

And now the tale turns to Seigramoe rand his nine knights who are
searching for Merlin, but without success (687); then to Ewein and
his knights, who also vainly seek Merlin (688) but meet the maiden
and go to the assistance of the dwarf, who has overcome four knights
and sent them to Arthur; last of all the story speaks of Gawein,
who has separated from his knights and is continuing the search
alone (689).   As he is riding silently along, he meets a damsel
splendidly mounted, and passes her without a salute.   She stops her
palfrey and tells him that he is a vile knight so to pass her without
uttering a word.   He begs her forgiveness, but she tells him to

remember another time to salute a lady or a damsel. For his punishment he shall be like the first man he meets (690). A little later, Gawein meets the damsel and the dwarf, and salutes her courteously. After going a short distance the dwarf changes to his original form, and becomes a young knight of great beauty, while Gawein becomes a dwarf (691). In this guise, however, he continues the quest for Merlin, going all through the realm of Logres and at length to Little Britain. As he is riding through the forest at Broceliande, he hears Merlin speaking, but cannot see him (692). Merlin says that he can never come forth from the place where he is, but that she who has enchanted him can come and go as she likes (693). Merlin comforts Gawein by telling him that he shall soon regain his form, and so he departs glad and sorrowful. As he rides on his way he again meets the damsel whom he had passed without saluting (694). She pretends to be struggling with two knights and cries to Gawein for help. He smites the knights (695) till the damsel cries, " Enough, Sir Gawein, do no more." Then on his promise never to fail to salute a lady she restores him to his original form. He kneels and says that he is her knight for evermore. After taking leave of her he rides to Cardoell, arriving at the time appointed, on the same day as Ewein and Seigramore. Then he tells all his adventures and the fate of Merlin (697).

Whilst they are rejoicing over Gawein, the damsel enters leading the knight who was a dwarf. She presents him to King Arthur, who makes him a companion of the Round Table. Then the story says no more of Arthur and his company, and turns to Ban and Bors. After Arthur takes leave of the two brothers they dwell with joy in Benoyk. To Ban is born a son who is surnamed Lancelot, and to Bors a son named Lyonel, and another called Bohort. All three win great renown by their prowess (698). After the birth of Bohort, Bors falls sick at Gannes, deprived of the help of Ban, who is kept at home by his enemies and finally conquered by the Romans, till he has only the Castle of Trebes left, and this he loses afterwards by the falsity of his seneschal whom he brought up from childhood (699).

IV.

VARIOUS FORMS OF THE MERLIN LEGEND.

THE prose romance of *Merlin*, as we have it in our fifteenth-century English version, is a translation of a French prose romance which had assumed substantially its final shape early in the thirteenth century. The prose romance is but one of a variety of forms in which much of the material of the romance has been preserved. An enumeration of these forms will show to what extent this branch of the Arthurian legend entered into the literature of the Middle Ages and of later times. The arrangement according to language is not the best in all respects, for it groups together pieces produced under widely different conditions, but the practical convenience is considerable. In this account it will be desirable to give a list not only of the pieces that acquaint us with the history of Merlin, but also of such pieces as the prophecies and other works attributed to him. We can thus get at the outset a general view of the wide range of the legend, though we must reserve a number of questions relating to the Celtic, Latin, French, and English forms for more extended discussion in later sections. In such a sketch as this, exhaustive treatment is not attempted.

A.—Celtic.

1.—A few Welsh poems purporting to belong to the sixth century contain an obscure account of a bard of the name of Myrddin. This name is the exact phonetic equivalent of the Merlin of the romances. Upon the direct development of the romance these poems, as we shall see, had no influence; but possibly some traits of character in the Merlin of the romances are due to legends relating to Myrddin. The Breton ballads relating to Marzin have a very doubtful claim to antiquity. Some critics do not hesitate to pronounce them modern forgeries.[1]

2.—Of Geoffrey of Monmouth's *Historia Regum Britanniæ* there exist Welsh translations, once supposed to be originals.

3.—The Irish translation of Nennius' *Historia Britonum*, though made in the eleventh century, was entirely without influence on the development of the legend.

B.—Latin.

The Latin forms are for our purpose more important than the Celtic, even though the legend is essentially Celtic in many of its elements.

1.—Nennius, *Historia Britonum* (ninth century).

2.—Geoffrey of Monmouth, *Historia Regum Britanniæ* (1135-1147). This repeats with considerable additions the story told by Nennius, and adds a large number of prophecies.

3.—*Gesta Regum Britanniæ*.[2] This anonymous chronicle,[3] in more than 4500 Latin hexameters, follows closely Geoffrey of Monmouth's *Historia*, and only now and then reveals any individuality. The portion devoted to Merlin is included in verses 2052-3005.

4.—*Vita Merlini* (about 1148),[4] usually attributed to Geoffrey of Monmouth.

5.—*Prophecy of Merlin Silvester* (in ten lines), known as the *Prophecy of the Eagle to Edward the Confessor*. This and other [5] short prophecies attributed to Merlin Silvester, as well as the prophecy of Merlin Ambrose (Book VII. of Geoffrey's *Historia*), were often copied separately, and are preserved in

---

[1] *Cf.* i. 86.

[2] *Cf.* Ward, *Catal. of Romances*, i. pp. 274-277; Kölbing, *Altenglische Bibl.* iv. p. cvii. This poem was published by Francisque Michel, Cambridge, 1862.

[3] It is hardly necessary to cite the various Latin chronicles in prose, as they are discussed later.

[4] *Cf.* Ward, *Catal. of Romances*, i. pp. 278-288.

[5] *Cf. ibid.* i. pp. 320-324.

numerous manuscripts.[1] (Ward, *Catal. of Romances*, i. pp. 292-338.)

6.—Prophecy about Scotland, in thirty leonines.[2] (Ward, *Catal. of Romances*, i. p. 299.)

7.—San-Marte (*Sagen von Merlin*, pp. 265-267) printed a Latin prophecy in sixty lines of halting dactylic hexameters (published also by Muratorius, *Rerum Italicarum Scriptores*, t. viii. pp. 1177-1178) attributed to Merlin, and belonging to the time of the Emperor Frederick II. This was one of a number of political prophecies directed against the Popes.[3]

8.—San-Marte also printed [4] twelve four-line stanzas of a Latin imitation of a Welsh war song, based largely on Geoffrey's *Historia*.

9.—A Latin version of the larger prose romance of *Merlin* was *printed* [5] in Venice in 1554.

10.—Besides the pieces above mentioned, the following are attributed by Bale and somewhat later by Fabricius to Merlin Ambrose[6]: 1. *Super arce Vortigerni*; 2. *Epitaphium sexti Regis*; 3. *Contra Vortigerni Magos*; 4. *Super quodam Cometa*.

As for the Latin commentary on the prophecies of Merlin

---

[1] The Prophecies possess interest for our immediate purpose only in so far as they show how powerfully the name of Merlin continued to influence the writers of successive generations, but I cannot discuss the questions which these singular productions suggest. In the works on Merlin by Francisque Michel and Villemarqué will be found enough to satisfy a reasonable curiosity in the matter. The Prophecies are referred to with more or less respect by a score of chroniclers, among whom we meet such names as Giraldus Cambrensis, Orderic Vital, Matthew Paris, Roger of Hoveden, William of Newburgh, Froissart, John Fordun, and others. The French *Prophéties de Merlin* are said to have been translated from the Latin. *Cf.* Ward, *Catal. of Romances*, i. pp. 371-373; P. Paris, *Les Romans de la Table Ronde*, i. p. 58.

[2] Printed in the Rolls ed. of Pierre de Langtoft's *Chronicle*, ii. pp. 450, 451. The MS. of the prophecy belongs to the 13th or the 14th century.

[3] For a further account of the influence of Merlin in Italy see Ward, *Catal. of Romances*, i. p. 372, where additional bibliographical references are given.

[4] *Sagen von Merlin*, pp. 207-209.

[5] Geoffrey's Latin Prophecies were first printed in Paris in 1508, and reprinted in 1517.

[6] *Cf.* F. Michel, *Vita Merlini*, p. lv.; Michel also calls attention to a fragment of four lines preserved by John Price in *Hist. Brit. Defensio*, p. 121.

by Alanus de Insulis,[1] and other Latin illustrative writings, they lie outside of our limits.

C.—French.

1.—The first appearance in French literature of the Merlin legend is in translations of Geoffrey of Monmouth's *Historia*.[2] Of these the earliest version was that of Geoffrey Gaimar, which has entirely disappeared. Most popular was the version by Wace, whose *Brut* appeared in 1155. Several other versions, some of which are preserved in fragmentary form, attest the popularity of the lively *Historia* of Geoffrey of Monmouth. The so-called *Münchener Brut* is an anonymous fragment of which only the beginning is preserved.[3] Another anonymous version is the *Chanson de Brut*, preserved in a thirteenth-century manuscript. This is in five fragments, and is "written as a chanson de geste, in monorhymed tirades of alexandrines. There are 3360 lines remaining."[4] In a fourteenth-century manuscript is a poem of 258 lines translated from Geoffrey. It begins with the story of Vortiger, and breaks off at the point where Merlin is preparing to explain the meaning of the fight of the dragons.[5] Still another version is found in the first part of the Anglo-French Chronicle of Pierre de Langtoft, which, however, had little or no influence on the development of the legend. Pierre slightly condenses Geoffrey's *Historia* and adds some minor particulars.[6]

[1] PROPHETIA anglicana, sive vaticinia et praedicationes Merlini Ambrosii, ex incubo (ut hominum fama est) ante annos 1200 circiter in Anglia nati, a Galfredo Monumetensi latine conversa, una cum vii. libris explanationum in eandem prophetiam Alani de Insulis. Francofurti-ad-Mœnum, 1603. Small 8vo.

[2] To avoid repetition I reserve further discussion for a later section.

[3] Edited by C. Hoffmann and K. Völlmöller, Halle, 1877. Still another fragmentary version in rhyming octosyllabic verse exists in the form of *tirades* with assonances. *Cf.* Kreyssig, *Gesch. der franz. Lit.* i. 155.

[4] Ward, *Catal. of Romances*, i. 272.

[5] *Ibid.* i. 384. See also Villemarqué, *Myrdhinn*, pp. 422-431; Kölbing, *Altenglische Bibl.* iv. pp. cviii., cix.

[6] Langtoft lived during the reign of Edward I., and probably died in the reign of Edward II. *Cf.* T. Wright's ed. of L.'s Chronicle (Rolls Series), vol. i. p. xii. Lond. 1866.

2.—Robert de Borron's poem of *Merlin* belongs to the end of the twelfth century. Of this has been preserved only a fragment of 504 lines. The *Merlin* was intended as a continuation of the poem of *Joseph d'Arimathie.*

3.—At the end of the twelfth or the beginning of the thirteenth century, Robert de Borron's poem of *Merlin* was reduced to prose. This is the first branch of the romance of *Merlin*, and is the source of chapters i.-vi. in the English version.

4.—Several thirteenth and fourteenth century continuations of the short prose *Merlin* exist, but they have never been fully described.[1] Paulin Paris called the ordinary continuation the *Book of Arthur.*

5.—Prophéties de Merlin.[2] Translated from the Latin by " Mestre Richart d'Yrlande," at the command of the Emperor Frederick II. " These prophecies are quite unconnected with those in Geoffrey of Monmouth's *Historia*; and such as are not purely romantic relate more to the affairs of Italy and of the Holy Land than to those of France or Germany, and hardly at all to those of England."[3]

6.—We have in a manuscript of the thirteenth or fourteenth century an Anglo-French "prophecy of Merlin about the six kings that are to follow King John, who are here called the Lamb of Winchester, the Dragon of Mercy, the Goat of Carnarvon, the Boar of Windsor, the Ass with Leaden Feet, and the Accursed Mole."[4]

7.—In 1455 Geoffrey of Monmouth's *Historia* was translated into French prose by Jehan Wauquelin of Mons.[5]

---

[1] These versions I have discussed in treating of the manuscripts.

[2] In Brit. Mus. Add. MS. 25,434; end of thirteenth century. Imperfect at beginning and end.

[3] Ward, *Catal. of Romances*, i. 371–373.

[4] *Ibid.* i. 299.

[5] *Ibid.* i. 251–253.

8. — The first printed edition of the large prose *Merlin*
appeared in 1498, and was followed by numerous others. [1]

[1] I give the editions in the order of their appearance :—

1498. The Romance and the Prophecies, printed for Anthoine Verart, Paris,
The copy in the Bibliothèque Nationale is a small folio in black letter, containing
three volumes bound in one, the first two containing the Romance, and the third the
Prophecies. These last are, however, as Ward remarks, printed " in a strange state
of disorder." This is the rarest and choicest of the printed editions, and it has on
the title-page a large illustration of the General Resurrection, and at irregular
intervals woodcuts of a battle (seventeen times repeated), and of Christ asleep in the
ship (on last page). The colophon at the end of voL iii. gives the date : " Cy
finissent les prophecies Merlin nouuellement imprime a paris lan mil. iiii. cccc. iiii. xx.
xviii. pour Anthoine Verart demourant devāt nostre Dame De Paris a lymage saint
Jehan leuangeliste/ ou au palays au premier pillier deuant la chappelle ou lenchãte la
messe de messeigneurs de parlement." The same publisher brought out another
edition the same year. The forms of the letters prove that the second edition was
reprinted from the type used in the first edition, but reset.

1505 (2nd September). The Romance and the Prophecies were printed for
Michel le Noir at Paris, in three small quarto volumes, black letter.

1507. The same publisher brought out the same work in two quarto volumes,
black letter.[a]

1526 (June). The Prophecies were printed at Paris for Philippe le Noir in a
small quarto of two columns, black letter.

1526. In this same year the Romance and the Prophecies appeared in three
octavo volumes, black letter.

A quarto edition in black letter of the Prophecies, without date, but assigned
to the year 1526, was printed at Rouen for Jehan Mace of Rouen, Michel Angier
of Caen, and Richard Mace of Rouen. Brunet mentions a quarto edition in
black letter of the second volume of Merlin by the same publishers, who doubtless
also printed the first volume, and assigns the two to 1526. Another quarto edition
in black letter, also without date, appeared in three volumes, " Nouuellement
imprimes a Paris, pour le veufe feu Jehan Trepperel et Jehan Jeannot."

1528 (24th December). The Romance and the Prophecies were again printed for
Philippe le Noir in three small quartos, black letter, two columns.[b]

1535. Another edition of Merlin was printed by Jehan Mace from a fifteenth-
century manuscript. This was the last of the old editions.

1797. In this year appeared in Paris, in three volumes, 16mo., *Le Roman de Merlin
l'enchanteur, remis en bon français, et dans un meilleur ordre*, par S. Boulard.
Villemarqué gave a short analysis of the romance in his *Myrdhinn ou l'enchanteur
Merlin*,[c] and Paulin Paris a much longer and better one in the second volume of the
Romans de la Table Ronde.[d]

[a] Sommer (*Morte Darthur*, iii. 7, note) remarks that an edition appeared at Paris
in 1510 (?) and another at Rouen in 1520 (?). As his dates are conjectural, I do not
know whether he has in mind the editions I have cited under the year 1526.

[b] But *cf*. F. Michel, *Vita Merlini*, p. lxviii., and Brunet, *Manuel du Libraire*,
art. *Merlin*.

[c] Printed in Paris in 1861, and dated ahead so as to appear new in 1862.

[d] Paris, 1868.

Allusions to Merlin are not infrequent in French literature.[1] Thus Chrestien de Troyes in the *Roman d'Erec et Enide*[2] has :

> " En mi la cort sor .i. tapit
> Ot .xxx. muis d'esterlins blans,
> Car lors avoient à cel tens
> Corréu dès le tens Merlin
> Par toute Bretaigne esterlin."

Merlin is also mentioned in Gautier's continuation of Chrestien's *Conte du Graal*,[3] as well as in the prose *Queste du Saint-Graal.*

Guillaume le Clerc, a thirteenth-century *trourère*, in *Li Romans des Aventures Fergus* refers to

> " Noquestan
> U Merlin's sejourna maint an."[4]

In *Claris et Laris* Merlin is mentioned by name (l. 22,931), and elsewhere referred to as he, " Qui tout set, tout fet, et tout oit "; and he is called the " sages Mellins " in the *Roman de l'Escoufle*.[5] Merlin's exploit of bringing over the great stones to Salisbury Plain is touched upon in the *Roman du Hen*. The author of the *Conte du Perroquet* makes some use of the story of Merlin and alludes to the Prophecies, though he makes but slight reference to other Arthurian literature.[6] The enchanter plays a large part in *Les grandes et inestimables Cronicques du*

Strangely enough there does not exist a single modern edition of this famous work. The first part, which extends to the coronation of Arthur, is included in the edition of the Huth MS. published (1886) for the *Société des Anciens Textes Français* ; but the manuscript is a poor one, and the first part contains only about one-seventh of the entire romance. A proposal to print in *fac-simile* a 14th century vellum MS. (Brit. Mus. Add. 10,292) of the ordinary *Merlin* was made by Dr. H. Oskar Sommer in the *Academy* (1891), and in vol. iii. of his *Studies on the Sources of* Malory's *Morte Darthur* (London, 1891), but nothing has appeared as yet.

[1] For several of these allusions I am indebted to Michel's *Vita Merlini*, pp. lxxxiii.–lxxxv.

[2] B. N. MS. fr. 7498⁴, last leaf but one, col. 2, last verse.

[3] *Cf.* Nutt's *Studies*, p. 18, p. 43.

[4] B. N. MS. fr. 7595, fol. 442*b*, col. 1.

[5] *Cf.* G. Paris, *Hist. Litt. de la France*, xxx. p. 132 ; F. Michel, *Vita Merl.*, p. lxxxv.

[6] *Hist. Litt.* xxx. p. 104.

grant et enorme geant Gargantua (1532), in which both Merlin
and Arthur are introduced, but no longer in a serious mood.
The spirit of burlesque which gives such a flavour to *Don
Quixote* had long before begun to find ridiculous the old
romances with their interminable wonders.[1]

Since the close of the mediæval period Merlin has suffered
neglect in France. Except for Jacques Vergier's (1657–1720)
versified tale of *l'Anneau de Merlin*[2] and Edgar Quinet's
strange prose poem of *Merlin l'Enchanteur*[3] (1860), there is
little or nothing in modern French literature to remind us of
the place that the great enchanter held in the literature and
the thought of the Middle Ages. The group of Merlin legends
recently put together by Méras is a mere collection of exercises
for teaching boys French syntax![4]

D.—Provençal.

From allusions to Merlin in the *Cabra juglar* of Giraud de
Cabrareira, as well as in the *Guordo* of Bertrand de Pâris de
Roerge, Francisque Michel inferred the existence of the romance
of *Merlin* in Provençal.[5] This opinion was justified by the
publication in 1883 of the fragments of a Provençal translation
of the romance of *Merlin*.[6] But, as Chabaneau remarks (p. 4):
"Allusions to Merlin are very rare in Provençal poetry.

---

[1] *Cf. e.g.* Chaucer's *Rime of Sire Thopas.*

[2] See his poems, Paris, 1750, 2 vols., 12mo.

[3] Paris, 1860, 2 vols., 8vo.

[4] Merlin l'Enchanteur, Légende. Exercices sur la Syntaxe pratique de la Langue française par B. Méras. New York and Boston, 1888, 94 pp., 12mo.

[5] Cf. *Vita Merlini*, Introd. pp. lxix.-lxxi.

[6] *Fragments d'une traduction provençale du roman de Merlin*, publiés par Camille Chabaneau, Paris, 1883. 8vo. Pièce. The MS. was found in the archives of the Commune of Epine—a "double leaf of parchment detached toward the end of the sixteenth century or later from a handsome thirteenth-century MS., which contained a translation of the French romance of *Merlin*." F. 1 contains the amour of Uter with Ygerne, from near the beginning of the incident to the point where Uter prepares to besiege the Duke of Tintagel; f. 2 tells the story from the death of Uter to the episode of the sword enclosed in the anvil. *Cf.* Chabaneau, pp. 3, 4. The fragments differ slightly from the version of B. N., MS. fr. 747.

Birch-Hirschfeld (*Ueber die den provenzalischen Troubadours bekannten epischen Stoffe*, p. 55) can find but three. I do not remember to have seen others."

E.—Italian.

The earliest Italian translation of the French romance of *Merlin* is the *Historia di Merlino*, made in 1379, and printed in a folio edition at Venice in 1480.[1] The Life and Prophecies were printed in a quarto volume at Florence in 1495. Two other quarto editions appeared at Venice, one in 1507 and the other in 1529; and two octavo editions, one in 1539 and one in 1554.[2] The popularity of Merlin is further shown by allusions in Dante's *Divina Commedia*, in Ariosto's *Orlando Furioso* (c. 3 and c. 26),[3] in Bojardo's *Orlando Innamorato* (1. 3), and in the works of writers of lesser fame.

F.—Spanish.

The romance of Merlin was early translated into Spanish, and printed at Burgos in 1498, under the title : *El baladro del sabio Merlin cō sus profecias.* Only the first nineteen chapters, which tell the story up to the coronation of Arthur, have the same subject-matter as the *Merlin* of Robert de Borron. After that point this version agrees in many particulars with the continuation found in the Huth MS.,[4] but affords among other rarities a translation of at least a part of the lost *Conte du brait.* In 1500 appeared a folio edition of *Merlin y demanda del Santo Grial*, printed at Seville. Merlin's celebrity in the Iberian peninsula is attested by allusions scattered

---

[1] Reprinted at Bologna, 1884, 8vo. *Cf.* criticism by Kölbing, *Altenglische Bibliothek*, iv. p. cxi. *Cf.* also, *ibid.* p. cxxix.

[2] *Cf.* Michel, *Vita Merlini*, Introd. p. lxviii.; Brunet, *Manuel du Libraire*, art. *Merlin.*

[3] In the third canto of O. F. the poet tells of the grotto that Badamante visits, where Merlin is buried, and where he predicts to his visitor the coming glories of the house of Este.

[4] Published by G. Paris and J. Ulrich for the *Soc. des. Anc. Textes Français.* See *Introd.* pp. lxxii.-xci.

through the older Spanish literature, some of which are found in the *Historia de la Reyna Sebilla*,[1] in *Don Quixote*, and the famous romance of *Don Belianus*.

G.—Portuguese.

The Portuguese *Merlin* contains, according to M. Gaston Paris, "the third part of the compilation of which the Huth MS. has preserved to us the first two."[2]

H.—Netherland.

In the year 1261, the poet Jacob van Maerlant translated the *Graal* and the prose *Merlin* under the title : *Historie van den Grale* and *Merlijns Boeck* (*circâ* 10,400 ll.).   He added among other things a trial of Satan.   His work was continued by Lodewijc van Velthem (1326) in his *Boec van Coninc Artur*, which is a close translation of the *Licre du roi Artus* (25,800 ll.).[3]

I.—German.

Some of the romances of the Round Table, as, for instance, the Holy Grail, found an early welcome in Germany, but it was not till 1478 that Ulrich Fürterer, a poet of the court of Albrecht IV., duke of Bavaria, wrote a long verse romance " on the knights of the Round Table and the Holy Grail, in which he recounted also the history of Merlin."[4]   Nothing else worthy of mention[5] appeared till 1804, when Friedrich von Schlegel translated from an early edition (1528) a considerable part of the French prose romance.   Scarcely anything is omitted up to the point (p. 256) where Arthur goes to the assistance of Leodegau.

---

[1] Michel notes an allusion in this romance to an adventure of Merlin not found in the French prose *Merlin*.   *Vita Merl:*, Introd. pp. lxxxviii.-xc.

[2] *Romania*, xvi. p. 585.

[3] Paul, *Grundriss d. germ. Philologie*, B. II. pp. 458, 459.   *Cf.* also *Germania*, xix. p. 300 ; Kölbing, *Altenglische Bibl.* iv. p. cxi., p. cxxviii.   The work of the two poets has been published by J. van Vloten under the title : *Jacob van Maerlant's Merlijn*, Leiden, 1880-1882.

[4] Michel, *Vita Merl.*, Introd. p. lxxii.   For the poem itself see *Altdeutsche Gedichte*, ii. p. 263 ; *Der Theure Moerlin* (F. F. Hofstäter).

[5] The play entitled *Die Geburt des Merlin* is a translation of William Rowley's *Birth of Merlin*, London, 1662, 4to.   See *Nachträge to Shakspeares Werken*, Bd. I. 1840, 8vo.

After this point Schlegel devotes his few remaining pages (which are very small) to the most important incidents in Merlin's later career, his relations with Nynianne (*sic*), and his tragic end. In 1829 Uhland wrote his short ballad of *Merlin der Wilde*.[1] Three years later Karl Immermann attempted to unite in his drama of *Merlin: a Myth*,[2] the leading motives of the Faust legend with those of the Holy Grail, but he failed to awaken popular interest in the great enchanter. This piece closes the Merlin literature in German.[3]

J.—Icelandic.

1.—*Merlinus-Spá*: or the prophecy of Merlin. This is "an early versified paraphrase [in two parts, of 290 and 459 verses respectively] of Geoffrey of Monmouth's well-known prophecy, the text of which is freely treated and amplified by one who knew some, at least, of the old Heroic Lays."[4] The author was a monk, *Gunnlaug Leifsson*.

2.—The Breta-Sögur is a translation of Geoffrey's *Historia* condensed and altered.[5]

K.—English.

I will here outline the history ·of the legend from its first introduction into English down to the present. The relations of the prose romance to the French original will best be treated in another section; but I shall here venture a somewhat more extended discussion of the English forms of the legend than I have given to those of the other literatures.

1.—The earliest mention of Merlin in an English book is in Laʒamon's *Brut*[6] (ll. 12,884–19,961), written about the

---

[1] *Cf.* Holland, *Ueber Uhland's Ballade " Merlin der Wilde."* Stuttgart, 1876.

[2] Düsseldorf, 1832, 8vo.

[3] Yet the appearance in Vienna (about 1888) of a new opera on Merlin by Karl Goldmark shows that the legend has not lost its vigour. *Cf. The Opera Glass.*

[4] Vigfusson and Powell, *Corpus Poeticum Boreale*, ii. pp. 372–379.

[5] *Cf.* Ward, *Catal. of Romances*, i. pp. 304–305; Kölbing, *Altenglische Bibliothek*, iv. p. cviii.

[6] Ed. by Sir F. Madden. London, 1847. 3 vols. 8vo.

year 1205. The *Brut* is in large measure a translation of
Wace's *Roman de Brut*; but although Laȝamon expanded his
work to more than double the size of the original, he added
scarcely anything [1] to the story of Merlin.

2.—Robert of Gloucester's *Chronicle* appeared at the end
of the thirteenth century, about a century after Laȝamon's
Brut, but Robert's book, in so far as it touches the history
of Merlin (ll. 2271–3480), is a translation of Geoffrey of
Monmouth's *Historia*.[2]

3.—Robert of Brunne's *Chronicle* (1338) follows Wace in
the legendary portion [3] of the story; but Robert's variations
from his French original are trifling.

4.—The chronicles above mentioned are dull enough, and can
lay but slight claim to be called literature. The earliest really
literary use of Merlin in English is in the long verse romance
entitled *Arthour and Merlin*, which was translated from a
French original as early as the first quarter of the fourteenth
century, and possibly even earlier.[4] This is among the most
important of the romances of Merlin, as well for its intrinsic
merit as for its relations to the great prose romance. Judged
by a reasonably severe standard, many passages are tiresome
enough. The author is still too dependent upon his source;

---

[1] *Cf.*, however, Kölbing, *Altenglische Bibl.* iv. p. cxii, note. In l. 23,845 is an
allusion to Merlin not found in Wace. The passage from l. 23,305 to l. 23,354
occupies in Wace only six lines.

[2] *Cf.* K. Brossmann, *Ueber die Quellen der me. Chronik des Robert von Glouces'er*,
Breslau, 1887; Kölbing, *Altenglische Bibliothek*, iv. p. cviii. The Chronicle was
edited for the Rolls Series by W. A. Wright, London, 1887, 2 vols., 8vo.

[3] ll. 6989–9768 relate to Merlin. The portion of the Chronicle based on Wace
was edited by Dr. F. J. Furnivall, for the Rolls Series, under the title, *Robert of
Brunne's Story of England*, Lond., 1887, 2 vols., 8vo. *Cf.* A. W. Zatsche, *Ueber
den ersten Theil der Bearbeitung des Roman de Brut des Wace durch Robert Mannyng
of Brunne*, Reudnitz-Leipzig, 1887.

[4] *Cf.* Kölbing, *Altenglische Bibliothek*, iv. p. lx. The author is not certainly
known; but Kölbing thinks him identical with the author of *Kyng Alisaunder* and
Richard Coer de Lion (p. lx. *sqq.*), though he is not quite certain about the second
piece (p. ciii.).

but in more than one feature the *Arthour and Merlin* marks a
distinct advance over the narrative literature that preceded it.
The poem is about as long as the first nine books of *Paradise
Lost*, but is nevertheless a fragment, which breaks off after the
victory gained by Leodegan, Cleodalis, Arthur, Ban, and Bohort,
over King Rion and the giants.[1] The last lines are:—

> " þai maden gret blis and fest,
>   And after ȝeden hem to rest." [2]

The story so closely resembles the prose romance that Ellis's
analysis of the poem might almost be taken for an analysis of
the prose romance. There are, however, striking differences,
some of which I will note. The poem begins by telling of
Constans and Vortigern,[3] and the tower which the latter constructed.[4] The poem describes in 628 lines what is related in
the prose romance in about six pages. The story of the rich
man's daughter who is deceived by the devil[5] is brought in
later (l. 799 *sqq.*). In dramatic effect the poem is in this
instance much inferior to the prose romance. As some of the
minor differences, we note that in the poem[6] Merlin is five years
old when brought before Vortigern ; in our romance, seven
years old. In the poem the boy Merlin, while being conducted
to the king, laughs[7] three times, apparently without cause.

---

[1] As printed for the Abbotsford Club in 1838 from the Auchinleck MS. in the
Advocates' Library in Edinburgh, the poem consists of 9772 lines in short rhyming
couplets. Of this poem Ellis gives a long analysis (pp. 77–142, Bohn's ed., of
Specimens of Early English Metrical Romances). He follows the Lincoln's Inn MS.
No. 150. The poem has been re-edited by Kölbing in vol. iv. of the *Altenglische
Bibliothek*, Leipzig, 1890. Kölbing's edition contains 9938 lines, and differs in
the numbering of the lines from the earlier edition. My references are to Kölbing's
edition. Kölbing discusses in detail (pp. cvii.-cl.) the relations of the poem to the
English prose version and others. Most of my comparison was made before Kölbing's
edition appeared.

[2] The poem parallels more or less exactly the prose romance as far as p. 358, l. 28.
This would indicate a possible loss of eight or nine thousand lines.

[3] The poem calls him *Fortiger*.

[4] The poem thus begins with what is related in Chapter II. of the prose romance,
p. 23.

[5] The devils' council begins at l. 640.   [6] ll. 1375-1381.   [7] l. 1342.

The occasion of the third outburst is, however, that the king's chamberlain is a woman in the disguise of a man, with whom the queen has fallen in love.[1] In the prose version Merlin laughs but twice. According to the poem,[2] the Magi when brought before the king and confronted by Merlin plead that they have been deceived by the signs in the sky. Merlin says that his father the devil had evidently planned thus to destroy his son. Of this turn of the incident the prose romance (p. 39) knows nothing. Among the important omissions of the poem is that of the bringing over of the great stones from Ireland,[3] as well as all account of Merlin's visits to Nimiane.[4] The Holy Grail is scarcely referred to, though not altogether forgotten.[5]

Among the additions to the poem we should not overlook the charming verses on the seasons, and the pretty little by-play between Arthur and his young bride as he goes forth to battle:

> þat ich day paramour,
> Guenore armed king Arthour;
> At ich armour, þe gest seit þisse,
> Arthour þe maiden gan kisse,
> Merlin bad Arthour, þe kyng,
> þenche on þat ich kisseing,
> When he com in to bataile;
> "Ʒis," he seyd, "Merlin, saunfaile."[6]—ll. 8677-8684.

---

[1] *Cf.* the story of Grisandol in the prose romance, pp. 422-437.

[2] l. 1573 *sqq.*

[3] *Cf.* ll. 2150-2180.

[4] She is named once (l. 4446) along with Morgein, who

> "Woned wiþ outen Niniame,
>   þat wiþ hir queint gin
>   Bigiled þe gode clerk Merlin."

With this compare the prose version p. 185.

[5] *Cf.* ll. 8902-8918.

[6] *Cf.* prose version, p. 323, where Merlin laughs because they have not kissed each other. Then Arthur takes the maiden in his arms and kisses her sweetly, as he should.

What has been adduced is sufficient to prove either that the English prose romance is based upon an original differing considerably from the original of the verse romance, or that the English translator of the prose romance purposely varied and expanded his original. The English prose romance is, however, elsewhere shown to be an almost slavish translation of the French prose version. There is enough general agreement to show that the basis of the poem and of the prose romance is in essential features the same, and enough difference to prove that the two versions cannot be based on exactly the same original. I imagine the poem to be based upon one of the numerous French prose continuations of the original prose romance of Merlin. The author refers to his source as the "boke,"[1] and once to the *Brout*,[2] which must be the *Brut*, but of course only a small portion of this poem can be referred to Wace. It is barely possible that the original was in French verse, but of this I feel by no means certain.[3]

[1] l. 2581 ; l. 4434 ; l. 4719 ; l. 5785, etc.

[2] line 2730.

[3] The essential likeness of the two English versions, along with striking differences, appears plainly in a comparison of the list of knights : —

The Poem, ll. 3067–3106.	Number of knights.	The Prose Merlin, p. 108.	Number of knights.
1. Lot	500	1. Loth	500
2. Nauters of Garlot	700	2. Vrien of Gorre	400
3. Vrien of Gorre	25,000	3. Ventres of Garlot	700
4. Carodas of Strangore	600	4. Carodas Brenbras of Strangore	600
5. Yder	30 × 20 = 600	5. Aguysas	500
6. Angvisant	500	6. Ydiers	400

In the first great tournament the best knights, according to the poem (ll. 3591–3601), are : Lucan the boteler, Kay, Grimfles, Maruc, Gumas, Placides, Driens, Holias, Graciens, Marlians, Flaundrius, Sir Meliard, Drukius, Breoberuis. The prose version (p. 135) mentions the following : Gifflet, Lucas the boteller, Marke de la roche, Guynas le Bleys, Drias de la foreste sauge, Belyas, Blyos de la casse, Madyons le crespes, Flaundryns le blanke, Grassien, Placidas le gays.

5.—A later version of a portion of this romance is contained in four manuscripts, which differ considerably.[1] The romance begins with the story of King Constance and "Fortager," tells of the birth of Merlin and his wonderful deeds till the death and burial of Uter Pendragon. According to Ward:[2]

The rebel kings who fight against Arthur, with the number of the accompanying knights, are:—

POEM, ll. 3725-3773.	Number of knights.	PROSE, pp. 145-146.	Number of knights.
1. Clarion of Norþ-Humberland	7000	1. Duke Escam of Cambenyk	5000
2. Brangores of Strangore .	5000	2. Tramelmens of North Wales	6000
3. Cradelman of Norþ-Wales	6000	3. Clarion	3000
4. King of the Hundred Knights	4000	4. King with the hundred knights	3000
5. Lot of Leonis and Dorkaine	7000	5. Loth of Orcanye and Leonoys	7000
6. Carodas of the Round Table	7000	6. Carados of Strangore .	7000
7. Nanters of Garlot . .	6000	7. Ventres of Garlot . .	7000
8. Vrien	6000	8. Vrien of Gorre . .	7000
9. Yder	5000	9. Ydiers of Cornewaile .	6000
10. Angvisaunt of Scotland .	6000	10.	
11. Sestas, Erl of Canbernic .	5000	11.	

Still more remarkable is the agreement in the lists of the princes and knights who came to the help of Leodegan. Poem, ll. 5410-5498: 1. Ban; 2. Bohort; 3. Arthour; 4. Antour; 5. Vlfin; 6. Bretel; 7. Kay; 8. Lucan þe boteler; 9. Grifles; 10. Marec; 12. Drians of þe Forest sauage; 13. Belias þe lord of Maiden castel; 14. Flaundrin; 15. Lamuas; 16. Amores þe broun; 17. Ancales, 18. Bliobel; 19. Bleoberiis; 20. Canode; 21. Aladanc þe crispe; 22. Islacides; 23. Lampades; 24. Ierias; 25. Cristofer of þe roche norþ; 26. Aigilin; 27. Calogreuand; 28. Angusale; 29. Agrauel; 30. Cleades þe fondling; 31. Gimires of Lambale; 32. Kehedin; 33. Merangis; 34. Goruain; 35. Craddoc; 36. Claries; 37. Blehartis; 38. Amandanorgulous; 39. Osoman; 40. Galescounde; 41. Bleherris; 42. Merlin; 43. Leodegan. Cf. the list in the prose romance, p. 212.

[1] The MSS. are:— a Lincoln's Inn Library, MS. 150, containing 1980 lines. b Bishop Percy's Folio MS., Brit. Mus. Add. 27879, containing nine parts and 2378 lines. c Brit. Mus. Harl. MS. No. 6223, containing 62 lines. d Oxford, Douce MS. No. 236, containing 1278 lines. Kölbing remarks (Altengl. Bibl. iv. p. xvii.) that Douce MS., No. 124, is a very careless copy of the version of the Auchinleck MS. Kölbing prints L and D with the variants of P and H (Altengl. Bibl. iv. 275-370). P is printed in Bishop Percy's Folio Manuscript, edited by Hales and Furnivall, Lond. 1867, vol. i. pp. 422-496. For the relation of the later version to the other versions see Kölbing, iv. pp. cliii.-clxxii. ; Hales and Furnivall, i. pp. 419-421. Other details are given by Kölbing, iv. pp. xvii.-xviii. ; Ward, Catal. of Romances, i. 385, 386; and in Arthour and Merlin (edited by Turnbull for the Abbotsford Club, Edin. 1838), pp. x.-xiii.

[2] Catal. of Romances, i. 386.

"The events relating to Merlin are fuller than those given by Geoffrey of Monmouth and Wace, and they agree with those given by Robert de Borron, in the prose romance of Merlin. The present version is probably translated from a French poem."

It is hardly necessary to remark that the birth of Merlin with which Robert de Borron's romance begins, is in this verse romance brought in after a long account of "Fortager" and the sons of Constance, and that minor differences are numerous.

6.—From the middle of the fourteenth century Merlin seems to have been in favour in England. Laurence Minot (1352) begins one of his political songs entitled,

> "How Edward at Hogges vnto land wan,
>   And rade thurgh France or euer he blan."

with the words—

> "Men may rede in Romance right
>   Of a grete clerk þat Merlin hight;
>   Ful many bokes er of him wreten,
>   Als þir clerkes wele may witten;
>   And ʒit in many priué nokes
>   May men find of Merlin bokes.
>   Merlin said þus with his mowth,
>   Out of þe north into þe sowth
>   Suld cum a bare ouer þe se,
>   þat suld mak many man to fle," etc.

A few years later (1355–1362) Thomas Grey in his old French *Scalachronica* mentions Thomas of Erceldoune, and ranks him along with William Banastre and Merlyne.[1] In *Sir Gawayne and the Green Knight* (about 1360) there is a mere allusion to Merlin (l. 2448).

---

[1] The various points of contact of the legend and the prophecies of Merlin with Thomas of Erceldoune, are pointed out by Alois Brandl in vol. ii. of the *Sammlung engl. Denkmäler in kritischen Ausgaben*, Berlin, 1880, 8vo. For example, Merlin's love for Nimiane is paralleled by Thomas's love for a nymph.

In the famous *Process of the Sevyn Sages* the eleventh tale bears the title *Herowdes and Merlin*.[1] Then in the metrical romance of Sir Gowghter[2] we read near the beginning—

> "Sum tyme the fende hadde postee
> For to dele with ladies free
> In liknesse of here fere,
> So that he bigat Merlyng and mo,
> And wrought ladies so mikel wo,
> That ferly it is to here."—ll. 7–10.

A little farther on are these very singular lines—

> "Þis chyld wiþin hur was no nod*ur*,
> But eyvon *M*arlyon halfe brod*ur*,[3]
> For won fynd gatte hom bothe."—ll. 97–99.

On this romance A. Brandl remarks—

"Gegenüber der französischen Quelle, deren Kern durch einen reich verzweigten Stammbaum auf das indische Märchenbuch Sendabad zurückgeht, hat der englische Bearbeiter manches vereinfacht und seinen Landsleuten näher gebracht, namentlich aber den Zauberer Vergil in den nationalen Merlin verwandelt."[4]

Towards the end of the fourteenth century (1387) the Latin *Polychronicon* of Ranulf Higden, written early in the reign of Edward III., was translated into English by John of Trevisa. The *Polychronicon*, as its name implies, is a compilation bringing

---

[1] See the second M.E. version, ed. T. Wright, Lond., 1845, l. 2323. *Cf.* Kölbing, *Altenglische Bibl.* iv. p. civ.

[2] It would be interesting to compare the legend of *Merlin* with that of *Robert the Devil*. *Cf.* K. Breul's *Sir Gowther*, Oppeln, 1886, which contains an investigation of the legend of *Robert the Devil*.

[3] Brit. Mus. MS. Reg. 17, B. xliii, f. 118, reads:

> "The childe with-yn) hire was non) other,
> But Marlynges half brother :
> On) fende gat hem bothe."

[4] Paul's *Grundriss der germ. Philologie*, ii. 635.

together in mediæval fashion a vast amount of historical material, but it contains nothing new about Merlin.[1]

7.—No important literary use was made of Merlin during the remainder of the fourteenth and till about the middle of the fifteenth century, when some unknown scholar translated (*c.* 1450–1460) the great prose romance of *Merlin* from the French prose redaction of Robert de Borron's poem and the ordinary continuation known as the *Book of Arthur*. This is the romance which is the central point of our investigation.

8.—About the same time (1450 ?) Henry Lonelich, skinner, made a rhyming version of the French prose *Merlin* from a manuscript closely allied to that from which the prose version is translated. The metrical romance contains, according to Kölbing,[2] about 28,000 lines, and forms a part of MS. 80 of Corpus Christi College, Cambridge. The beginning is at f. 88*b*, col. 1, and is as follows :—

> "Now gyneth the Devel to wraththen him sore,
> As Aftir scholen ʒe herkene & here wel More,
> whanne that Oure Lord to helle wente
> and took Owt Adam with good Entente
> and Also Eve and Ek Othere Mo,
> þat with him he likede for to han tho.
> and whanne þe develis behelden this,
> Moche drede and Merveille they hadden, I-wis.
> So as Aftyrward longe beffelle,
> to-gederis they Conseilled, the develis, ful snelle
> and token hem to-Gederis In parlement,
> the Maister Develis be On Assent,
> and seiden : " what Mester Man Is he, this,
> that doth vs here Al this distres ?

---

[1] The doggrel rhyming Latin verses, which carefully distinguish Merlin Ambrose from Merlin Silvester, are based on Giraldus Cambrensis.

[2] *Altenglische Bibliothek*, iv. p. xix. Kölbing prints (pp. 373-478) the first 1638 lines, which parallel the prose *Merlin* pp. 1-23, and gives in his introduction a minute account of the poem.

> we Mown not Aȝens him Maken defens,
> whanne he is Owht In Owre *presens*
> and bynemeth vs that we scholde haue,
> and for hym non thing mowe*n* we kepe*n* save."

I have examined the first 6200 lines of the poem,[1] and find a remarkably close general agreement between it and the prose romance.   All the incidents are the same, and the difference in details is very slight.   This agreement suggests three questions: First, is Lonelich's *Merlin* a mere versification of the English prose version? or, secondly, is the prose version based on Lonelich's romance? or, thirdly, are both versions based on exactly the same French original?

We have first to note that the verse romance is considerably more prolix[2] than the prose; but the prolixity is largely due to unskilful padding of the verse.   Of course, we do not expect exact verbal agreement between a verse and a prose romance, even though translated from the same French original, and we cannot draw satisfactory conclusions from minor variations in phrases, or even from the omission of sentences.   The exigencies of metre lead a halting versifier into many strange paths.   But if the two translators had been really one, or if one had borrowed from the other, or if the French manuscript had been the same in both cases, we should have considerable verbal agreement in phrases and sentences, as well as in numerals and proper names.

A considerable number of passages show almost exact verbal agreement, but this seems to be due to the similarity of the source rather than to actual borrowing by one English version from the other, for the diction as a whole is so distinct in the

---

[1] These were furnished me by Dr. Furnivall in a MS. copy. This copy ends at l. 43 of f. 111.

[2] By a rough calculation I estimate the first 6200 lines to contain not far from 43,000 words: the prose version does not much exceed 35,000 words.

TABLE I.

English Prose.	Lonelich.	Huth Merlin.
x monthes; ij yere ago or more; xij monthes (p. 15).	ten monthes; two jeres old; xviij monthes (ll. 999–1101, f. 92b).	nuef mois; un an; en l'eage do dis et uit mois (p. 20).
xl dayes (p. 16).	xl dawes (l. 1105, f. 92b).	quaranto jours (p. 22).
viij dayes (p. 16).	viij dayes (l. 1116, f. 93).	set jours (p. 22).
to the ve day (p. 18).	xv dayes (f. 93b).	a lo quinsainno (p. 25).
iij men (p. 21).	tweyne men (f. 94b).	dous hommes (p. 29).
xij (p. 25).	xij (f. 95b).	douzo (p. 35).
two noble men; tow godo men (p. 25).	two good men; tweyne goode Men (f. 95b).	deus preudommes (p. 35).
xij (p. 26).	xij (f. 96).	li proudommo (p. 36).
iiij fadomo of height (p. 27).	the heythe of fowre Roddis (f. 96).	douzo (p. 37).
vij in nombre (p. 28).	sevene thero were (f. 96b).	trois toises u quatre (p. 38).
viij dayes of respyte (p. 28).	viij dayes of Respyt (f. 96b).	set (p. 39).
xij (p. 29).	xij (f. 96b).	oucoro jour dusqu'a onze jors (p. 40).
xij; xij; xij (p. 31).	xij; xij; xij (f. 97).	douze (p. 43).
		douzo (p. 45; hero written but once, but pronouns supply tho lack).
xj (p. 47).	xj (f. 102).	onsime (p. 72).

a C stedes, a C palfrayes, and a hundred faucons (p. 50).	An hundred destreres & as Many of palfray and An hundred fawkowns (f. 103).	Et nous le terrons de lui et treu l'en donrons chascun an dis chevaliers, et dis damoisieles et dis faucons et dis levriers et cent palefrois (p. 79).
withinne these vj dayes (p. 53).	with Inne sixe dayes (f. 103b).	en sis jours (p. 84).
on the vje day (p. 53).	to the xvj day (f. 103b).	au sisime jour (p. 85).
The xj day of Iuyne (p. 54).	Atte the Elloveneth day (f. 104).	L'onsime jour de jung[net] (p. 87).
two dayes (p. 54).	tweyne dayes (f. 104).	deus jours (p. 87).
the thirde day (p. 54).	On the thrydde (f. 104).	au tierch jour (p. 87).
xl winter (p. 59).	two and fowrty ʒer (f. 105).	(No equivalent for " xl winter ").
fifty knyghtes (p. 60).	fyfty knyghtes (f. 105b).	cinquante des plus proudomes (p. 96).
viij days (p. 61).	viij dayes (f. 105b).	uit jours (p. 97).
thre yere (p. 61).	two yere (f. 105b).	plus de deus ans (p. 98).[1]
the xje iour of Pentecoste (p. 67).	xi day aftyr pentecost (f. 107a).	un jour après (p. 102).
xl dayes (p. 70).	fowrty dayes (f. 107b).	quaranto jours (p. 105).
vj monethes (p. 80).	Sixe Mownthes (f. 110).	sis mois (p. 115).

[1] The Huth *Merlin*, p. 98, l. 26 *sqq.* has no equivalent for the passage in the English prose version, from p. 61, l. 31 to p. 63, l. 29 ; and the subsequent lines in the French do not exactly agree with the English.

two versions that this in itself is a strong argument against
a common authorship.

<table>
<tr><td align="center">ENGLISH PROSE.</td><td align="center">LONELICH.</td></tr>
<tr><td>'That shall I telle the,' quod merlin) " (p. 32).</td><td>" 'That schal I the telle,' quod Merlyne " (f. 97b).</td></tr>
<tr><td>" He ycleped hym maister, for that he was maister to his moder " (p. 33).</td><td>" and Maister he clepid him for this manere, For Maister to his Modir he was Every where " (f. 97b).</td></tr>
<tr><td>" to god I comaunde yow" (p. 33).</td><td>" I comande ȝow to God " (f. 97b).</td></tr>
<tr><td>" and axed a-noon) how they hadde spedde " (p. 35).</td><td>" And Axede of hem how they hadden sped " (f. 98b).</td></tr>
<tr><td>" And, sir, the peple that were ther-at cleped this vessell that thei hadden) in so grete grace, the Graal " (p. 59).</td><td>" Sire, this peple Clepede this vessel
The Sank Ryal oþer ellys Seint Graal " (f. 105).</td></tr>
</table>

The agreement in the numerals is very close, but there are
some trifling variations which indicate that the two translators
based their work upon slightly different manuscripts. I give
a list of some of the numerals, and add for comparison the same
as found in the Huth *Merlin*. In contrast with the French, the
two English versions show striking agreement. See Table I. p. 54.

More striking differences are found in the names ; and these
seem unmistakably to indicate that the two versions are independent, and based upon slightly different French manuscripts.
I pass over most of the differences in spelling ; for while the
forms in the two versions follow pretty regularly unlike types,
there are too many variations in the English prose text itself
to make an argument satisfactory that is based on mere
orthography.

<table>
<tr><td align="center">ENGLISH PROSE.</td><td align="center">LONELICH.</td></tr>
<tr><td>Loth (p. 23).</td><td>Omitted (f. 95).</td></tr>
<tr><td>Constance (p. 24).</td><td>Costantyn (f. 95).</td></tr>
</table>

ENGLISH PROSE.	LONELICH.
The three sons of Constance are: (1) Moyne, (2) Pendragon, (3) Vter (p. 24).	The three sons of Costantyn are: (1) Costantyn, (2) Awrely Ambros or Pendragon, (3) Vter (f. 95).
Vortiger (p. 24), *et passim*.	Fortager (f. 95), *et passim*.
Gawle (p. 25).	Wales (f. 95*b*).
Benoyc, that now is cleped Bourges (p. 25).	Boorges (f. 95*b*).
Constance (p. 41).	Constantyn (f. 100*b*).
Aungys (p. 50).	Hangwis (f. 103).
Ventres (p. 179).	Newtris (f. 135).
Gawein　　,,	Gawenet　　,,
Gaheret　　,,	Garrers　　,,
Gaheries　　,,	Gaheryes　　,,
Cardoell in Walys (p. 180).	Kerdyf In Wales (f. 135).

More important still are such differences as appear in the following passages :—

(1) At l. 49 of Lonelich's version we read : "And hem also anoynteth with oynement." The English prose has no reference to ointment.

(2) At l. 241, l. 256, and l. 1064 of the poem we read that the erring maiden was to be stoned. The prose version (p. 5, p. 16) knows nothing of the stoning.

(3) In the poem (ll. 1286–1292), the judge says—

> "ȝif thou konne proven that thou seist pleyn,
> Thy modyr from brenneng schalt thou save,
> And al thyn owne axeng thou schalt have ;
> But, natheles, and it be, as thou dost telle,
> Thanne schal I don brenne bothe ful snelle,
> Bothe myn owne modyr and ek thyn,
> And bryngen hem bothe to a schort fyn."

The prose version (p. 18, ll. 24–27) has—

"Tho gan the Iuge to be right wrath, and seyd : 'Yef thow canste do so, then haste reserved thy moder fro brennynge ; but wyt thow well, yef thow canste not prewe this vpon hir, I shall brenne bothe the and thy moder to-gedere.'"

(4) In Lonelich's version (ll. 1465–1467) we read—

> " For sweche spirites as they be
> Ben icleped Equibedes, I telle the,
> And from the eyr into the erthe they gon."

The Huth *Merlin* (i. p. 28) has—

" Je sui fieus d'un anemi qui engingna ma mere. Et saces que ceste maniere d'anemis ont a non Ekupcdes, et repairent en l'air."

Yet in the English prose *Merlin* (p. 20) the proper name is omitted—

" I am the sone of the enmy that begiled my moder with engyn, and their repair is in the air."

(5) Lonelich writes (ll. 1667–1676)—

> " and hos that wil knowen In Certaygne
> what kynges that weren In grete Bretaygne
> Sethen that Cristendom thedyr was Browht,
> They scholen hem fynde hos so that it sowht,
> In the Story of Brwttes book ;
> there scholen ȝe it fynde and ȝe welen look.
> which that Martyn de Bewre traunslated here
> From latyn Into Romaunce In his Manere.
> but leve we now of Brwtes book,
> and after this storye now lete vs look.
> In Bretaygne somtyme A kyng there was
> That Costantyn was clepid, In that plas."

The English prose (pp. 23, 24) has—

" And he that wiłł knowe the lyf of kynges whiche were in the grete Bretayne be-fore that cristendom͛ come, be-holde the story of Bretons. That is a boke that maister Martyn͛ traunslated oute of latyn͛, but heire rested this matere. And turneth to the story of Loth, a crysten kynge in Bretayne, whos name was Constance."

This passage is exceedingly important in that Lonelich's version mentions Martyn de Bewre.[1] This translator is

---

[1] B. N. MSS. fr. 105; 9123 " Martins de bieure." The others, in so far as they name *Martins* at all, are: B. N. MS. fr. 749," martins de roescestre"; Bib. de l'Arsenal, MS. 3482, " martins de rocestre"; B. N. MS. fr. 344," Maistre martins de rouain."

mentioned in but two of the French MSS., and these two, while representing very closely the version followed by the translator of the English prose, are not in every detail coincident with it.

The differences between the English prose version and the metrical version by Lonelich compel us to answer in the negative the three questions with which we started, and admit no other conclusion than that the two translators worked independently upon different French manuscripts having almost, but not perfectly, identical readings.[1]

9.—Of all the older Arthurian literature none exceeds in interest to the English reader the *Morte Darthur* of Sir Thomas Malory (1469). This was first printed by Caxton in 1485, and speedily became one of the most popular books in England. When we compare the *Romance of Merlin* with the *Morte Darthur*, we find that for a little distance the two stories run in almost parallel channels, though there is less agreement than one might expect, and this, though scattered throughout the *Merlin*, is confined almost wholly to the first five books of the *Morte Darthur*.[2] The points of contact may be briefly pointed out in detail. The story opens in the *Morte Darthur* with the amour of Uter Pendragon and Igrayne. In nine pages and a half Malory arrives at Arthur's coronation and the feast which he held at Pentecost.[3] Many of the

---

[1] Kölbing's view (*Altenglische Bibl.* iv. p. clxxxix.) is slightly different. He concludes that Lonelich's poem and the English prose version, "von einander, ganz unabhängig, auf *denselben* frz. text, die prosa-auflösung von Robert de Boron's epos, als quelle zurückgehen." Kölbing would perhaps hardly care to have the words "Robert de Boron's epos" understood to mean that Robert's poem is the source of the romance after the coronation of Arthur.

[2] There are twenty-one books in all. My references are to H. Oskar Sommer's edition, Lond. 1889, Vol. I. *Text*. For a minute account of the relations of the *Morte Darthur* to the *Merlin* see Sommer's third volume, *Studies on the Sources*, pp. 14-58.

[3] In the *Merlin* (p. 108) the feast was held after the middle of August. *Cf. Morte Darthur*, i. pp. 35-44.

incidents are substantially the same as in the *Merlin*, but much abridged. Merlin's origin is passed over without remark, and he is introduced in the first chapter as a personage well known: " Wel my lord faid Syre Vlfius/ I fhall feke Merlyn/ and he fhalle do yow remedy that youre herte fhalbe pleafyd." Up to the end of B. I. chap. xvi. there is considerable general agreement in the incidents of the two versions, though the *Morte Darthur* gives a very brief account of what is told in the *Merlin* with many words and manifold variations. Chapter xvii. has some incidents found in the *Merlin*, but much altered. From this point up to chap. xxvii. is only here and there an incident that reminds one of the *Merlin*. In chap. xxvii. (p. 74) is the message of King Ryons, who sends for Arthur's beard. In *Merlin* this occurs not far from the end (p. 619) of the story. The war with the Romans as related by Malory in the fifth book of the *Morte Darthur* agrees only in confused outlines with the version in *Merlin*. According to Malory the war occurs after Merlin is enclosed in the rock. In our version Merlin is at Arthur's side assisting him with wise counsels. In the *Morte Darthur*, in the same chapter and on the same page (B. IV. ch. i. p. 119) in which the tragic end of Merlin is described,[1] Lancelot is spoken of as a child at the court of King Ban his father. But at the beginning of the war with the Romans the child has become a famous knight, and plays a part like that of Gawain in the *Merlin*.[2] In the prose *Merlin*, however, Lancelot is not yet born.[3] In the fight with the giant on Mount St. Michel, Malory (B. V. ch. v.) adds the picturesque detail that there " were thre fayr

---

[1] The account in the *Merlin* (p. 681) differs considerably from that in the *Morte Darthur*.

[2] As Sommer points out in the *Academy* of Jan. 4, 1890, Malory does not follow the ordinary *Merlin* in his account of the war with the Romans, but rather the same source as *La Morte Arthure*, edited by Brock for the E.E. Text Soc.

[3] P. 698. Cf. *Morte Darthur*, B. II. ch. xix. p. 90 ; B. IV. ch. i. p. 119, l. 19 ; B. IV. ch. xix. p. 143, l. 26.

damoysels tornynge thre broches whereon were broched twelue yonge children late borne like yonge byrdes." Of this our version knows nothing. In minor details and in phraseology the two versions differ continually, even when the agreement is closest, and after a certain point the two narratives are entirely different. The *Morte Darthur* hurries at once to the later career of Arthur and his knights. The *Merlin* relates with endless detail the incidents of Arthur's early life, and introduces us to a large number of the characters who figure in the *Morte Darthur*. This masterpiece of poetic prose, which Sir Walter Scott pronounced the best romance in our language, far exceeds in literary merit the confused and prolix *Merlin*; but this, as affording in effect an introduction to the *Morte Darthur*, must always retain a real interest. Even considered by itself, the *Merlin* has in more than one passage a nameless charm and beauty in comparison with which the *Morte Darthur* is distinctly inferior, though the heights occasionally reached in the *Merlin* make us see only more plainly the barren wastes through which much of the narrative creeps.

10.—In addition to the long prose and verse romances we have a considerable number of prophecies attributed to Merlin in English verse of the fifteenth century. One of these contains 278 lines, and is a translation from French prose of Merlin's *Prophecy of the Six Kings that are to follow King John*.[1] Another prophecy[2] of three hundred lines relates to the year "M.CCCC.L. and moo." Three Scottish prophecies in alliterative verse, attributed to Merlin, are found "in a collection of prophecies partly composed, partly adapted from earlier compositions, at various periods between 1513 (the date of Flodden Field) and 1550, together with some later additions."[3] Some

---

[1] Ward, *Catal. of Romances*, i. p. 309.
[2] *Ibid.* i. p. 325.
[3] *Ibid.* i. pp. 334-336.

of the prophecies in the collection are assigned to Thomas of Erceldoune[1] and others.

11.—At the end of Caxton's *Chronicle* is a little poem on Merlin printed by Wynkyn de Worde in 1498, of which I cite the more interesting portions. This poem is a translation of a Latin poem in Higden's *Polychronicon*.

> At Neuyn in Northwales
> A lytell ylonde there is
> That is called Bardysay.
> Monkes dwelle there alway,
> Men lyue so long in that hurst
> That the oldest deyeth fyrst.
> Men say that Merlyn there buryed is,[2]
> That hyght also Syluestris
> There were Merlyns tweyne,
> And prophecyed beyne,
> One hyte Ambrose and Merlyn
> And was ygoten by gobelyn
> In Demecia at Carmerthyn,
> Vnder kyng Vortygeryn ;
> He tolde his prophecye
> Euen in Snowdonye
> Atte heede of the water of Coneway
> In the syde of mount Eryry,
> Dynas Embreys in Walsshe
> Ambrose hylle in Englysshe.
> Kyng Vortygere sate on
> The watersyde and was full of wone,
> Then Ambrose Merlyn prophecyed
> Tofore hym ryght tho.

[1] On the relation between Merlin's prophecies and those of Thomas of Erceldoune see J. A. H. Murray's ed. of Thomas of Erceldoune for the E.E. Text Soc. 1875 ; Ward's remarks in the *Catal. of Romances*, i. pp. 328-338 ; Brandl in Zupitza's *Sammlung engl. Denkmäler in kritischen Ausgaben*, ii. pp. 12-41.

[2] According to another tradition Merlin is buried at Drummelzier in Scotland. See J. S. Stuart Glennie's *Arthurian Localities*, p. lxxii.

What wytte wolde wene
That a fende myght get a childe ?
Some men wolde mene
That he may no such werke welde.
That fende that goth a nyght
Wymmen full ofte to gyle,
Incubus is named by ryght ;
And gyleth men other whyle,
Succubus is that wyght.
God graunt vs non such vyle.
Who that cometh in hyr gyle
Wonder happe shall he smyle,
With wonder dede
Bothe men and wymen sede,
Fendes woll kepe,
With craft and brynge an hepe ;
So fendes wylde
May make wymmen bere childe.
Yet neuer in mynde
Was childe of fendes kynde,
For withouten eye
Ther myght no suche childe deye,
Clergie maketh mynde,
Deth sleeth no fendes kynde ;
But deth slewe Merlyn,
Merlyn was ergo no goblyn.

12.—In the sixteenth century interest in Merlin is evidenced by the publication in 1510 by Wynkyn de Worde of *A Lytel Tretys of the Byrth and Prophecyes of Merlin*. The celebrated printer issued another edition in 1529, and John Hawkyns a third in 1533.

13.—The numerous chronicles written in the sixteenth century detail with more or less fulness the exploits of the enchanter, but they tell nothing new. We find, however, in the sixteenth-century literature, in so far as it turned for

inspiration to the romances or to the legendary history of
Britain, that Merlin was one of the convenient "properties"
of the poets.[1] We meet him in Warner's *Albion's England*
(1586), which is full of early British legends. In a splendid
passage of the *Faery Queene*[2] Spenser tells of the wall of brass[3]
with which Merlin began to surround the city of Caermarthen
just before he was lured to his grave in the rock by the
wiles of the fair temptress.

14.—In 1603 appeared for the first time in print[4] some
old alliterative Scottish prophecies attributed to Merlin, along
with prophecies by Thomas the Rhymer and others. In these
prophecies we read (i. ll. 114-120)—

> " When the Cragges of Tarbat is tumbled in the sey,
>   At the next sommer after sorrow for euer :
>   Beides bookes haue I seene, and Banisters also,
>   Meruelous Merling and all accordes in one :
>   Meruelous Merling is wasted away,
>   With a wicked woman, woe might shee be ;
>   For shee hath closed him in a Craige on Cornwel cost."

[1] In Robert Chester's *Love's Martyr* (Lond. 1601 ; reprinted by the Rev. A. B.
Grosart for the New Shakspere Soc. Lond. 1878), the " true legend of famous King
Arthur " is introduced. Merlin naturally appears, but he is made responsible for
nothing except the birth of Arthur.

[2] B. III. canto 3, stanza 6 *sqq.* The argument of the third canto is :

> " Merlin bewrays to Britomart
>   The state of Arthegall,
>   And shows the famous progeny
>   Which from them springen shall."

Other references to Merlin occur, F. Q. I. canto 9, st. 4, 5, where Merlin is
represented as visiting " Old Timon " who had taken Arthur at his birth to bring up.
Other references occur B. II. c. 8, st. 20 ; B. III. c. 2, st. 18, 21.

[3] *Cf.* Giraldus Cambrensis, *Itin. Cambr.* i. 6 ; Holinshed's *Chron.* i. 129 ;
Camden's *Brit.* p. 734.

[4] This collection has been several times reprinted, 1615, 1680, 1833. The last
edition bears the title—" Collection of Ancient Scottish Prophecies, in alliterative
verse, reprinted from Waldegrave's edition, M.DC.III. Edinburgh ; printed by
Ballantyne and Co., M.DCCC.XXXIII. 4to." Sir Walter Scott made considerable use
of these prophecies. *Cf.* also section 10, *ante*, and Ward, *Catal. of Romances*, i. pp.
334-336.

A little later (ll. 170–172) we find—

> " As Bertlingtones bookes, and Banister us telles,
> Merling and many more, that with maruels melles,
> And also Thomas Rymour in his tales telles."

In the second of these prophecies (ll. 63–65) we read—

> " Oft this booke haue I seene, and better thereafter,
> Of Meruelous Merling, but it is wasted away,
> With a wicked woman, woe might it be."

In 1612, Michael Drayton brought out the first eighteen books of his *Polyolbion*—a poetical description of England—and related the various legends connected with the places described. Thus he sings of "Stonenge," of the wall of brass that the magician would fain have built about Caermarthen, of his imprisonment in a cavern, and of the spirits that " a fearful horrid din still in the earth do keep."[1]

In Song the Fifth (vol. ii. pp. 757, 758), he tells of Merlin's birth, but speaks sceptically of the incubuses.[2] In Song the Tenth (vol. iii. pp. 842, 843) he devotes twenty-four lines to Merlin and his prophecies.[3]

Ben Jonson, though he had scornfully referred in *The New Inn* (act i. sc. 1) to the Arthurian stories, raises Merlin from his tomb, and lets him take part in the *Speeches at Prince Henry's Barriers*.[4]

---

[1] Song the Fourth, vol. ii. p. 735, Lond. 1753. This is a passage of twenty lines.

[2] Selden gives in a learned note (p. 763) the grounds of objection to their existence. We may remark that Selden (vol. ii. p. 746) follows Giraldus Cambrensis in distinguishing Merlin Ambrose from Merlin Silvester.

[3] In Drayton's *Remarks to the Reader*, May 9, 1612, he says : " In all, I believe him most, which, freest from affection and hate (causes of corruption), might best know, and hath with most likely assertion delivered his report. Yet so, that, to explain the author, carrying himself in this part an historical, as in the other a chorographical Poet. I inferr oft, out of the British story, what I importune you not to credit. Of that kind are those prophecies out of Merlin sometimes interwoven ; I discharge myself ; nor impute you to me any serious respect of them."—*Works*, ii. p. 649.

[4] *Works*, pp. 577-580, Dyce's ed. *The Old Dramatists*.

All through the seventeenth century Merlin enjoyed a certain popularity, which showed itself in a variety of ways. In 1641 appeared in London his *Life*, written by Thomas Heywood, the most prolific dramatist of the time, under the following title: " *The Life of Merlin, sirnamed Ambrosius, his Prophisies and Predictions interpreted; and their Truth made good by our English Annals.*" [1]

. Twenty-one years later William Rowley wrote a tragicomedy entitled *The Birth of Merlin; or, The Child hath found his Father*,[2] in the composition of which the publishers declared that Shakspere had assisted; but of this there is no proof.[3]

It is well known that Dryden, as well as Milton, intended to write an Arthurian epic, but never carried out the plan. Yet Dryden went so far as to write a dramatic opera [4] entitled *King Arthur, or The British Worthy*, in which Merlin figures as one of the characters. The author drew freely on his invention, and reproduced very little of the Arthur or Merlin of the romances. As Sir Walter Scott well observes: "He [Arthur] is not in this drama the formidable possessor of Excalibur, and the superior of the chivalry of the Round Table; nor is Merlin the fiend-born necromancer of whom antiquity related and believed so many wonders. They are the prince and magician of a beautiful fairy tale, the story of which, abstracted from the poetry, might have been written by Madame D'Aunois." [5]

The epic was reserved for Sir Richard Blackmore, who

---

[1] Reprinted, Caermarthen, 1812. 8vo. London, 1813.

[2] London, 1662. 4to. Reprinted in *The Doubtful Plays*, Tauchnitz, Leipzig, 1869. The second half of the title of Rowley's play has sometimes as a variant, *The Child has lost his Father*.

[3] Ward, *Eng. Dram. Lit.* i. pp. 468, 469, gives an analysis of the play, and rejects Shakspere's participation; *cf.* also, Halliwell-Phillipps' *Outlines of the Life of Shak.*, p. 193.

[4] Acted and published in 1691.

[5] Dryden's *Works*, Scott's ed. viii. p. 110; *cf.* also Ward, *Eng. Dram. Lit.* ii. p. 523.

touched the last refinement of dulness in his *Prince Arthur*, published in ten books in 1695. Merlin figures scarcely at all in the poem (B. vii. p. 202 *sqq.*), and then in a character absurdly out of keeping with all traditions. The worthy doctor depicts a British sorcerer who had been driven out of the British State and had sided with the Saxons. The magician essayed to help the Saxon Octa, but suddenly,

> "A Warmth Divine his Spirits did invade,
> And once a Sorcerer a Prophet made.
> The Heav'nly Fury *Merlin* did constrain
> To Bless, whom he to Curse design'd in vain."—p. 205.

Twice he thus plays the part of Balaam, then flees before the angry Octa (p. 207), and is seen no more.

In 1736 appeared two attempts to dramatize a portion of the story of Merlin. The first was a mere alteration by Giffard [1] of Dryden's *King Arthur*, and bore the title *Merlin or the British Inchanter, and King Arthur the British Worthy ; A Dramatic Opera*. The second piece is a versified drama preserved in a fragment without a title-page (pp. 33–40) and entitled *The Royal Chace, or Merlin's Hermitage and Cave*. [2] In the same group of revivals of Merlin, is to be counted the pantomime opera, *Merlin in Love*, which the poet and dramatist Aaron Hill (1685–1749-50) ventured to write. [3] This production, of very slender merit, practically closes the list of the older literary works in which Merlin figures. Yet one might

---

[1] Of Giffard we know little. William Cushing remarks (*Anonyms*, p. 423, Cambridge, U.S.A., 1890) that he was "an actor, and long the manager of the old theatre in Goodman's Fields ; under his management Mr. Garrick made his first appearance in London." Here the piece was first acted ; and it was published in 8vo., London, 1736.

[2] The copy I refer to is in the British Museum. The date and place of publication are to some extent conjectural, but it is reasonably certain that the play appeared in London in 1736.

[3] See vol. i. of his *Dramatic Works*. London, 2 vols., 8vo.

probably glean from the poets and prose-writers a considerable number of allusions not here noted.[1]

Besides these serious attempts to make literary use of the great enchanter, there appeared in the course of the seventeenth and eighteenth centuries a considerable number of general prophecies and almanac predictions which were fathered upon the national prophet. Merlin's name had long ceased to be a name to conjure with, but nothing was more natural than to take advantage of his celebrity in order to help the sale of catchpenny pamphlets of a prophetical character. A good type of the prophet of that day was William Lilly (1602-1682), the most celebrated of the English astrologers of the seventeenth century.[2] He won notoriety at the time of the Puritan uprising against Charles I., and under the name of *Merlinus Anglicus* published among many other predictions *England's Propheticall Merline foretelling to all nations of Europe.*

Lilly's prophecies were forerunners of a long series of predictions, the titles of which I will enumerate without discussion. It will be noted toward the close of the list that the prophetic character is well-nigh lost :—

1.—A Prophesie [of Merlin] concerning Hull in Yorkshire, 1642. 4to.
2.—The Lord Merlin's Prophecy[3] concerning the King of Scots; foretelling the strange and wonderfull Things that shall befall him in England. As also The time and manner of a dismal and fatall Battel. Lond., Aug. 22, 1651. 4to.
3.—Merlin Reviv'd, or an old Prophecy found in a Manuscript in Pontefract Castle in Yorkshire. (In verse.) Lond. 1681. Another ed. 1682. Fol.

[1] For example, Pope has four allusions to Merlin :—
   " Did ever Proteus, Merlin, any witch."—Sat. III. 152.
   " Extols old Bards, or Merlin's Prophecy."—Sat. V 132.
   " When Merlin's Cave is half unfurnish'd yet."—Sat. V. 355.
   " Lord, how we strut thro' Merlin's Cave, to see."—Sat. VI. 139.
[2] His *Introduction to Astrology* even appeared in a new edition : Lond. 1832, 8vo.
[3] This was an old prophecy presented to Queen Elizabeth in 1582.

4.—The mystery of Ambros Merlins, Standard-bearer, Wolf, and
last Boar of Cornwall, with sundry other misterious prophecys
. . . . . . unfolded in the following treatise on the signification . . . . . . of that prodigious comet seen . . . . . . anno
1680, with the blazing star, 1682 . . . . . . Written by a
lover of his countrys peace. Lond. (1683), fol.

5.—Catastrophe Mundi; or Merlin reviv'd, in a Discourse of
Prophecies and Predictions, and their remarkable accomplish-
ment; with Mr. Lilly's Hieroglyphics exactly cut. By a
Learned Pers[on]. Lond. 1683, 12mo.

6.—Merlin reviv'd, in a Discourse of Prophecies and Predictions,
and their Remarkable accomplishment, with Mr. Lilly's Hieroglyphics; also a collection of all the Ancient Prophecies,
touching the Grand Revolution like to happen in these Latter
Ages. Lond. 1683, 12mo.

7.—Merlini Anglici Ephemeris; or, Astrological Judgments for the
Year 1685 . . . . . . London, Printed by J. Macock for the
Company of Stationers, 1685, 8vo.   .

8.—In the year 1709 Swift threw out "A Famous Prediction of
Merlin, the British Wizard. Written above a thousand years
ago, and relating to the year 1709. With explanatory notes
by T. Philomath." With regard to this prophecy Swift
observes, after a passing jibe at the almanac-maker, Partridge:
"I found it in an old edition of Merlin's prophecies, imprinted
at London by Johan Haukyns, in the year 1530, p. 39. I set
it down word for word in the old orthography, and shall take
leave to subjoin a few explanatory notes." [1]

9.—Merlinus liberatus. An Almanack for the Year of our blessed
Saviour's Incarnation 1723 . . . . . . by John Partridge. [2]
London, Printed by J. Roberts for the Company of Stationers,
12mo.

10.—Merlinus liberatus . . . . . . London: Printed by R. Reily,
for the Company of Stationers, 1753: 1761. 12mo.

---

[1] Swift's *Works*, vol. viii. pp. 480-484, Scott's ed.
[2] This is the Partridge just referred to, who was the laughing-stock of the
wits associated with Swift. *Cf.* Scott's *Prose Works*, vol. v. p. 199.

11.—Merlin's Life and Prophecies . . . . . . His predictions relating
to the late contest about . . . Richmond Park. With some other
events relating thereto, not yet come to pass, etc. London,
1755, 8vo.

12.—A Prophecy of Ill. ["A political satire."] London, 1762, 8vo.

13.—A prophecy of Merlin. An heroic poem concerning the wonderful success of a project, now on foot, to make the River from
the Severn to Strond navigable. Translated from the original
Latin, annexed with notes explanatory. London, 1776, 4to.

14.—Merlinus Liberatus. An Almanack. By John Partridge [pseud.],
London, 1819–1864, 16mo.

15.—The Philosophical Merlin: being the translation of a valuable
manuscript, formerly in the possession of Napoleon Buonaparte
. . . . . . enabling the reader to cast the Nativity of himself
. . . . without the aid of Tables . . . . . . or Calculations.
Part I. [The second part never appeared.] London, 1822, 8vo.

16.—Urania; or the Astrologer's Chronicle and Mystical Magazine.
Edited by Merlinus Anglicus, jun. [R. C. Smith.] London,
1825.[1]

In the miscellaneous pamphlets just cited the fame of the
great prophet had sunk to its nadir; but with the rise of
Romanticism Merlin again found a place of honour. Early in
the present century Sir Walter Scott introduced him as a
leading character into one of the most graceful of his romantic
poems, *The Bridal of Triermain* (1813).

The great enchanter Merlin had long been resting in his grave

---

[1] In addition to these pamphlets, all of which bear a more or less prophetic
stamp, there are several other fugitive productions, which I cannot describe more
precisely, but which may be classed with the English Ephemerides. Such are:
*Merlin's Almanack and Prognostications, Merlin's Prognostications, The Mad-
merry Merlin, The Royal Merlin*, etc.

Even in our own day Merlin's name has not infrequently served as a
pseudonym.[a] Under this name Alfred Tennyson contributed two poems to the
Examiner (Lond. 1852) with the titles: *The Third of February*, 1852, and *Hands
All Round*. Of less note are Merlin = Milner; Merlin the Second = David Henry.
Merlin was the pseudonym of Dr. Alex. Wilder, from 1864 to 1870 the New York
correspondent of the Boston *Daily Advertiser*.

[a] *Cf*. Cushing's *Initials and Pseudonyms*, Art. *Merlin*.

in the rock, when Gyneth, the fair daughter of Gwendolen and Arthur, was offered in marriage to the knight who should prove himself bravest in the tournament. From all sides the knights of the Round Table gathered for the contest. As the combat thickened, the proud maiden saw without pity one knight fall after another, till at length young Vanoc, of the race of Merlin, died at her very feet. Then suddenly arose out of the earth, in the midst of the lists, the form of Merlin, who with stern gesture pronounced sentence upon her—

> " Thou shalt bear thy penance lone
> In the valley of Saint John,
> And this weird shall overtake thee ;
> Sleep, until a knight shall wake thee,
> For feats of arms as far renown'd
> As warrior of the Table Round."
>
> —CANTO II. STANZA xxvi.

For five hundred years the maiden slept her enchanted sleep within a mighty castle, till at length she was awakened by the Baron of Triermain, Sir Roland de Vaux, who braved the dangers of the Hall of Fear, and defied the snares

> "Spread by Pleasure, Wealth, and Pride."
>
> —CANTO III. STANZA xxxvi.

When he entered the magic bower where the maiden slept in her ivory chair, she awoke suddenly from her slumber, while the magic halls melted away amid the flash of lightning and the roll of thunder. But safe in the arms of the bold knight lay the princess, and with him she went to be his bride.

The two leading motives of the piece—the summoning of an enchanter, and the magic sleep of a princess who is to be awakened by a brave knight—are familiar and threadbare enough ; but Scott, while missing some of the naïve simplicity of the verse romance of the Middle Ages, has invested the narrative with a grace and beauty not often found in his models.[1]

Very different from Scott's somewhat conventional enchanter is the Merlin of Tennyson's tale of *Vivien* (1859), in which the poet tells how Merlin was beguiled by the wily temptress who had vainly endeavoured to seduce " the blameless king." The story is too familiar to need recalling ; but we may note that in this poem Tennyson differs widely from the sources that he usually follows so closely. Nowhere in the old romances does the character of Vivien appear in such a malignant light. In the prose romance of *Merlin* (p. 681) she desired to have him ever with her, and for this she wrought upon him the enchantment that he had himself taught her; and while it seemed to him that he was in the fairest and strongest tower in the world there were few hours of the day or of the night when she was not with him. But though the maiden went in and out when she would, Merlin never came forth from the fortress in which he was imprisoned.

According to Malory's *Morte Darthur* (B. IV. ch. 1), Nyneue, the lady of the lake, imprisoned Merlin in a rock wrought by enchantment. He had been tempting her to give him her love, but " she was euer passynge wery of hym, and fayne wold haue ben delyuerd of hym."

---

[1] Scott alludes to Merlin and the Lady of the Lake in *Kenilworth*, chap. xxx., and makes use of Merlin in his ballad on *Thomas the Rhymer*, Part III.

The novelist Thomas Love Peacock introduces Myrrddin Gwyllt (*sic*: the name should, of course, be Myrddin Wyllt, or Merlin the Wild) into his romance of *The Misfortunes of Elphin* (1829). Merlin here takes part in a song-contest with the other Welsh bards, and sings the *Avallenau* or *Song of the Apple-trees*. (Reprinted, Lond. 1891.)

In a ballad of unknown age, a " Fragment of Child Rowland and Bard Ellen," the eldest brother of the lost maid Ellen goes to the Warluck Merlyn (*Myrddin Wyldt, sic*) and asks his advice. Merlin gives the desired instructions. Child Rowland proceeds to the Castle of Elfland, rescues his sister from the king, and brings back her and the two brothers in search of whom she had gone. The portion of the ballad relating to Merlin is lost, but has been supplied from an oral narration. *Cf. Eng. and Scottish Ballads*, ed. by F. J. Child, i. 416–423. Boston, 1857.

Tennyson has borrowed little more than the hint of his leading motives. Yet this poem, steeped as it is in the personality of the poet, gives us a picture of the last days of Merlin which, in its depth and colour, may be sought elsewhere in vain. The mysterious charm of the old Celtic legend has here lost none of its glamour; and while the venomous insinuations of the wily harlot well-nigh destroy the beauty of some passages, yet the strange spell that one feels in *The Lady of Shalott* and *The Passing of Arthur*, recurs now and again in this legend of the enchanted sleep of Merlin.

Merlin has inspired nothing of recent years to compare with *Vivien*, but the enchanter figures once more in Tennyson's *Merlin and the Gleam* (1889) and in a poem by Robert Buchanan —*Merlin and the White Death*.[1]

We are perhaps hardly bound to notice the appearance of Merlin in Mark Twain's burlesque romance, *A Yankee at the Court of King Arthur*, though it is to be feared that the irreverent mind of this unheroic century will find as much entertainment in the farcical burlesque as in the serious romance of six centuries ago.

V.

THE DEVELOPMENT OF THE EARLY FORMS OF THE LEGEND.

We have traced in outline the Merlin legend in the various forms which it has assumed in the literature of Europe. We must now go back a little, and endeavour to follow in some detail the development of the legend from the earlier forms. But before we can study the legend itself we are compelled to consider briefly the genuineness and authenticity of the literary documents in which it is contained. For the sake

[1] In *Once a Week*, 10 : 251.

of convenience we will glance first at the Latin sources, and then pass to the Welsh literature. The first name to consider is Nennius.

It is not easy to overestimate the importance for the history of the Arthurian romances, and especially for the history of Merlin, of this obscure little chronicle. One can find in the extant Celtic literature little or nothing that throws light on the sources of the romantic Merlin legend. But in this short recital we have in embryo[1] one of the most characteristic and interesting portions of the legend afterwards developed in the French romance. It is in fact, as de la Borderie remarks, "the first and the most ancient collection of the popular legends of Britain, which later gave birth to the romances of *Brut*, of *Merlin*, of *Arthur*—in a word, the immense cycle of the chivalric epics of the Round Table."[2] We may then agree with Milton that Nennius is " a very trivial author," without losing sight of the immense importance of the *Historia Britonum* in the development of the legendary history of Britain. It will therefore be worth our while to pause for a moment and review the varying opinions that have been advanced with regard to the authorship and the age of the book.

As to the authorship, we need scarcely remark that Nennius is a mere name used, as de la Borderie suggests, to cover our ignorance of the real author. For a time Gildas was credited with the book, but this hypothesis is now universally abandoned. Among other conjectures we may note that Paulin Paris[3] supposed the *Historia Britonum* to be the work of an Armorican which was brought into England early in the twelfth century. But critics are now generally agreed that this little chronicle

---

[1] *Cf.* de la Borderie, *L'Hist. Brit. attribuée à Nennius*, p. 69. " Ici [cap. 40] commence le récit d'une merveilleuse aventure, germe de tout ce qu'on a écrit plus tard sur le fameux Merlin et ses fameuses prophéties."

[2] *L'Hist. Brit.* etc. p. 83.   [3] *Les Romans de la Table Ronde*, I. p. 36.

is "essentially an insular creation."[1] Mr. Skene supposes that the *Historia* was "originally written in British in Cumbria or *y Gogled*[*d*] (the North), and was afterwards translated into Latin."[2] It is of course made up of several parts of varying age. If we exclude the interpolations we have, according to de la Borderie,[3] the original core of the work, which may be analyzed as follows :—

1. Descriptio Britanniae.
2. Origo Britonum Scotorumque.
3. Britannia sub Romanis.
4. Historia Guortigerni.
5. Arthuri gesta.

For our immediate purpose we are concerned chiefly with the "Historia Guortigerni."

The age of the Chronicle has given rise to a great variety of opinions. In the preface to his text of Nennius, Mr. J. Stevenson (Eng. Hist. Soc. 1838) remarks (p. v.) : "We may despair of being able to decide, with any degree of accuracy, either as to the age, the historical value, or the authorship of this composition." In Skene's opinion "The text of the *Historia Britonum* was first put together . . . as early as the seventh century."[4] His opinion is followed in Glennie's Essay on Arthurian Localities[5] (pp. xxxvii. and cvii.). Nash,

---

[1] De la Borderie, *L'Hist. Brit. attribuée à Nennius*, p. vii. We ought not, however, entirely to overlook Wright's remark (*On the Lit. Hist. of Geoff. of Monmouth*, Lond. 1848, 4to.) that the earlier manuscripts of Nennius appear to have been written abroad, and in fact never to have been in England, but to have been brought from France.

[2] Cf. *Encyc. Brit.* 9th ed. 1876, art. *Celtic Lit.* "*Y Gogledd*," notes M. Phillimore, "was technically used for all Britondom north of Wales in the Middle Ages and before."

[3] *Hist. Brit. attribuée à Nennius*, p. 27. For a general estimate of the value of Nennius, see Skene's *Celtic Scotland*, i. p. 152. Both Mr. Skene and Dr. Guest accept the historical authority of Nennius. I much regret not to have seen Mr. Phillimore's articles and notes in *Y Cymmrodor*, vols. ix. and xi., on various points connected with Nennius and Merlin.

[4] *Four Ancient Books of Wales*, i. pp. 58-60.

[5] Printed for E.E.Text Soc. in Part III. of the *Merlin*. Lond. 1869.

in his introduction to the *Romance of Merlin*, thinks that the *Historia* was "probably written as early as the eighth century."[1] By far the larger proportion of later critics have fixed upon the ninth century. Schoell, writing in 1851, made a strong argument[2] in favour of the year 822 A.D. He is followed by de la Borderie[3] and by Ebert.[4] The interpolated Prologue[5] of the *Historia* (sec. 2) assigns the date of the compilation to the year 858 A.D., but this is not accepted by the critics. Gaston Paris criticizes de la Borderie's argument, and rejects the date 822 for 878.[6] In the *Histoire Littéraire de la France* (xxx. p. 4), G. Paris merely remarks that the *Historia* was composed in the ninth century. Paulin Paris had already taken the same ground,[7] though confessing that the earliest manuscripts were of the twelfth century. Still more cautious than these critics are those who merely say that the pseudo-Nennius was put together between the seventh and the ninth centuries.[8] Ten Brink[9] speaks of the age of the

---

[1] Part I. p. ii. E.E.Text Soc. Lond. 1865.

[2] C. G. Schoell, *De Ecclesiasticae Britonum Scotorumque historiae fontibus*, p. 35. Berlin, 1851.

[3] *L'Hist. Brit.* etc.   Paris, 1883, p. 20.

[4] *Allgem. Gesch. der Litt. des Mittelalters im Abendlande.* Leipzig, 1887, Bd. iii. p. 387.   [5] *Cf.* De la Borderie, p. 12.

[6] *Romania,* xii. 368-70. "A primo anno quo Saxones venerunt in Britanniam usque ad annum quartum Mervini regis supputantur anni ccccxxix." Now, 449+429=878. "Il écrivait donc en 878." M. Paris selects for his purpose a Mervin who died in 903, and began (perhaps) to reign about 874. His fourth year would be, then, 878.

[7] *Les Romans de la Table Ronde,* i. 38.   [8] *Encyc. Brit.*, art. *Romance,* xx. 638.

[9] *Gesch der engl. Lit.* i. 169.   Berlin, 1877.   Mr. Phillimore, who is recognized as the best authority on Nennius, sends me the following note on the date of Nennius: "One of the two oldest MSS. of Nennius (Harl. 3859, now said by Mr. E. M. Thompson to be of the early 12th century), which contains the short Welsh chronicle and Anglo-Saxon Genealogies (briefly known as the *Saxon Genealogies* or *Genealogiae*), has annexed to it, in the same or contemporary hands, Welsh annals and genealogies (only found in this MS.) which must, from the way they end, have been written between 954 and 988, as I have shewn in *Y Cymmrodor*, vol. ix., in my preface to these *Annales Cambriae* and Old Welsh Genealogies from Harl. MS. 3859." Now this MS. and its three sister MSS (de la Borderie, who adds other MSS. containing these *Genealogiae Regum Saxonum*, is altogether wrong: the MSS.

Historia as highly doubtful, and possibly not much earlier than Geoffrey of Monmouth, but in this opinion he has little or no following.

We see, however, that in spite of considerable differences of opinion, the critics are agreed in placing Nennius earlier than Geoffrey of Monmouth, and, with few exceptions, in the ninth century. As already remarked, the question as to the historical value of Nennius is for our purpose of no great importance; but we must take the *Historia Britonum* as the original source of one of the most characteristic of the legends relating to Merlin,[1] and as the only original we can find for much of Geoffrey's *Historia*.

De la Borderie does, indeed, attempt to make out a case for the so-called *Historia Britannica*, which he would like to regard as the intermediate link between Nennius and Geoffrey; but he has succeeded in convincing few besides himself. The fragments of this very dubious history date, according to him, from the year 1019 A.D.[2] "Like the *Historia Britonum* of Nennius,

in question either do not contain them or are not MSS. of Nennius) are very similar, except for the unique additions to one of them, and must, as can be proved, all go back immediately to one prototype. This prototype, ergo, must be older than 954. But this edition of the *Saxon Genealogies* is necessarily more modern as an edition (though it may be preserved in other MSS.) than the edition of Nennius without the said Genealogies, but with other accretions to the original work. Now this older edition is the one of which MSS. are most numerous. Moreover, the "*Sax.-Gen.*" edition, besides its accretion of the Sax.-Gen., has the orthography of the Welsh names modernized from the older edition. But the older edition has already accretions (the *Mirabilia*) and changes, which mark it off as more modern than the edition of the Vatican MS. (the oldest known), which is *said* to be of the tenth century. We may, therefore, judge how far beyond 954 Nennius can be certainly predicated to be. But take 954 as the earliest possible date for the composition of Nennius (which it is not, by far), and, as Geoffrey of Monmouth's *Historia* was issued 1120-1130, or thereabouts, there is a difference of 170 or 180 years."

[1] I do not, of course, deny that some of the elements of the legend may be older than Nennius. See the notes on the Sources.

[2] *L'Historia Britannica avant Geoffroi de Monmouth*, p. 103. A few pages later he urges the following reasons : "Entre *l'Historia Britonum* de Nennius et *l'Historia Regum* de Geoffroi, il a nécessairement existé une forme intermédiaire de la légende des origines bretonnes. Cette forme constituait un livre appelé *Historia Britannica*,

the *Historia Britannica*," he remarks, "is the work of the imagination of the insular and not of the Armorican Britons."[1] Now then, argues de la Borderie, "the book of Nennius, the *Historia Britannica*, the work of Geoffrey, represent the three successive stages of the legend in its development from the British sources. Nennius, or the *Historia Britonum*, is the egg ; the *Historia Britannica* is the chicken ; the *Historia Regum Britanniae* is the superb and noisy (bruyant) cock, who chants his fanfare to the great orchestra."[2] He goes on to suggest[3] that the *Historia Britannica* is the identical book that was brought from Britain by Walter, archdeacon of Oxford,[4] for the use of Geoffrey of Monmouth. Britain, we are told, means the British (Welsh) portion of the Island of Great Britain, as opposed to the English portion.

It must be confessed that this is a large theory on a very narrow basis. We have but four small pages of the *Historia Britannica*. One paragraph is given to Arthur : of Merlin, we find no mention. How so careful a critic as de la Borderie could have propounded a theory so lacking in proof is not easy to see. As Gaston Paris points out,[5] if this Anglo-Latin book existed and was known in Armorica, English historians of that day might fairly be expected to know of

dont l'existence est constatée et testée en 1019 par le prêtre Guillaume, auteur de la *Vie de saint Gouëznou*. Mais—comme l'œuvre de Nennius, forme rudimentaire de la légende, comme le livre de Geoffroi qui en marque l'épanouissement,—cette forme intermédiaire appartient exclusivement, par son inspiration et sa rédaction aux Bretons de l'île, et il n'est nullemeut prouvé—au contraire—que l'exemplaire qu'en posséda Gautier d'Oxford sortît de l'Armorique," etc.—*Ibid.* p. 108.

[1] *Ibid.* p. 99.   [2] *Ibid.* p. 102.   [3] *Ibid.* pp. 102–107.

[4] "Ce Gautier, surnommé *Calenius*, est un personnage assez mystérieux. Henri de Huntingdon (*De Contemptu Mundi*, § 4, éd. Arnold, p. 302), l'appelle 'superlative rethoricus.' On lui attribue une continuation de *l'Hist. regum* de Gaufrei pendant quarante ans, qui ne s'est pas retrouvée. Il figure en 1129 avec son ami *Gaufridus Artur* (ce surnom ne fut donc pas donné à Gaufrei pour son *Historia*) dans les chartes de fondation de l'abbaye d'Oseney près d'Oxford (*v.* Dugdale, *Monasticon* vi. 251)."—G. Paris, *Romania*, xii. 373. This note is based on one by Sir F. Madden. See further, Ward's *Catalogue of Romances*, i. pp. 218, 219.

[5] *Romania*, xii. 371, 372.

its existence. Yet William of Malmesbury, writing in 1125, "declared positively that he could find for the ancient history of the island no other sources than Beda and Gildas : indeed, except the pseudo-Nennius used by William himself and by Henry of Huntingdon, no other source was known up to the appearance of Geoffrey's book (1136) ; and when this appeared, the accounts that it contained of the victories of Arthur in Gaul were to everybody a revelation, which Henry of Huntingdon and others accepted with as much confidence as surprise, (but) which William of Newburgh and others rejected with contempt. Furthermore, Geoffrey, proud of the possession of the Breton book which his friend Walter had brought him, declares that the English historians, not having the documents that he possesses, can say nothing concerning the British kings of which his history alone knows." With no great injustice, therefore, M. Paris ends his criticism by calling the *Historia Britannica* " ce fantôme de ce livre imaginaire." We may, then, pass directly to Geoffrey of Monmouth.

It is quite unnecessary to go into detail in treating of the life of Geoffrey of Monmouth.[1] For our purpose it is enough to note that he was an ecclesiastic who became Archdeacon of Monmouth, that from 1152 to 1154, the year of his death, he was Bishop of St. Asaph, and that between 1130–1150 he wrote three works now generally[2] accepted as his—the *Prophetia Merlini* (before 1136),[3] the *Historia Regum Britanniæ* (about 1136),[4] and the *Vita Merlini* (between 1140 and 1150).

---

[1] On the whole the best account of him is in Ward's *Catalogue of Romances*, i. pp. 203-222.

[2] But not universally, as we shall see a little later.

[3] Ward, *Catalogue of Romances*, i. 207.

[4] G. Paris, *Hist. Litt. de la France*, xxx. pp. 4, 5. Various dates are assigned for the *Hist. Reg. Brit.* :—

(1) Low and Pulling's *Dict. of Eng. Hist.*, 1130 A.D.

(2) Ten Brink, *Gesch. der engl. Lit.* i. 168, 1132-1135 A.D.

The *Prophetia* was afterwards incorporated with the *Historia*, of which it now forms the seventh book.[1]

The first question naturally arising with regard to each of these books is: From what materials are they constructed? In searching for the sources of Geoffrey's *Historia* it is hardly possible to advance far.[2] The most obvious source is the *Historia Britonum* of Nennius. As for the British book brought from the Continent by Archdeacon Walter of Oxford, we know nothing about it, and we gain little by multiplying conjectures

(3) *Encyc. Brit.* xx. p. 643—"The Round Table romances had their starting-point in Geoffrey's *Historia*, first published in 1138-39, revised and republished in its present form in 1147."

(4) Ward, *Catal. of Romances*, i. 209—"The first edition of Geoffrey's *Historia* was certainly completed by the end of 1138."

(5) Paulin Paris and Sir F. Madden, 1135-1147 A.D.

(6) *Cf.* Arnold, Introd. to Henry of Huntingdon's *Historia Anglorum* (Rolls Series), pp. xxii., xxiii.

[1] On the *Prophecies*, Professor Henry Morley has the following remark, the last clause of which is a good example of the baseless statements that have found their way into so many works on the literature of the period we are treating:—"Afterwards he made alterations, and formed the work into eight books; to which he added Merlin's *Prophecies* translated out of Cymric verse into Latin prose."—*English Writers*, iii. 45.

[2] "Assurément il a beaucoup,—et très pauvrement,—inventé; mais il s'est appuyé, en beaucoup de points, sur des légendes galloises, sur des contes populaires qu'il a arbitrairement rattachés à des noms de rois (Lear, Bladud, etc.)."—G. Paris, *Romania*, xii. 372.

Compare with the above note the following:—

"That Geoffrey drew his materials from British sources, and did not coin any of them, seems to us the legitimate conclusion to be drawn from a careful study of the whole subject. His book is, however, a compilation and not a translation, at all events no book now exists which can be regarded as his original, while all the *Bruts* or chronicles are posterior to Geoffrey's book and based upon it."—*Encyc. Brit.* 9th ed., art. *Celtic Lit.*

On the specific question of the origin of Geoffrey's *Merlin*, A. Brandl remarks:—

"Ähnlich bunt mag Geoffrey die Figur des Merlin, des Propheten beim letzten Brittenkönig Vortigern, zusammengestellt haben, mit Elementen aus der Legende von St. Germanus, aus druidischer Mystik, aus Daniel und den *XV. Signa ante judicium*, nach deren Art Merlin schliesslich den Weltuntergang weissagt."—Paul's *Grundriss der germ. Philologie*, ii. 621.

For further details, see the discussion of the question whether we have to deal with one Merlin or two, and the discussion of the sources of Robert de Borron's *Merlin*.

with regard to it. Paulin Paris[1] supposed that the Latin chronicle of Nennius was the original text or a translation of the famous British book. Of course this is not impossible, but hardly probable.[2]

Gaston Paris finds the origin of Geoffrey's *Historia* in the

---

[1] *Romans de la Table Ronde*, i. 38. Geoffrey, remarks M. Paris, merely expanded Nennius, writing a line for a word, and a paragraph for a sentence, and pieced out the whole with the help of his Latin reading, Vergil, Ovid, etc.

[2] Those who are interested in the question may follow it up in Ward's *Catalogue of Romances*, i. p. 214 *sqq.*, where the views of P. Paris are controverted, and the whole matter discussed at length. Mr. Ward thinks that a Breton book may have existed :—

"But there are really some grounds for supposing that Walter left behind him a book, resembling Geoffrey's *Historia*, yet distinct from it, though there is nothing to prove whether it was his own composition or the book which he brought from abroad."—p. 214.

"The Breton book, then, we hold, was not a mere copy of Nennius. At the same time it is evident that whoever drew up the scheme of the present *Historia* had the work of Nennius before him, and made arbitrary changes in certain facts derived from it."—p. 217.

Mr. Ward remarks further on the origin of Geoffrey's *Historia* : "But the Arthur legend had travelled south, and had been immensely developed, before the days of Geoffrey. At all events, it was not he who invented the fiction, that Arthur was born and mortally wounded in Cornwall. The monks of Laon,[a] who visited Cornwall in 1113, were shown rocks called Arthur's Chair and Arthur's Furnace, and were told that this was his native land, 'secundum fabulas Britanorum regis Arturi'; and at Bodmin they narrowly escaped bloodshed when they refused to believe that Arthur was still alive. (See Hermannus, *De miraculis S. Mariæ Laudunensis*, book ii. 15, 16, republished by Migne, *Patrologia*, tom. 156, col. 983.) These monks also inform us that similar Arthurian fables were rife in Brittany. Finally, considering that Geoffrey's Arthur is a grandson of an Armorican prince, and that his Armorican cousin Hoel is his brother in arms both at home and in Gaul; and considering that Cadwalader finds a last hope for his degenerate Bretons in the princes of Armorica ; one can hardly doubt Geoffrey's deriving much of the latter part of his *Historia* from Breton sources. Whether he followed (or, as he terms it, translated) any regular book, or whether he collected materials and arranged them himself, can never be completely decided."—*Ibid.* i. 217, 218.

Mr. Ward's opinion may be compared with that of M. Gaston Paris :—"Je suis au contraire tout à fait de l'avis de M. de la Borderie sur la seconde question qu'il traite, celle de la provenance galloise et non bretonne, des fables de Gaufrei. Celui-ci prétend à trois reprises avoir trouvé l'histoire des rois bretons dans un livre écrit *Britannico sermone*, que lui avait fait connaître son ami Gautier, archidiacre d'Oxford. Il ment certainement, car on a prouvé qu'il reproduisait textuellement des phrases latines d'écrivains antérieurs, et que par conséquent il ne traduisait pas du Gallois. Il se contredit d'ailleurs: il prétend à un endroit (xii. 20) qu'il a simplement

[a] On the visit of the monks of Laon, compare Zimmer, *Zeits. für franz. u. Lit.* xiii. p. 106.

Historia Britonum of Nennius taken as a groundwork, and supplemented by the tales told him by his friend Walter of Oxford, and by his own recollections of Welsh legends. Gaston Paris even admits the existence of a British book, for "the forms of many of the proper names of the *Historia Regum* are often more archaic than those of Nennius";[1] but M. Paris is careful to remark that Geoffrey did not translate from the Welsh.

traduit le livre gallois (*in latinum sermonem transferre curavi*), et à un autre (xi. 1) il dit qu'il écrit tant d'après ce livre que d'après les récits de Gautier (*ut Gaufridus in Britannico prefato sermone invenit et a Gualtero Oxinefordensi audivit*). La vérité est à mon sens, dans cette dernière phrase. C'est avec *l'Historia Britonum* d'une part et les récits de son ami Gautier, ainsi que ses propres souvenirs de contes gallois d'autre part que Gaufrei a composé son roman. Quant au fameux livre gallois, il a existé : les formes de beaucoup de noms propres de *l'Historia regum*, formes souvent plus archaïques que celles de Nennius . . . . . et que Gaufrei n'a pu inventer, montrent qu'il a eu sous les yeux des documents fort anciens ; en quoi ils consistaient, et s'ils contenaient autre chose que des listes de noms propres, c'est ce qu'il faudrait étudier de près. Mais pourquoi, en parlant de ce livre, Gaufrei dit-il que Gautier le lui a 'apporté de Bretagne' (*ex* Britannia advexit)? On a compris jusqu'à present que *Britannia* désignait ici la Petite-Bretagne." G. Paris follows de la Borderie in thinking Great Britain to be meant, and indeed the whole of it, and not Wales, as de la Borderie supposed. He continues :—"L'explication du problème est, à mon sens, bien plus simple. Toute la difficulté repose sur ce point : puisque Gaufrei était en Grande-Bretagne, comment pouvait-on lui apporter un livre de Grande-Bretagne ? Mais il y a pétition de principe. Rien ne nous prouve que Gaufrei fût en Grande-Bretagne quand il écrivait son livre, et il y a même des vraisemblances pour qu'il fût en Normandie. Si Gaufrei était en Normandie, on comprend très bien qu'il prétende que le livre gallois qu'il dit traduire lui a été apporté de Grande-Bretagne par Gautier d'Oxford, et ainsi disparaît toute difficulté sur ce passage. Un mot encore sur les sources de Gaufrei. Il avait très probablement trouvé dans quelque cloître de Normandie un exemplaire de *l'Historia Britonum*, et, croyant cet ouvrage inconnu en Angleterre, il s'était mis à l'exploiter, en s'aidant de divers auteurs latins, pour en tirer sa grandiose mystification. Il reçut sans doute, pendant qu'il y travaillait, la visite de son ami Gautier d'Oxford, qui lui apporta quelque document gallois, et tout deux arrangèrent en commun l'imposture qui devait avoir tant de succès : il fut convenu que Gautier aurait apporté à Gaufrei une histoire complète des rois bretons, qui contenait toutes les belles choses que celui-ci allait apprendre au monde. On a vu que Gaufrei n'avait même pas su soutenir ce mensonge sans se contredire. Tout ce qui, dans son livre, n'est pas tiré de *l'Historia Britonum* (ou d'autres ouvrages latins) repose, sauf ce qui pouvait se trouver dans le document en question, sur l'invention ou sur les contes populaires gallois, recueillis par Gautier et par lui. C'est à la critique à s'efforcer de discerner ce qui doit être attribué à l'une ou à l'autre de ces provenances."—*Romania*, xii. 372-375.

[1] *Romania*, xii. 372, 373.

From all this discussion may be inferred, as in the case of Nennius, the need of extreme caution in the construction of a theory designed to explain all the facts. Nothing really convincing is to be deduced from the evidence. Some of the theories advanced are not impossible; and with this comfort we must be as content as we can.

As for the *Vita Merlini*, it also has been the subject of much discussion.[1] Mr. Ward (*Catalogue of Romances*, i. 278-288) gives an excellent account of the arguments in favour of its genuineness, which is not now seriously questioned by most scholars.[2]

[1] For instance, in the *Encyclopaedia Britannica* (9th ed.) some of the contributors affirm, while others deny, its genuineness. In the article on *Romance* we read concerning Geoffrey of Monmouth: "His poem on the *Life and Prophecies of Merlin* was a separate work, published in 1136–1137, and again in 1149"; while in the article on Geoffrey of Monmouth we read: "Internal evidence is fatal to the claims of the second," *i.e.* the *Vita Merlini*.

Henry Morley (*English Writers*, iii. p. 44) says: "There has also been improperly ascribed to him [Geoff. of Mon.] a life of Merlin, in Latin hexameters."

Compare with these authorities the opinion of Gaston Paris:—

"Gaufrei, quelques années après *l'Historia*, composa un autre ouvrage, la *Vita Merlini*, poème assez élégamment écrit, où des traditions historiques bretonnes se mêlent à des contes venus d'orient ou courant dans les écoles, et qui n'a pas été sans influence sur quelques romans français postérieurs."— *La Litt. Française au moyen Âge*, p. 90.

Also: "Gaufrei composa en hexamètres latins sa *Vita Merlini*, dans laquelle il mêla des notions de géographie et d'histoire naturelle, empruntées aux écrivains classiques, à des contes populaires bretons dont la plupart se retrouvent ailleurs, et à quelques nouvelles prédictions."—*Hist. Litt. de la France*, xxx. p. 5.

Paulin Paris had already advanced about the same opinion (*Romans*, i. 77) in opposition to the views of Thomas Wright and Francisque Michel. He says:—

"Il faut absolument en conclure que le poëme a été composé avant les romans, c'est à dire de 1140 à 1150. Ainsi tout se réunit pour conserver à Geoffroy de Monmouth l'honneur d'avoir écrit vers le milieu du douzieme siècle, le poëme *De Vita Merlini* après *l'Historia Britonum* que semble continuer le poëme pour ce qui touche à Merlin, et avant le roman français de *Merlin*, qui devait faire un poëme d'assez nombreux emprunts."

[2] The earliest printed edition appeared in 1833 for the Roxburghe Club, under the editorship of William Henry Black. This edition was fortunately limited to forty-two copies; for it was as bad as bad could be. The second, and in fact the only edition based upon the manuscripts,[a] is that of Wright and Michel, since

[a] G. Paris, *Hist. Litt. de la France*, xxx. p. 5, says there is but one MS.; but *cf.* Ward's *Cat. of Romances.*

For convenience we may defer all further account of the *Vita Merlini* and the other Latin sources till we have examined the extant Celtic literature that tells us of Myrddin the Bard. Here, too, we find it necessary in the first place to determine the genuineness of the Welsh poems that touch upon Myrddin. We cannot here attempt an exhaustive discussion, but we may trace in a few words the varying attitude of critical opinion toward the few poems that concern the question before us, and set in order the results of the investigations which none but advanced Celtic specialists are competent to make. The data are so meagre that we may perhaps never hope to get more than a probable solution of the difficulties starting up at every turn. There is here a tempting field for an ingenious constructive critic, for in this matter one can conjecture much and prove little.

One caution, however, we should observe from the outset. We must not forget that it is one thing to find in Welsh poems of doubtful age a meagre account of a bard named Myrddin, and in a modern Breton ballad or two the figure of Myrddin[1] the Bard and Myrddin the Enchanter, and quite another thing to show that these throw any real light on the legend as we find it in the French prose romance of Merlin. If we accept the genuineness of the poems ascribed to Myrddin or which make mention of him,—and there is really no great harm in doing so,—we have advanced scarcely a step in tracing out the source of the legend as found in Nennius, in Geoffrey of Monmouth's *Historia*, or in any of the translations or imitations of Geoffrey's *Historia*. As the investigation proceeds, we shall hardly be

San-Marte did no more than to reprint the text and annotate it. Our edition of the *Vita Merlini* really dates, therefore, from 1837, when it appeared under the title: "Galfridi de Monumeta . . . . Vita Merlini. Vie de Merlin attribuée à Geoffroy de Monmouth . . . par Francisque Michel et Thomas Wright. Parisiis, Silvestre, London, W. Pickering, 1837." This edition has become rare.

San-Marte follows Michel and Wright in rejecting Geoffrey of Monmouth as the author, and thinks the poem to have been written soon after 1216. *Die Sagen von Merlin*, p. 271.   [1] Or Marzin.

able to escape the conclusion that—whether or not we accept Geoffrey's story of the Breton book—he based his work upon materials almost, if not quite, independent of any preserved to us in Welsh literature. This Welsh literature is of great interest in that it shows us how the legendary history might have arisen, but it affords a very slender basis for a working theory as to the origin of the French romance.

In studying the Celtic literature we shall find it to be no small gain in clearness to put aside at the' outset all that is conceded to have nothing to do with either Myrddin or Merlin. The Celtic literature is preserved in three great groups—the Gaelic, the Breton or Armorican, and the Welsh.

I. The first of these groups, the Gaelic, has nothing original relating to Myrddin or Merlin, and it became possessed of the legend of Merlin only through translation. The only piece relating to Merlin of which we have any knowledge in Irish literature is the eleventh-century version of Nennius; while not till many generations later was the verse romance of *Arthour and Merlin* translated into Irish prose.[1] The fact that so scanty use was made of the legend, even in its borrowed form, is a sufficient proof that the historical bard and the legendary prophet were strangers to the great body[2] of old Irish literature.

II. It would hardly be necessary to consider the extant Armorican literature at all, were it not that Villemarqué, in a series of studies[3] in Celtic literature, made great capital out of Marzin ballads that he pretended to have found in Brittany.

---

[1] *Cf.* F. Michel, *Vita Merlini*, p. lxxxii.

[2] How great this body of Irish literature is may be seen from the estimate of a learned German, who has calculated that to publish all the Irish literature, inclusive of MSS. from the eleventh to the sixteenth century, would require about a thousand volumes, 8vo. *Cf.* Jubainville, *La Litt. Celtique*, i. 43.

[3] Th. Hersart de la Villemarqué, *Contes Populaires des anciens Bretons.* 2 vols. Paris, 1842; *Barzaz-Breiz, Chants Populaires de la Bretagne . . . . avec une traduction française.* 2 vols. Paris, 1846; *Poëmes des Bardes Bretons du 6ᵉ siècle.* Paris, 1850; *Les Romans de la Table Ronde.* 1 vol. Paris, 1860, 3rd ed. ; *Myrdhinn ou l'Enchanteur Merlin, son histoire, ses œuvres, son influence.* Paris, 1862 (actually printed, 1861).

Modern criticism rejects the ballads relating to Marzin the Bard[1] and Marzin the Enchanter, and pronounces them "impositions, of which," as Mr. Phillimore assures me, "no original or basis has been found in the country." The authenticity of the *Barzaz-Breiz*, as a whole, has been the subject of considerable discussion, but the question does not belong here.[2] We are chiefly concerned to know that the literature of Brittany is scarcely older than the fifteenth century,[3] and that it maintained its precarious existence only by borrowing from the Latin and the French.[4] We cannot deny the possible existence of Armorican literary documents more ancient than any now extant, but we are quite in the dark as to what they may have contained concerning Merlin. Even though we were to grant that the ballads on Marzin, instead of being modern forgeries, are based on genuine Breton traditions, we should find them of little service for our purpose. Considered as contributions to folklore they would then possess a certain degree of interest, but the assistance they would render in determining out of what materials our romance was formed would be exceedingly slight.[5]

---

[1] Villemarqué asserted the forged poem on Marzin the Bard to be earlier than the age of chivalry, and to belong to a time between the sixth and the tenth century. San-Marte, on the other hand, was inclined to refer it to the fourteenth century (*Sagen von Merlin*, p. 230), and to regard it, along with the short poem on Marzin the Enchanter, as an interesting proof that Merlin was known in a twofold character among a people who, like the insular Britons, regarded Merlin as one of their own countrymen.

[2] Anyone interested in this question may study it in the following discussions:— (1) Le Men, *Athenæum*, April 11, 1868, p. 527. (2) D'Arbois de Jubainville, *Bibl. de l'École des Chartes*, 3e sér. t. iii. p. 265–281; t. v. p. 621 .... (3) *Idem. Rev. Archéol.* t. xx. (4) *Idem. Rev. Critique*, 16 Févr. and 23 Nov. 1867, 3 Oct. 1868. (5) Liebrecht, *Gött. Gelehrte Anzeigen*, 7 April, 1869. (6) Jubainville, *Encore un mot sur le Barzaz-Breiz*, Paris, 1873. (7) *Rev. Celtique*, t. ii. (8) Sayce, *Science of Language*, ii. p. 86.

[3] W. D. Whitney, in *Language and the Study of Lang.* p. 218, says that one or two brief works go back to the fourteenth century, or even farther.

[4] Jubainville, *La Litt. Celtique*, vol. i. Introduction, p. 42.

[5] We are dealing primarily with origins, but we may note that Merlin figures in a Breton drama entitled *Buhez Santez Nonn, or Life of Sainte Nonne and of her son St. Devy* (F. Michel, *Vita Merlini*, p. lxxxiii.), and that very recently Louise d'Isole

III. In the face of these facts we must therefore confine our attention to the remaining branch of Celtic literature—the Cymric or Welsh. This, however, affords us much less light than might be desired. The most detailed accounts of Merlin Ambrosius[1] that we find in Welsh literature are contained in the so-called *Bruts*,[2] but these need detain us only a moment; for we need no longer refute Villemarqué's opinion[3] that the

has brought out a poem entitled *Merlin*, poème breton, 2ᵉ éd. revue et corrigée, avec une preface de Louis Frechette, Paris, 1877, 12mo. The *Buhez Santez Nonn* has been recently edited with a translation in the *Revue Celtique*.

[1] Or *Myrddin Emrys*. In referring to Welsh literature I shall usually adopt this spelling. On the form of the name Mr. E. G. B. Phillimore sends me the following note:—"The only possible variant in modern Welsh is *Myrddin Emrais*. *Ambrosius* makes both *Emrys* and *Emrais* in Welsh: in Middle and Old Welsh these would be written with an *i* or *y*, or even an *e* for the *y*, and a regular *ei* with a possible variant *e* for the modern *ai*; of course, some people—archaic purists who despise the modern *ai*—would spell Emre*is* now. As to *Myrddin*, it is the *only* form in current Welsh. *Dd* in modern Welsh is equal to the *th* in *the*, *that*, *this*, etc. In Old and Middle Welsh they had practically no character for it; the barred *d* (ð, ẟ or the like) occurring, but being very rare. In the sixteenth and seventeenth centuries both the ẟ and the *dh* were used, but finally disused for the *dd*. For the *y* of *Myrddin*, *e*, *i*, or *y* would be used in Old and Middle Welsh. The sound is that of French mute *e*: in the oldest Welsh would probably be written *o*, but *Mordin* does not occur. It was often written ; from the sixteenth to the eighteenth century by certain scholars and writers. *Myrdin* is simply the *Middle Welsh* orthography. *Marzin* is Villemarqué's deliberate Bretonization of the word. They have not the sound of *d* in Breton, except, I believe, in one or two sub-dialects: *z* takes the place in usual Breton of both sounds, *th* in *the*, and *th* in *thing*. The barred ẟ of Professor Rhŷs' Hibbert Lectures is meant to guide people who are puzzled by the barbarous Welsh *dd*. Nor have they in Breton the "obscure" sound of Welsh ; so Villemarqué altered it into *a*, their nearest sound. Skene's Welsh orthography is not consistent. He uses modern, Middle, and Old Welsh forms promiscuously and indiscriminately."

[2] Mr. Phillimore notes that "*Brut* is derived, not from an originally Welsh word, but from the word *Brutus* through Norman-French or English. It was used to mean a chronicle in these languages, and derived from *Brutus*, as in Wace's *Brut*. Originally it meant a chronicle beginning with Brutus or the like. The history of the transference of the word to Welsh is all that is obscure. In Rhŷs and Evans' *Bruts from the Red Book of Hergest* (Oxford, 1890), this question is gone into in u note in the preface. The word *Brut* for a chronicle occurs in Welsh before it does in English MSS., but that proves nothing."

[3] *Romans de la Table Ronde*, p. 25; *L'Enchanteur Merlin*, note, p. 99. San-Marte, however, held the same opinion, *Die Sagen von Merlin*, p. 16; and strangely enough, de la Borderie (*Hist. Brit. attribuée à Nennius*, p. 35) refers to "le *Brut er Brenined* (xᵉ siècle) et son amplificateur latin, Geoffroi de Monmouth (xiiᵉ siècle)."

Brut y Brenhinoedd (or the *Brut Tysilio*) was the British original of Geoffrey of Monmouth's *Historia*. This, like the other *Bruts*, is later[1] than Geoffrey of Monmouth, and obviously based upon his work.[2]

The Welsh Triads make mention of Myrddin, but they are of no great importance for our purpose. The details are discussed in the footnote.[3]

Mr. Phillimore remarks that "*er Brenined* is a gross blunder for *y Brenhinoedd*—the usual plural of *Brenin* 'a king'—though *Brenhinedd* also occurs in Middle Welsh; *y* means *the; er* does not exist."

[1] P. Paris, *Romans de la Table Ronde*, i. 38; G. Paris, *Romania*, xii. 373; *Encyc. Brit.* 9th ed., art. *Celtic Lit.*

[2] De la Borderie, *Les Véritables Proph. de Merlin*, p. 75, p. 124.

[3] On the Triads Mr. Phillimore sends me the following note:—

"The Triads simply consist of parts or characters taken from early (pre-seventh century) Cymric, and rarely Cornish, history and legend grouped by threes according to some salient characteristic, *e.g.* 'The three liberal kings were so and so,' etc.; 'The three felon axe-blows were so and so,' etc." "There are several collections of the Triads, the two oldest existing in MSS. of the thirteenth and fourteenth centuries (call these two *a* and *b*), and others (with a few new ones not found in *a* and *b*) in MSS. of the fifteenth century. All or most of these collections were pieced together by Robert Vaughan, of Hengwrt, the great Welsh collector of MSS., who died about 1667. He used some versions of the fifteenth century, which have never been published, and one at least which I cannot trace. Let us call this mosaic (*c*). Now, sometime—*when* it cannot exactly be said, but between 1600 and 1800—some one got hold of a great many—not all—of the old versions of the Triads, and also of a later (probably fifteenth-century) compilation called the 'Triads of the Twenty-four Knights,' and served them up with much additional detail and verbiage, and occasionally with important new matter, mostly not found elsewhere. This version, the fullest of all, was first printed in the *Myvyrian Archaiology*, vol. 2, and no MS. of it older than the eighteenth century is known to exist, though I do not believe that it was then concocted. Call this (*d*). Now (*d*) is often known, most misleadingly, as 'The Welsh Triads' or 'The Welsh Historical Triads' *par excellence*. I may add that—1. Robert Vaughan's piecework version (*c*); 2. the Red Book of Hergest version (*b*); and 3. the late or spurious *rechauffée* version (*d*), are printed in this order in the *Myvyrian Archaiology*, and are thence quoted by Rhŷs in his Hibbert Lectures as Versions 1, 2, 3, respectively (*b* has since been printed with absolute correctness).

Now, with this light let us come to what Skene says (and de la Borderie purports to quote or refer to in *Les Véritables Prophéties de Merlin*). In *Celtic Scotland*, vol. I. pp. 23, 24, we read: 'Among the Welsh documents which are usually founded upon as affording materials for the early history of the country, there is one class of documents contained in the Myvyrian Archaiology which cannot be accepted as genuine. The principal of them are the so-called Historical Triads, which have been usually quoted as possessing undoubted claims to antiquity under

A word ought to be given to the *Mabinogion*, though we really get from them no light on Myrddin.   These are a collection of prose tales, a number of which tell of Arthur and the knights of his court.   Merlin (Myrddin) is not mentioned

the name of the Welsh Triads . . . .   In a former work [p. 24] the author in reviewing these documents [the said Triads and others with which we have nothing to do here, many of which were certainly not concocted in the eighteenth century as Skene thought] merely said, " It is not unreasonable, therefore, to say that they must be received with some suspicion, and that very careful discrimination is required in the use of them."   He does not hesitate now to reject them as entirely spurious.'   Skene here appends a footnote (No. 15) with the very reservation which de la Borderie ignores — 'See *Four Ancient Books of Wales*, vol. I. pp. 30-32. In rejecting the Welsh Triads which have been so extensively used, the author excepts those Triads which are to be found in ancient MSS., such as the Triads of the Horses in the Black Book of Caermarthen; those in the Hengwrt MS. 536, printed in the *Four Ancient Books of Wales*, vol. II. p. 457; and those in the Red Book of Hergest.'

Skene says also in the work cited, I. p. 172, in a note (No. 11) : 'The author confines himself as much as possible to Welsh documents before his [Geoffrey of Monmouth's] time, and the so-called Historical Triads he rejects as entirely spurious.'   Also at pp. 195, 196 he says (end of p. 195) : 'The Welsh Triads say that the Picts came from Llychlyn, which is Scandinavia.' . . . . (p. 196 end) : 'The Welsh Triads which contain the passage referred to may now be regarded as spurious.'   The passage referred to, with much other ethnological matter, occurs in (*d*), but in *no other* collection of Triads.   Skene further says in note 50 on p. 197 : 'Neither does he refer to the so-called Historic Triads, because he considers them spurious; but among the genuine " Triads of Arthur and his Warriors" ' [these are those contained in the Hengwrt MSS. 54 and 536].   '*Ib.* [in the *Four Ancient Books of Wales*] vol. II. p. 457, there is one to this effect : " Three oppressions came to this island and did not go out of it " ' ' (p. 8).

What Skene means, and what I mean, by 'genuine' is, that the authors wrote down actual tradition or legend which they found to hand ; by 'spurious,' that the authors invented some at least of what they record, out of their own heads.   The genuine Triads do not purport to be written at any particular date.   The oldest MSS. are of about 1225 and 1275 for (*a*), and 1300-1325 for (*b*), but contain archaisms and errors of transcription which carry them back each, say, from fifty to a hundred years in their present form.   But how much older some of the Triads may or may not be no one can say !   Of course (*d*) is genuine in so far as it copies the older Triads, which it mostly does.   Some of its additions and alterations are demonstrably spurious, and the rest cannot be relied upon unless and until corroborated from other sources which have not the same taint.''

In the light of Mr. Phillimore's remarks we note that we have two Triads relating to Merlin, both from version (*d*).

The first I quote is No. 125, which " is entirely peculiar to (*d*)."   This enumerates : " Three principal bards of the Isle of Britain, Myrddin Emrys, Myrddin, son of Morvryn, Taliessin, chief of the bards."   *Cf.* also J. Loth, *Les Mabinogion*, II.

by name, but the combat of the white with the red dragon is found in the story of Llud and Llevelis, much the same as in Nennius and Geoffrey of Monmouth. Criticism has not yet said the last word with regard to the age and authenticity of these tales.[1] But the three romances of *Owein and Lunet, Peredur ab Evrawc, Geraint and Enid*, agree in many essentials with the three French romances of Chrestien de Troyes,—the *Chevalier au Lyon, Perceval le Gallois, Erec et Enid*,—all of which were produced in the last half of the twelfth century.[2] Still, according to Loth,[3] "the three *Mabinogion* are no more

p. 268; F. Michel, *Vita Merlini*, p. xvi.; and *The Ancient Laws of Cambria*, translated from the Welsh by William Probert, 1823, p. 413, Triad 125.

The second (*d*) (No. 10) tells of : "Three complete disappearances from the isle of Prydein .... the second is that of Myrddin, the bard of Emrys Wledig, and of his nine Cylveidd, who directed their way by sea toward the House of Glas." *Cf.* J. Loth, *Les Mabinogion*, II. pp. 277, 278. This Triad, as Mr. Phillimore observes, "takes. and amplifies *one* subordinate incident from (*a*), copied thence in (*c*), No. 34; but everything concerning Merlin is only in (*d*). Nor does *difuncoll* mean necessarily 'complete *disappearances*': *col* is a loss, not a disappearance, and *difancoll* (*difangoll* now) means 'utter loss,' whether disappearance or destruction. The Isle of Britain was the consecrated term for the undivided Britondom of the sixth and seventh centuries."

These two Triads just quoted are very late, and, in Mr. Phillimore's opinion, worthless. He adds: "The only allusion to Merlin or his works which I can find in the genuine Triads are in the Triads of Hengwrt MSS. 54 and 536, Skene's *Four Ancient Books of Wales*, ii. 265—'The third (concealment and disconcealment [a] of the Isle of Britain was) the dragons which Llud, son of Beli, buried (al. concealed) in Dinas Emreis, in Eryni.' (Eryni roughly answers to Snowdonia.) There is the same statement in one of the Red-Book Triads; but nothing more that I can find."

[a] "This is not the best word, but it means the uncovering of what has been concealed."

[1] Mr. Phillimore says of the *Mabinogion*, that they are conceded to be Celtic, "excepting the versions of Ywein, Perceval, and Erec, and perhaps the Llud and Llevelis. The stories and incidents are purely Celtic, though here and there you will get a lay figure dragged in from France, as you will from Ireland and other non-Welsh countries. I dare say the manner of telling the Tales may have been indirectly influenced by the French story-tellers, but that is the utmost. As for Llud and Llevelis, it occurs intercalated in some of the Welsh translations or adaptations of Geoffrey of Monmouth, but is a Welsh addition to the Latin of the original text."

[2] *Cf.* Loth, *Les Mabinogion*, i. p. 13; also G. Paris, *Hist. Litt. de la France*, xxx.

[3] *Les Mabinogion*, i. p. 15.

translated from Chrétien de Troyes than the poems of Chrétien de Troyes are translated or imitated from them. They all mount to one common source, that is to say, the French romances written in England and based upon British legends; the originals have disappeared, and we have preserved nothing of them but mutilated imitations. It would perhaps be going too far to affirm that the three *Mabinogion* are literally translated from the French, but it is very evident that they follow closely a French source. As for the primitive basis of these tales, it is generally admitted to be of Celtic origin. The Celtic legends of the country of Wales were early known by the Normans after the conquests of England."

I have touched upon the *Mabinogion*, not because the tales yield us much information with regard to Merlin (Myrddin), but because they yield so little. It is certainly rather surprising that a long series of Celtic stories, several of which tell us of Arthur, should make no reference to the great Merlin (Myrddin), unless, indeed, some one chooses to see in this very fact a slight confirmation of the historical character of the bard Myrddin of the sixth century, who had not (as one might urge) been invested in genuine works of Celtic imagination with the legendary character that the enchanter Merlin assumes in the Latin chronicles and the French romances.

There remain to be examined the Welsh poems that contain allusions to Myrddin. If we accept these poems as genuine works of the sixth century, we have nothing more than a few obscure fragments, the full import of which is perhaps even yet not rightly interpreted.

The publication of Old Welsh texts is comparatively recent.[1] It began in 1764, when the Rev. Evan Evans brought out his *Specimens of the Poetry of the Ancient Welsh Bards*. Twenty years later, Edward Jones published his *Musical and Poetical*

---

[1] *Cf.* Skene, *Four Ancient Books of Wales*, i. pp. 4-18.

Relics of the Welsh Bards. Following this work appeared in 1792 Dr. Owen Pughe's collection, *The Heroic Elegies and other Pieces of Llywarch-Hen.* The first really important publication of old Welsh poems was made in the year 1801, when the first two volumes of the *Myvyrian Archaiology* (sic) *of Wales* were published by Owen Jones, a London furrier, Edward Williams (Iolo Morganwg) a stone-mason, and William Owen, later known as William Owen Pughe. A third volume followed in 1807.[1] The lively controversy which at once arose over these poems— helped on doubtless by the recollection of the extravagant claims made for MacPherson's pseudo-Gaelic Ossian — was for a time brought to an end by the publication in 1803 of Sharon Turner's *Vindication of the genuineness of the Ancient British Poems of Aneurin, Taliessin, Llywarch-Hen, and Myrddin,* though, as Gaston Paris remarks, he really proved nothing. Since Turner's day critical opinion has vibrated between alternate acceptance and rejection of these poems. Villemarqué, although a strenuous defender of the Celtic origin of the Merlin (Myrddin) legend, preferred to regard Brittany as the original home of the bard, and did not hesitate to affirm that none of the poems attributed to Myrddin could be accepted as genuine.[2] In 1849 Thomas Stephens published a careful study of these old poems in his *Literature of the Kymry.* He, too, refused to accept any of the poems as genuine products of the sixth century.[3] Still more careful and critical was the investigation of the entire subject of early Welsh literature by W. F. Skene in the *Four Ancient Books of Wales* (1868). Here appeared all of the texts of the poems in

----

[1] The whole reprinted in one volume, royal 8vo. Denbigh, 1861, and in one volume, small 4to. Denbigh, 1870.

[2] "On ne peut pas citer une seule pièce, une seule strophe originale de ce barde : toutes portent des traces nombreuses de remaniements."—Villemarqué, *Poèmes des Bardes Bretons,* q. v.

[3] *Cf.* Skene, *Four Ancient Books of Wales,* i. 12.

question with a literal translation,[1] and a series of critical dissertations on the genuineness of the poems. This was the first discussion of the matter on the basis of a really critical text. Mr. Skene's investigations led him to the following conclusions: "That the bards to whom these poems are in the main attributed are recorded as having lived in the sixth century, is certain. We have it on the authority of the *Genealogia*[2] attached to Nennius, written in the eighth century.[3] That this record of their having lived in that age is true we have every reason to believe, and we may hold that there were such bards as Taliessin, Llywarch-Hen, and Myrddin at that early period, who were believed to have written poems."[4]

Mr. Skene is recognized as a foremost authority on this question, but his views have not won entire acceptance.[5] Yet even if we accept all the poems as genuine and ancient, and include the interpolations as well as the evidently spurious poems rejected by Mr. Skene, we have but a shadowy outline of the personality of the Bard Myrddin. For the sake of

---

[1] By the Rev. D. Silvan Evans and the Rev. Robert Williams : *cf.* i. 7–17.

[2] The passage referred to is found in the ordinary editions of Nennius, sec. 62. "At that time Talhaiarn Cataguen was famed for poetry, and Neirin and Taliesin and Bluchbard and Cian, who is called Guenith Guant, were all famous at the same time in British poetry " (Gunn's translation, edited by J. A. Giles). There is no mention of Myrddin in Nennius. Mr. Phillimore adds that " Llywarch-Hen is not mentioned either by the author of the ' Genealogia.' The old identification of Llywarch (Old Welsh *Loumarch* or Leumarch) with Bluchbard is too insane ! *et Neirin* is a mistranslation of the Welsh *Aneirin*, *a* in Welsh meaning *and*. The MSS. read *Tat Aguen*, not *Cataguen* (modern Welsh *Tad Awen*, Pater Poeseos). Guenith Guant, now Gwenith Gwawd. The ' Genealogia ' attached to Nennius have nothing to do with Nennius. They were merely accidentally tacked on an edition of Nennius represented by only four very nearly related MSS. They are a distinct work entirely."

[3] On this date compare our discussion of Nennius, *ante.*

[4] *Four Ancient Books*, i. 184.

[5] *Cf.* for example, the article on *Celtic Literature* in the *Encyc. Brit.* 9th ed. 1876. G. Paris remarks on these poems — "Je suis très porté, pour ma part, à croire qu'il n'y a rien d'authentique du tout, mais on ne pourra le décider que quand on aura appliqué à ces productions bizarres l'instrument de la critique philologique." —*Romania*, xii. 375.

clearness we can perhaps hardly do better than to take up in
order each of the Welsh poems that in any way refers to
Myrddin. Of these poems eight[1] have been attributed to
Myrddin; but they are not all accepted as genuine by either
Mr. Skene or M. de la Borderie; nor do these two eminent
critics exactly agree with each other as to what is genuine
and what is spurious.

These differences of opinion as to just which of these poems
were indubitably composed in the sixth century are not re-
assuring to one who naturally defers to the judgment of
recognized specialists in things Celtic. In such a case a lay-
man can hardly do more than silently to place the conflicting
opinions side by side, and move on. In our examination we
may best begin with the two poems that are least doubtful—
The Dialogue between Myrddin and Taliessin, and the *Avallenau*.[2]

I.—The *Dialogue between Myrddin and Taliessin* adds but
little to our knowledge. Its chief importance for our purpose
is that it helps to establish the existence of a bard bearing
the name Myrddin.[3] He is represented as talking with
Taliessin concerning the battle of Arderydd, and expressing
sadness at the slaughter.[4]

---

[1] *Cf.* de la Borderie's list in *Les Véritables Proph. de Merlin*, p. 57 (ed. 1884),
with that given by F. Michel, *Vita Merlini*, pp. liv., lv. Also Skene, *Four Ancient
Books of Wales*, i. p. 222.

[2] Skene, *Four Ancient Books of Wales*, i. pp. 222, 223; de la Borderie, *Les
Véritables Proph. de Merlin*, p. 116. De la Borderie remarks also, p. 81 — "Quoi
qu'il en soit, dans le *Dialogue de Taliésin et de Merlin* et dans les *Afallenau* du
Livre Noir, nous avons (nous croyons l'avoir prouvé) deux poèmes historiques fort
curieux, dont l'authenticité, l'attribution à Merlin, ne sauraient souffrir plus de
difficulté que celle des poèmes attribués jusqu'ici sans contestation sérieuse—par
M. Stephens lui-même—à Lywarch-Hen et à Taliésin."

[3] *Cf.* J. Loth, *Les Mabinogion*, ii. p. 268, note.

[4] It will be instructive to put, side by side, the translation of the *Dialogue between
Myrddin and Taliessin*, as given by Davies[a] and followed by San-Marte,[b] and the
translation of the same, as given in Skene's *Four Ancient Books of Wales*.[c] A few
specimens will suffice.

[a] *Mythol.* p. 549.   [b] *Die Sagen von Merlin*, pp. 138-140.   [c] Vol. i. pp. 368-370.
This translation is by Rev. D. Silvan Evans. (See i. 17.)

In the sixth stanza Taliessin speaks :

> " The host of Maelgwn, it was fortunate that they came—
>   Slaughtering men of battle, penetrating the gory plain,
>   Even the action of Ardderyd [Arderydd], when there will be
>   a crisis,
>   Continually for the hero they will prepare."

In the eleventh stanza Myrddin says :

> " Seven-score generous ones have gone to the shades ;
>   In the wood of Celyddon they came to their end.
>   Since I, Myrd[d]in, am next after Taliessin,
>   Let my prediction become common."

II.—*The Avallenau*, observes Mr. Skene, contains passages (already pointed out by Stephens), "which could not have

	DAVIES.	SKENE.
	Myrddin.	*Myrddin.*
I.—	How great my sorrow ! How woful has been the treatment of Kedwy and the boat ! Unanimous was the assault, with gleaming swords. From the piercing conflict, one shield escaped.—Alas, how deplorable !	How sad with me, how sad ! Have Cedwyv and Cadvan perished? Glaring and tumultuous was the slaughter; Perforated was the shield from Trywruyd [Tryfrwydd].[a]
	Taliessin.	*Taliessin.*
II.—	It was Maelgwn, whom I saw, with piercing weapones (*sic*) before the master of the fair herd. His master will not be silent.	It was Maelgwn that I saw combating. His household before the tumult of the host is not silent.
	Myrddin.	*Myrddin.*
III.—	Before the two personages they land in the celestial circle—before the passing form, and the fixed form over the pale white boundary. The grey stones they actually remove. Soon is Elgan and his retinue discovered—for his slaughter, alas ! how great the vengeance that ensued !	Before two men in Nevtur will they laud, Before Errith and Gurrith on a pale white horse. The slender bay they will undoubtedly bear away. Soon will his retinue be seen with Elgan. Alas! for his death a great journey they came.

[a] " This is the Trifruit of Nennius."— E. G. P.

been written prior to the time of Henry II."; but these
passages seem to be "interpolations in an older poem."[1] At
best we learn from this poem very little about the personality
of the bard,[2] though more than from any other of the Welsh
poems.[3]

In addition to these two poems there are a few others
of more doubtful age and authenticity, which mention
Myrddin and ascribe to him various qualities.

III.—The *Porchellanau* or *Hoianau*—one of the poems of

---

[1] *Four Anc. Books*, ii. pp. 316, 317. *Cf.* de la Borderie, *Les Vérit. Proph. de Merlin*, pp. 62. Skene's text of the *Avallenau* contains 86 lines; San-Marte's, *Die Sagen von Merlin*, pp. 62–78, has 185 lines.

[2] To avoid repetition I will cite nothing at this point from this poem, as I have reserved it for comparison with the *Vita Merlini*.

[3] M. de la Borderie (*Les Véritables Proph. de Merlin*, p. 72) gives the following account of the *Avallenau*:—"Le barde nous apprend qu'il a été riche, honoré par le roi Gwend[d]oleu, guerrier vaillant dans la forêt de Kelyddon et portant le collier d'or à la bataille d'Arderyd[d]; qu'il a connu les enivrements de l'amour et s'est, avec une jeune fille, promené autour de la tige du pommier tant célébré dans ses vers, c'est-à-dire à la cour du roi, père du jeune exilé dont il annonce le rétablissement (ci-dessus, st. 4, 5, 7). Puis sont venus les jours mauvais. Gwend[d]oleu, son protecteur, ne s'est plus trouvé en état de soutenir sa fortune. Merlin a eu le malheur de causer la mort du fils de Gwendyz, que l'on croit avoir été sa sœur et la femme de R[h]yd[d]erch. De là le disgrâce où il est tombé vis-à-vis de R[h]yd[d]erch, de ses serviteurs et de Gwendyz; disgrâce qui l'afflige profondément. Ces chagrins et ces malheurs ont fini par lui déranger l'esprit. Il a erré—ou bien il a cru errer—longtemps et péniblement, parmi les ténèbres et en compagnie des spectres, dans la forêt de Kelyddon. Aussi appelle-t-il maintenant la mort, espérant ainsi entrer dans le cortège splendide du roi des rois (st. 4, 5, 6, 7). Il semble toutefois reprendre raison, vie et espoir, en songeant au triomphe prochain du jeune prince en qui, nous le répétons il y a tout lieu de voir le fils ou l'héritier de Gwend[d]oleu. Un point à noter : Merlin ne parle point de sa vieillesse. Or, quand ils atteignaient cet âge, les bardes bretons du VIe siècle—par exemple Lywarch-Hen—ne cessaient de le dire et de geindre sur leurs cheveux blancs, quelquefois en très beaux vers, mais sans jamais craindre de se répéter.

Donc [!] Merlin n'était pas vieux quand il faisait sa pièce des *Pommiers* [Avallenau] plusieurs années après la bataile d'Arderyd[d]."

The argument that Myrddin could not have been old because he does not talk precisely like some other bard is certainly a surprising one. We have at most but a few lines with which to construct the entire portrait of Myrddin ; and from the purely negative considerations presented by M. de la Borderie we are not warranted in drawing so important an inference.

the Black Book of Caermarthen—is rejected by Mr. Stephens and Mr. Skene as being spurious and late.   Like the *Avallenau*, it contains passages not earlier than the time of Henry II.,[1] and really contains nothing to warrant it in being placed earlier than Geoffrey of Monmouth.   De la Borderie, however, regards it as containing a few fragments of Merlin's (Myrddin's) work imbedded in a mass of interpolations.[2]

Myrddin is not mentioned by name in the form, but there is a prediction that,

"All the Cymry will be under the same warlike leader ;
   His name is Llywelyn, of the line
   Of Gwynedd, one who will overcome."—STANZA I.

And the speaker says of himself :

"Little does R[h]ydderch Hael know to-night at his feast
     What sleeplessness last night I bore ;
   The snow was up to my knees owing to the wariness of the chief,
     Icicles hung to my hair : sad is my fate ! "—STANZA X.

"Thin is my covering, for me there is no repose,
   Since the battle of Ardderyd [Arderydd] it will not concern me,
   Though the sky were to fall, and sea to overflow."—STANZA XXV.[3]

IV.—*Dialogue between Myrddin and his sister Gwenddydd* [4] (the *Cyvoesi*).

---

[1] *Four Ancient Books of Wales*, ii. 316.   Mr. Skene also remarks, i. 209, that the poem "must have been composed either in whole or in part in the reign of Henry II."

[2] *Les Vérit. Proph. de Merlin*, p. 100, p. 116.   A little earlier he remarks, p. 95 : "Force nous est donc d'admettre l'existence d'un poème primitif des *Hoianau*, œuvre de Merlin, envahi aux xi⁰ et xii⁰ siècles par des interpolations successives qui, s'étendant de proche en proche d'une strophe à l'autre, ont fini par dévorer et détruire la pièce entière."

[3] For the entire poem see *Four Anc. Books*, i. 482.

[4] The English translator spells the name of the bard *Myrdin*.   De la Borderie spells the name of the sister *Gwendyz—Les Vérit. Proph. de Merlin*, p. 57.   Mr. Phillimore remarks that the name should have been Bretonized *Gwenzyz*.

If we could accept this dialogue as genuine,[1] we should get considerable information from it with regard to Myrddin, but in all probability it is a late piece of work, and consequently of little value for our purpose. Some of the passages are instructive, in that they show how little we learn from these Welsh poems even when they are most specific [2]—

MYRDDIN II. Since the action of Ardderyd [Arderydd] and Erydon,
      Gwend[d]ydd, and all that will happen to me,
      Dull of understanding, to what place of festivity shall I go?

GWENDDYDD III. I will address my twin-brother [3]
      Myrd[d]in, a wise man and a diviner.

M. XII. As Gwenddoleu was slain in the bloodshed of Ardderyd [Arderydd],
      And I wonder why I should be perceived.

G. XIII. Thy head is of the colour of winter hoar;
      God has relieved thy necessities.

---

[1] Mr. Skene, *Four Anc. Books*, i. pp. 234–241, rejects it as spurious, and adds: "The form of the prophecy in the *Hoianau* is obviously the same as that in the third part of the *Cyvoesi*, which I consider to have been produced in South Wales in the twelfth century." And de la Borderie in turn observes: "A nos yeux, si l'on excepte les quinze dernières stances (117–131), dont nous parlerons plus loin, les *Kyvoësi* est une insipide rapsodie chronologique fabriquée au xiie ou au xiiie siècle par un barde pédant, qui avait sous les yeux Nennius, Geoffroi de Monmouth, Caradoc de Lancarvan."—*Les Vérit. Proph. de Merlin*, pp. 83, 84.

[2] For the entire poem see *Four Anc. Books*, i. 462 *sqq.* The Roman numerals in the passages I quote refer to the stanzas.

[3] On this passage the Rev. T. Price (*Literary Remains*, i. 143, quoted in *Four Anc. Books*, ii. 424) has an important remark: "It is worthy of note that Gwenddydd in this dialogue addresses Myrddin by the appellation of Llallogan, twin-brother . . ." Now this will explain a passage in the Life of St. Kentigern, in which it is said that there was at the court of R[h]ydderch Hael a certain idiot named *Laloicen* who uttered predictions. "In curia ejus quidam homo fatuus vocabulo Laloicen;" and in the *Scotichronicon* it is stated that this Laloicen was *Myrddin Wyllt*. By connecting these several particulars, we find an air of truth cast over the history of this bard, as regards the principal incidents of his life, and there can be no reason to doubt that some of the poetry attributed to him was actually his composition."

Mr. Ward also touches upon the same matter in discussing Cott. MS. Titus A. xix. "The prose narrative (at f. 74) of the meeting of Merlin and St. Kentigern (or St. Mungo, the patron saint of Glasgow) may perhaps belong to the imperfect

> M. xiv. Heaven has brought a heavy affliction
> On me, and I am ill at last.
>
> G. xvii. Since thou art a companion and canon
> Of Cullaith . . . . .
>
> M. xx. Since my reason is gone with the ghosts of the
> mountain,
> And I myself am pensive.
>
> G. xxiv. Since Gwenddoleu was slain in the bloodshed of
> Ardderyd [Arderydd], thou art filled with dismay.
>
> G. lxii. Myrd[d]in fair, of fame-conferring song.

life of St. Kentigern which follows it (f. 76*b*). This narrative has been abridged by Walter Bower (or Bowmaker), last abbot of Inchcolm (d. 1449), and inserted in his enlarged edition of the Scotichronicon of John Fordun, lib. iii. cap. xxxi. (see Royal 13, E. x. f. 58, and Walter Goodall's edition, of 1759, vol. i. p. 135). But Bower has omitted the pith of the story. Merlin does not receive the sacrament on the first day of meeting; but one day he comes to the "Mellodonor" (or Molendinar) brook, near Glasgow, demanding the sacrament, and saying that his death is at hand. He is asked three times how he will die, and each time gives a different answer. Still, St. Kentigern is at last persuaded to administer the sacrament to him. Now it has happened, once upon a time, that he was caught and bound by the petty king ("regulus") Meldredus; that he laughed at seeing the king take an apple-leaf out of his wife's hair; that he was promised freedom if he would state the cause of his laughter, and that he then told of the queen's adultery in the orchard. The queen, in revenge, ordered some shepherds to keep a look-out for him. They see him coming away from St. Kentigern, and pursue him with sticks and stones. He falls dying over a bank of the Tweed near Drumelzier, and is impaled on a salmon-stake in the water. Thus he dies by the three deaths that he has prophesied. The laugh at seeing the apple-leaf and the prophecy of the three different deaths are stories introduced into the poem; but in the poem it is not his own death that Merlin prophesies.'

The prose narrative begins: "Eo quidem in tempore quo beatus kentegernus heremi deserta frequentare solebat. contigit die quadam illo in solitudinis arbusto solicite orante. vt quidam demens nudus et hirsutus et ab omni bono destitutus. quasi quidam toruum furiale transitum faceret secus eum qui lailoken vocabatur. quem quidam dicunt fuisse Merlynum." f. 74. It ends: "Porro opidum istud distat a Ciuitate Glascu quasi xxx* miliaribus. In cuius campo lailoken tumulatus quiescit.

> 'Sude perfossus. lapidem perpessus. et vndam?'
>
> Merlinus triplicem fertur inisse necem." f. 75*b*.

>   —*Catalogue of Romances*, i. p. 291.

The *Acta Sanctorum* for January tells us with regard to St. Kentigern: "De eius aetate id solum possumus statuere, vixisse seculo a Cristi nativitate sexto, circiter annum 560, nam tum S. Columba floruit, quem illius fuisse aequalem constat."— vol. i. p. 815.

> G. cxii. My twin-brother, since thou hast answered me,
>   Myrd[d]in, son of Morvryn the skilful,
>   Sad is the tale thou hast uttered.
> M. cxxii. The Creator has caused one heavy affliction :
>   Dead is Morgeneu, dead is Mordav,
>   Dead is Morien : I wish to die.
> G. cxxiii. My only brother, chide me not ;
>   Since the battle of Ardderyd [Arderydd] I am ill.

V.—*Yscolan*[1] is the shortest of the eight poems sometimes attributed to Myrddin, and is rejected as spurious both by Mr. Skene and M. de la Borderie, though the latter believes it to be a poem of the seventh century. But whatever its age it tells us nothing at all about Myrddin.

VI.—*Prediction of Myrddin in his tomb.*[2]

This is unquestionably as late as the end of the thirteenth century, and cannot be by Myrddin. In any case nothing important is to be learned from a poem which tells us merely—

> " I have quaffed wine from a bright glass with the lords of
>   fierce war ;
> My name is Myrd[d]in, son of Morvryn."

There remain a few fragments which call for a word of comment. In the *Book of Taliessin* (*Four Anc. Books*, i. 436) we find by an unknown writer a single allusion[3] to Myrddin in the poem entitled *The Omen of Prydein the Great*, " Myrd[d]in fortells these will meet, in Aber Peryddon, the stewards of the kings," ll. 17, 18.

The poem on the Birch-trees contains nothing at all on Myrddin. It neither mentions his name nor alludes to him in any way. Skene regards it as " one of the spurious

---

[1] De la Borderie, *Les Véritables Proph. de Merlin*, p. 100, p. 108. For the translation see *Four Anc. Books*, i. p. 518. *Cf.* also, ii. pp. 318, 319, note.

[2] Called in the *Four Anc. Books*, i. 478, *A Fugitive Poem of Myrd[d]in in his Grave*. *Cf.* ii. p. 17 ; de la Borderie, *Les Vérit. Proph. de Merl.* p. 116.

[3] *Cf.* J. Loth, *Les Mabinogion*, ii. p. 268.

poems attributed to Myrddin which were composed in the twelfth century.[1] Last of all we have the poem called by de la Borderie *Les Fouissements*, which, besides being late, adds nothing to our knowledge of Myrddin.

We have now examined all of the extant Welsh literature that gives any hint as to the personality of Myrddin. We have found the record scanty at the best, and of not too convincing authenticity. Important is the fact that the supernatural element is not introduced, though it may be implied in the gift of prophecy. We here see Myrddin merely as a warrior-bard, who laments in moving words the death of his friends in battle. Our next step will take us to the Latin *Vita Merlini*, which we must compare with the Welsh poems. We shall discover a few points of likeness, but we must guard against overestimating the correspondences. Where the resemblance is not purely accidental there is scarcely enough to argue actual borrowing.

In the *Vita Merlini*[2] we find in the main a conception of Merlin very different from that in Geoffrey's *Historia*. This difference appears clearly in an analysis of the poem. If

---

[1] *Four Anc. Books*, ii. p. 334. Translation, i. p. 481. *Cf.* de la Borderie's remarks on this and other poems of its class in *Les Vérit. Proph. de Merlin*, p. 109.

[2] Ward (*Catal. of Romances*, i. p. 286) gives a very good summary of the contents, but he does not bring out the fact that the mad bard identifies himself (ll. 681-683) with the prophet who explained to Vortigern the combat of the two dragons. "The main action of this poem begins after the battle of Ardderyd [Arderydd]; which seems to have been fought in A.D. 573, between the great chief of the Pagans in Scotland, Gwend-dolen,* on one side, and Maelgwn Gwynedd, R[h]ydderch Hael, and Aedan son of Gafran, on the other. Gwenddolen* was killed; R[h]ydderch established himself as King of Strathclyde, and recalled St. Kentigern from Wales to become Bishop of Glasgow: and Aedan was inaugurated King of Dalriada (Argyle and the Isles) by St. Columba. The battlefield was near two small hills, still called the Knows of Arthuret, on the western bank of the Esk, about nine miles north of Carlisle."

Cf. *The Four Ancient Books of Wales*, by W. F. Skene. Edinburgh, 1868. Vol. i. pp. 65-67. "Merlin is here described as a King of the South Welsh. Guennolous, King of Scotland, is defeated by Peredurus, the leader of the North Welsh, in conjunction with Merlin and Rodar, King of the Cambrians. Merlin, though his side wins the day, goes mad at the sight of the slaughter, and flies into the woods. He is enticed home by his wife Guendoloena, and by his sister Ganieda,

* [Guenddoleu.]

we take the facts in the life of Merlin in the order in which
they are presented in the *Vita Merlini* we find that he was—

1. A king and prophet.   l. 21.

2. That he

"Demetarumque superbis,
Iura dabat populis, ducibusque futura canebat."   ll. 21, 22.

3. That in a strife between several princes,
"Venerat ad bellum Merlinus cum Pereduro.   ll. 31, 32.
Rex quoque Cumbrorum [1] Rodarchus."

4. That at the sight of the slaughter,
"Hoc viso, Merline, doles, tristesque per agmen.   l. 38.
Commisces planctus, tali quoque voce remugis."

Merlin breaks out into lamentation.

who is married to Rodarcus.   Several wild incidents follow, but finally Ganieda
builds a great house in the woods for Merlin.   Telgesinus (Taliessin) visits him ; and
they discourse together of the wonders of nature, and recall the day when they conveyed King Arthur in a boat steered by Barinthus (or Barrindeus, abbot of Druim-
cuillin, and a friend of St. Brandan's) to 'Insula Pomorum' (Avalon), where the
king's wounds were tended by Morgain and her sisters."

The Caledonian Forest, to which Merlin fled, is thus described by J. Rhŷs (*Celtic
Britain*, p. 225) : "The Caledonian Forest is found to have been located by Ptolemy
where there is every reason to suppose it really was, namely, covering a tract where
we are told that a thick wood of birch and hazel must once have stretched from the
west of the district of Menteith, in the neighbourhood of Loch Lomond, across the
country to Dunkeld.   It is this vast forest that probably formed, in part at least,
the boundary between the Caledonians and the Verturiones or the Brythons of
Fortrenn."

Skene (*Four Anc. Books of Wales*, i. 54) remarks : "The seventh battle [of
Arthur] was ' in silva Caledonis, id est, Cat Coit Celidon '—that is, the battle was so
called, for *Cat* means a battle, and *Coed Celyddon* the Wood of Celyddon.   This is
the Nemus Caledonis that Merlin is said, in the Latin *Vita Merlini*, to have fled to
after the battle of Ardderyth, and where, according to the tradition reported by
Fordun (B. iii. ch. xxvi.), he met Kentigern, and afterwards was slain by the shepherds
of Meldredus, a regulus of the country on the banks of the Tweed, 'prope oppidum
Dunmeller.'   Local tradition places the scene of it in Tweeddale, where, in the
parish of Drumelzier, anciently Dunmeller, in which the name of Meldredus is
preserved, is shewn the grave of Merlin.   The upper part of the valley of the Tweed
was once a great forest, of which the forests of Selkirk and Ettrick formed a part,
and seems to have been known by the name of the *Coed Celyddon*."

See also Skene's *Celtic Scotland*, i. p. 86.

[1] V. R. Cambrorum.

5. That Peredur and his companions vainly endeavour to
quiet Merlin :

"Solatur Peredurus eum, proceresque ducesque.   1. 68.
Nec vult solari nec verba precantia ferre."

6. That after three days of weeping and fasting Merlin
flees to the forests, and becomes a wild man of the
woods, forgetful of himself and of his friends :

" Iam tribus emensis defleverat ille diebus.   1. 70.
Respueratque cibos ; tantus dolor usserat illum :
Inde novas furias, cum tot tantisque querelis
Aera complesset, cepit, furtimque recidit ;
Et fugit ad silvas, nec vult fugiendo videri,
Ingrediturque nemus, gaudetque latere sub ornis;
Miraturque feras pascentes gramina saltus.
Nunc has insequitur, nunc cursu præterit illas.
Utitur herbarum radicibus; utitur herbis ;
Utitur arboreo fructo, morisque rubeti.
Fit silvester homo, quasi silvis editus esset.   1. 80.
Inde per aestatem totam ; nullique repertus,
Oblitusque sui, cognatorumque suorum,
Delituit, silvis obductus more ferino.
At cum venit [h]yems herbasque tulisset et omnes
Arboreos fructus, nec quo frueretur haberet ;
Diffudit tales miseranda voce querelas."

7. That his complaints are heard by a passer-by who comes
from the court of Rodarchus :

" Ecce viatori venit obvius alter ab aula.   1. 121.
Rodarchi regis Cumbrorum, qui Ganiedam
Duxerat uxorem, formosa coniuge felix.
Merlini soror ista fuit, casumque dolebat
Fratris, et ad silvas et ad arva remota clientes
Miserat, ut fratrem revocarent."
One said he had seen Merlin
" Inter dumosos saltus nemoris Calidonis."

8. That Merlin is persuaded to return to his wife and sister :
  "Et veniunt pariter laetantes regis in urbem.   l. 214.
  Ergo fratre suo gaudet regina recepto,
  Proque sui reditu fit coniunx laeta mariti."

9. But that he shortly goes mad again :
  "At postquam tantas hominum Merlinus adesse.   l. 221.
  Inspexit turmas, nec eas perferre valeret ;
  Cepit enim furias, iterumque furore repletus
  Ad nemus ire cupit, furtimque recedere quaerit."

10. That after a time he flees again to the woods :
  "Et petiit silvas nullo prohibente cupitas."   l. 385.
  Some time later he is again brought to Court.

11. That one day he utters various prophecies, and adds :
  "Haec Vortigerno cecini prolixus olim.   l. 681.
  Exponendo duum sibi mistica bella draconum
  In ripa stagni quando consedimus hausti."

12. That he then asks his sister to send for Telgesinus to
  come to him ; and the two wise men discourse a
  long time together on problems of nature :
  "Quid ventus nimbusve foret," etc.   l. 734.

At l. 982, Merlin begins with the betrayal of Constans, and recounts the history of Uter and Ambrosius, Vortimer and Arthur, and the treason of Modred. The story of Ygerne is passed over in silence. This résumé of the *Historia* extends to l. 1135.

In what follows (ll. 1136–1529) we are told of the discovery of a spring, by the drinking of the water of which Merlin's reason was restored. Then follows a considerable discourse with Telegesinus, and some prophecies.

The origin of a considerable part of the *Vita Merlini* is not very difficult to trace. As Gaston Paris remarks : " The author mingles notices of geography and natural history borrowed from classical writers with popular British tales, the greater portion of which are found elsewhere."[1] Exactly how much of the material is Celtic is uncertain. There is a certain vague correspondence between parts of the *Vita* and parts of the *Avallenau* and the (spurious) *Hoianau*. Merlin has long conversations in the *Vita* with Telgesinus; and Myrddin engages in conversation with Taliessin in a short Welsh dialogue, probably ancient. These correspondences may not be accidental, but they are not so definite as to argue actual borrowing, to say nothing of actual translation.[2] Of course, Geoffrey uses names that appear in Welsh literature, as for instance, in the following passage; but these had doubtless become common literary property in his day :—

1. 26. " Dux Venedotorum Peredurus bella gerabat
          Contra Guennoloum Scotiae qui regna regebat."

Peredur is referred to in one of the Gododin Poems of

---

[1] *Hist. Litt. de la France*, xxx. p. 5.

[2] San-Marte (A. Schulz) very well points out the general relations in which the *Vita Merlini* stands to Welsh literature, but he pushes his conclusions farther than most careful critics can follow him. He remarks: " Als eine besondere Eigenthümlichkeit, zumal in dieser Zeit, wo schon die französische Romanpoesie sich Merlins bemächtigt hatte, deren Kenntniss auch unserm Dichter nicht abgeht, ist jedoch hervorzuheben, dass er [der Autor] wesentlich der wälschen Tradition von Merlin Caledonius anschliesst, und eine Kenntniss der wälschen Literatur verräth, welche man bei den französischen und englisch-normannischen Dichtern sehr selten findet. Er hat indess den Stoff ziemlich frei behandelt, und die Tradition nach seiner Bequemlichkeit gestaltet. Merlin ist hier Prophet, aber auch zugleich König der nördlichen Britten. Sein Gegner ist nicht, wie bei den Barden des dreizehnten Jahrhunderts, der gegen ihn aufgehetzte Rhydderch (Rodarchus, dux Cumbrorum) der vielmehr als Bundesgenosse auftritt, sondern Guennolous, König von Schottland, der indess in der wahren wie fabelhaften Geschichte dieses Reiches vergebens gesucht wird. Der Verlust dreier Brüder in der Schottenschlacht treibt ihn zum Wahnsinn und wilden Leben im kaledonischen Walde. Ganieda, nicht Gwenddydd, heisst seine Schwester, und Guendoloëna seine Gattin, und der mythische Gwendoll au der Barden ist verschwunden, wie auch den mitauftauchenden Taliesin nicht jener neodruidische Mysticismus desselben, sondern die Glorie klassischer Wissenschaft umschwebt, deren Quellen nachzuweisen, fast überall uns geglückt ist."—*Die Sagen von Merlin*, p. 272.

Aneurin [1] (stanza 31), as "Peredur with steel arms," and he appears also in the *Mabinogion* as the hero of one of the tales.

It would be very difficult to prove that Geoffrey made extended use of any Welsh literature now extant. The following passages from the *Hoianau*, the *Avallenau*, and the *Vita* contain all the parallels I have been able to discover.

THE HOIANAU.

Stanza IX.

To us there will be years and
   long days,
And iniquitous rulers, and the
   blasting of fruit.

Stanza XXIV.

The dales are my barn, my corn
   is not plenteous;
My summer collection affords me
   no relief.

Stanza II.

Till Cynan [2] comes to it, to see its
   distress,
Her habitations will never be
   restored.

VITA MERLINI.

Deficiunt nunc poma michi, nunc
   cetera quaeque.
Stat sine fronde nemus, sine fructu;
   plector utroque,
Cum neque fronde tegi valeo, neque
   fructibus uti.—ll. 95–97.

Donec als Armorico veniet temone
   Conanus
Et Cadwalladrus Cambrorum dum [3]
   venerandus.—ll. 967, 968.

---

[1] Skene, *Four Anc. Books of Wales*, i. p. 386.

[2] Referring to the prophecy found in the *Avallenau* and the *Hoianau* of the coming of Cadwaladyr and Cynan, Skene remarks (*Four Anc. Books*, i. p. 241): "In the later form of the prophecy Cynan and Cadwaladyr come from Armorica. Thus, in the *Vita Merlini* Geoffrey says :—

> The Britons their noble kingdom
> Shall for a long time lose through weakness,
> Until from Armorica Conan shall come in his car,
> And Cadwaladyr, the honoured leader of the Cymry.

And the prophecy can only have assumed this shape after the fictitious narrative of Cadwaladyr taking refuge in Armorica was substituted for his death in the pestilence, and the scene of his return is placed in South Wales, whence this form of prophecy emerged." Mr. Phillimore suggests that Cadwaladyr is preferably Cadwaladr.

[3] For *dux*.

THE AVALLENAU.[1]   VITA MERLINI.

I.

Sweet apple-tree of delightful branches,

Budding luxuriantly, and shooting forth renowned scions.

Tres quater et iuges septenae poma ferentes

Hic steterant mali; nunc non stant.[2]—ll. 90, 91.

I will predict before the owner of Machreu,

That in the valley of Machawy[3] on Wednesday there will be blood,—

Joy to Lloegyr of the blood-red blades.

Hear, O little pig! there will come on Thursday

Joy to the Cymry of mighty battles,

In their defence of Cymminawd, with their incessant sword-thrusts.

On the Saxons there will be a slaughter with ashen spears,

And their heads will be used as balls to play with.

I prophesy truth without disguise,—

The elevation of a child in a secluded part of the South.

II.

Sweet apple-tree, a green tree of luxurious growth,

How large are its branches, and beautiful its form!

And I will predict a battle that will make me shriek

At Pengwern, in the sovereign feast, mead is appropriate.

III.

Sweet apple-tree, and yellow tree,

Grow at Tal Ardd, without a garden surrounding it;

[1] *Black Book of Caermarthen*, xvii. Skene, *Four Ancient Books of Wales*, i. pp. 370-373.

[2] San-Marte, in commenting on l. 90 of the *Vita Merlini*, remarks: "*Tres quater*. Die Zahl stimmt zwar nicht mit *Avallenau* i.; doch ist die Beziehung darauf klar, und die Kenntniss jenes Gedichts beim Autor sicher vorauszusetzen."—*Die Sagen von Merlin*, p. 316. Doubtless most readers would like to feel as sure as San-Marte.

[3] Mr. Phillimore states: "The vale of the Machawy (now spelt 'Bachowey') is in S. Radnorshire. A great battle was fought there near Pain's Castle, toward the end of the twelfth century, and three thousand men were killed. See Giraldus Cambrensis' works for this slaughter."

And I will predict a battle in Prydyn,
In defence of their frontier against the men of Dublin ;
Seven ships will come over the wide lake,
And seven hundred over the sea to conquer.
Of those that come, none will go to Cennyn,
Except seven half-empty ones, according to the prediction.

IV.

Sweet apple-tree that luxuriantly grows !
Food I used to take at its base to please a fair maid,
When, with my shield on my shoulder, and my sword on my
     thigh,
I slept all alone in the wood of Celyddon.
Hear, O little pig ; now apply thyself to reason,
And listen to birds whose notes are pleasant :
Sovereigns across the sea will come on Monday ;
Blessed will the Cymry be, from that design.

V.

Sweet apple-tree that grows in the glade !
Their vehemence will conceal it from the lords of R[h]ydderch ;
Trodden it is around its base, and men are about it.
Terrible to them were heroic forms :
Gwenddyd[d] loves me not, greets me not ;
I am hated by the firmest minister of R[h]ydderch ;
I have ruined his son and his daughter.
Death takes all away, why does he not visit me ?
For after Gwenddoleu no princes honour me ;
I am not soothed with diversion, I am not visited by the fair ;
Yet in the battle of Ardderyd [Arderydd] golden was my
     torques,
Though I am now despised by her who is of the colour of
     swans.

VI.

Sweet apple-tree of delicate bloom,
That grows in concealment in the woods !

At break of day the tale was told me,
That the firmest minister is offended at my creed,
Twice, thrice, four times, in one day.
O Jesus! would that my end had come
Before the death of the son of Gwend[d]ydd happen on my hand !

VII.

Sweet apple-tree, which grows by the river side !
With respect to it, the keeper will not thrive on its splendid
    fruit.
While my reason was not aberrant, I used to be around its
    stem
With a fair sportive maid, a paragon of slender form.

THE AVALLENAU.

Ten years and forty, as the toy of
    lawless ones,
Have I been wandering in gloom
    and among sprites.
After wealth in abundance and
    entertaining minstrels
I have been (here so long that) it
    is useless for gloom and sprites
    to lead me astray.

VITA MERLINI.

Et fugit ad silvas, nec vult
    fugiendo videri,
Ingrediturque nemus, gaudetque
    latere sub ornis ;
Miraturque feras pascentes gra-
    mina saltus.
Nunc has insequitur, nunc cursu
    praeterit illas.
Utitur herbarum radicibus; utitur
    herbis ;
Utitur arboreo fructu, morisque
    rubeti,
Fit silvester homo, quasi silvis
    editus esset,
Inde per aestatem totam ; nulli-
    que repertus,
Oblitusque sui, cognatorumque
    suorum,
Delituit, silvis obductus more
    ferino.—ll. 74-83.

I will not sleep, but tremble on account of my leader,

My lord Gwenddoleu, and those who are natives of my country.

After suffering disease and longing grief about the words[1] of
Celyddon,

May I become a blessed servant of the Sovereign of splendid
retinues !

VIII.

Sweet apple-tree of delicate blossoms, which grows in the
soil amid the trees !

The Sibyl foretells a tale that will come to pass—

A golden rod of great value, will, for bravery,

Be given to glorious chiefs before the dragons ;

The diffuser of grace will vanquish the profane man ;

Before the child, bold as the sun in his courses,

Saxons shall be eradicated, and bards shall flourish.

IX.

THE AVALLENAU.   VITA MERLINI.

Swect apple-tree, and a tree of
crimson hue,

Which grow in concealment in the
wood of Celyddon;

Though sought for their fruit, it
will be in vain,

Until Cadwaladyr comes from the   Donec ab Armorico veniet temone
conference of Cadvaon,   Conanus [2]

To the Eagle of Tywi and Teiwi   Et Cadwalladrus Cambrorum dum[3]
rivers ;   venerandus.—ll. 967, 968.

And until fierce anguish comes
from Aranwynion,

And the wild and long-haired
ones are made tame.

---

[1] But the original has *coed keliton*.

[2] *Cf.* " Cadwalladrus vocabit Conanum, et Albaniam in societatem accipiet."
—Geoff. of Monmouth, *Prophecy of Merlin*, l. 92.

[3] For *dux*.

THE AVALLENAU.   X.   VITA MERLINI.

Sweet apple-tree, and a tree of crimson hue,	"Non," Merlinus ait, "non sic gens illa recedet,
Which grow in concealment in the wood of Celyddon;	Ut semel in nostris ungues in-fixerit ortis:
Though sought for their fruit, it will be in vain,	Regnum namque prius populosque iugabit et urbes,
Until Cadwaladyr comes from the conference of Rhyd Rheon,	Viribus atque suis multis domina-bitur annis.
And Cynan to meet him advances upon the Saxons;	Tres tamen ex nostris magna vir-tute resistent,
The Cymry will be victorious, glorious will be their leader.	Et multos periment, et eos in fine domabunt:
All shall have their rights, and the Brython will rejoice,	Sed non perficient,[1] quia sic sen-tentia summi
Sounding the horns of gladness, and chanting the song of peace and happiness!	Iudicis existit, Britones ut nobile regnum

THE AVALLENAU.

Sweet apple-tree, and a tree of
    crimson hue,
Which grow in concealment in
    the wood of Celyddon;
Though sought for their fruit, it
    will be in vain,
Until Cadwaladyr comes from the
    conference of Rhyd Rheon,
And Cynan to meet him advances
    upon the Saxons;
The Cymry will be victorious,
    glorious will be their leader.
All shall have their rights, and
    the Brython will rejoice,
Sounding the horns of gladness,
    and chanting the song of peace
    and happiness!

VITA MERLINI.

"Non," Merlinus ait, "non sic
    gens illa recedet,
Ut semel in nostris ungues in-
    fixerit ortis:
Regnum namque prius populosque
    iugabit et urbes,
Viribus atque suis multis domina-
    bitur annis.
Tres tamen ex nostris magna vir-
    tute resistent,
Et multos periment, et eos in fine
    domabunt:
Sed non perficient,[1] quia sic sen-
    tentia summi
Iudicis existit, Britones ut nobile
    regnum
Temporibus multis amittant de-
    bilitate,
Donec ab Armorico veniet temone
    Conanus,[2]
Et Cadwalladrus Cambrorum dum[3]
    venerandus;
Qui pariter Scotos, Cumbros, et
    Cornubienses,
Armoricosque viros sociabunt foe-
    dere firmo;
Amissumque suis reddent diadema
    colonis,
Hostibus expulsis, renovato tem-
    pore Bruti,
Tractabuntque suas sacratis legi-
    bus urbes.
Incipient reges iterum superare
    remotos,
Et sua regna sibi certamine sub-
    dere forti."[4]—ll. 958–975.

---

[1] V.R. proficient.   [2] V.R. Conais.   [3] For *dux*.   [4] *Cf.* San-Marte, *Die Artussage*, p. 92.

With very trifling exceptions this is the entire extent of Geoffrey's indebtedness in the *Vita* to such of the Welsh literature as has come down to us. At best it would be difficult to prove from the correspondences between these Welsh poems and the *Vita* that Geoffrey had ever seen them.[1] Surely we may admit that some of the Welsh poems refer to the battle of Arderydd, and that the *Vita Merlini* does the same, without being compelled to assume that the *Vita* is based upon them. From a variety of considerations we may conclude that a considerable part of the *Vita* is in the last analysis Celtic, but further than this we can hardly go. The Welsh poems that we have may be mere fragmentary representatives of a large body of Welsh literature now irretrievably lost, but perhaps still in existence in the time of Geoffrey. It is possible, if not certain, that Geoffrey had access to a considerable mass of floating unwritten tradition based, it may be, in part on old poems that have long since perished. Probably none of these poems were directly employed in the composition of the *Vita Merlini*; but a set of parallel traditions, based in part on the same events referred to in the Welsh poems, may have formed the groundwork of those portions of the Latin poem which tell of Merlin's madness and of his discourse with Taliessin.

VI.

THE TRANSITION TO FRENCH LITERATURE.

HAVING now taken a general survey of the Latin and Celtic sources that are extant, and that can therefore be directly examined, we are prepared to see how the legend passed into the literature of France, and thence into the other literatures of Western Europe. But before entering upon this question

---

[1] *Cf.* on this matter P. Paris, *Romans de la Table Ronde*, i. p. 45.

we ought to glance at what M. Gaston Paris calls the *matière de.Bretagne*.[1] Unfortunately we cannot trace the growth of the legend in Armorica. The Breton literature, considerable of which doubtless existed at an early period, has not been preserved except in the form of early French[2] and Icelandic translations, and none of these relate in any way to Merlin. The existence of a large body of unwritten tradition, which kept a precarious existence on the lips of *jongleurs* and harpers,[3] is not open to question. But to what extent the popular imagination modified the original material can, in the absence of literary documents, be only a field for conjecture. But while we are unable to trace directly the Armorican literature in its various forms, we have from a variety of sources evidence of the existence of Breton *lais*, in which perhaps the germ of many of the later French romances is to be sought. Without question there existed both in greater and lesser Britain before Geoffrey of Monmouth wrote his *Historia*, and perhaps before *Nennius* composed his little chronicle, a considerable body of songs embodying popular legends.[4] Some of these recitals undoubtedly found their way into Geoffrey's *Historia*. It is probable, too, that the publication of his book and of the numerous translations brought to light a great number of songs or *lais*, as well as prose legends which had been known only in obscure corners or had at most been sung and related by wandering harpers in passing from castle to

---

[1] *Hist. Litt. de la France*, xxx. p. 14. By *Bretagne* he means Great Britain : cf. *Romania*, xii. p. 373; and p, 82, *ante*.

[2] Such, for example, as the *Lais* of Marie de France.

[3] The existence of British harpers is attested by a number of the classical writers, as, for example, Athenæus, Cæsar, Strabo, Lucan, Ausonius, Fortunatus, etc., who thus show that the wandering gleemen of the twelfth and thirteenth centuries were not a new creation. *Cf*. P. Paris, *Romans de la Table Ronde*, i. p. 7.

[4] " Rien ne saurait scientifiquement nous empêcher de croire à l'antériorité des chants bretons sur la chronique de Nennius, chants dont un certain nombre sont si profondément celtique."—*Les Épopées françaises*, L. Gautier. Quoted by Hucher, *Saint-Graal*, i. 2. *Cf*. also P. Paris, *Romans de la Table Ronde*, i. p. 47.

castle. As soon as the *Historia* crystallized some of this material into literary form, the example once set was followed by a great variety of versifiers and prose-writers, whose activity extended through several generations. A part, at least, of these songs may have related to Arthur and the Round Table as well as to his Court, and they would naturally penetrate into the courtly circles which alone could substantially reward the singer. The stories embodied in these songs must have passed from lip to lip in the form of prose tales, and, once introduced into the quick-witted French and Norman society, the progress of assimilation must have been rapid.[1]

---

[1] The details of the process are unknown, and have naturally led to conflicting views. M. Gaston Paris expresses himself as follows:—"En effet, en dehors du monde des clercs, dans lequel Gaufrei de Monmouth avait introduit, en l'arrangeant à sa mode la légende arthurienne, elle avait pénétré, sous des formes variées et par des canaux divers, dans la société chevaleresque. Dès devant la conquête de l'Angleterre par les Normands, les musiciens gallois avaient, semble-t-il, franchi les limites de leur patrie pour venir exécuter chez les Anglo-Saxons eux-mêmes ces 'lais' qui depuis eurent un si grand charme pour le public français. C'est ainsi du moins qu'on peut expliquer que Marie de France désigne le sujet de deux de ses lais à la fois par un mot breton et un mot anglais (*bisclavret, garwall; laustic, nihtegale*), celui d'un autre seulement par un mot anglais (*gotelef*), et que le breuvage amoureux qui causa la passion de Tristan et d'Iseut porte, dans le poème de Béroul, le nom anglais de *lovendris* (les traits particuliers que le prêtre anglais Layamon, dans sa traduction du *Brut* de Wace, ajoute à la legende d'Arthur s'expliquent peut-être autrement). Mais ce fut surtout chez les nouveaux maîtres d'Angleterre que les chanteurs et musiciens bretons trouvèrent un accueil empressé ; ils ne tardèrent même pas à passer la mer, et de nombreux témoignages, qui ne dépassent guère la fin du xiie siècle, nous les montrent à cette époque exécutant avec grand succès leurs lais dans toutes les grandes ou petites cours de la France du Nord. Ces 'lais bretons' étaient des morceaux de musique accompagnés de paroles ; la musique, la 'note,' comme on disait, y jouait le rôle principal ; toutefois les paroles avaient leur importance, et les auditeurs qui ne comprenaient pas le breton éprouvèrent naturellement le besoin de savoir ce qu'elles voulaient dire. Elles se référaient toujours, mais peut-être sans la raconter précisément, à quelque histoire d'amour et généralement de malheur. On mit ces histoires en vers français, et nous avons ainsi conservé une assez riche collection de lais bretons, que n'ont plus rien de musical, et qui sont tous composés en vers de huit syllabes rimant deux par deux. Un seul est en vers de six syllabes. . . . . Mais la plupart des lais sont réellement fondés sur des contes celtiques. D'ordinaire, les aventures qu'ils racontent ne reçoivent aucune détermination de temps ou de lieu. . . . . Les lais ne furent pas les seul véhicules par lesquels les fictions celtiques pénétrèrent en masse au xiie siècle, dans la société polie d'Angleterre et de France, et y suscitèrent une poésie nouvelle. Déjà les vers de

The oft-quoted passage from the *Chanson des Saisnes* shows

Wace cités plus haut nous ont montré à l'œuvre les conteurs et les 'fableurs' brodant à qui mieux sur le fond des aventures de la Table ronde.''—*Hist. Litt. de la France*, xxx. pp. 7-9.

The case against the theory proposed by M. Gaston Paris is stated[a] " by Prof. Foerster in the introduction to his recently published edition of Chrétien's *Erec*, and at greater length by Prof. Zimmer.[b] Without going into details, let it suffice to say, that, on the negative side, the latter challenges the production of any evidence to show, that Welsh bards or minstrels used to sing to the Saxons in England before the Norman Conquest, or even after that event to either Normans or Saxons at a time early enough for the purpose of M. Paris' argument. He contends that the term 'lais bretons' and 'la matière de Bretagne' had nothing to do with Wales, but everything with the Bretons and Brittany. Then as to the lays and the romances, and the suggestion that the latter are derived from the former, he denies it, partly because neither he nor Foerster knows of any lays which can be said to have been originally Arthurian ; partly also — and this brings us to the positive side of Zimmer's contention—because he is convinced that the romances were based on stories in prose rather than in verse. He even goes so far as to call attention to what he considers an ancient and far-reaching distinction between Celts and Teutons, namely, that while the Teutonic way of dealing with the heroic was to express it in the form of an epic poem, the Celtic ideal was that of an epic story in prose. To suit the Norman the Celtic originals had not only to be translated into his language, but also transformed into the epic form of his predilection. The versification was his own business, or that of his French neighbours; but the translation was quite a different matter, belonging to an antecedent stage, and this is believed by Zimmer to have been gradually done, in the first instance, by the Bretons of the eastern portion of Brittany when they gave up their own Brythonic speech to adopt Norman French in its stead, and when their nobles became dependent on Normandy.

Accordingly Dr. Zimmer lays great emphasis on the difference between the Arthur of the romances, whom he tries to trace to Breton sources, and the Welsh Arthur whom Nennius, for instance, mentions hunting the *Porcus Troit*. This, however, does not go quite far enough, as the rôle he assigns to the Normanized Bretons of east Brittany does not exclude the Welsh from playing a similar rôle with regard to the Normans later, namely, after the advent of the latter into Wales: witness the case of the Welshman Bledri. The twofold Brythonic origin of the romances makes itself perceptible in a way which the readers of these chapters may have already noticed, especially in the matter of proper names. Looked at from our point of view, the latter divide themselves into two groups :—1. Well-known names like Gauvain and Modred, the forms of which do not admit of being explained as the result of misreading or miscopying of Welsh originals : they may be the French forms which the Normanizing Bretons gave them—without the direct intervention of scribes or literary men of any kind—when they adopted French as their language.

---

[a] I borrow for convenience the summary of the argument from the *Studies in the Arthurian Legend* (pp. 374-376) by Prof. Rhŷs.

[b] In *Gött. gelehrte Anzeigen* for 1890, pp. 488-528, pp. 785-832 ; and *Zeitschrift für französische Sprache und Litteratur*, xii. pp. 231-256.

what a hold this material had already got upon the writers
of romance :—

> "Ne sont que troi materes a nul home entendant
>   De France, de Bretagne, et de Rome la grant ;
>   Et de ces troi materes ni a nul semblant
>   Li conte de Bretagne sont et vain et plaisant." [1]

At the outset this material, in the opinion of Gaston Paris,
came from England, and thence was carried into France, either
directly by the British singers and story-tellers, or by means
of Anglo-Norman story-tellers ; or already put into verse in
the lays and the Anglo-Norman poems." [2]   But the part
played by Armorican Britain must not be overlooked.   A more
or less lively intercourse was kept up between Armorica [3]
and Great Britain, and it is quite probable that the Arthurian
and Merlin legends were almost as well known in Armorica as

2. Names like Gonemans, Bron, and Palomydes, together with place-names like
Aroie, which readily admit of being explained from Welsh originals: these mostly
belong to the romances more or less closely connected with the story of the Holy
Grail, which itself we have endeavoured to trace to Welsh sources.   This opens up
a new and difficult question, which may be confidently left to future research."

· For the sake of comparison I add the following passage from Kreyssig's *Gesch. der
franz. Lit.* i. pp. 78, 79 : —"Einen ganz andern Character als die *chansons de geste*
tragen die nunmehr zu betrachtenden *romans*.   In ihnen haben wir das Resultat der
Berührung der französischen Normannen und der englischen Kelten zu sehen ; von
diesen haben sie die Vorliebe für das Wunderbare, Übersinnliche, Geheimnisvolle,
Mystische, den Glauben an Riesen, Zwerge, Feen, Zauberer, Drachen ; von jenen
den chevaleresken Zug, die keine Gefahr scheuende Tapferkeit, die Betonung des
Motivs der Liebe, der in den Heldengedichten nur spärlich Raum gelassen ist.   In
ihnen ist der ritterliche Geist zur vollsten Entwickelung gelangt, und es ist wohl
angezeigt sein Wesen in kurzen Zügen darzustellen, da die Kenntniss desselben
zum Verständniss der sein Gepräge tragenden Litteraturproducte unumgänglich
notwendig ist."

[1] *Cf.* P. Paris, *Romans de la Table Ronde*, i. p. 17.

[2] G. Paris, *Hist. Litt. de la France*, xxx. p. 14.

[3] "Une autre source de transmission des légendes bretonnes a été la Bretagne
armoricaine.   Sans parler de la communauté d'origine et des incessantes relations des
émigrés bretons avec l'île mère, notamment avec la Cornouaille anglaise, il y avait
eu une nouvelle émigration de Bretons armoricains en Angleterre au commencement
du dixième siècle, émigration considérable, mais, qui, pour beaucoup des émigrants,
ne fut pas définitive."—J. Loth, *Les Mabinogion*, i. p. 16.

in the heart of Wales itself.   At any rate, it is hardly open to
question that these British chants and tales are older [1] than any
of the French romances in prose or verse [2]; and we may suppose
that, while the French romances were growing up on all sides,
these British tales were diffused in France and England "under
the double form of the *lai* and the story," from the " first
half of the twelfth century till toward the middle of the
thirteenth." [3]

Wace recognized the existence of this material in speaking
of the Round Table, which Geoffrey of Monmouth had not
mentioned, and significantly adds that of this the Britons tell
many a fable.   He had doubtless an independent acquaintance
with Breton legends; for he mentions in the *Roman de Rou*
the wonderful fountain of Broceliande, and says that he has
visited the spot without discovering any marvels.

We may, then, grant at once that Geoffrey of Monmouth was
not the originator of the material of the French romances,[4] but
we may suppose that his work gave the necessary impetus for
the literary development of the legends he had told.   His
popularity is evidenced by several translations [5] of his *Historia*
into French verse.   The first by Geoffrey Gaimar (1145) has
disappeared without leaving an enduring trace.   But in 1155,
about a decade after Geoffrey of Monmouth had given the final
touches to his *Historia*, Wace [6] translated the whole into

[1] *Cf.* P. Paris, *Romans de la Table Ronde*, i. p. 21.

[2] On the general subject of the Breton *lais* see *Hist. Litt. de la France*, xviii.
p. 773; xix. p. 712; xix. p. 791; xxiii. p. 61; xxiii. p. 76; xxiii. p. 114;
xxviii. p. 375; xxviii. p. 385; xxix. p. 498; xxx. pp. 7-12; *Romania*, vii. p. 1:
Romania, viii. p. 29.—*Strengleikar* (Icelandic version), pp. 57, 67, 82.

[3] *Hist. Litt. de la France*, xxx. p. 12.

[4] *Cf.* G. Paris, *Hist. Litt. de la France*, xxx.

[5] *Cf.* the list in the enumeration of the French forms of the legend, p. 37, *ante*.

[6] The peculiar difficulty attending this whole investigation is well illustrated by
such a series of misstatements as is found in a single sentence from the *Encyc. Brit.*
(iv* ed.), art. *Geoffrey of Monmouth*: "Geoffrey's *Historia* was the basis of a host
of other works.   It was abridged by Alfred of Beverley (1150), and translated into

octosyllabic rhyming verse, and opened to those writers who had but a slender acquaintance with Latin an orderly grouping of materials that were capable of indefinite expansion.

In so far as Merlin is concerned, Wace is little more than a translator of Geoffrey. The diffuseness of the translator in his versified descriptions of feasts and battles entitles him to no great credit for inventiveness; and his only real addition [1] is his account of the establishment of the Round Table.[2] This, however, belongs more to the history of Arthur than to that of Merlin.

Wace's *Roman de Brut* was put into French prose shortly after its appearance,[3] and then recopied, imitated, and translated so frequently that the versions in English as well as in French have not yet been properly edited. Up to the last quarter of the twelfth century no French writer seems to have ventured to make independent use of the materials for romance that lay scattered in such profusion. But after Wace's *Brut* had made this material familiar to French writers the period of production began. Our limits make it impossible for us to do more than to follow closely the origin of the prose romance of Merlin.

For the purposes of our examination we may note that the prose *Merlin* divides itself into two very unequal parts. The first part comprises about one-seventh of the whole, and represents what was in all probability the original romance of *Merlin*.[4] The second part deals more particularly with King

Anglo-Norman verse by Geoffrey Gaimar (1154), and then by Wace (1180), whose work, *Li Romans de Brut*, contained a good deal of new matter.'' The few facts that we have of the life of Wace are found for the most part in the autobiographic hints that he gives in the *Roman de Rou*, ll. 5315-5329; 10440-10453; 16526-16537.

[1] *Cf.* Ten Brink, *Gesch. der engl. Lit.* i. p. 177. Ward, *Catal. of Romances*, i. p. 261.

[2] L. 9998. The account of Merlin is practically closed at l. 9022, where Merlin, Ulfin, and the King resume their real persons after the visit to Ygerne. Wace's account of Merlin begins about l. 7490, where Vortigern's tower is mentioned.

[3] Villemarqué, *Les Romans de la Table Ronde*, p. 5.

[4] This matter is fully treated in the discussion of the MSS.

Arthur. The first part ends with the coronation of Arthur. This event the romancers took as a point of departure for a number of versions widely differing in character. Our English translation is based on the continuation most in vogue. For convenience, therefore, we may first deal with the original romance, and then make a more detailed survey of the continuations. We can then best treat the question of the authorship of the latter portion of the romance.

The original French romance of *Merlin* was in verse, and was probably written as early as the last decade of the twelfth century, if not earlier. The *Merlin*, as already noted, was intended to serve as a connecting link[1] between two other poems, *Joseph d'Arimathie* and *Perceval*. Of these poems we have the first entire[2]; of the second, we have a fragment of 504 lines; of the third,[3] we have nothing in verse, but we possess a fourteenth-century prose version much altered, in a unique manuscript of the Bibliothèque Nationale in Paris.[4] The poem of *Merlin* was early reduced to prose,[5] and then furnished the incidents of the short romance of *Merlin*. M. Gaston Paris,[6] following Birch-Hirschfeld, thinks that the prose *Perceval* published by Hucher[7] is based upon a poem by Robert de Borron. The conclusion is reasonably certain, though we know nothing of the prose-writer.

The few known facts of Robert's life have been brought

---

[1] G. Paris, *Merlin*, Introd. p. ix.

[2] Ll. 1–3514.

[3] Nutt, *Holy Grail*, chap. ii., gives a summary of all three, but the summary of the *Merlin* on p. 64 D is not taken from the poem (which in the extant fragment does not contain all the matter summarized), but from the prose romance.

[4] No. 4166, Nouv. acq. fr.

[5] *Cf*. P. Paris, *Romans de la Table Ronde*, i. p. 355. The MS. of the poem of the *Joseph* and the *Merlin* is unique (Bib. Nat. MS. fr. 20,047), and small enough to be carried in the pocket. The only published edition is that of F. Michel, Bordeaux, 1841.

[6] *Merlin*, Introd. i. p. ix.

[7] *Le Saint-Graal*, i. pp. 415–505.

together in an attempted chronological sequence ;[1] but of his personal history, the date of his birth, the circumstances in which he wrote, his relations to the other writers of his time, the extent of his education, and the opportunities he had for becoming acquainted with the legends which he reproduced in verse—of all this we can say very little that is certain.[2] He mentions in his poem (ll. 3488–3494)—

> "Mon seigneur Gautier in peis,
> Qui de Mont Belyal estoit,"

and tells us that from Gautier he had learned the story of the Graal. The meaning of these lines has been variously interpreted ; but the most probable explanation is that which takes the words *en peis* and *estoit* to refer to the decease of Gautier (Walter) in 1212. This was thirteen years after he had left France for Italy and the Holy Land, where he had been made Constable of Jerusalem. Robert de Borron had been in Walter's service sometime between 1170 (?) and 1190, and perhaps during the entire period. In these years[3] he wrote the first draft of his poem ; and the second draft, in all probability, after Walter's death in 1212. This second draft is the one that we possess.

Now follows an obscure period in which the exact sequence of events cannot be traced. But in any case, though we

---

[1] *Cf.* P. Paris, *Romans de la Table Ronde* ; G. Paris, *Merlin*, i. Introd. ; Hucher, *Le Saint-Graal*, i. Introd. ; Nutt, *Studies on the Legend of the Holy Grail*, Index ii. Mr. Nutt gives, on the whole, the most coherent account.

[2] *Cf. Romania*, x. p. 601. His name is variously written (*cf.* Nutt's *Studies*, p. 5): "Messires Roberz de Beron" (*Joseph d'Arimathie*, l. 3461) ; "Meistres Robers dist de Bouron" (l. 3155). The prose romance writes "Roberz de Borron," "de Boron," etc. M. Gaston Paris writes "Robert de Boron."

[3] Nutt, *Studies*, pp. 6, 7. Ten Brink, *Gesch. der engl. Lit.* i. p. 215, supposes Robert to have written in the sixties of the twelfth century. As a curiosity of literary history, we may note that San-Marte regarded Robert de Borron as a thirteenth-century adapter of earlier prose versions of the *Saint-Graal. Cf.* Nutt, *Studies*, p. 99.

cannot fix the precise year in which each production took shape, we may believe that in the course of two generations or less after Robert de Borron began to write, the most important of the prose romances were, if not already written, at least in their main outlines, already conceived.[1] None of these romances can be said to have been finished at any particular time; for in most cases each new copyist felt at liberty to substitute something of his own for whatever was not exactly to his liking.

As already remarked, the prose romance of *Merlin* is a more or less faithful reproduction of the poem of Robert de Borron. As a specimen, I have placed the beginning and the end of the *Merlin* fragment side by side with the French prose and the English prose.

[1] *Cf.* Nutt, *Studies*, p. 6.

Robert de Borron's Merlin.	French Prose.	English Prose.
B.N. MS. fr. 20,047.	B.N. MS. fr. 105, f. 126.	
f. 55b, l. 7.		p. 1, ll. 1–11.

ROBERT DE BORRON'S MERLIN.

B.N. MS. fr. 20,047.

f. 55b, l. 7.

l. 3515.

Mout fu li Ennemis courciez
Quant Enfer fu ainsi brisiez;
Car Jhesus de mort suscita,
En Enfer uint et le brisa.
Adam et Eue en ha gité
Ki là furent en grant uiuté;
O lui emmena ses amis
Lassus ou ciel, en Paradis.
Quant Deable ce aperçurent,
Ausi cum tout enragié furent.

l. 3525.

Mout durement se merveillierent
Et pour ce tout s'atropelerent,
Et disoient: "Qui est cist hon
Qui ha teu uertu et tel non?
Car nos fermetez ha brisies,

FRENCH PROSE.

B.N. MS. fr. 105, f. 126.

Moult fu li annemis iries quant nostre sires ot este en enfer et il en ot iete[1] adam et eue et tant des autres comme a lui plot.[2] Quant li Anemi virent ce si en orlent moult grant enuie.[3] Si sassamblerent et distrent.[4] Qui est cils hom qui[5] si nous a enforciez que fermetez ne riens que[6] nous euissons ne puet estre contre lui gardce quil ne[7] feist ce que lui pleut.[8] Nous ne cuidions pas que nuls homs deust[9] naistre (f. 126b) de femme quil ne fust nostre et si nous destruit ainsi. Comment est il nez quant[10] il n'i a nul delit domme ne riens ensi comme nous auons eu dautre homme.

ENGLISH PROSE.

p. 1, ll. 1–11.

Fvħ wrothe and angry was the Deuoħ, whan that oure lorde hadde ben in helle, and had take oute Adam and Eve, and othere at his plesiere; and whan the fendes sien that, they hadden right grete feere and gret merveile; thei assembleden to-gedire and seiden: "What is he this thus vs supprisiħ and distroyeħ, in so

Les portes d'Enfer depecies :
Riens n'auoit force encontre lui,
Ne de par nous ne par autrui ;
Car il feit tout quanque lui pleit,
Pour nului son uoloir ne leit.

.

l. 3535.

Ceci au meins bien cuidions
Qu'en terre ne uenist nus hons
Qui de cors de femme nachist,
De ne pouoir fuir pouist ;
Et cist ainsi nous ha destruit,
Qu'il Enfer ha leissié tout uuit.
Comment puet estre d'omme nez
Ne concéuz ne engenrez
Que delit én n'i auuns
Si cum en autre auoir soluns ?''

I add a collation of the more important readings of B.N. MSS. fr. 747, f. 77, col. 2 (A), and 24,394, f. 108 (B).

[1] Gite (A) ; gete (B).
[2] tant com li plot (A) ; tant *com* il li plot (B).
[3] merueille (A) ; poor et ml't grant merueille (B).
[4] dirent (A).
[5] qui nos a eforciez car en nos permeter rien (A) ; qui si nossorpuet (B).
[6] qui fust repost *je raie* contre lin *parce que plus loin ecla manque dans* (A).
[7] non face (A) ; *contrester* qhil non flist (B).
[8] plaist (A) ; plot (B).
[9] poist (A) ; peust (B).
[10] que nosni auons conçu nul delit de nul homo terrien, ainsi com nos auons ueu *et* seu de toz autres homes (A) ; que nos nauons veu en lui nul delit terrien ensi com nos auons veu de tos autres hommes (B).

moche that oure strengthes ne nought ellis that we haue may nought withholde hym, nor again hym stonde in no diffonce ; but that he doth aH that him lyketh, we ne trowed not that eny man might be bore of woman, but that he sholde ben oures ; and he that thus vs distroyeth, how is he born in whom we knewe non erthely delyte.''

ROBERT DE BORRON'S MERLIN.	FRENCH PROSE.	ENGLISH PROSE.
l. 3991.	B.N. MS. fr. 105, f. 128, col. 1. ll. 12–38.	p. 6, ll. 21–29.

ROBERT DE BORRON'S MERLIN.

l. 3991.

La uielle dist : "ma douce suer,
Vous estes bien gitée puer.
La uostre grant biauté mar fu,
Qu'einsi auez trestout perdu;
Car iameis ioie en uostre uio
N'arez en ceste compeignie.
Meis se uous sentu auiez
La ioie as autres, et sauiez
Qués deduiz autres femmes unt.

l. 4000.

Quant aucques leur amis sunt,
Certes, ne priseriez mie
Vostre eise une pomme pourrie ;
Se saviez quele eise auuns
Quant aucques nos amis suns,

FRENCH PROSE.

B.N. MS. fr. 105, f. 128, col. 1.
ll. 12–38.

Diex bele amie se uous sauiez comme *grant* ioie[1] autres femmes ont, *uous* ne priseriez rions quan*que* vous auez. Nous auons tele ioie tant comme *nous* sommes en compaignie d*om*mes que nous amons que se nous nauions que vne aumonne[2] de pain si scrio*n*s nous plus aise que uous nestes que se nous auio*n*s[3] quan-

[1] MS. 24,394, f. 109b, col. 1, la ioie.
[2] aumosne.
[3] nos auies.

ENGLISH PROSE.

p. 6, ll. 21–29.

"Now, feire lovo," quod she, "yef ye knewe what ioye other wemen haue, ye sholde preyse litiH alle othir thynges ; ffor we haue oche ioye when we be in companys of men that we loven, that yef we hadde but a mosseH brede, we haue more ioye and delyte than ye haue with alle the delicatys of the worlde.

Car nous summes en compeignie
Que nous amuns; c'est boeuno nie.
Vn peu de poin mieuz ameroie,
Se delez mon ami estoie,
Que ne feroie uos richesces

l. 4010.

Que gardez à si granz destresces.
N'est si granz eise, ce me semble,
Comme d'omme et de femme en-
  semble.
Bele amie pour toi le di;
Car dou tout as à ce failli,
Et si te direi bien pour quoi;
Ta suer est ainz née de toi
Et pour li se pourchacora,
[S]i qu'einçois de toi en aura.

.   .   .   .
.   .   .

quil a en cost pays.[1]   Que nant dont
ioie de femme qui na ioie demme?
Bele amie io le di pour *nous* que ia
point nen auerez ne ne saurez que
ioie demme sera.   Si uous dirai *pour*
quoi *vostre* suer si est aisnce de vous
si en aura auant a son oez que[2] ele
sueffre ne ne veille que nous en aicz.
Et quant ele en aura si ne li chaudra
de vous.   Ainsi auez uous perdue la
ioie de *nostre* bel cors qui tant marg fu.

[1] siecle Die que nant.
[2] vos en aies point.

Fye! what ioye hath a woman with-
oute man?   Ffeire love, this I seye
for yow that knowen not what it is
to be in mannes company, and I will
telle you why: youre suster is elder
than ye, and so she wolde alwey
holde yow as her sogeet, so that she
myght haue all, and so shold ye loose
youre tyme, and the ioye of youre
feire body."

A comparison of the three parallel texts shows how closely and yet with what considerable variations the prose adapter has handled his original. It is, however, by no means certain that we have the earliest French prose version of the poem, and we can therefore make allowances for a second paraphrase based, it may be, upon the first one. As for the English version, it is based upon a French text differing slightly from those texts that have come down to us.

VII.

THE FRENCH MANUSCRIPTS OF THE PROSE MERLIN.

In the following list I have arranged in chronological order all of the manuscripts of the French prose *Merlin* [1] that are mentioned in the numerous catalogues I have consulted. After grouping the manuscripts according to age, I have endeavoured to point out in detail some of the relations existing among the more important ones. The generic grouping is always a perilous task; and I shall not insist too strongly upon the family resemblances that I find. I need hardly add that I make no pretence to an absolutely exact chronological arrangement, though in the main it will be found, I think, that the older manuscript has the earlier place. Until we have established such a chronology, and know how many hands retouched the original work, we can, of course, scarcely hope to understand precisely the relations of one version to another. We should, however, not forget that a late manuscript may represent a very

---

[1] One might be led to think from Dr. Sommer's remarks on p. 7 of his *Studies on the Sources* of Malory's *Morte d'Arthur* that we have but three or four MSS. of the *Merlin ordinaire*. I hardly understand what he means (p. 14) where he speaks of "all MSS. and editions presenting the same version." He cites for the *Merlin* only the Huth MS., Brit. Mus. Add. 10,292, and Harl. 6340, though he had already mentioned MS. 747 of the Bibl. Nat. (p. 7).

early copy now lost, and thus give a more primitive version (though in modernized phraseology) than a manuscript actually older.   The original version seems to have been lost,[1] and it can be tentatively reconstructed only by laborious critical comparison.   There now exist the following French manuscripts of the prose *Romance of Merlin*.   Some of these represent only the first part (ch. i.-vi.), some only the second part (ch. vii.-xxxiii.), and some are mere fragments.[2]

1.* Paris, Bib. Nat. MS. fr. 337, Anc. No. 6958, xiii. cent.   Incomplete at the beginning and the end.   Contains only the *Book of Arthur*, and after f. 115, col. 1, l. 28, presents a unique version, differing entirely from all the other texts.[3]

2.* Paris, Bib. Nat. MS. fr. 747, Anc. No. 7170, xiii. cent.   Contains prose romance of *Joseph*, or the *Saint-Graal*, and the *Merlin*, complete.[4]

3. Paris, Bib. Nat. MS. fr. 748, Anc. No. 7170, Fonds de Cangé, No. 4, middle of xiii. cent.   Contains *Roman de Josephe ou du Saint-Graal*,[5] and the first part of the *Romance of Merlin*.   Incomplete at the end.   Parallels the English version with some variations up to the words, "On witson even be comen coun-[seile of all the barons]," p. 106, l. 31.   For our purpose this

---

[1] There is a bare possibility that B.N. MS. fr. 337 may be the original version of the *Book of Arthur*, but this is not at all certain.

[2] The * indicates that the manuscript is more fully discussed further on.

[3] *Cf.* G. Paris, Introd. to *Merlin*, i. p. xxiv. note.   An edition of this MS. is to be published by the *Société des Anciens Textes*.   This version is interesting, too, in that it mentions "maistre Gautiers mape" (f. 152, col. 2), and tells us that he had translated the book from Latin into French at the request of King Henry, who richly rewarded him.   Credat Judæus!

[4] "La leçon est bonne et des plus complètes."—P. Paris, *Les MSS. Franç.* vii. p. 1.   "Le plus ancien et le meilleur, si nous ne nous trompons, de ceux qui nous ont conservé ce texte."—G. Paris, Introd. to *Merlin*, p. viii.   G. P. here refers specifically to the *Merlin* based on Robert de Borron's poem.

[5] P. Paris, *MSS. Franç.* vi. p. 2, observes that this is a "Volume fort précieux en ce qu'il contient le même récit en prose que M. Francisque Michel a publié en vers d'après le Manuscrit de Saint-Germain, No. 1987.   Le texte en prose paraît unique comme le texte en vers.   Le roman de Merlin commence au f. 18 r.   Il diffère peu des leçons ordinaires, et n'est continué que jusqu'au couronnement d'Artus."

manuscript is of no especial importance, as it belongs to the group of manuscripts which differ so widely (f. 28*b*, col. 2) from the English version at one point (p. 23).

4. Paris, Bib. de l'Arsenal, MS. fr. 2996, Anc. No. 225 B.F., xiii. cent. Contains *Le Petit Saint-Graal ou Josephe d'Arimathie* and the first branch of *Merlin*. Very badly defaced at the end. Last page almost illegible. The legible portion parallels the English version up to p. 105. This manuscript presents the ordinary readings of the MSS., and varies (f. 25*b*–f. 26, col. 1), as do so many of the other MSS., from the English version at p. 23. It may be classed with Bib. Nat. MS. fr. 748 (No. 3 of our list).[1]

5. Paris, Bib. de l'Arsenal, MS. fr. 2997, Anc. No. 229 B.F., xiii. cent. Contains the first branch of the *Romance of Merlin*, followed by the *Petit Saint-Graal*.[2] This manuscript calls for no special remark. Some pages are hardly legible, but the readings in general are not peculiar. The French parallels the English up to the end of Chapter vi. p. 107, but like Bib. Nat. MS. 748 it differs (f. 8) from the English version at p. 23 (*cf.* No. 3 of our list). At the end of the *Saint-Graal* Merlin is called *Mellin*.

6.* Paris, Bib. Nat. MS. fr. 344, Anc. No. 6965, middle of xiii. cent.[3] Contains *Saint-Graal, Merlin, Lancelot, La Quête du Saint-Graal.*[4] As far as f. 182, col. 2, l. 36, the French parallels the English version (p. 521, l. 31); then rapidly condenses the remainder of the story, and ends with f. 184, col. 1, l. 26. The first column on the page is filled up with a miniature, and two lines of the *Lancelot*. The second column begins with a miniature and the two opening lines, which are repeated from the first column.

7. Paris, Bib. Nat. MS. fr. 2455, xiii. cent. Contains *Saint-Graal* (ff. 1-338) and a very short fragment of the beginning of the prose *Merlin*, nine long lines and four and a half short ones.

8.* Paris, Bib. Nat. MS. fr. 770, Anc. No. 7185,*3.3.* Fonds de Cangé, No. 6, middle of xiii. century. Contains *Saint-Graal, Merlin*

---

[1] For a further description see *Cat. des MSS.* (Bibl. de l'Arsenal) iii. p. 186.

[2] *Ibid.* iii. p. 186.

[3] *Cf.* Hucher, *Le Saint-Graal*, i. p. 23.

[4] *Cf.* P. Paris, *MSS. Franç.* ii. p. 365.

complete, *Chronique de la Conquéte de Jérusalem par Saladin*.[1] This version closely resembles that of Bib. Nat. MS. fr. 95 (No. 9 of this list), but may perhaps be older.

9.* Paris, Bib. Nat. MS. fr. 95, Anc. No. 6769, xiii. cent. Contains *Saint-Graal, Merlin* complete, *Roman des Sept Sages, Légende de la Pénitence d'Adam*.[2]

10.* Paris, Bib. Nat. MS. fr. 24,394, Notre Dame, No. 206,[3] xiii. cent. Contains *Saint-Graal* and *Merlin* complete.

11.* Paris, Bib. Nat. MS. fr. 110, Anc. No. 6782.[4] End of xiii. cent.[5] Contains *Saint-Graal, Merlin* complete, *Lancelot*.

12.* Paris, Bib. Nat. MS. fr. 749, Anc. No. 7171, Fontainableau No. 733, etc. End of xiii. cent. Contains *Roman de Josephe ou du Saint-Graal, Merlin* complete. Paulin Paris remarks[6] that this text is good, and contains several episodes of the *Merlin* not found in all the old manuscripts. The last nine *laisses* of the *Merlin*, are lost.

13. Paris, Bib. Nat. MS. fr. 423, Anc. No 7024, Anc. Bib. Mazarin No. 116, Morceau No. 14. End of xiii. cent. Paulin Paris calls this a " curious abridgement of the romances of the *Saint-Graal* and of *Merlin*. The last leaves are wanting."[7] There is no formal division between the *Petit Saint-Graal* and the *Merlin*, except that a new paragraph is begun. The French parallels the English up to the middle of p. 23, but at this point differs by giving the version which says that "when the two books are put together they will be *.i. bel liure*."

14.* Paris, Bib. Nat. MS. fr. 19,162, S.G. fr. 1245, xiii.-xiv. cent. Contains *Saint-Graal* and *Merlin* complete.

15. London, Huth MS.[8] End of xiii. or beginning of xiv. cent. Contains the prose *Joseph d'Arimathie*, the prose Merlin

---

[1] *Cf.* P. Paris, *MSS. Franç*, vii. 130, 131.

[2] *Ibid.* i. 120.

[3] Mentioned by P. Paris, *Romans de la Table Ronde*, ii. 352.

[4] Described by P. Paris, *MSS. Franç.* i. 145.

[5] *Cf.* Hucher, *Le Saint-Graal*, i. 23.

[6] *MSS. Franç.* vi. 3.

[7] *Ibid.* iv. 65-67.

[8] Fully described by G. Paris, Introd. to *Merlin*, i. pp. i.-viii.

(Eng. chap. i.-vi.), and a unique continuation of the *Merlin*. This version agrees less closely with the English version than several of the other French texts do.

16.* Paris, Bib. Nat. Nouv. acq. fr. 4166. Written 1301 A.D. Contains *Joseph d'Arimathie*, the first branch of *Merlin* (Eng. chap. i.-vi.), and a unique continuation of the *Merlin*, known as the prose *Perceval*, which has been published by Hucher.[1]

17. Rennes, Bib. publique, MS. 147.[2] Copy begun 1302–1303 A.D.

18.* Paris, Bib. Nat. MS. fr. 105, Anc. No. 6777. End of xiii. or beginning of xiv. cent.[3] Contains *Joseph d'Arimathie* and *Merlin* complete.

19.* Paris, Bib. Nat. MS. fr. 9123, suppl. fr. 11. xiv. cent. Contains *Joseph d'Arimathie* and *Merlin*. This manuscript, though later and somewhat better preserved, is almost exactly like MS. fr. 105 in its readings. The two MSS. agree in having rubrics as headings for the chapters, a feature not found in many of the MSS. of *Merlin*. These two MSS. seem on the whole to represent more nearly than any of the others the French original of the English romances. The details of the proof will be found in the subsequent discussion.

20.* London, Brit. Mus. MS. Add. 10,292. Early xiv. cent. Contains *Saint-Graal*, *Merlin*,[4] complete. This MS. may be classed with Bib. Nat. MS. fr. 24,394, Bib. Nat. MS. fr. 96, and Bib. Nat. MS. fr. 19,162.[5] Of course this general agreement does not preclude minor differences due to the caprice or negligence of the copyist.

21.* Paris, Bib. de l'Arsenal, No. 3482, B.F. 235, xiv. cent. Contains *Merlin* (both branches), *Lancelot*, *la Queste du Saint-Graal*, *la Mort du Roi Artus*. Several leaves are missing: the whole

---

[1] *Le Saint-Graal*, i. pp. 415–505.

[2] F. Michel, *Vita Merlini*, p. lxxi., gives the number as 148. See also *Description, Notices et Extraits des MSS. de la Bibl. de Rennes* par Domenique Maillet, Rennes, 1837, 8vo., pp. 133, 134. This MS. and the late Brussels MS. are the only ones that I have not examined.

[3] P. Paris, *MSS. Franç.* i. 140, 141 ; Hucher, *Saint-Graal*, i. 21.

[4] Described in Ward's *Cat. of MSS.* i. 343. *Cf.* Sommer's note, *Morte Darthur*, iii. 7.

[5] Nos. 10, 14, 24, of this list.

of *cahiers* xv. and xvi.; in *cahier* viii. two leaves; in ix. two
leaves; in xii. one leaf; in xviii. one leaf; in xx. one leaf; in
xxii. two leaves; in xxiii. one leaf; in xxv. two leaves.[1]

22. Paris, Bib. Nat. Coté dons, No. 1638. Don de M. Piot.[2] xiv.
cent. Fragment of the romance of *Merlin* in eight leaves,
numbered 25-32. The French represents accurately the English
version from Eng. p. 59, l. 22, to p. 81, l. 28. With one exception
the paragraphs begin at the same point in the French and the
English, and in that case there is a variation of but a single line.

23.* Paris, Bib. Nat. MS. fr. 98, Anc. No. 6772. xiv. cent. Contains *Saint-Graal, Merlin*, complete, *Lancelot*.[3]

24.* Paris, Bib. Nat. MS. fr. 96, Anc. No. 6770. End of xiv. cent.
Contains *Saint-Graal, Merlin*, complete, first part of *Lancelot*.
Agrees closely with Bib. Nat. MS. fr. 24,394 (No. 10 of this
list), but the language has been modernized in the copying.[4]

25.* Paris, Bib. Nat. MS. fr. 117-120, Anc. No. 6788-6791. End
of xiv. cent.[5] Contains *Saint-Graal, Merlin, Lancelot*. The
Merlin is found in No. 117, and is very complete.

26. Brussels, Bib. Royale MS. fr. 9246, 1480 A.D. Contains *Joseph
d'Arimathie* and *La Vie de Merlin*.[6]

27. Paris, Bib. Nat. MS. fr. 113, Anc. No. 6784. End of xv. cent.
Contains *Saint-Graal*; the first branch of *Merlin*, representing
the first six chapters of the English version; *Lancelot*. The
French text is abridged, modernized, and otherwise altered.[7]

28. London, Brit. Mus. Harl. 6340, xv. cent. paper MS. Contains
Merlin, complete. The version is considerably modernized, and
according to Ward[8] is written at greater detail than the text of
the printed edition (2 vols. Paris, 1498), but containing the

---

[1] *Cf. Cat. des MSS. Bib. de l'Arsenal*, iii. pp. 382, 383.

[2] Cf. *Romania*, 1878, vii. p. 157.

[3] *Cf.* P. Paris, *MSS. Franç.* i. p. 129.

[4] *Ibid.*, i, p. 125, p. 127.

[5] Hucher, *Le Saint-Graal*, i. 23, assigns this MS. to the xiv. or xv. century.
Cf. P. Paris, *MSS. Franç.* i. 154-156.

[6] This MS. I have not seen; but as it was transcribed twenty or thirty years
after our translation was made, I imagine that my loss is not great.

[7] *Cf.* P. Paris, *MSS. Franç.* i. 152-154.

[8] *Cat. of Romances*, i. 344.

same adventures, only with two additional chapters, viz. that of the dwarf knight and that of the birth of Lancelot.[1] Besides being too late to have been used as the basis of our translation, this manuscript is a copy of a version which omits numerous passages contained in the English translation as well as in several of the French MS.   Such omissions may be verified by comparing E. p. 176 with Fr. f. 83, col. 1 ; E. p. 179 with f. 83*b*, col. 1 ; E. p. 187, l. 8 – l. 18 with f. 85*b*, col. 2 ; E. p. 189 with f. 86, col. 1, etc.   The test passage, f. 21*b*, col. 2 and f. 22, col. 1, differs from the English, p. 23, in giving the expanded version and in omitting to mention "Maister Martins."[2]

29. Paris, Bib. Nat. MS. fr. 332, Anc. No. 6954.   Beginning of xvi. cent.   Contains *Merlin*, complete.   The language is modernized so as to represent the speech of the xv. century.[3]   Besides being too late for our purpose, the minor variations from the English version exclude this version from being regarded as the original. It differs from the English in giving the expanded version for Eng. p. 23, and in making no mention of "Maister Martins." Other differences may be found by comparing E. p. 485 with f. 223, col. 2 ; E. pp. 576–578 with f. 261*b* – f. 262, etc.

THE MERLIN A COMPOSITE ROMANCE.

At this point, before venturing on a further classification, we can most conveniently consider the facts which indicate that the *Romance of Merlin* as we have it is a composite of several romances.

---

[1] On this Sommer (*Morte Darthur*, vol. iii. p. 7) remarks "The fact is that both texts [Harl. and Add. 10,292] are exactly alike, representing only different stages of the French language ; both, therefore, contain more than the printed [French] *Merlin*."

[2] This MS. may be compared with Bib. Nat. MS. fr. 24,394.

[3] *Cf.* P. Paris, *MSS. Franç.* ii. 340. To the MSS. noticed above I may add three MSS. mentioned in the *Romania* for 1873, vol. ii. pp. 51, 53, 55 as existing in the Este collection (in Italy) of the fifteenth century.

(1) " 6(20). Libro uno in francexe, chiamado Merlino,—in carta membrana, coverto de chore roso."

(2) " 43 Libro uno chiamado Merlino—in membrana, coverto de chore roso—in francexe."

(3) " Liber Merlini—in membranis. '

In the year 1868, about a third of a century after the publication of his first work on the Arthurian romances, Paulin Paris expressed the opinion [1] that the romance of *Merlin* was made up of at least two principal parts by different writers, the first part [2] extending to the corouation of Arthur ; the second, comprising the remainder of the romance. At first sight the division appears somewhat arbitrary, but closer study makes it extremely probable.[3] At any rate, the scepticism with which I was disposed at the outset to regard the theory has almost entirely vanished. As the details of his argument are but little known to English readers, I will venture to reproduce concisely what is to be urged in favour of his view. Paulin Paris presented his arguments in several different forms at different times, but they may be reduced to the following :—

1.—At the close of the original romance of *Merlin* [4] we are told that Arthur after his coronation held the land and the kingdom for a long time in peace. But in the romance as we have it the rebellion against Arthur follows immediately after. It is hardly probable that a writer would so contradict himself in the course of a few lines.

2.—At the end of the poem of *Joseph d'Arimathie* Robert de Borron had promised to take up the adventures of Alain le Gros when he had read the large book of the *Graal* where they are related. Now, in one of the manuscripts of *Merlin*,[5] after telling of the coronation of Arthur, the author says he is going to tell of Alain, and when done with him to return to Arthur. This promise is not kept in any version which has come down to us; and these closing lines are omitted in all the other

---

[1] In *Les Romans de la Table Ronde*, i. p. 356 sq. ; ii. pp. 101–103, etc.

[2] Chapters i.-vi. of the English version.

[3] *Cf.* also Kölbing, *Altenglische Bibl.* iv. p. cxxviii.

[4] P. 107 of the English translation.

[5] Bib. Nat. MS. fr. No. 747, f. 102, back. The other MSS. containing both branches of the romance make no formal break at this point, though in most cases they begin a new paragraph.

manuscripts. They are evidently the prose equivalents of the concluding verses of the poem of Merlin. All the versions pass at once to the rebellion of the barons who disdained the young king.

From these and other data Paulin Paris concludes: 1. That Robert de Borron had nothing to do with the Book of the *Saint-Graal*, written at the very same time when he composed *Joseph d'Arimathie*; 2. that after becoming acquainted with the *Graal* he intended to continue the history of Alain le Gros, if not of Bron and Petrus; 3. that the writers who came after Robert de Borron, finding the story of Alain fully told in the *Graal*, set aside Robert's poetic version (assuming that it really existed) and substituted for it the history of Arthur,[1] which they harmonized as well as they could with the *Merlin*.

M. Paris finds additional confirmation for his theory in the numerous contradictions between the first portion of the romance and the second :—

1.—In the original romance the Duke of Tintagel[2] left several daughters, the eldest of whom married Loth, King of Orkanie, while another daughter, the illegitimate Morgain, was put to school. In the continuation we find that Ygerne had been twice married before espousing Uter-Pendragon. Of this double marriage were born five daughters: the Queen of Orcanie, wife of Loth; the Queen of Garlot, wife of Nautre (Ventres)[3]; the Queen of Wales (Gorre), wife of Urien; the Queen of Scotland, widow of Briadan, and mother of King Aguisel (Aguysas); finally, the wise Morgain, surnamed *le fee*.

2.—In the short romance of Robert de Borron, Merlin had made a golden dragon as a standard just after the battle of

---

[1] Paulin Paris uniformly refers to the *Livre d'Artus*, or shortly, the *Artus*.

[2] Strangely enough we find in the second part (Eng. p. 177) the name of " Duke Hoel of Tintagel " given as the husband of Ygerne. This is not found in the first part. Geoffrey of Monmouth has, of course, *Gorlois*.

[3] I need not remark that the forms of the names are so various in the MSS. that no two writers on the Arthurian romances are quite agreed as to which forms to adopt.

Salisbury, won by the brothers Pendragon and Uter. In the continuation Merlin makes the dragon for Arthur (Eng. p. 115) instead of for his father. This argument is, however, not very convincing, as there is no reason why Merlin may not have made two dragons as well as one.

3.—According to Robert de Borron, Kay was made steward or seneschal at the time when Arthur took the sword out of the stone (Eng. p. 104). In the continuation, observes Paulin Paris, it is at the moment of attacking the six rebel kings that Arthur confides to Kay, his foster-brother, the office of seneschal (Eng. p. 116).

I must confess that as the two passages appear in the English I can see no real contradiction at this point. The English reads as follows :—

"And be counseile of the archebisshop̄ and certeiɲ of the barouɴs, Kay was made stiwarde," p. 104.

"Thaɲ toke the kynge the dragoɲ and yaf it to Kay, his stiwarde, in soche forwarde that he be chef banerer of the reame of logres euer while his lif doth dure," p. 116.

4.—Paulin Paris instances[1] also the confusion introduced by the Round Table of Leodegan, and observes that the continuator of Robert de Borron's narrative was content to follow the ancient lays without regard to the contradictions.

We may then, argues Paulin Paris, regard it as well established[2] that we have in the large romance of *Merlin* at least two romances. The first ends at the coronation of Arthur, and represents the original poem of Robert de Borron—a poem written to link the poem of *Joseph d'Arimathie* with the (lost) poem of *Perceval.* To this original romance were added several continuations, one of which became more popular than the others,

---

[1] *Romans de la Table Ronde,* ii. pp. 126, 127.

[2] For a continuation of these arguments, see the remarks by Gaston Paris in the Introduction to the *Merlin* published for the *Soc. des Anc. Textes,* 1886.

and furnished the text for the early printed editions. In the following pages I will sketch briefly these different versions.

It is not impossible that other continuations of the romance existed that have not been preserved. Those that we have are found in the following manuscripts :—

> 1. Bib. Nat. MS. fr. 337 (list No. 1).
> 2. Bib. Nat. MS. fr. 344 (list No. 6).
> 3. Bib. Nat. Nouv. acq. fr. 4166 (list No. 16).
> 4. Huth MS., London (list No. 15).
> 5. Bib. Nat. MS. fr. 98 (list No. 23).

The continuation known as the vulgate, or the *Merlin ordinaire*, appears in a considerable number of manuscripts which exhibit only minor variations. The reason for treating any of these versions separately is one of convenience only.

1. *Bib. Nat. MS.* fr. 337.

On this manuscript Paulin Paris remarks that it is the one which before all others should be consulted by those who would well understand the history of the Enchanter Merlin.[1] The volume has lost the original beginning and the end, and begins, " with the court that King Arthur holds immediately after his coronation," and " ends with the combat of Gawein with Oriol, king of the Saxons." For a considerable distance this version runs parallel with the ordinary version, and in many cases agrees almost word for word with it. But this text (MS. 337), after describing the amour of Guyomar with Morgain le fee, breaks off abruptly (f. 115, col. 1, l. 28), and returns to speak of King Arthur and the Knights of the Round Table. The ordinary French text[2] (represented by the English version p. 509) introduces at this point King Loth and his sons as starting

---

[1] *MSS. Franç.* ii. p. 343. He gives a short analysis of the special features of this version in *Romans de la Table Ronde*, ii. p. 393 sqq.

[2] *Cf.* Bib. Nat. MS. fr. 747, f. 186, col. 1.

out on their mission to the feudatory princes. The entire remainder of the narrative in MS. 337 and in the vulgate is essentially different, though here and there is a passage which points to a common source. In the unique portion (of MS. 337) which follows the point of divergence, the wars with the Saxons, and the personal adventures of Seigramor, of Yvain, of King Arthur, and especially of Gawein, are dwelt upon at great length, and with an infinity of detail. There are, however, four hundred pages (pp. 108-508) of the English version that contain essentially the same narrative as appears in the first 115 leaves of this manuscript. It is true that the minor variations are such as to preclude the possibility of this version having been actually used by the English translator; for there are numberless differences in forms of names, in numerals, in omitted sentences, and added phrases.[1] Yet multitudes of passages are almost literally coincident, and show clearly that all the versions, in so far as they agree at all, were copied with mere individual variations from one original. This manuscript is one of the very earliest of those that have been preserved to us, though it may in turn have been based upon a version still earlier.

If now we take up the later unique portion of the romance, and add it to the portion which agrees with the vulgate, we have a romance far exceeding in length any of the existing versions.[2] We cannot go into the details of this unique French version, but must be content to note a few of the more

---

[1] *Cf.* for instance, the list of knights, f. 29, col. 2, with that of the English version, p. 212; the description of Gonnore, f. 33*b*, with that on p. 227 of the English version; f. 107*b*, col. 1, with English, p. 485. These are by no means the most divergent of the passages that might be cited.

[2] In the entire MS. are 294 leaves or 588 pages (14½ × 10⅝in.) of two columns each, which would be equal to about 1030 pages of our English translation. If we were to add the first branch of the *Merlin*, we should have, say, 1130 pages, and still have an unfinished romance! The unique portion is equal in amount to about 625 pages of the English translation: that is, it lacks only about 75 pages of being as long as the entire English version.

remarkable passages. In reading the ordinary *Merlin* and the *Book of Arthur*, the attentive reader remarks several passages in which the writer promises to explain something more fully later ·in the narrative. For instance, after describing the amour of Guyomar with Morgain le fee, the writer adds (p. 509)—"But after it knewe the quene Gonnore, as ye shull here tell." In the ordinary version there is no further reference to the matter. But in MS. 337, f. 187, col. 2, the narrator returns to the adventure as he had promised (f. 114*b*, col. 2) and describes the visit of Merlin to Morgain le fee after her disappearance from the court, and tells how he comforts her. Now, on p. 508 of the English translation, we read of Morgain le fee that " she was a noble clergesse, and of Astronomye cowde she I-nough, for Merlin hadde hir taught; and after he lerned hir I-nough, as ye shull heren afterward." But we do not " heren afterward," except in the unique French version of MS. 337, in which we find that he teaches her many things, and she in turn almost makes the enchanter prefer her to Nimiane his love.

On p. 527 of the English translation (that is, in the portion not represented in this unique French version) we read of the reproof that king Loth gives Agravain for his impure thinking, and then we find a passing reference to an unpleasant accident which befell the young man, " as the booke shall yow devyse here-after." In all the subsequent story, however, we discover no further reference to the matter; while MS. 337, f. 255, col. 1, gives the story in full, though with some variation. For instance, in the English version (p. 527) we read " that he langwissid longe a-boue the erthe for the vilonye that he dide to a mayden, that rode with hir frende, with whom he faught till that he hadde hym discounfited and *maymed of oon of his armes*." The French has (f. 255) " il li trenchast la teste."

The inference from these facts is obvious: Whoever under-

took to write the later portion of the romance of *Merlin* worked
over an older version, and was too careless to notice the incon-
sistencies and contradictions of one part of his narrative with
another. This older version may have been that of MS. 337,[1]
from which the later writer borrowed now and then a hint.
Paulin Paris sees in this special version evidence that it was
composed earlier than the *Lancelot*.[2] This suggestion, however,
raises a question that may safely be left till we have the
promised edition of MS. 337.

To determine exactly the influence that this special version
had upon the composition of the last third of the *Book of Arthur*,
is not easy without a printed text. But, as already noted, the

---

[1] *Romans de la Table Ronde*, ii. p. 397.

[2] Compare the remarks of Gaston Paris (Introd. to *Merlin*, p. xxiv.) on the
priority of the *Lancelot* over the *Book of Arthur*. I cannot discuss the question,
but I shall be surprised if critical comparison of the texts when they are published
will altogether justify G. Paris. I note merely a few of the passages in the *Merlin*
and the *Lancelot* where the two romances refer to the same incidents :—

1.—The birth of Merlin is recounted in the *Lancelot*, part i., chapter vi. : " Cõe
merlin fut ẽgẽdre du dyable. *Et* cõe il fut amoureux de la dame du lac " (ed. of
1488), but with difference enough, as P. Paris remarks,[a] to show that the *Merlin*
and the *Lancelot* are not by the same author.

2.—The death of Lancelot is referred to in an interpolated passage[b] of the
Merlin (p. 147).

3.—The trouble that Guyomar caused the realm of Logres, " as the tale shall
reherse here-after," is referred to in the *Merlin* (pp. 316, 317).

4.—The marvels that Guynebans performs for a maiden (*Merlin*, p. 361 *sqq.*)
are paralleled in the *Lancelot*.[c]

5.—The origin of Morgain's hate for the queen (*Merlin*, pp. 508, 509) is explained
in the *Lancelot*.[d]

6.—The adventure of Agravain and his cure (*Merlin*, p. 527) are touched upon in
the *Lancelot*.[e]

7.—The adventure of Ban at the castle of Agravadain (*Merlin*, ch. xxx) is
paralleled in the *Lancelot*.[f]

8.—The loss of the castle of Trebes (*Merlin*, p. 699) is described at the beginning
of the *Lancelot*.

An incident not found in the *Merlin* is referred to in the *Lancelot*. Reference
is there made to the *Perron Merlin*, " where Merlin had killed the two enchanters."
Ibid. iii. 287.

[a] *Cf.* B. N. MS. 24,394, f. 149b, col. 2.   [b] *Romans*, iii. 23.   [c] *Ibid.* v. 311.
[d] *Ibid.* iv. 292, 293.   [e] *Ibid.* iii. 326–332; iv. 47 (*cf.* B. N. MS. 337, f. 255).
[f] *Ibid.* v. 309, 324–325.

later writer seems to have taken a hint here and there. For
instance, a sort of variant of the adventure of king Ban at the
castle of the Lord of the Marsh (Eng. chap. xxx.) is found at
f. 184*b*, with the difference that in this French version the
niece plays the leading part instead of the daughter, and that
the setting of the two incidents is not the same. To inquire
particularly into the motives for the rejection of so much of this
old version would lead us too far. If the reason lay in the
salacious quality of many of the incidents, one might ask why
the adventure of Guyomar and Morgain le fee should have been
retained, especially as it is apropos of nothing, and occurs at the
very point where the ordinary version begins to differ from this
one. But taken as a whole the ordinary version is not so highly
seasoned with realistic love adventures as the version it replaced,
which is an almost continuous catalogue of lechery. A more
plausible explanation, perhaps, is that after the old version had
been written, the *Lancelot* appeared and some writer conceived
the plan of recasting the *Merlin* as an introduction to the
Lancelot. There are some difficulties in this view, but
M. Gaston Paris regards it as probable.[1] Whatever our view
of the relative age of the two versions, the one which the
sense of the Middle Ages fixed upon as preferable seems, in
spite of incoherency and needless details, to possess more connection and to move forward more definitely toward the end
than this crude and formless congeries of adventures.

2. *Bib. Nat. MS.* fr. 344.

The only peculiarity worthy of special attention in this
manuscript is that after f. 182, col. 2, l. 36, the story is suddenly
compressed into a few pages, so that the end is reached on

---

[1] This may well be true of that part of the *Merlin* between pp. 509 and 699; but
as for the part between pp. 107 and 509 there may be more doubt. The interpolations
are numerous, and they need critical handling with the help of a critical text before
the question can be settled.

f. 184, col. 1.[1]   This fact would of itself be sufficient to exclude this manuscript from being regarded as the possible original of the English translation, even though we took no account of minor differences.   Yet these smaller differences are considerable, in spite of frequent verbal agreement.   For instance, the important passage f. 85*b*, col 2. ; Eng. p. 23, is much longer in the French than in the English ; nor is this contraction due to the English translator, for we find the same in MS. 105. Exceedingly interesting is it, however, to find mentioned at this point "maistre Martins," whose name does not appear in most of the texts, though it is found in the English translation :—

" *Et* ki voudroit nomeir les rois q*ui* deuant i furent *et* lor uie uoldroit oir, si gardaist en lestoire de bretaigne q*ue* len apelle brutus, ke maistre martins de rouain retrait de latin en romans."

In the English version (p. 23) the reader is referred to a book on the history of the Britons that "maister martyn t*r*aunslated out of latyn."   As most of the manuscripts omit this name, its

---

[1] The corresponding portion in the English version extends from p. 521, l. 31, to p. 699.   Comparing the two versions, we find the parallel almost complete as far as f. 182, col. 2, l. 36 ; Eng. p. 521, l. 31, when Elizer, son of King Pelles, sets out accompanied by a squire.   But in place of the long series of adventures related in our version we have a short account of his proceeding directly to Carlion, where Arthur and his Queen, King Ban, and King Bohors receive him with honour, and tell him of the embassy of Loth and his sons to the princes.   While they are talking, the news comes to Ban and Bohors that King Claudas is ravaging their country.   They at once take their departure, and without stopping go to their own country (" *et* san vont droit au lor terres," f. 182*b*, col. 1).   All this is, of course, a wide variation from the English version.   Then the story turns again to King Loth and his four sons. The King gets Minoras the forester to send messengers to the princes, and then goes his way, meets the princes and secures their promise of help.   After this he returns to Arthur at Camelot, where Elizer is knighted.   The princes come to help Arthur against the Saxons, and succeed in defeating them before the City of Clarence, after which they kneel before Arthur and ask pardon for their rebellion.   He forgives them, and they become his men.   Here the tale ends, f. 184, col. 1.

This short version I incline to regard as a condensation rather than an earlier and less diffuse narrative, though I find it not easy to see why some incidents should be passed over while others are retained.   A possible reason for the abridgment is that the copyist wished to save parchment for the *Lancelot* and the *Quête du Saint-Graal* which follow.

presence here would seem to indicate that this manuscript stands in somewhat closer relations than do the other manuscripts to the family of manuscripts on which our English translation is based. The long passage with regard to the Saint-Graal in this manuscript may have been condensed into a form like that from which the English passage was translated, or possibly the shorter version may be the original; but this seems hardly probable, as the longer version is found in Bib. Nat. MS. fr. 747, which is perhaps the oldest text of the first portion of the romance.[1]

As in the case of so many other manuscripts, the verbal differences alone are sufficient to compel the rejection of this version as the actual working original of the English translation. For instance, in the list of knights (E. p. 212; French, f. 122, cols. 1 and 2) we have such differences as: "And the forthe was Antor"—"et li quars ector ces alvouez"; "the ix⁰ was Gifflet"—"li.ix. li fiz do de carduel." Conclusive also is the variation in the French passage quoted in the English version (p. 485) and what we find here (f. 175, col. 1, l. 6).

" *Et* li heraut comansent a crier, et cil crioz darmes per-mi ces rans. ' or i paurait qui bien lon ferait. or iert veus qui bien lon ferait.'"

3. *Bib. Nat. Nouv.* acq. fr. 4166.

This unique manuscript is of peculiar interest, as it supplies a missing link in the history of the French Arthurian romances. It contains the prose romance of *Joseph of Arimathea*, the romance of *Merlin* up to the coronation of Arthur, and the romance of *Perceval*,[2] which exists only in this prose version. Gaston Paris regards these three romances as prose versions of the three poems of Robert de Borron.[3] This conclusion is reasonably certain as regards the first two, and not improbable

---

[1] *Cf.* G. Paris, Introd. to *Merlin*, p. viii.
[2] *Cf. Romania*, viii. p. 478.
[3] Introd. to *Merlin*, i. p. ix.

as regards the last, but perhaps we have not sufficient evidence
for a final judgment. The *Merlin* does not differ widely from
the ordinary texts, though the verbal differences are often
considerable. The manuscript is beautifully executed, but it
would have excited comparatively little attention, were it not
for the unique *Perceval*, which adds one more continuation
to the *Merlin*.[1]

4. *Huth MS.*, London. [2]

This manuscript, like the one just noticed, contains a unique
continuation of the original romance of *Merlin*. The point of
divergence is the coronation of Arthur. In the opinion of
Gaston Paris this version, "like the ordinary continuation
of the *Merlin*," was made "for the purpose of connecting the
Merlin of Robert de Borron with the *Lancelot* and other compositions."[3] The principal interest that it possesses for us is
that it contains the original of a portion of Malory's *Morte
Darthur*.[4]

5. *Bib. Nat. MS.* fr. 98.

This, perhaps, hardly deserves to rank as a special version.
The entire manuscript contains the *Saint-Graal*, *Merlin*, *Lancelot*,
and along with the *Merlin* the so-called *Prophecies*, singularly
dovetailed into the ordinary text of the long romance.
Variations from the English version are scattered throughout
the text.   On f. 138*b*, col. 2, the longer version,[5] with no
mention of "maister Martyn," is given instead of that found
in the English text, p. 23. The list of knights (f. 173, col. 2,
and f. 173*b*) agrees more closely with the list in the translation

---

[1] The *Perceval* has been published by Hucher in *Le Saint-Graal*, i. pp. 415–505;
see an analysis in Nutt's *Studies on the Legend of the Holy Grail*, pp. 28–32.

[2] Edited by G. Paris and Jacob Ulrich for the *Soc. des. Anc. Textes*, two vols., 8vo.
Paris, 1886.

[3] *Introd.* p. xxvii. Many further details of interest are found pp. xxiii.-L.

[4] See Sommer's ed. *Studies on the Sources*, vol. iii.; London, 1891. *Introd.*
p. 7 *sqq.*

[5] Essentially the same as in Bib. Nat. MS. fr. 95.

on p. 212, than do the lists in many of the other manuscripts. Still, we have such variations as: "Le ix^e le fil le Duc de Carduelz, marech de la roche" (f. 173, col. 2), and "the ix^c was Gifflet" (Eng. p. 212), etc. The French passage quoted on p. 485 of the English translation differs considerably from the same passage in this manuscript, f. 222*b*, col. 1, l. 19, which reads : "Et li herralz commencerent a crieir permi ces rens, or y paira qui bien fera et honour auoir voulra," though of course the difference is almost wholly verbal. Even less difference appears between the French quoted on p. 563 of the English translation and the version of this manuscript (f. 239, col. 1).

In the list of knights (f. 241*b*), MS. 98 presents essentially the same version as the English text (p. 576 *sqq.*). In Bib. Nat. MS. fr. 95, however, a much more contracted version is found (f. 313). Many other passages agree almost word for word,[1] so that were it not for the violent interjection of the *Prophecies* towards the end this manuscript would agree about as closely with our English version as do most of the other manuscripts. The union of the *Prophecies* with the text of the romance is not very skilfully made. The *Prophecies* are merely cut into fragments and pieced in as follows :—The first passage begins on f. 250, col. 1, l. 19, and extends to f. 258, col. 1, l. 27. Then the *Merlin* begins again, and continues to f. 276, col. 1, l. 14. The *Prophecies* then recommence, and extend to the end of the romance, f. 287*b*. The next leaf begins with the *Lancelot.*

Some changes in the *Merlin* were necessarily made, in order to accommodate the *Prophecies.* We find in this version no account of the enchanted tower in which Merlin is confined by his love (Eng. p. 681), nor of Arthur's charge to Gawain

---

[1] *Cf.* f. 263*b*, col. 2, with Eng. p. 639, which tells of the twelve princes sent by the Emperor Luce to Arthur. At the end of the paragraph the English is a little more concise than the French. *Cf.* also the account of Merlin as harper, Eng. p. 615, with f. 258*b*, col. 1.

to go in search of Merlin (Eng. pp. 680–682). This French
version, however, tells us of the dwarf who was dubbed a
knight (Eng. p. 682), and conducts him to the court of King
Arthur. Then follows: "Mais atant se tait or li conte deulx
a parler, et retorne a parleir dez propheciees de merlins"
(f. 276, col. 1). Of Merlin we hear no more, except as he
answers the questions of Antoine. The adapter does not allow
Merlin to enter upon his enchanted sleep, for the obvious reason
that he is needed for the *Prophecies.*[1]

Having thus examined and dismissed the versions that
evidently could not have served as the actual working originals
of the English translation, we have yet to consider the manuscripts which substantially represent the English translation.
To enter into a minute comparison of the variations in the
different French manuscripts would swell our pages to in-
ordinate proportions, and would be of little real gain to the
reader.[2] Until several of the more important manuscripts
have been properly collated and printed, any comparison dealing
largely with details will be more confusing than helpful. I
shall attempt, therefore, in the following pages merely to trace
in a rough sketch the chief lines of divergence, and tentatively
to group the different versions. By a series of approximations

[1] The strange French romance known as the *Prophéties de Merlin* might, as
Gaston Paris remarks (Introd. to *Merlin*, p. xxv. note), be regarded as another
continuation of the original romance of *Merlin*. In these *Prophecies* there is far
more said than done; and the burden of the talk falls upon Merlin and Bishop
Antoine. I have not taken especial account of the Prophecies, but they exist in a
considerable number of MSS. and in printed editions of the fifteenth and sixteenth
centuries. It may be worth while to note that MS. 5229 (old No. 236) (xiv.-xv.
cent.) in the Bibl. de l'Arsenal, catalogued as *Histoire de Merlin*, is nothing but the
Prophecies.

[2] As one minor difference, I note that, except in a few MSS., the paragraphs do not
begin at the same points. Sommer's remark to the contrary (*Morte Darthur*, iii.
p. 7) was based upon study of a small proportion of the MSS.

we may finally select the version which on the whole is most closely represented by the English text, but we must not expect to find complete agreement.

It will add to clearness if we set aside at the outset as many of the remaining manuscripts as are plainly to be excluded. We thus dismiss as mere fragments—Bib. Nat. MS. fr. 2455 (list No. 7); Bib. Nat. MS. fr. 423 (list No. 13); Bib. Nat. Coté dons, No. 1638 (list No. 22). We may also reject the manuscripts that contain nothing more of the romance than the paraphrase in prose of Robert de Borron's poem of *Merlin*. There can be no doubt that the translator used one of the complete versions of what we may call the vulgate *Merlin*; for the English version bears no marks of having been pieced together with the short *Merlin* of one manuscript and the *Book of Arthur* from another manuscript, but presents in the main a closely literal translation of one of the French versions. Furthermore, each of the manuscripts containing the first branch only of *Merlin* (pp. 1–107) differs too widely in several essentials to allow us to accept it as the actual basis of the English translation. The manuscripts which we exclude are the following :—

Bib. Nat. MS. fr. 748 (list No. 3); Bib. de l'Arsn. MS. fr. 2996 (list No. 4); Bib de l'Arsn. MS. fr. 2997 (list No. 5); Bib. Nat. Nouv. acq. fr. 4166 (list No. 16); Bib. Nat. MS. fr. 113 (list No. 27).

After these deductions there still remains a considerable number of manuscripts which call for more extended discussion. In many particulars they all agree most surprisingly with the English version. From all of them may be selected long passages which are almost literally reproduced in the English translation. On the other hand, certain other critical passages differ widely from the English text; and these I have taken as points of departure in my tentative classification.

If we were fortunate enough to have but a single authentic version of the French romance, the task of determining what is due to the translator and what to the original would be sufficiently simple. Since, however, the *Merlin* was one of the most popular romances of the Middle Ages, it has been preserved in so great a number of manuscripts that we are embarrassed by our riches.

Our plan involves taking up the manuscripts in something like chronological order and classifying them. Some repetition is inevitable, but I will avoid it to some extent by cross-references.

1. Bib. Nat. MS. fr. 747 (list No. 2).

The verbal differences between this version and the English translation are enough of themselves to compel us to reject it from the list of possible originals. More important than mere verbal disagreement are some of the differences which I now proceed to note. The French and the English run closely parallel, with here and there a verbal difference, as far as Eng. p. 23. Then follows in the French (f. 82, col. 2, l. 29) a passage of twenty-two lines not represented at all in the translation. This evident interpolation is not found in all the manuscripts (*cf.* MS. 105), and is introduced in order to justify the attempted fusion of the two romances of the *Saint-Graal* and the *Merlin*. At the end of the *Saint-Graal* (f. 77, col. 2, l. 15) we find the words—

"Et retorne a une autre estoire de merlin, q*ue* il conuient aioute*r* a fine force auec lestoire del sai*n*t g*r*aal porce q*ue* branche en est *et* li apartient. Et come*n*ce mesires roberz de bor*r*on cele branche en tel maniere. Ml't fu iriez li annemis q*ua*nt nostre sire ot este en enfer."

In the interpolated passage (f. 82, col. 2, l. 41) the same matter is again referred to—

"Et q*ua*nt li dui liure seront assamble sen i aura .i. biau, et li dui seront une meisme chose, fors tant que ie ne puis pas dire ne retraire ne droiz nest les priuces paroles de iosoph *et* de ihū crist. Einsi dist mes sires roberz de borron qui cest conte retrait," etc.

In this passage, furthermore, no mention is made of the mysterious "maister Martyn" of our English version. He is mentioned in but few French MSS.; and one of the few (B. N. MS. fr. 105) stands in other particulars in closer relations with our English version than do any of the other French texts.

On f. 84*b* begins an interpolation of ninety-two lines relating to the *Saint-Graal*, a passage which differs considerably from our English version (pp. 32, 33).

The most interesting feature of this manuscript is, that it sharply marks off the *Romance of Merlin* (Eng. pp. 1–107) from the *Book of Arthur* which follows. On f. 102, at the end of the *Merlin*, is the passage in which Robert de Borron formally terminates the *Romance of Merlin*. There are nine lines and a half on f. 102*b*; the remainder of the page is blank.[1] The *Book of Arthur* begins at the top of f. 103.

I shall content myself with the mention of a few other differences between this version and the English translation. The list of knights (fr. f. 125, col. 2; Eng. p. 212) differs so widely in the two versions that to exhibit all the variations I should have to copy the whole. For instance, the French has—"li neuiemes li filz do de carduel"; the English, "the ix[e] was Gifflet "; "li onziemes gurnay li bloiz," which hardly represents the English, "the xj. drias de la forrest sauage."

___

[1] Paulin Paris makes much of this formal mark of division, as being designed to indicate the limits of the original *Romance of Merlin*. He is probably justified in his inference, but there is a bare possibility that this *blank* is due to the practice common in the Middle Ages of dividing the work of transcription among several copyists. Another blank of a column and a half (f. 188*b*) occurs without any break whatever in the story. Most of the MSS. take no more account of this transition to the *Book of Arthur* than to begin a new paragraph. In one or two cases even this slight break is omitted.

In the list of kings and princes (Eng. pp. 643, 644) the French
(f. 215, col. 1) differs considerably in the numerals, and
altogether omits Ydier and Aguysans.

It would be easy to furnish additional proofs that this
manuscript did not serve as the basis of our translation. Yet
in several points it is more in harmony with the English
version than, for example, B. N. MS. fr. 24,394, which omits
passages found in the English (pp. 146, 147, 187, 188, etc.),
and also in MSS. 747, 105, etc.

2. *Bib. Nat. MS.* fr. 770 (list No. 8).

This manuscript shows a large number of striking resemblances to B. N. MS. fr. 95, but still has a considerable
individuality. MS. 770 cannot be the original of our translation, but it is interesting in that it mentions " maistre
martins " (f. 127*b*, col. 1, l. 12)—

" Mais q*u*ant il morront p*a*rler il naront talent de moi ocirre. *et* Ie
men irai auec aus, *et* tu ten iras es p*a*rties ou cil so*n*t q*ui* ont le saint
vaissel, et tous iors mais sera volentiers tes liures ois, *et* qui vaurra
sauoir la uie des rois qui e*n* la grant br*e*taigne furent ains que la
crestientez i venist, si regart e*n* lestoire des br*e*tons. ce*st* en vn liure
q*ue* maistre martins de beures tr*a*nlata de lati*n* en romans. Mais ata*n*t
se taist ore li contes de ceste cose *et* retorne a lestoire. Or dit li
contes quil ot vn roi en br*e*taigne qui eut a no*m* coustans."

As in MS. 95, the list of knights shows remarkable agreement with the English (p. 212), but there are some differences.
For instance, in the English the twenty-second knight is
" Placidas ly gays," in the French, " Ierohas " (f. 174*b*, cols. 2
and 3) ; but the English has also " the xxiiij Ierohas lenches,"
the French, " Ierohas de la*n*ches."

The two French passages quoted in the English translation
exhibit verbal differences, not due to the English transcriber.

For the first passage (Eng. 485) we have (f. 249*b*, col. 3, l. 35)—
"*et* li hiraut *comencent* a crier or i p*ar*ra q*ui* bien le fera or ert
veu." Compare also Eng. p. 563, with the French (f. 271,
col. 2, l. 9)—

"*Et* il les fist si fu tcus li contes chou est li *commencemens* des
auentures dou pais. p*ar* quoi li mcrvilleus lyons fu aterre *et* q*ue*
fils de Roi *et* de Roine destruira *et* *conuenra* quil soit li mieudres
ch*evaliers* qui lors sera cl mond*e*."

A conclusive proof that this version did not serve as the
basis of our translation is, that MS. 770, like MS. 95, gives the
contracted version of the list of the princes (f. 274, col. 2,
Eng. p. 576 *sqq.*), a list which is expanded in MS. 98 and
several other MSS. iu the same way as in the English version.

3. *Bib. Nat. MS.* fr. 95 (list No. 9).

This is, perhaps, the most gorgeous of all the manuscripts
of *Merlin*, and from the beauty of the miniatures and the
illuminated letters seems to belong to the latter part of the
thirteenth century, if not to the early part of the fourteenth.
In many passages it stands as close to the English version as
any of the manuscripts, but it contains additions and omissions
enough to compel us to reject it. For instance, it does not
mention "maistre Martins," and presents the following
passage[1] as the equivalent for the English version (p. 23) :—

"Et quant tu aueras ta paine achieuee et tu scras tex come dois
estre en la compaingnic del saint graal. lors sera tes liures aioins au
liuro ioseph. si sera la cose bien esprouuee de ma paine ct de la
toie si en aura diex mcrchi se lui meisme plaist. et cil qui loront

---

[1] This passage may be compared with the one at the end of the *Saint-Graal*
(f. 113*b*, col. 1)—" Chi se taist ore li contes de toutes les lingnies qui de cclidoine
issirent et retorne a une estoire de Merlin, qui conuient a fine force aioster a lestoire
del saint graal, por ce que la branche i est et li apartiens. et comence mesires
Robiers en tel mauiere come uous pores oir sil est qui le uous die."

proieront nostre signor por nos. et quant li doi liure seront ensamble si i aura .i. biau liure. Et li doi seront une meisme cose, fors tant que ne puis pas dire ne retraire les priuees paroles de ih'u c'st et de ioseph." (f. 123, col. 2.)

On the other hand, the list of the forty-three knights (f. 192*a*) shows in the forms of the names and in the order a striking agreement with the English (p. 212). Even the variants are remarkable for the particulars in which they agree. The English has, for example, "The xxix. Agresianx, the nevew of the wise lady of the foreste with-oute returne." The French omits the name, and reads, "Li uintenoefismes fu li fieus a la sage dame de la forest sans retour." As the thirty-second knight the English has "kehedin de belly"; the French, "Kehedins li biaus." Most of the other variations in the two lists are mere differences of spelling.

Without burdening our pages with minor differences, such, for example, as Eng. 563 and Fr. f. 309*b*, col. 1, we find convincing proof that neither this manuscript nor exact copies of it could have been used by the English translator, when we compare the list of the princes who come to Salisbury Plain (Eng. pp. 576–578) with the list in the French (f. 313 *a* and *b*). The two versions agree almost word for word, except that the English adds a ʹline or two of description to each knight. These additions amount to about nineteen lines to the page (p. 576½ – p. 577½), and are found in MS. 98, f. 241*b*, in MS. 105, and others. The evident explanation is, that MS. 95 represents a group of thirteenth-century MSS. afterwards expanded by a copyist who was also an author.

4. *Bib. Nat. MS.* fr. 24,394 (list No. 10).

This manuscript is remarkable for striking points of agreement with the English version, and for equally striking omissions. I have space for but a small portion of the variants.

I give them in the order of their occurrence :—English, p. 15, "x. monthes"; French, f. 112, "ix. mois." Eng. p. 15, "xij. monthes"; Fr. f. 112, "xviij. mois." Eng. p. 61, "thre yere"; Fr. f. 129, col. 2, "plus de ij. ans." Considerable other verbal differences occur between Eng. pp. 60, 61 and Fr. f. 128*b* – f. 129. This MS. agrees essentially with MS. 95 in presenting the longer version (f. 114*b* – f. 115) in place of the one found in the English translation, p. 23. In giving the list of kings who came to Arthur's court the English (p. 108) mentions six, the French but five [1] (f. 141*b*, col. 1).

The French version (f. 149*b*, col. 2) omits a passage extending in the English version from "Now, seith the boke" (p. 146, l. 27) to "Now, seith the boke" (p. 147, l. 30). Two other omitted passages are Eng. p. 187, ll. 8–18 (*cf.* Fr. f. 157*b*, col. 1); Eng. p. 188, ll. 5–11 (*cf.* Fr. f. 157*b*, col. 2). Characteristic variations and omissions appear in the following passages :—

ENG. pp. 176, 177.

"And so com) the renou*n* in to the hoste that the*D* durste not ride that wey with̄oute grete foyson) of peple. And so on) that part the kynge Ydiers kepte hem so streyte that the*D* myḡt haue no socour*e* of no vitaile.

"The tother Citee that the*D* ȝede to stuffe was cleped Wydesans, and thedir ȝede the kynge Ventres of Garlot and ledde with̄ hym knyḡtes that were lefte of the hoste."

FR. f. 155*b*, col. 1.

"Si reuint li reno*n*s en lost si q*ui*l nosere*n*t mie cele part cheualch*er* sans mo*n*t gra*n*t fuison de gent.

"Lautre cite q*ui*l e*n*uoiere*n*t garnir si ot a non huidesant. A cele ala li rois nantres de garlot si e*n* amena auoec lui .M.ij. homes de cels qu*i* furent remes e*n* la bataille."

---

[1] All six are named in MS. 747, f. 111, col. 1; f. 119*b*, cols. 1 and 2; in MS. 105, etc.

A little lower down the page we find—

ENG. p. 177.

"and the wif of kynge Ventres was suster to kynge Arthur on his moder side, Ygerne, that was wif to Vterpendragon, and wif also to Hoel, Duke of Tintagell, that be-gat basyne, the wif of kynge Ventres; and upon this basyne be-gate he his sone, that was so gode a knyght and hardy, as ye shall here her-after, and how he was oon of the C.C.l. knyghtes of the rounde table, and oon of the moste preysed, and his right name was Galashyn."

FR. f. 155*b*, col. 1.

"et la feme al roi nantre fu [f. 155*b*, col. 2] seror le roi artu de par sa *mere* ygerne, q*ui* auoit este fille al duc hoel de tintaioel. Si ot a no*n* blaisine et de li ot li rois nantres son fil, q*ui* puis fu compai*n*s de la table roonde, et fu nomes p*ar* son droit no*n* galescin."

ENG. p. 179.

"kynge loot wente to the Citee of Gale with M̈ⁱⁱⁱ. knyghtes."

FR. f. 156, col. 1.

"li rois loth sen ala a une chite a .M̈.ⁱⁱⁱ. *com*batans."

In the list of knights (Eng. p. 212, Fr. f. 163*b*, cols. 1 and 2) we find—

ENGLISH.

No. 2. "Boors de Gannes."
No. 9. "Gifflet."
No. 18. "blioberis."
No. 21. "Aladan the crespes."
No. 29. "Agresianx, the nevew of the wise lady," etc.

FRENCH.

"Bohors ses fr*e*res."
"gyrfle le fil do de cardoel."
"bliobleris de gannes."
"mcleadant."
"Agreucil, le fil a lasage dame," etc.

The English p. 519 has an unusual reading—

FR. f. 239, col. 2.

"and therfore now telle hym that he shall fynde me ther on seinte Berthelmewes day."

"Or li dites qu*i*l mi i trouera le ior de la no*st*re dame en septembre."

On p. 525 the English agrees with the French—

<table>
<tr><td style="text-align:center">ENGLISH.</td><td style="text-align:center">FR. f. 241, col. 1.</td></tr>
<tr><td>"the kynge Looth of Orcanye sendith hym to wite that he sholde be with hym at Arestuell in Scotlonde on oure lady day in Septembre."</td><td>"que li rois loth dorcanie li mande si comme uos aues oi quil soit encontre lui a arestuel en escoche le ior de la nostre dame en september."</td></tr>
</table>

Wide variations may be pointed out in abundance, as well as almost literal agreement. In the list of princes who come to Salisbury (Eng. pp. 576–578), this Fr. version (f. 254*b*, col. 1 to f. 255, col. 1) supplies all the omissions of MS. 95. The slight variations in the Roman numerals were probably due to haste in copying. Interesting, too, it is to find such agreement as in the following passage, for some of the manuscripts that on the whole agree much more closely with the English version omit the descriptive word *breton*.

<table>
<tr><td style="text-align:center">ENG. p. 615.</td><td style="text-align:center">FR. f. 265, col. 2.</td></tr>
<tr><td>"and he harped a lay of Breteigne ful swetely that wonder was to here."</td><td>"et il harpoit .i. lai breton tant doucement que ce estoit melodie a escouter."[1]</td></tr>
</table>

The unexpected agreement with the English version of such a manuscript as B. N. 24,394, makes difficult a thoroughly satisfactory grouping of the different versions. A long process of collation must precede any such classification.

5. Bib. Nat. MS. fr. 110 (list No. 11).

This version agrees with the English translation in several particulars, more closely than does MS. 24,394; but it makes no mention of "maistre Martins," and has the passage (f. 50, col. 3) omitted from the English, p. 23. The lists of knights

---

[1] MS. 117, f. 141*b*, col. 1, gives the same version as this French text; while Arsn. MS. fr. 3482, B. N. MS. fr. 105, etc., omit the word *breton*.

(Eng. p. 212 ; Fr. f. 82, cols. 1 and 2) agree in the main, though
the French has some words of description not reproduced in the
translation.   Other lists—*e.g.*, Eng. pp. 576–578, Fr. f. 142*b*–
f. 143; Eng. pp. 593, 594, Fr. f. 145*b*; Eng. p. 616, Fr. f. 149,
col. 3—show very close agreement.   The two passages quoted
from the French (Eng. p. 485, Fr. f. 126*b*, col. 1; Eng. p. 563,
Fr. f. 140*b*, col. 1) agree, except for a letter or two, with MS.
24,394, f. 230, col. 1 ; f. 251, col. 2, l. 15.

6. *Bib. Nat. MS.* fr. 749 (list No. 12).

At the beginning of the *Merlin* we find above a row of five
miniatures the rubric : " Chi co[m]ence lestoire de merlin
que mesire robers de borron translata."   This manuscript
mentions (f. 132, col. 2) " mesire martins de roescestre," who
appears in the English version (p. 23) as " maister Martyn."
Nowhere else, except in Arsn. MS. 3482, is he called Martin of
Rochester,[1] though a certain *Martin* is mentioned in a few other
manuscripts.[2]   This passage gives the long version, a part of
which does not appear in the English (f. 132, col. 2)—

" *et* quant li doi liure seront ensamble. si aura .i. bel liure *et* li dui
seront une meisme chose fors tant q*ue* ie ne puis pas dire ne drois nest
les priuces p*a*roles de ih'u crist *et* de ioseph nest cel tans nauoit encore
gaires rois crestiens en engleterre.   Ne de ceuls qui i auoient este ne
me tient a retraire fors tant come a cest conte monte *et* qui valroit[3] oir
conter les rois qui deuant furent, *et* lor vie volroit oir si qui fist *et*
regardast[4] en lestoire de bretaigne que on apelle brutus q*ue* mesire
martins de roescestre tr*a*nslata de latin en romans ou il le troua si le
porroies[5] sauoir vraiement."

---

[1] Paulin Paris remarks (*Romans*, ii. p. 36) : " I know no other mention of this
Martin of Rochester, rival of Pierre de Langtofte and of our Wace."

[2] *Cf.* p. lxviii.

[3] vouroit : P. Paris.   [4] regarde : P. P.   [5] porra : P. P.

Other minor variations forbid us to suppose that the English translator used this version, or a copy of it, though the resemblances are at times surprisingly close. In the list of knights (Eng. p. 212; Fr. f. 195, col. 1) the names are meant to be alike, except that in the English we have "the xlj. bleoris the sone of kynge Boors," and in the French, "li xli.isme fu banins li filleus au roi bohort de gausnes."

In the passages quoted from the French, the first (Eng. p. 485) differs in but one essential word—*bien* for *checun*—

FR. f. 275, col. 2, l. 32.—"*et* hiraut comencent a crier | chi est li honors darmes or i parra qui b*i*en le fera | "

The second passage (Eng. p. 563) shows more variation—

FR. f. 300, col. 2, l. 22.—"*et* il les fist si fu i teus li contes. ce sont ichi les aue*n*tures dou pais qui par le me*r*uilleus lion fu a te*r*re, *et* qui fu fieus de roi *et* de roine destruira *et* co*n*uen*r*a quil soit castes *et* li mieudres chr's q*ui* soit aillors el monde."

In the list of princes (Eng. pp. 576–578), the French (f. 305) gives the expanded version, in the main the same as in the English version, though with some variations in the numerals and the descriptive details. For example, Eng. p. 576, "kynge Belynans of south wales"; Fr. (col. 2), "rois belinans de norgales." I could multiply examples, but those already given must suffice. In classing this version we must place it with the small group of manuscripts that most closely represent the English, though the coincidence is not so great as in MS. 105. Perhaps it stands in closest relation to Arsn. MS. fr. 3482. The manuscript breaks off at f. 330*b* with the words translated in the English by "and whan the [kynge saugh this]," p. 667, l. 27.

7. *Bib. Nat. MS.* fr. 19,162 (list No. 14).

This manuscript may be classed with MS. 24,394. For Eng. p. 23 this MS. (f. 152*b*)[1] gives the ordinary version, differing from the English, with no mention of "maistre Martins." The list of kings (f. 187, col. 1) is the same as in MS. 24,394 (*cf.* Eng. p. 108). The equivalent of line fifth on p. 143 of the English is omitted from MS. 19,162, f. 197, col. 2. The passage corresponding to Eng. p. 145, l. 15 to Eng. p. 150, l. 29 is lost from the French manuscript between f. 197 and f. 198, so that we cannot tell whether the passage on pp. 146, 147 is omitted as in MS. 24,394. But this version, like MS. 24,394, omits a line corresponding to a line in the Eng. p. 176, as well as the words "of Gale" (Eng. p. 179). So, too, the passages, Eng. p. 187, ll. 8–18, Fr. f. 208, col. 1 ; Eng. p. 188, ll. 5–11, Fr. f. 208, col. 2. In the list of knights (Eng. p. 212, Fr. f. 216, col. 2) the version is essentially that of MS. 24,394. On f. 313*b*, col. 1, the usual version "de la *nostre* dame septembre" appears in place of "Berthelmewes day" of the Eng. p. 519. For the Eng. pp. 576–578 this manuscript gives the usual expanded version.

8. *Brit. Mus. MS.* Add. 10,292[2] (list No. 20).

This version may be classed with MS. 24,394, as is evident from the regular variations that appear in the two versions.

ENGLISH.	FRENCH.
p. 15. " x. monthes."	f. 79, col. 1. " ix. mois."
" xij. monthes."	" xviij. mois."

---

[1] Most of the leaves are not numbered.
[2] This is the MS. selected by Sommer for his edition of the romance of *Merlin*.

For Eng. pp. 22, 23 the French, f. 80*b*, col. 3 to f. 81, col. 1, gives the ordinary expanded version, with no mention of "maistre Martins."

The list of kings, with the number of attendant knights (Eng. p. 108), agrees exactly, except that the French, f. 101*b*, col. 1, omits the name of Ydiers. On f. 108, col. 2, the French has nothing corresponding to about a page of the English (pp. 146, 147). On f. 113, col. 1, the French omits a line and a half found in the English, p. 176 (bottom), as well as in MS. 105. On f. 113, col. 2, the French version of Eng. p. 177 is confused, and not so exact as MS. 105. On f. 114*b*, col. 2, the French omits the passage found in the Eng. p. 187, ll. 8–18. From f. 114*b*, col. 2 is omitted the equivalent of Eng. p. 188, ll. 5–11. The list of knights,[1] f. 120, cols. 1 and 2, agrees closely with the English, p. 212, but with such variations as—No. 9, "Gifflet" in the English for "Giffles le fil do de carduel"; No. 29, "the nevew" for "le fil." The passage quoted from MS. 10,292 on pp. 700, 701 of the *Merlin* of the E.E.T.S., agrees almost word for word with B. N. MSS. fr. 96 and 24,394.

9. *Bib. Nat. MS.* f. 96 (list No. 24).

This manuscript closely agrees at most points with B. N. MS. 24,394. I give below a few of the data which compel us to reject this version as the original of our translation—

ENGLISH.		FRENCH.	
p. 15.	"x. monthes."	f. 63, col. 2.	"ix. mois."
	"xii. monthes."		"xviii. mois."
p. 61.	"thre yere."	f. 74, col. 1.	"plus de .ii. ans."

---

[1] For the entire list see Malory's *Morte Darthur* (ed. Sommer), vol. iii. pp. 55, 56, *Studies on the Sources.* Sommer prints also the lists from the Auchinlech MS. of the English verse *Merlin*, from Harl. MS. 6340, and from the English prose version.

For the English of p. 23 the French (f. 65*b*, col. 1) gives the ordinary expanded version, with no mention of "maistre Martins." On f. 82, col. 2, Ydiers is omitted from the list of kings (Eng. p. 108). The French also omits (f. 87*b*, col. 2) the passage corresponding to Eng. p. 146, l. 27 to p. 147, l. 30. From f. 155*b*, col. 1, the French omits a line corresponding to the English, p. 176 (bottom). At this point MS. 96 and MS. 24,394 agree word for word. The English, p. 177, differs widely from the French, f. 91*b*, col. 1 (*cf.* MS. 24,394). From f. 91*b*, col. 2, the same omission occurs as in MS. 24,394 (*cf.* Eng. p. 179). The list of knights, f. 96*b*, is essentially that of MS. 24,394, and agrees closely with the English, p. 212. Wide differences between the English, pp. 438, 439, and the French, f. 134, are found in the numerals, a few of which I select—

<table>
<tr><td align="center">ENGLISH.</td><td align="center">FRENCH.</td></tr>
<tr><td align="center">" xij. kynges."</td><td align="center">x.</td></tr>
<tr><td align="center">" xij. princes."</td><td align="center">" x. roys et d'un duc."</td></tr>
<tr><td align="center">" xij. kynges."</td><td align="center">x.</td></tr>
</table>

Numerous points of difference might be noted, but we need not multiply words. There can be no doubt that this MS. presents essentially the same version as Brit. Mus. MS. Add. 10,292 and B. N. MS. 24,394. On comparing MS. 96, f. 176*b*, col. 2, l. 8, to f. 177, col. 1, with MS. 10,292, f. 216, col. 3, I found the two agreeing almost word for word, except that MS. 96 has later forms for almost all the words.

10. *Bib. Nat. MS.* fr. 117 (list No. 25).

This cannot be taken as the exact original of the English version, though many passages agree almost word for word. For the English of p. 23, MS. 117, f. 55*b*, col. 1, gives the ordinary expanded version, and does not refer to "maistre Martins." In the list of kings (Eng. p. 108; Fr. f. 73, col. 1) the French mentions "Constant qui estoi[t] roi descosse," while the English has "Aguysas." The French omits "Ydiers." The list of knights (Eng. p. 212; Fr. f. 86b, col. 2) differs very widely. The amour of Guyomar and Morgain (Eng. p. 508) is much abridged in this MS. (f. 126b, col. 2). The bits of French on p. 485 and p. 563 of the English version agree closely with the corresponding passages in this MS. (f. 123b, col. 2; f. 134, col. 2). This MS. has the expanded version (f. 136, col. 2 to 136b, col. 1) of the list of princes (Eng. pp. 576–578), and, except in a few of the numerals and other minor details, agrees closely at this point with the English. On p. 620 of the English we have: "Whan the archebisshop hadde redde this letter"; while the French has: "Quant larchevesque de brise ot les lettres leues" (f. 142, col. 2).[1] The name again occurs in the French a little later (f. 145, col. 2 : *cf.* Eng. p. 640). Our English version does not once mention the archbishop by name, though his name appears in many of the French MSS. as well as in Geoffrey of Monmouth. On the other hand, MS. 117 omits much; for example, nearly the whole of the equivalent of Eng. p. 616 (Fr. f. 141, col. 2), including all of the list given in the English and found even in MS. 24,394.

11. *Arsenal MS.* No. 3482 (list 21).

In spite of the very defective state of this manuscript, it has for us more value than some of those better preserved. It is not the exact original of our translation, but it agrees so closely in a great number of passages that I have merely collated with other manuscripts the transcripts I had made from this version

---

[1] So, too, in MS. 24,394, f. 266b, col. 2.

before examining B. N. MS. 105. In a number of passages, however, I must confess that this version is widely at variance with the English. The test passage of the English, p. 23, appears in this MS. (p. 14, col. 3) in part in the usual expanded form, but with the addition of the rare version found in the English translation, suggesting that anyone who is interested in the history of the Britons may study it—

"en lystoire de bretaigne *que* len appele bretus, que mesires martins de rocestre translata de latin en francois, ou la trouua si la porrez sauoir uraiement. En cel temps en i auoit .i. qui estoit constan*s* apeles," etc.

The numerals afford a peculiarly delicate test of agreement; for the Roman notation used in the manuscripts is far more liable to errors of transcription than the Arabic. The variations in the numerals of this MS. and of the English translation are great enough, but not so striking as in some other MSS. For instance (Fr. p. 62, col. 3), the names of the six kings who came to Arthur's court after his coronation are here given as in the English (p. 108), with the exact number of knights accompanying each king. Even Ydiers is mentioned, though omitted from many of the MSS. I have prepared long lists of the numerals in the French and the English, but omit them for lack of space.[1] In many cases the difference is quite as striking as the agreement, though this manuscript shows less variation than most of the others.

When we turn to the passages that are found in the English, although omitted from several of the French MSS., we learn to

---

[1] Differences in the numerals may be found by comparing Eng. p. 15, Fr. p. 9; Eng. p. 61, "thre yere," with Fr. p. 41, col. 1, "pl*us* de .ii. ans"; Eng. p. 145, Fr. p. 81, col. 2; Eng. p. 146, Fr. pp. 81, 82; Eng. p. 184, "xiiij. dayes," with Fr. p. 101, col. 1, "entre ce et quin*s*aine": Eng. p. 187, Fr. p. 102; Eng. p. 188, Fr. p. 103; Eng. p. 576, Fr. p. 271; Eng. p. 643, Fr. p. 306, etc.

appreciate more highly the agreement that we here find. Of
the following passages all are omitted from MS. 24,394, MS. 98,
etc., yet are found both in the English and in MS. 3482.

<table>
<tr><td align="center">ENGLISH.</td><td align="center">FRENCH.</td></tr>
<tr><td>p. 146, l. 27 to p. 147, l. 30.</td><td>p. 82, cols. 2 and 3 to p. 83, col. 1,
ll. 1–5.</td></tr>
<tr><td>p. 176, last line.</td><td>p. 97, col. 1.</td></tr>
<tr><td>p. 179, "to the Citee of Gale
with M^l iij knyghtes."</td><td>p. 98, col. 2, "a la cite de gales
a tout M^iiii combatans." The
words "de gales" are fre-
quently omitted from the
MSS.</td></tr>
<tr><td>p. 187, ll. 8–18.</td><td>p. 102, cols. 2 and 3.</td></tr>
<tr><td>p. 188, ll. 5–11.</td><td>p. 103, col. 1.</td></tr>
</table>

On the other hand, the English account (pp. 252–257) of
King Clarion of Northumberland, and his battles with the
Saxons, is more extended than the account in the French
(p. 135). The name of the "arceuesques del brice" is here
given (Fr. p. 295, col. 2; Fr. p. 304, col. 3) as in MS. 117, etc.,
though omitted from the English (p. 620, p. 640). A remarkable reading occurs on p. 243, col. 2, "et ie uous di certainement
que il mi trouuerra le ior de la saint bertelemi." The English
reads (p. 519), "and therfore now telle hym that he shall
fynde me ther on seinte Berthelmewes day." The mention
of St. Bartholomew's Day is rare, most of the manuscripts
preferring the reading, "our lady day in September."

Enough evidence has been adduced to show that while this
version can hardly be taken as the exact original of the English
translation, the similarity is very great. I will add at this
point a few passages, which are, however, no more remarkable
for their agreement than hundreds of others to be found in this
manuscript.

(*a*) FR. p. 112, col. 2.

" car il porte el somet[1] dune lance .i. dragon petit, ne guieres grant, qui auoit la queue longue de toise et demie et toute tortice; et auoit la gueule baee[2] si grant quil uous fust auis que la langue qui dedens estoit se branlast[3] tousiours, et li sailloient estan-celes et brandons de feu parmi[4] la gueule en lair."

ENG. p. 206, ll. 16–19.

" for he bar a dragon that was not right grete, and the taile was a fadome and an half of lengthe tortue; and he hadde a wide throte that the tounge semed braulinge euer, and it semed sparkles of fier that sprongen vp in-to the heire out of his throte."

(*b*) FR. p. 114, col. 3.

" et li dragons que il portoit rendoit parmi la gueule si grant brandon de feu quil sourmontoit amont en lair, que cil qui estoient sus les murs de la cite enueoient la clarte de demie liue loing *et* de plus."

ENG. p. 210, ll. 8–10.

" and the dragon that Merlin bar caste oute gret flames of fierc, that it sparkled vp in the ayre, that thei vpon the walles of the town saugh the clernesse of the light half a myle longe."

(*c*) FR. p. 199, col. 1.

" Ilec peust len ucoir maint riche garnement *et* mainte enseigne dor et de soie qui au uent ueuteloit,[5] et li airs estoit dous et soues, et li pais biaus et delitables, car moult i auoit fores et praeries ou cil oiseillon[6] chantoient par mains[7] langages,"[8] etc.

ENG. p. 384, ll. 29–33.

" Ther myght oon haue seyn many a riche garnement and many a fressh baner of riche colour waue in the wynde, and the seson was myri and softe, and the contre feire and delitable, ffor many feire medowes and forestes ther woren, in whiche these briddes singen with lusty notes and cler," etc.

Note.—I have collated the two passages (*a*) and (*b*) with B. N. MS. fr. 105. Some slight variations of the first passage are found. The second reappears almost literally. (*c*) Cf. B. N. MS. fr. 105, f. 251*b*, col. 3.

(*a*) f. 191*b*, col. 3.

[1] " Quar . . . portoit ou sommet de la.

[2] basse bee . . . estoit ains *que* la langue.

[3] se branlast touz.

[4] parmi la gueule en haut en lair."

[5] venteloient.   [6] oiselet.

(*b*) f. 193, col. 2.

" et li dragons que il portoit rendoit parmi la gueule si grant brandon de feu qui seurmontoit amont en lair, que cil qui estoient sus les murs de la cite en veoient la clarte de demie lieue loing et de plus."

[7] maint.   [8] langaies.

(*d*) Fr. p. 287, col. 3. Eng. p. 604, ll. 26 to p. 605, l. 8.

" Ne el chastel nauoit que une seule entree, et estoit si estroite que dui cheualier a cheual ni alassent mie li uns en coste lautre se aenuis non. Par desus cel mares[1] auoit une chauciee de leus en leus ainsint comme del lonc dune lance de pierre et de sablon faite. et de chaus *et* ert espesse et bien faite li remanans des fautes estoit de fust et de planches, pour ce que se besoins uenist au chastel que len ostast les planches si que nus ne peust outre passer. *et* au chief deca[2] la chauciee auoit une eue courant auques rade. mais ele ne portoit pas nauie. Deuant le pie de cele chauciee auoit .i. pin .i. petit ensus de leue dedens .i. praelet qui tenoit bien lespasse dun quartier de terre ou de plus. ou lerbe estoit haute et bele. et li pins estoit [p. 288] biaus et grans et si bien ramus que il peust bien auoir en lombre de lui .c. cheualiers et estoit si gentement duis et si iointement que lune branche ne passoit lautre de hautesce. A une branche de cel pin qui tant estoit biaus et gens comme li contes le deuise pendoit .i. cors diuuire bende dor a une chaenne dargent, que cil sonnoient qui el chastel uoloient herbegier ou qui tres-passoient par illec pour demander iouste. A ces .ii. choses seruoit le cor."

" In to this castell was but oon entree, and that was so streite that two horse myght not ther-on mete, oon beside a-nother; and a-bove this marasse was a chauchie fro place to place of the breede of a spere lengthe, made of chalke and sande stronge and thikke and wele made, and this cauchie was of lengthe a stones caste, and the remenaunt was made of plankes and of tymbir, so that noon ne myght passe ouer yef the plankes hadde be take a-wey; and at the ende of the cauchie was a grete water, but ther-to com no shippes; but it was right feire and plesaunt, and good fisshinge; be-fore the foot of this cauchie was a pyne tre a litill fro the water in a medowe of the space of an acre [p. 605] londe or more, where-ynne the grasse was feire and high, and the pyne tre was right feire and full of bowes, so that oon branche passed not a-nother of height, and vpon a braunche of this pyne was hanged by a cheyne of siluer, an horne of yvorie as white as snowe, ffor that thei sholde it sowne that com for to be herberowed in the castell or elles who that passed forth by that wolde aske Iustinge. Of these two thinges served the horne that ther was hanged."

[1] chastel ! (B. N. MS. fr. 105, f. 318*b*, col. 1).
[2] de la.

(e) FR. p. 293, col. 3 ; p. 294,
col. 1.

ENG. p. 614, l. 35 ; p. 615, l. 24.

"Tandis com il [1] estoient en tel
feste *et* en tel deduit [2] *et* en tel
ioie si comme keus aportoit le
premier mes deua*n*t le roi artus
et deuant la ro [p. 294] guenieure
entra leens la plus bele forme
do*m*me qui onques mais fust [3] ueue
en nule terre de crestiens [4] en une
cote de samit uermeille ceins dun
bandre de soie a membres dor a
pierres precieuses qui getoient si
grant clarte [5] que to*us* li palles
en flamboia. [6]   *et* [7] ot uns cheueus [8]
sores une corone dor en son chief
comme rois et ot [9] une harpe a son
col qui toute estoit dargent et les
cordes dor. et il estoit si biaus de
cors et de uis et de membres que
onques nule si bele riens ne fu
ueue. mais itant li empira son
uis [10] que il ne ueoit goute. non
pourquant les iex auoit biaus et
clers en la teste. et auoit a sa
ceinture loie .i. petit [11] chienet a
une chaenne dargent qui li estoit
atachie a .i. coler de soie a
membres dor et le mena cil chiens
droitement deuant le roy artus et
il harpoit [12] .i. lay [13] si doucement
que 'ce estoit droite melodie a
escout*er* et el refret [14] de son lay
saluoit le roi artus et sa co*m*paignie.
si lesgarda li rois artus et la roine
guenieure *et* tuit et toutes a
merueilles. et keus li seneschaus
qui le p*re*mier mes aportoit
sentarda grant piece dasseoir le
deuaut le roy tant estoit ententis

"And as thei were in this ioye,
and in this feste, and kay the
stiward that brought the firste
mese be-fore the [p. 615] kynge,
ther com in the feirest forme of
man that euer hadde thei seyn
be-fore, and he was clothed in
samyte, and girte with a bawdrike
of silke harnysshed with golde
and preciouse stones, that all the
paleys flamed of the light, and
the heir of his hede was yelowe
and crispe with a crowne of golde
ther-on as he hadde ben a kynge,
and his hosen of fin scarlet, and
his shone of white cordewan orfraied, and bokeled with fin golde ;
and hadde an harpe abowte his
nekke of siluer richely wrought,
and the stringes were of fin golde
wire, and the harpe was sette
with preciouse stones ; and the
man that it bar was so feire of
body and of visage that neuer hadde
thei sein noon so feire a creature ;
but this a-peired moche his bewte
and his visage for that he was
blinde, and yet were the iyen in
his heed feire and clier ; and he
hadde a litill cheyne of siluer
tacched to his arme, and to that
cheyne a litill spayne was bounde
as white as snowe, and a litill
coler a-boute his nekke of silke
harneysed with golde ; and this
spaynell ledde hym strieght before the kynge Arthur, and he
harped a lay of Breteigne full

a celui regarder. si se test atant li contes ici endroit a parler deuls et retorne au roy rion des illes,"

swetely that wonder was to here, and the refraite of his laye salewed the kynge Arthur, and the Quene Gonnore, and alle the other after; and kay the stiward that brought the first cours taried a-while in the settinge down to be-holde the harper ententifly. But now we moste cesse of hem a-while, and speke of the kynge Rion."

I add a collation of the more important variations of B. N. MS. fr. 98, f. 258*b*, col. 1 (A); and B. N. MS. fr. 105, f. 321*b*, col. 2 (B)—

[1] *comme* ilz (A); [2] desduit einsi *comme* keux li seneschault (A); et en tel bandoun (B); [3] fuit (A) (B); [4] cristiens empiire (A); [5] et si grant resplendissement (B); [6] et enenlumina (B); [7] cil iouencel (A); [8] ung crespe cheueux (A); [9] si auoit pendue; [10] et sa byaulte (A); [11] petit (*omitted*, B); [12] et puez prist a harper (A); [13] .i. lai breton tant doucement *que* ce estoit melodie a escouter (B. N. MS. fr. 24,394, f. 265, col. 2); [14] et en la fin de son refrain (A).

12. *Bib. Nat. MS.* fr. 105 (list No. 18).

This manuscript is, for our purpose, more important than any of the others, for it presents the version most nearly resembling the version of the English text. An almost literal copy of this version is found in Bib. Nat. MS. fr. 9123 (list No. 19). The two manuscripts agree in having rubrics as headings for the chapters, a feature not found in many of the MSS. of *Merlin*, and, indeed, lacking in the English MS. of *Merlin*. The passages taken especially as test passages, where the English contains a considerable amount of matter lacking in a number of the French texts, are all found in MS. 9123, as well as in MS. 105. I give a few references. MS. 9123 has the contracted

version for Eng. p. 23, and mentions as the author of the
history of the Britons a certain "Martins de Bieure." The
essential identity with the English version may be seen by
comparing Eng. pp. 146, 147 with Fr. f. 143; Eng. p. 176,
Fr. f. 152, col. 3; Eng. p. 177, Fr. f. 152, col. 3; Eng. p. 179,
Fr. f. 153, col. 1; Eng. p. 187, ll. 8–18, Fr. f. 155; Eng. p.
188, ll. 5–11, Fr. f. 155b, col. 2; Eng. p. 212, Fr. f. 162b, col. 3
to f. 163, col. 1.   Same version as in MS. 105: Eng. p. 229,
Fr. f. 167b, col. 3 to f. 168, col. 1; Eng. p. 485, Fr. f. 244b,
col. 1; Eng. p. 509, Fr. f. 251b, col. 2; Eng. p. 563, Fr. f. 266,
col. 3; Eng. p. 576, Fr. f. 269b to f. 270; Eng. p. 616, Fr. f.
280, col. 2. The closing pages, except for a letter here and
there, are exactly as in MS. 105.

We turn now to MS. 105. This manuscript betrays innu-
merable evidences of haste in copying,[1] but in its main features
it approaches most nearly to the original from which the
English translation was made.

The English translation of the test passage (pp. 22, 23) is
based on a version slightly differing from this one, but the
agreement is more striking than appears in any of the other
French versions.

<table>
<tr><td>Fr. f. 133b, col. 1.</td><td>Eng. p. 22, l. 35.</td></tr>
</table>

"Blaises quist ce que mestier
li fu, et quant il ot tout quis et
assamble si li commenca a conter
les amours de ihesu crist et de
joseph darimachie, si comme eles
auoient este et de pierre et de

"Blase sought all that hym
mystered to write with, and when
he was all redy, Merlyn be-gan to
telle the loynge of Ihesu [p. 23]
Criste and of Iosep Abaramathie,
like as thei hadden ben of

---

[1] Especially noticeable is the omission of the substantive verb and of descriptive
words. Compare, for instance, Eng. p. 508: "Whan Guyomar entred in to the
chambre ther as was Morgain the ffee, he hir salued full swetly"; Fr. f. 289b,
col. 2: "Quant guyomar entra en la chambre ou morgain si li salua moult
doucement."

pol, et des autres compaignons si comme il sestoient departi, et le fenissement de joseph et de tous les autres. puis li conta comment dyables apres toutes ces choses furent auenues prirent *con*seil de ce quil auoient perdu les pouoir quil souloient auoir sus les ho*m*mes et sus les femmes, et coument li prophete leur auoi*n*t mal fait, et comment il prirent conseil que il feroient *vn* homme qui auroit leur sens et leur memoire dengignier les gens. et tu as oi par ma mere, et par autrui la paine que il y mirent a moi faire. mais par leur folie moult il perdu.

Elayn) and of Pierow, and of othir felowes like as they weren) departed, and the fynyshment of Ioseph and of alle other. And after he tolde hym that whan) alle thise thynges were don), how the deu-elles toke theire counseile of that they hadde loste their power that they were wonte to haue over man *and* woman), and how the *p*rophetes hadden) hyndred here purpos, and how they were acorded to purchase a man, that sholde haue their witte and mynde to disceyve the peple. ‘And thou hast herde be my moder, and also be other, the trauayle that they hadden) to begete me ; but throughֿ theire foly, they alle loste their trauayle.’

CHAPTER II.

“ Ensi deuisa merlins ceste oeuure, et la fist fere a blaise. Et comment sen esmerucilla blaises de ce que merlins li disoit. *et* toutes uoies ses paroles bo*n*nes il entendi moult uole*n*tiers. Et endentres quil [f. 133*b*, col. 2] tendoient a ceste chose fere uint merlins a blaise si li dist, Il te conuient a souffrir de ceste chose *et* ie la souffrerai encore grigneur. blaises demanda comment ? Merlins li dit. ie serai enuoiez querre deuers occident. et cil qui me uenront querre aro*n*t enconuent a leur seigneur que il locirront. Mais q*ua*nt il morront parler il naro*n*t talent

“ Thus devised Merlyn this boke, and made Blase to write it, which hadde ther-of so grete me*r*veile that he wolde not telle it to no *p*ersone, and alwey hym thought that his tales weren gode, and therfore he herkened hem gladly. In the menetyme that they entended a-boute this mater, come Merlyn to Blase, and seyde : ‘Thow moste haue grete traueyle a-boute the makynge, and so shal͘l I haue moche more.’ And Blase axed, ‘How ?’ Merlyn) seyde : ‘I shal͘l be sente after to seche oute of the weste, and they that shul͘l come to seche me haue graunted their lorde that they

MS. 105, f. 133*b*, col. 2.

"de moi occirre et ic men irai auec eulz et tu ten iras es parties ou cil sont qui ont le saint uessel. et touz iours mais sera volentiers tes liures oiz. et qui uoudra sauoir la vie des roys qui en la *grant* bretaigne furent ains q*ue* la crestientez venist si *regarde* en lystoire des roys breto*n*s. cest uns liures que martins de bieure tranlata de latin en roumans. Mais ore se taist li contes de ceste chose et retorne a la uraie hystoire"

shull me sle, but wha*n* thei come and here me speke they shull haue no will me to sle. And I shall go with hem; and thow shalt go in to that p*a*rtyes, where they be that haue the holy vessell. And euer hereafter shall thy boke gladly be herde, and he that will knowe the lyf of kynges whiche were in the grete Bretayne be-fore that cristendo*m* come, be-holde the story of Bretons. That is a boke that maister Marty*n* traunslated oute of laty*n*, but heire rested this matere. And turneth to the storye of Loth, a cryste*n* kynge in Bretayne [p. 24] whos name was Constance. This Constance regned a grete tyme, and hadde thre sones, the first hight Moyne, and the tother Pendrago*n*, and the thirde Vter.'"

There are, of course, variations. If we compare Eng. pp. 32, 33 with the French f. 137, col. 3 to 137*b*, col. 2, we find that the manuscript has an interpolation of 92 lines relating to the *Saint-Graal*, not exactly reproduced in the English. On the other hand, the omissions of MS. 24,394, and others, are here supplied. Compare, *e.g.*, Eng. pp. 146, 147 with f. 173*b*, col. 2 to f. 174, col. 2 [1]; Eng. p. 176, Fr. f. 182*b*, cols. 2 and 3 ; Eng. p. 177, Fr. f. 182*b*, col. 2. The passage relating to the

---

[1] This passage (Eng. pp. 146, 147), remarks Sommer (*Le Morte Darthur*, vol. iii. p. 44, note), is not found in the French originals. His mistake was due to his examining an insufficient number of MSS., for, as I have already shown, it is found in several.

son of king Ventres is here given exactly, though strangely
mixed in some of the versions. Eng. p. 179 reads :

"That than) the kynge loot wente to the Citee of Gale with M̅iij
knyghtes and fightynge men)";

Fr. f. 183*b*, col. 1 :

"que li roys loth sen ala a la cyte de gales a tout M̅iij combatans."

Many MSS. omit the words " de gales."   Eng. p. 187, ll. 8–18
is found in Fr. f. 186, and Eng. p. 188, ll. 5–11, in Fr. f. 186,
col. 3.

The passage Eng. p. 229, l. 13 *sqq.*, differs somewhat from
the French f. 199, col. 3, which here is closely like MS. 24,394.
But MS. 105 has the words omitted from many versions—

"la plus sage dame de la bloie bretaigne,"

and thus parallels the English :

" the wisest lady of alle the bloy breteyne."

A slight difference appears also on comparing Eng. p. 509
with Fr. f. 289*b*, col. 3. The two French passages quoted in the
English text have not the precise form that they bear in MS.
105.   Compare the version Eng. p. 485 with Fr. f. 282, col. 2 :

"*Et* li heraut *c*omencierent a crier. ici est loneur des armes. or i
para qui bien le fera ";

Eng. p. 563 with Fr. f. 306, col. 1 :

"Cest yci li commencemens des auentures du pays par quoi li
*m*erueilleus lyons fu aterre, et que fils de roy *et* de royne destruira et
couuendra que il soit chastes et li mieudres cheualiers qui lors sera el
monde."

This version mentions the " archeuesq*u*es del brice " (f. 323*b*,
col. 2), while the English has merely "the archebisshop"
(p. 620, p. 640, etc.).

In a manuscript so carelessly copied we must not look for exact agreement with the English version; but for that very reason we must attach considerable importance to the agreement we do find.   Nearly all the manuscripts are at variance with the English p. 15.   Here the numerals are the same:

ENGLISH.	FRENCH.
p. 15. "x. monthes."	f. 130*b*, col. 3. "x. mois."
"ij. yere."	"xij. mois."
"xij. monthes."	"ij. ans."

The names and the numerals, Eng. p. 108, exactly agree with those in the French, though at this point most MSS. vary widely in the numerals, and omit the name of Ydiers.   Less exact agreement appears Eng. pp. 145, 146; Fr. f. 173, col. 2 to f. 173*b*, col. 1.   In the list of knights, Eng. p. 212; Fr. f. 193*b*, col. 3 to f. 194, col. 1, there are such differences as—

ENGLISH.	FRENCH.
No. 4, Antor.	Artus qui le nourri.
No. 9, Gifflet.	li filz au duc de cardueil.
No. 19, Canide.	Canot de lisse.
No. 30, Chalis.	Dyales lorfenin.

Other lists showing considerable variation appear, Eng. pp. 576–578, Fr. f. 309*b*, col. 2; Eng. p. 616, Fr. f. 322.   The latter is a characteristic specimen.   I omit all but the most essential details.

ENGLISH.	FRENCH.
Palerens xv.	fariens dirlande xv.
Tasurs xij.	sapharins xij.
Brinans xiiij.	ramedons xiij.
Argans xj.	arganz xiij.
Taurus xj.	thaurus xj.
Kahadins x.	kaamin x.

After this comparison we need scarcely devote more space to illustrative passages.   There is, on the whole, none of the manuscripts of *Merlin* showing more general agreement with the English version than does MS. 105. Yet the verbal differences are so great as to compel us to reject even this version from being regarded as the one actually followed by the English translator. Nevertheless, very large portions of this missing French version were literally transcribed by the writer of MS. 105, as may be seen by a glance at passages where the English translator copied the French words without translating them at all.

ENGLISH.	FRENCH, MS. 105.
p. 2, l. 14, and when we hadde assaied hym.	f. 126*b*, col. 2, omitted. (In Huth *Merlin*, p. 2, "et quant nous l'eusmes essaiié.")
p. 3, l. 19, This riche man had grete plente of bestes and of other richesse.	f. 127, col. 1, Cil riches homs auoit moult grant plente de bestes et dautres richeces.
p. 4, l. 5, and seide a worde of grete ire.	f. 127, col. 2, et dist vne fole parole que sa grant ire li fist dire.
p. 7, l. 21, Ye shall abandon yow to alle men.	f. 128, col. 2, vous *uous* haban-donnerez aus ho*m*mes.
p. 8, l. 32, full humble to god.	f. 128*b*, col. 1–col. 2, moult humilians enuers dieu.
p. 10, l. 26, confessed and repen-tant.	f. 129, col. 2, confes et repentanz.
p. 27, l. 33, be force of clergie.	f. 135*b*, col. 1, par force de clergie.
p. 34, l. 7, grete doel.	f. 138, col. 2, grant duel.
p. 40, l. 1, Thus delyuered Mer-lyn the Clerkes.	f. 140, col. 3, Einsi se deliura merlins des clers.
p. 40, l. 3, the significaunce of the two dragouns.	f. 140, col. 3, la senefiance des .ij. dragons.
p. 59, l. 29, thus be these two tables convenable.	f. 148*b*, col. 2, ai*n*si sont ces .ij. tables conuenables.
p. 147, Merlin maunded that all the harneise and armoure sholde be trussed in males.	f. 149*b*, col. 2, si *commanda* M. q*ue* tos li ha*r*nois fust trousses e*n* males.

Of like sort are many of the instances of tautology in the English text, though in some instances the fault appears to belong to the translator :—

<table>
<tr><td>ENGLISH.</td><td>FRENCH.</td></tr>
<tr><td>p. 5, l. 1, Fvll wrothe and angry was the Deucll.</td><td>f. 127, col. 1, Moult fu li anne-mis iries.</td></tr>
<tr><td>p. 5, l. 28, And so he taught and enformed hem here creaunce and feith.</td><td>f. 127b, col. 2, Moult les aprist bien li preudons et enseigna se eles le uousissent croire.</td></tr>
<tr><td>p. 7, l. 33, full hevy and pensif, makynge grete doell and sorow.</td><td>f. 128, col. 3, Molt fu irie et moult fist grant duel.</td></tr>
<tr><td>p. 8, l. 19, kepe the fro fallynge in to grete ire or wrath.</td><td>f. 128b, col. 1, tu te gardes de cheoir en grant ire.</td></tr>
<tr><td>p. 22, l. 8, lest thow me disceyve and be-gyle.</td><td>f. 133, col. 3, que tu ne me puisses engignier ne deceuoir.</td></tr>
<tr><td>p. 615, l. 29, triste and sorowfull.</td><td>Omitted from MS. 105, f. 322, col. 1. (MS. 24,394, f. 265, col. 2, l. 30, reads, "tristes et dolans.")</td></tr>
<tr><td>p. 627, l. 9, the grete mortalite and slaughter.</td><td>f. 325b, col. 2, la grant mortalite et la grant occision.</td></tr>
<tr><td>p. 632, l. 36, I haue yow hider somowned and assembled.</td><td>f. 327, col. 3, omitted.</td></tr>
<tr><td>p. 643, l. 2, the king hem yaf riche yeftes and presentes.</td><td>f. 330, col. 2, si leur donna li roys de moult riches dons.</td></tr>
<tr><td>p. 643, l. 32, Whan the kynge this vndirstode he was gladde and ioyfull.</td><td>f. 330b, col. 1, Et quant li roys lentendi si en ot molt grant ioie.</td></tr>
<tr><td>p. 656, l. 32, with grete force and vigour.</td><td>f. 334b, col. 3, a force et a vigour.</td></tr>
<tr><td>p. 674, l. 35, and he a-bode gladde and myrye.</td><td>f. 341, col. 1, et il demoura en son chastel liez et ioians.</td></tr>
<tr><td>p. 680, l. 4, and he hir taught and lerned so moche.</td><td>f. 342b, col. 2, et il li endist et enseigna.</td></tr>
<tr><td>p. 682, l. 35, Whan kynge Arthur hadde a-dubbed the duerf by the preier and request of the damesell, and she had hym</td><td>f. 343b, col. 1, a cele heure que li roys artus ot adoube le uain cheualier par la proiere a la damoisele, quele len mena ainsi</td></tr>
</table>

<table>
<tr><td>[p. 683], ledde as ye haue herde gladde and ioyfull . . . . .
[thei] entred in to a feire launde that was grete and large.</td><td>comme vous auez oi moult liee et moult ioianz . . . . . .
[il] entrerent en vne lande qui moult estoit longue et large.</td></tr>
</table>

The net result of the entire investigation of the manuscripts is negative. In other words, we have proved that the English version is not translated word for word from any of the extant French versions, though most of them tolerably represent the story as a whole, and many of them agree almost literally in a large number of passages with the English version. Two of the MSS. (MS. 105 and MS. 9123) agree on the whole more closely with the English than do any of the others, and these two doubtless belong to the family of MSS. of which one was used by the translator of our version. I must confess, then, that I have not found the exact original, but I am firmly convinced that the English version is a slavish translation of a fourteenth-century[1] manuscript, now lost, and that a careful collation of all the extant MSS. might enable us to find a French equivalent for almost every word of the translation.[2]

[1] M. Paul Meyer, Director of the École des Chartes, to whom I submitted the French passages quoted in the English version, pp. 485, 563, assured me that the forms were those of the fourteenth century.

[2] As for the version of the printed editions, it need not detain us long.[a] The earliest edition did not appear till 1498, more than a half-century after our translation was made, and so, of course, can be of importance only in so far as the version of the printed text may represent an older manuscript original. At the beginning of my search for the version used by the English translator I compared paragraph by paragraph the English text and the French edition of 1498, and found a general agreement in the incidents, but very considerable verbal differences, and at times important omissions. I cannot take room for examples, but refer the reader to Fr. vol. i. f. 130, Eng. p. 212; Fr. vol. ii. f. 1, Eng. p. 379; Fr. vol. ii. f. 58, Eng. p. 484. Near the end of the romance, Fr. f. 172, col. 2, a sharp divergence from the English version begins, and continues to the close[b] (f. 172b) of the romance.

[a] Cf. the remarks of P. Paris on the general value of the printed editions.— MSS. François, i. pp. 126, 127.   [b] Cf. Ward, Catal. of Romances, vol. i. p. 343.

VIII.

TWO MERLINS OR ONE?

After this long examination of the romance, we may now consider a question that naturally suggests itself: Have we to do with two Merlins or one? This question is of no great importance in itself, but it has held too large a place in the literary history of the legend to be dismissed with a word. The answer to this question involves a comparison of all the data. For the sake of clearness, therefore, it will be well, even at the expense of some repetition, to bring together whatever can be urged with regard to the separate existence of Merlinus Ambrosius and Merlinus Caledonius (Myrddin).

Of Merlin Ambrosius[1] the so-called sixth-century Welsh poems know nothing. In them there is no hint of the existence of the wonder-working Merlin of the romances. The Triads, as we have seen (pp. xcix.–c.), mention Myrddin Emrys (Merlin Ambrosius), Myrddin, son of Morvryn, and Taliessin as the three principal bards of Britain, and tell of the disappearance of Myrddin, the Bard of Emrys Wledig, and his nine bardic companions. But the importance of this material in the Triads is hardly greater than must be attached to what we find in Giraldus Cambrensis, and other writers of the twelfth century.

The introduction of Merlin Ambrosius into Welsh literature (as distinguished from oral tradition) seems to be due to the Welsh translation of Geoffrey of Monmouth's *Historia Regum Britanniae*, though of course the legend may have existed as

---

[1] On Merlin Ambrosius, Rhŷs (*Studies in the Arthurian Legend*, p. 162) remarks: "But under the name Ambrosius or Emrys were confounded the historical Aurelius Ambrosius and the mythic Merlin Ambrosius, in whom we appear to have the Celtic Zeus in one of his many forms."

a floating popular tradition for centuries earlier. The Irish translation of Nennius belongs to the eleventh century; but the legend of Merlin, as well as the history of Arthur, was an exotic which did not thrive on Irish soil. For our earliest knowledge of the exploits of Merlin Ambrose we are, therefore, limited to two sources—Nennius and Geoffrey of Monmouth.

All that Nennius has to tell is contained in cap. xl., xli., xlii., xlviii., and lxvi. of his *Historia Britonum*. He does not even give us the name of Merlin; for the boy who is born without a father, and who explains to the king why his castle walls do not stand, replies, on being asked his name, "I am called Ambrose,"[1] the British for which is Embries, that is, the leader.[2] The addition of the name Merlinus is due to Geoffrey of Monmouth, writing at least three centuries later than Nennius. Geoffrey treated the legend in two different forms, the first in the *Historia Regum Britanniae* (1135–1147), and the second in the *Vita Merlini*. In the *Historia* the entire account of the boy Ambrose, as given by Nennius, is transferred to Geoffrey's pages, but with some changes from the text of Nennius that we possess. These changes are due in part, it may be, to the manuscript version which Geoffrey used; but more probably to his own invention.[3]

---

[1] Nennius, cap. 42 : " ' Ambrosius vocor ' (id est, Embries Guletic ipse videbatur). Et rex dixit: ' De qua progenie es ? ' ' Unus est pater meus de consulibus Romanicae gentis.' " (San-Marte's text.)

[2] It is important to note that not only does Nennius fail to name Merlin, but, as is remarked elsewhere (p. ciii.), the author of the *Genealogies* tacked on to the work of Nennius does not even include Myrddin among the bards of Britain: (cap. 62) " Tunc Talhaern Cataguen (Tat Anguen) [Aguen] in poemate claruit, et Neirin et Bluchbard (Bluchbar) et Cian, qui vocatur Guenith Guant simul uno tempore in poemate Britannico claruerunt." *Cf.* San-Marte, *Die Sagen von Merlin*, p. 8.

[3] As already remarked, the name *Merlin* is not found in any of the Celtic manuscripts, but the Welsh name Myrddin is the exact phonetic equivalent of the Latin form. G. Paris, in his criticism of de la Borderie's *Les Véritables Prophéties de Merlin*, makes the following comments (*Romania*, xii. p. 375) :—" Pourquoi appelle-t-il le barde-prophète du vi[e] siècle *Merlin*? Ce nom est de l'invention de Gaufrei de Monmouth, qui sans doute a reculé devant le *Merdinus* qu'il aurait

The chief additions by Geoffrey[1] are the following:—

1. Nennius (cap. xl.) tells us that the king and his wise men, in seeking a place for a tower, came to a province called Guenet,[2] and, after examining the mountains of Heremus,[3] selected the summit of one of them as the site.—Geoffrey says merely that after going about the country they finally came to Mount Erir, and there began to build.

2. Nennius (cap. xli.) relates that the messengers who went out in search of the boy born without a father came to the field of Aelecti,[4] in the district of Glevesing, where they found some boys playing ball. Two of them began to quarrel, and one called the other a boy without a father. When the messengers inquired whether the child had ever had a father, the mother denied all knowledge of the manner of his conception, and assured them that the boy had no mortal father.[5] At this the boy was taken away to King Vortigern.

Geoffrey[6] tells us that the messengers found some young men playing before the gate of a city afterwards called Kaermerdin. As they played, two of the young men, whose names were Merlin and Dabutius, began to quarrel, when Dabutius reproached Merlin—"As for you, nobody knows what you are, for you never had a father." Then the messengers looked closely at Merlin, and asked the bystanders who the boy was. They

obtenu en latinisant le nom gallois, mais qui trouvait assurément dans la tradition une forme avec *d*, puisqu'il prétend que Caermerdin (Carmarthen, ancien Maridunum) doit son nom à Merlin." The name is variously written. Villemarqué, in his *Myrdhinn, ou l'Enchanteur Merlin*, p. 3, gives a partial list of the different forms: (1) Ancient British, *Marthin*; (2) Modern Welsh, *Myrdhin*; (3) Armorican, *Marzin*; (4) Scotch, *Meller*, *Melziar*; (5) French, *Merlin*. To these we may add: *Myrdin*, *Myrddin*, *Myrddhin*, *Merdhin ap Morvryn*, *Martinus*, *Merlinus Ambrosius*, *Merlin Wyllt*, *Merlinus Caledonius*, *Merlinus Sylvestris*, and *Merlinus Avilonius* (so named from the *Avallenau*). *Cf.* Nicolson, *Eng. Hist. Library*, pp. 31, 32. For the Welsh form, see p. xcvii., note 1, *ante*.

[1] The passages in Geoffrey's *Historia* that parallel the account by Nennius are: B. vi. 17, 18, 19 ; B. vii. 3, up to the point where the prophecy begins.

[2] Guined, Guoinet, Guenez.   [3] Heremi, Heriri, Eryri.   [4] Elleti, Electi, Gleti.

[5] Strangely enough, in the very next chapter (xlii.) the boy tells the king, "My father was a Roman consul."   [6] *Hist.* vi. 17.

replied that his father was unknown, but his mother was daughter to the king of Dimetia, and now a nun in St. Peter's church in that city. The messengers thereupon went to the governor of the city, and ordered him to send Merlin and his mother to King Vortigern. On being questioned by the king, the mother replied that the boy's father was a very beautiful young man, who had the power of talking with her while remaining himself invisible, and that he had several times lain with her in the shape of a man, and left her with child. The king wondered at the recital, and ordered his counsellor, Maugantius, to tell whether the story was possible. He said that numerous instances of a like description were known, and that possibly the boy had been begotten in the same way; for Apuleius, in his book on the Demon of Socrates, had mentioned those spirits, half men, half angels, which live between the earth and the moon, and which we call incubuses. These had been known to assume human shape and to lie with women.

3. Nennius relates (cap. xlii.) that on the next day after the boy had appeared before King Vortigern a meeting was held for the purpose of putting him to death. When the boy asked the reason of his being brought there, he learned that it was with the design of sprinkling with his blood the ground on which the tower was to be built. He then requested that the wise men by whose advice this was to be done might be brought thither. When they came, he questioned them as to what was hid under the ground where the tower was building. On their confession of ignorance, he foretold successively what was to be found— the pool, the two vases, the folded tent, the two sleeping serpents, one white and the other red—and explained the meaning of their combat.

Geoffrey gives in the main the same account,[1] but in his version the conversation with the king, the questions addressed

---

[1] *Hist.* vi. 19; vii. 3.

to the wise men, and the combat of the two dragons, occur on the same day, without the interval that we find in Nennius. Geoffrey substitutes two hollow stones for the vases of Nennius, and tells nothing about the folded tent in which the dragons slept. Geoffrey has the pond drained before the fight begins, while Nennius lets the combat commence at once.

From this point the agreement between Nennius and Geoffrey, in so far as Merlin is concerned, entirely ceases. The short explanation which Nennius gives of the meaning of the combat is omitted by Geoffrey, who, on the other hand, fills the greater part of his seventh book with the famous prophecies of Merlin. The remainder of Geoffrey's account of Merlin touches upon his relations with Aurelius Ambrosius and Uter-Pendragon—the two sons of Constantine. After Merlin has assisted Uter-Pendragon to win Igerna the name of the enchanter vanishes from Geoffrey's pages, except in two brief references[1] to his prophecies. In spite of these minor differences the accounts of Nennius and Geoffrey relate to the same personage: the additions merely show what progress the myth had made in the course of three centuries.[2] But if, now, we turn to Geoffrey's *Vita Merlini*, we meet a difficulty; for, although we still find the name Merlin, a small portion only of the account of him as given in the *Historia* is reproduced in the *Vita*, and the leading topic in the poem is the madness of Merlin the bard. Yet the identity of the bard with the enchanter is directly asserted in the poem.[3] With this matter we shall deal presently.

[1] *Hist.* xii. 17, 18.

[2] It would be interesting to compare the growth of the Merlin legend with the growth of other mediaeval legends. The Chanson de Roland in its finished form belongs to the latter part of the eleventh century, while the battle of Roncesvalles was fought August 15, 778. The legends attaching to Godfrey of Bouillon were evolved somewhat more rapidly.

[3] ll. 681–683. San-Marte remarks (*Die Sagen von Merlin*, s. 322) that from about l. 431 Geoffrey begins to confuse Merlin Ambrosius with Merlin Caledonius. Geoffrey says (l. 681 *sqq.*) that Merlin the bard is the same as he who once prophesied before Vortigern; but he omits all account of the paternity of Merlin as related in the *Historia*.

It may be worth our while briefly to review some of the opinions held on this question. One side contends stoutly for two Merlins. It is argued that there was an enchanter of the name of Merlin, who lived, if at all, in the time of Vortigern, king of Britain, about the end of the fifth century. His history contains elements more or less mythical. The other personage was a Welsh bard, named Myrddin, who lived in the sixth century, and who went mad with grief over his friends killed in the battle of Arderydd, in the year 573. As already remarked, Nennius knows only the fatherless boy who calls himself Ambrosius, or Embries Guletic.[1] Geoffrey of Monmouth repeats the story told by Nennius, adopts the name Ambrosius, and adds that of Merlinus.[2] His other additions in the *Historia* are merely supplementary, and in no essential particulars contradictory to the account in Nennius. In the *Vita Merlini* Geoffrey calls him Merlin throughout, but he tells us that "rex erat et vates," and though, as we have seen, he identifies[3] the Merlin of the *Vita* with the Merlin of the *Historia*, he surrounds the bard with a group of persons[4] unknown in the earlier work. The *Vita* can hardly be placed later than 1150; so that the identification of the bard with the enchanter was made at a very

---

[1] *Hist. Brit.* cap. xlii.

[2] In touching on these names M. Gaston Paris strangely says: "Ce double nom, *Merlinus Ambrosius*, ne se présente que dans la *Prophetia Merlini* de Gaufrei, que nous prenons ici sur le fait, accolant son *Merlinus* à l'*Aubrosius* [sic] de Nennius; dans le corps de son livre (publié après la Prophetia), il dit simplement *Merlinus*" —G. Paris, *Romania*, xii. 371, note. Yet Geoffrey has in the *Historia*, vi. 19 (San-Marte's edition, *Sagen von Merlin*, pp. 19, 20): "Tunc ait Merlinus, qui et Ambrosius dicebatur"; and four lines below: "Accessit iterum Ambrosius Merlinus ad magos." In the *Prophecy* we find (cap. i.) "de Merlino"; (cap. ii.) "Merlini"; and (cap. iii.) "Ambrosio Merlino." These are the only cases where the double name is mentioned.

[3] *Cf.* also George Ellis, *Eng. Hist. Library*, Lond. 1786, p. 31; F. Michel, *Vita Merlini*, pp. xviii., xix.; San-Marte, *Die Artussage*, p. 90.

[4] Such, for instance, as his sister Ganieda, ll. 122-124; Peredur, l. 31; Rodarchus, l. 32, etc. *Cf.* the later discussion in this section.

early stage of the literary development of the materials, be they legendary or historical, or both.

The first attempt[1] of which we have any record to make a *formal* distinction between Merlin the enchanter and Merlin the bard is due to Gerald de Barri, better known as Giraldus Cambrensis. In his *Cambriae Descriptio*,[2] written near the end of the twelfth century, we find the following (cap. xvi.): "Sicut et olim, stante adhuc Britonum regno, gentis excidium, et tam Saxonum primo, quam etiam Normannorum post adventum Merlinus uterque, tam Caledonius quam Ambrosius fertur vaticinando declarasse." After comparing the prophecies of Merlin with those of Scripture, he adds: "Merlini itaque prophetiam legimus, sanctitatem eius vel miracula non legimus. Obiiciunt, et quia prophetiae non extra se fiebant, quando prophetabant, sicut de Merlino Silvestri legitur, quod amens factus prophetabat, et de his similiter quasi arreptitiis, de quibus hic locuti sumus."

Also, in the *Itinerarium Cambriae*, i, 10, he refers to Caermardyn: "Sonat autem Caermardyn, urbs Merlini, eo quod iuxta Britannicam historiam ibi ex incubo genitus, inventus fuerat Merlinus." In ii, 6: "Ea nocte iacuimus apud Nevyn videlicet vigilia paschae floridi; ubi Merlinum Silvestrem diu quaesitum, desideratumque Archidiaconus Menevensis dicitur invenisse."

Most important of all is the passage in cap. viii.: "Non procul ab ortu (fluminis) Conwey in capite montis Eryri, qui ex hac parte in Boream extenditur, stat Dinas Emrys, i.e. promontorium Ambrosii, ubi Merlinus prophetavit, sedente super ripam Vortigerno. Erant enim Merlini duo, iste qui et Ambrosius dictus est, quia binomius fuerat et sub rege Vortigerno prophetavit, ab incubo genitus, et apud Caermerdhin inventus; unde

---

[1] That is, unless we assume the Triads to be older than we thought them.

[2] For all these texts, conveniently brought together, see San-Marte's *Sagen von Merlin* Zeugnisse, pp. 37–58.

et ab ipso ibidem invento denominata est Caermerdhin, i.e. urbs Merlini. Alter vero de Albania oriundus, qui et Celidonius dictus est, a Celidonia silva, in qua prophetavit, et Silvester, quia cum inter acies bellicas constitutus, monstrum horribile nimis in aera suscipiendo prospiceret, dementire coepit, et ad silvam transfugiendo silvistrem usque ad obitum vitam perduxit. Hic autem Merlinus tempore Arthuri fuit, et longe plenius et apertius quam alter prophetasse perhibetur."[1]

In another place[2] Giraldus repeated his distinction between the two Merlins, and remarked that the Caledonian Merlin was much less known than the other, and that it seemed to him worth while to collect and publish whatever information he could find about the man: "Erat itaque Caledonii Silvestris solum hactenus fama percelebris; a Britannicis tamen Bardis, quos poetas vocant, verbo tenus penes plurimos, scripto vero penes paucissimos vaticiniorum eiusdem memoria retenta fuerat."

Giraldus has some other references to Merlin, of much less importance. From Geoffrey's *Historia* he takes the account of Merlin's transfer of the great stones from Ireland to Stonehenge. He tells also of the wonderful Lech-lavar or talking-stone, with which vulgar tradition had connected a prophecy of Merlin, but whether of Merlin Ambrosius or Merlin Caledonius we cannot affirm, for the prophecy is not given by Geoffrey.

We must not make too much of negative evidence, but we note in the work of William of Newburgh (b. 1135 – 6? d. 1200?) an omission that seems a little surprising, if we

---

[1] San-Marte, *Die Sagen von Merlin*, p. 52.

[2] "Noch um 1180 scheint die wälsche Tradition bestimmt den Ambrosius und Merlin unterschieden zu haben, wie aus dem *Itinerarium* des *Giraldus Cambrensis* hervorgeht, der mit eben so ungemeiner Begier als Leichtgläubigkeit dergleichen Volkssagen sammelte, doch aber Gottfrieds *Chronik* einmal eine *fabulosa historia* nennt" (*Cambriae Descriptio*, cap. vii.). San-Marte, *Die Artussage*, pp. 91, 92.

assume that two Merlins were well known in his day. William
of Newburgh criticized very severely Geoffrey's *Historia* as
being full of falsehoods, and especially blamed the lively
churchman for introducing the prophecies of Merlin,[1] who was
fabled to have had a woman for his mother and a demon incubus
for his father. William makes, however, no mention of two
Merlins, and seems to know of Merlin Ambrosius only.

Some of the other data at our disposal are not easy to
interpret. For instance, in two old lives of St. Patrick—one
by Jocelyn, at the end of the twelfth century, and the
other doubtfully attributed to Beda—is an account of a certain
evil-doer, who, by the prayer of St. Patrick, was mysteriously
raised into the air and dashed to the ground a corpse.[2] Jocelyn
gives the man the name *Melinus*, while Beda (?) calls him
"mago quodam nomine Locri." It is, however, by no means
certain that our Merlin is here referred to at all. Mere identity
of name does not necessarily prove identity of personality.

Ralph de Diceto, who died in the year 1210, mentions Merlin
as a bard born of a demon incubus and a king's daughter, who
was a nun and lived in the city of Caermarthen. This account,
of course, merely follows Geoffrey's *Historia*.

In the course of the next hundred years no writer seems to
have thought the matter worth mentioning; for not until the
appearance of Ranulf Higden's *Polychronicon*, in the first half
of the fourteenth century, do we find any further attempt to
distinguish the magician of the time of Vortigern from the

---

[1] William refers with scorn to the "lying prophecies of a certain Merlin, to
which he (Geoffrey) has himself added considerably." Paulin Paris infers from
William's attitude that the Merlin legend was not very old at the time when Geoffrey
wrote. Cf. *Romans*, i. 65–72. Just here we may note Mr. Ward's remark
(*Catal. of Romances*, i. 210) on Henry of Huntingdon, that "though he appears to
have had no great taste for marvels, it is certainly odd that he never once mentions
the name of Merlin, as one would have anticipated if Merlin had made any great
figure in the first recension " (of Geoffrey of Monmouth's *Historia*).

[2] *Cf.* San-Marte, *Die Sagen von Merlin*, pp. 51, 52.

bard of the sixth century. The doggrel rhyming Latin verses[1] which Higden wrote on Merlinus Ambrosius and Merlinus Caledonius reproduce much of the phraseology of Gerald de Barri, and add really nothing to the solution of the question.[2]

Merlin is referred to by a number of other writers of the Middle Ages. Thus, Sigebertus Gemblacensis[3] mentions a prophecy of Merlin relating to Arthur; and the monk of Malmesbury who wrote the life of Edward III. remarks on the year 1315 that, in consequence of a prophecy of Merlin predicting the recovery of England by King Arthur, the Welsh raised frequent revolts. Merlin is in each case referred to as a well-known name, without any hint of the existence of a second Merlin.

The fourteenth-century *Scotichronicon* of John Fordun touches[4] on the Merlin of Geoffrey's *Historia* as—"quidam

---

[1]
  "Ad Nevyn in North Wallia   Dinas Emreys ut comperi
    Est insula permodica   Sonat collis Ambrosii
    Quae Bardisia dicitur,   Ad ripam quando regulus
    A monachis incolitur,   Vortiger sedit anxius.
    Ubi tam diu vivitur   Est alter de Albania
    Quod Senior praemonitur.   Merlinus, quae nunc Scotia;
    Ibi Merlinus conditur   Repertus est binomius,
    Silvestris ut asseritur.   Silvestris Calidonius,
    Duo fuerunt igitur   A silva Calidonia
    Merlini ut coniicitur   Qua prompsit vaticinia,
    Unus dictus Ambrosius   Silvestris dictus ideo,
    Ex incubo progenitus   Quod, consistens in praelio,
    Ad Kaermerthyn Demeciae   Monstrum videns in aere
    Sub Vortigerni tempore   Mente coepit excedere,
    Qui sua vaticinia   Ad silvam tendens propere
    Proflavit in Snaudonia.   Arthuri regis tempore
    Ad ortum amnis Coneway   Prophetavit apertius
    Ad clivum montis Erery,   Quam Merlinus Ambrosius."

Cf. further, F. Michel, *Vita Merlini*, pp. xix., xx.; and Nash, in the first volume (pp. xii., xiii.) of the *Merlin*, E.E.T.S.

[2] Higden does indeed tell us that the Caledonian Merlin lost his reason at seeing a phantom in the air instead of at the sight of his friends slaughtered in battle; but even this account is borrowed from Giraldus Cambrensis, and can at most be nothing more than a variant of the commonly received version.

[3] San-Marte, *Die Sagen von Merlin*, p. 54.   [4] iii. c. 17.

ex Cambria, Merlinus nomine, plura quasi prophetice cecinit ad intelligendum obscura,"[1] etc.

With this account we may compare that of Powel,[2] who, as Francisque Michel remarked,[3] lived at a time when "the prophecies of the British bard [?] still preserved their authority."

Toward the end of the sixteenth century, Buchanan, in his Scottish history, compares the Merlin of the time of Vortigern with Gildas, somewhat to the disadvantage of the former, and says that Merlin ought rather to be regarded as a great deceiver and a crafty old fellow than as a prophet. Buchanan, like several of the other writers we have examined, seems to know but one Merlin. Yet the distinction made by Giraldus Cambrensis is repeated early in the second half of the sixteenth century in Bale's *Illustrium Maioris Britanniae Scriptorum Catalogus*,[4] which gives (p. 48) an account of Merlinus Ambrosius, followed by one of Merlinus Caledonius (p. 59).

The elaborate commentary by Alanus de Insulis (*cf.* p. xlvii.)

---

[1] *Cf.* in Hearne's edition of Fordun, pp. 202, 212, 251, 709, 755, 1206, 1208, 1226. See also Mr. Ward's article on *Lailoken* in the *Romania* for 1893, pp. 510, 511, in which he shows how Fordun's work was interpolated later by Bower, who finished his revision in 1447.

[2] " Merlinus ipse natus est in Cambria, non ex incubo daemone (ut inquit Baleus), sed ex furtiva venere cuiusdam romani consulis cum virgine vestali in Maridunensi monalium coenobio, ut in Brevario apud Gildam habetur." He then goes on to give an abstract of Geoffrey of Monmouth, and continues: " Aliunde ergo per impostores asseritur eius conceptio, quam ex communi hominum officio et uso, ut facile deciperentur creduli. . . . Dicitur etiam quod suis incantationibus Utherum regem in Gorloidis Cornubiae ducis speciem transformaverit, ut Igernae uxoris potiretur amplexu et quod ex eo scelerato concubitu Arthurum et Annam genuerit ; sed de his prudentes iudicent. De Maridivi urbis nomine vide ea quae annotavimus supra in cap. x. lib. 1. Extant apud Galfridum Hist. Britannicae libro quarto [?] Merlini vaticinia, obscura quidem illa et nihil certi continentia, quae vel antequam eveniant, sperare, vel cum evenerint promissa, vera audeas affirmare. Praeterea ita composita sunt ut eadem ad multa diversarum, rerum eventa sensibus ambiguis et multiplicibus, circumflectere et accommodare quis possit. Et quanquam multi his et huiusmodi imposturis delusi et decepti perierint tamen hominum credulorum tanta est insania ut quae non intelligant, quovis sacramento, vere esse contendere non dubitent nec in manifesto interim deprehensi mendacio se coargui patiantur."— Quoted by F. Michel, *Vita Merlini*, pp. x.-xiii.

[3] *Vita Merlini*, p. x.   [4] Basiliae, apud Iohannem Oporinum (M.D.LIX.), fol.

on Merlin's prophecies was published in 1603; but neither this work nor Freytag's *Programma de Merlino Britannico*, printed in Naumburg in 1737, brought to light any new material relating to the question now before us. In 1748 Bishop Tanner gave a biography of the two Merlins in the Bibliotheca Britannico-Hibernica [1] (pp. 522–525). Nearly forty years later Bishop Nicolson published, in his *English Historical Library* [2] (pp. 31, 32), a careful bibliographical account of authorities on English history, and, in characteristically vigorous style, proved to his own satisfaction that all the supposed Merlins were really but one.[3] The rough-and-ready dogmatism of the Bishop failed to carry conviction to Sir Walter Scott; for, in his *Minstrelsy of the Scottish Border*,[4] he distinguishes Merlin

---

[1] Lond., 1748, fol.　　　　　　[2] Lond., 1786, fol.

[3] "Amongst these bards is to be reckoned their famous *Merlyn*; whose true name (says *Humph.* Lhuid) is *Merdhyn*, so called from *Caermarthen* [*Mariduno*], where he was born. This was so mighty a Man in his Time that our Writers have thought it convenient to split him into three. The first of these (Godfather to the two following) they call *Merlinus Ambrosius* or *Merdhyn Emrys*; who liv'd about the Year 480 and wrote several prophetical Odes, turned into Latin Prose by *Jeffrey* of *Monmouth*. The next is *Merlinus Caledonius*, who liv'd A.D. 570, wrote upon the same Subject with the former, and had the same Translator. The third is surnamed *Avalonius*, who liv'd under King *Malgocunus* (they might as well have made him Secretary to *Joseph* of *Arimathea*, says our great *Stillingfleet*); and yet my Author [a] goes gravely on, and affirms that he was an eminent Antiquary, but seems to mix too many Fables with his true story. They write this last, indeed, *Melchinus*, *Melkinus*, and *Merwinus*, and make him to live some time before the latter *Merlyn*. But this is all stuff, and he is manifestly the same Man or nothing. The most learned of the *British* Antiquaries agree that this *Myrdhyn ap Morvryn* (call'd from the country he lived in *Caledonius*, and *Sylvestris* from his Humour of leading a retired life in the woods) wrote a Poem called *Avallenau*, or the Apple-Trees, to his Lord *Gwendholen ap Keidio*; who was slain at the Battle of *Arderith*, in the Year 577. Some Fragments of this Poem were found at *Hengwyrt*, in *Meirionydshire*, by Mr. Lhwyd; who long since observed to me that from hence the Poet himself got the surname of *Avallonius*. If so, there's a happy Discovery made of one of the many foolish Impostures of the old Monks of Glassenbury: Who, to secure this famous Prophet to themselves, have made King *Arthur's* Tomb and their own Monastery to stand *in Insula Avallonia*. Soon after him came *Ambrosius Thaliessin*, whom *Bale* and *Pits* make to live in the Days of King *Arthur*, and to record his story."

[a] J. Pits, p. 97, *Hist. Regum Britannorum*.

[4] Edinburgh, 1833, vol. iv. pp. 141, 143.

the Wild from Ambrose Merlin, and to the former attributes
the Scottish prophecies.

Sixteen years later, in 1849, Thomas Stephens, in his *Literature of the Kymry* (p. 208 *sqq.*), reaffirmed the identity of
Merlin Caledonius with Merlin Ambrosius. His argument, in
brief, is as follows:—Nennius represents Myrddin Emrys as
a child who appears before King Vortigern, about 480 A.D. On
the other hand, the Myrddin ab Morvryn of the Welsh poems
is an old man who, about 570 A.D., is the brother-in-law of
Rhydderch Hael, one of the three victorious princes in the
battle of Arderydd.[1] In order to affirm the identity of the two
prophets, we must assume an age of more than ninety years;
but this was not exceptional in Wales. Then we have the
striking fact that the two prophets lived in North Wales and
North England—districts not widely separated—and that their
prophecies show considerable similarity. Furthermore, the
bards of the twelfth century and later took the prophecies of
Merlin Ambrosius, as given by Geoffrey of Monmouth, and let
them reappear as prophecies of the Caledonian Merlin, thus
showing that the two bards were held to be identical. This
conclusion was natural enough, for the father of the Caledonian
Merlin was known, while the traditional Myrddin Emrys was
a child without a father, and seemed therefore less real than
the bard whose father was named.

San-Marte seems to adopt the view of Stephens, for he concludes his summary of Stephens' argument in these words:
"Und so gelangt Stephens zu dem wohlmotivirten Resultat,
dass Merddin Emrys und Merddin ap Morvryn, Wyllt und
Silvester, wie Merlin der Barde, Zauberer, und Prophet nur
verschiedne Namen für eine und dieselbe Person seien."[2]

A different conclusion was reached by the French critic
Villemarqué. He regarded Merlin Ambrosius as a historical
personage, associated as a bard with King Aurelius Ambrosius.

---

[1] Fought in 573 A.D.   [2] *Die Sagen von Merlin*, p. 235.

By a singular series of etymological guesses, Villemarqué tried to establish a connection between the Breton *Marzin* and the Latin *Marsus*, son of Circe. Although he held that Myrddin the Welsh bard had really lived, he would not affirm that any of the poems attributed to him are genuine.

For several years after the appearance of M. de la Villemarqué's theory the only critic of note who touched on the Merlin problem was Mr. D. W. Nash.[1] His theory rejects altogether the view of Mr. Stephens and others, who hold that the "Merddin Emrys of Vortigern and Merddin the son of Morvryn must be taken to have been one and the same person, and that the latter is the one whose character formed the nucleus from which the other was developed." "Merddin Emrys" (Merlin Ambrosius) has in Nash's view no claim to be regarded as a historical character. To use again his words: "We ought, I think, to look upon the figure of the great enchanter as a pure work of fiction woven in with the historical threads which belong to this epoch of the Saxon wars in Britain."[2] On the other hand, he adds: "So far from being of unknown or mysterious birth, the pedigree of Merddin Caledonius is as well ascertained as that of any other British celebrity."[3]

Mr. Skene did not discuss this specific question in the *Four Ancient Books of Wales*,[4] but he established more firmly than before the historical character of a Welsh bard bearing the name of Myrddin.

The conclusion arrived at by Stephens, in his *Literature of the Kymry*, that Merlin Ambrosius, Merlyn Sylvester, and Merlin Caledonius were one and the same person, was adopted by M. Paulin Paris in his *Romans de la Table Ronde* (i. p. 80).[5]

---

[1] His short paper was prefixed to Part I. of the *Romance of Merlin* (1865), edited by Mr. Henry B. Wheatley for the E.E.T.S.

[2] pp. viii., ix.   [3] p. x.   [4] Edinburgh, 1868, 2 vols., 8vo.

[5] "Mais (dira-t-on, pour expliquer la différence des légendes) il y eut deux prophètes du nom de Merlin : l'un fils d'un consul romain, l'autre fils d'un démon incube ; le premier ami et conseiller d'Artus, le second, habitant des forêts ; celui-ci

His son, M. Gaston Paris, though less pronounced, seems to hold essentially the same opinion.[1]

The last critic that I shall cite, Mr. H. L. D. Ward,[2] regards the Merlin who was brought before Vortigern as purely legendary and mythical; while the Myrddin of the Welsh poems is historical, and is to be assigned to the latter part of the sixth century and the beginning of the seventh. In a paper published in the *Romania*[3] for 1893, pp. 504–526, Mr. Ward proves that a wild man of the name of Lailoken,[4] who lived in the time of St. Kentigern, is to be identified with Merlin Silvester, otherwise known as Merlin the Wild or Merlinus Caledonius. This wild man one day meets St. Kentigern and begs the good man to listen to him. Then he goes on to accuse himself of being the cause of the death of all those who were slain in the battle "inter

surnommé *Ambrosius*, celui-là *Sylvester* ou le *Sauvage*. L'*Historia Britonum* a parlé du premier, et la *Vita Merlini* du second. Je donnerai bientôt l'explication de tous ces doubles personnages de la tradition bretonne: mais il sera surtout facile de prouver à ceux qui suivront le progrès de la légende de Merlin que l'*Ambrosius* le *Sylvester* et le *Caledonius* (car les Écossais ont aussi réclamé leur Merlin topique) ne sont qu'une seule et même personne."

[1] "M. de la Borderie appelle toujours la *Vita Merlini* en vers, *Vie de Merlin le Calédonien*, et dit qu'elle a été écrite 'sur la fin du xiie siècle'; mais ce poème est sans aucun doute de Gaufrei de Monmouth, et a été par conséquent écrit avant 1154. Quant au surnom de *Caledonius* (ou plutôt *Celidonius*, ou Silvester) donné à Merlin, il ne figure pas dans le poème; il est de l'invention de Giraud de Barri (Itin. Kambr., ii. 8), qui, frappé de l'anachronisme qu'avait commis Gaufrei, a essayé,[a] à la façon des gens du moyen âge de tout concilier en supposant deux Merlin; mais la *Vita Merlini* dit expressément que son héros était le même qui avait jadis parlé à Wortigern."—*Romania*, xii. 375, 376.

[a] De même, pour concilier l'*Historia Britonum* avec Gaufrei, il dit: "*Merlinus qui et Ambrosius dictus est*, quia binominis fuerat."

[2] Author of the *Catalogue of Romances in the Department of MSS. in the British Museum*. This opinion I got from Mr. Ward in conversation, April 22, 1890.

[3] Mr. Ward prints in full the Latin texts that contain the account of Lailoken. The oldest of these, Cotton Titus A. xix., he places in parallel columns beside the later mutilated version in Bower's *Scotichronicon*. Of this oldest version Mr. Ward says that it was "written at the request of Bishop Herbert (and therefore before 1164) by a cleric of St. Kentigern's, who was apparently a foreigner."

[4] *Cf.* pp. cviii.-cxxi. above.

Lidel et Carwonnok," *i.e.* the battle of Arderydd (A.D. 573). A variety of detail establishes the essential identity of Lailoken with the Myrddin of the *Avallenau*. Moreover, a considerable part of the account of Lailoken is very like what we find in Geoffrey of Monmouth's *Vita Merlini*. Now, as we can hardly assume that the writer of the life of St. Kentigern invented the story out of nothing, we must believe that he used earlier material accessible as an oral tradition or in the form of a written narrative in prose or verse. The date (1164) of the oldest version of the life of Kentigern is, however, only about sixteen years later than that assigned to the *Vita Merlini*. Evidently, then, Geoffrey of Monmouth obtained access in some way to a life of St. Kentigern, with the accompanying account of Lailoken, and incorporated such features as served his purpose into his *Vita Merlini*. The variations in his poem from the story as it appears in the prose versions are what we might expect from a writer of Geoffrey's lively invention. The style of the earliest prose version, published by Mr. Ward in his article, suggests a Celtic origin.[1] Hence we may not improbably suppose that if Geoffrey's source was an oral tradition, he may have learned the story from some Welshman. The fact of chief interest, the identification of the historic Myrddin with Merlin Ambrosius, is brought out clearly by Mr. Ward.

"People had certainly begun to identify Lailoken [Myrddin or Merlin Silvester] with Merlin [Ambrosius] when the narrative in Titus A. xix. was written. It says of him: 'qui Lailoken vocabatur quem quidam dicunt fuisse Merlinum, qui erat Britonibus quasi propheta singularis, sed nescitur.' Again, Lailoken utters that prophecy about a triple death (in this case told of himself), which we regard as essentially Merlinesque, because we know it well in the French romance. And lastly, at the end of Part II., when it has been told

[1] *Cf.* Mr. Ward's note, p. 523.

how he was buried at Drumelzier in Tweeddale, 'in cuius campo lailoken tumulatus quiescit,' the following couplet is added :

> ' Sude perfossus, lapidem perpessus, et undam,
> Merlinus triplicem fertur inisse necem.'

In all other respects, Lailoken is very different indeed from the semi-daemon who attaches himself to the early kings of Britain. Kentigern describes him as a mere man, subject to cold and hunger, and liable to death. He is much more a madman than a prophet. He can never make the same statement twice over. No one pays much heed to his words until he has died the triple death he had prophesied ; and then a few of his other strange sayings are recalled to mind." (p. 512.)

The most instructive lesson to be drawn from this long discussion is the diametrical opposition in opinion of those who have studied the question most carefully. The materials are, in my judgment, too scanty to allow us to affirm or to deny absolutely the existence of an earlier as well as a later Merlin. If the story of the boy without a father be a myth, we may yet suppose that the myth enclosed some small kernel of truth, even though we may not hope to discover what the exact truth is. If we adopt Mr. Skene's opinion, and assign the Chronicle of Nennius (or portions of it) to the seventh century, or take the more common view which refers it to the ninth century, we may well suppose the author to have been conversant with British traditions relating to the bard Myrddin. If the whole early account of the Enchanter Merlin be legendary, we have nothing to prove that the legend [1] existed as a whole before the birth of the historical Myrddin of the sixth century. If it be a later growth than the time of the real Myrddin, we need have no more difficulty with the mythical features than we have with the mythical Charlemagne

---

[1] I have elsewhere taken account of the possible oriental element in the account given by Nennius. See supplementary notes.

of the *Chanson de Roland*, or the mythical traits added to the character of Godefroid de Bouillon in the *Chanson du Chevalier au Cygne*.

My own belief is, that the only really historical personage is the Welsh bard Myrddin, while the Merlin of Geoffrey of Monmouth's *Vita Merlini* is, as we have seen, the same personage with the addition of confusing details borrowed from the life of Merlin Ambrosius. I also incline to think that Merlin Ambrosius is for the most part legendary, but that what we actually know of him can scarcely be more uncertain. As for his name, Geoffrey borrowed the name *Ambrosius* from Nennius, and Merlin (Myrddin) from Welsh tradition. A slight amount of actual prophetic Welsh tradition, added to a much larger amount of prophecy concocted by Geoffrey himself, made up the book of Merlin's prophecies. I hardly think that Geoffrey of Monmouth knew at first-hand the Welsh poems which have come down to us. If he did, the use he made of them was exceedingly slight. On the other hand, if we suppose him to have got his acquaintance with Welsh legend mainly through oral tradition, we have little difficulty in accounting for the genesis of Merlin Ambrosius, and for the confusion of the two prophets in the *Vita Merlini*. We may suppose Geoffrey at first to have known vaguely of a Welsh bard or prophet, and to have heard the name of Merlin (Myrddin) connected with the story of a boy without a father. These slight hints were all that his active mind needed to enable him to string together the materials which floating tradition and his own imagination furnished him. Such, at any rate, is the conclusion gradually forced upon me in the progress of this investigation, but I should be glad to abandon this theory for one better grounded.

The question, then, stands very nearly where it did when we started; and it need not detain us much longer. We have found that Geoffrey of Monmouth was the first or among the first to assert the identity of Merlin Ambrosius with Merlin (Myrddin) the Caledonian, and that Giraldus Cambrensis was the first to assert explicitly that Merlin Ambrosius was not the same as Merlin the Caledonian. Since the time of Giraldus we have discovered no important materials (unknown in his day), while we have probably lost much then extant; so that, in spite of our more critical methods, we can scarcely do more than to balance probabilities and to confess our ignorance. As for the Welsh poems, it appears probable that at least portions may be referred to the sixth century, and that a Welsh bard of the name of Myrddin actually existed. In the interval between the death of Myrddin and the time when the short chronicle of Nennius was committed to writing a tradition had arisen of a wonderful diviner. This tradition may have owed something to floating tales concerning Myrddin, even though his name may not have been uniformly associated with them all. During this intermediate stage of development the mythical element was first introduced, but how long the mythical features had existed cannot be definitely fixed. Yet we may be well-nigh certain that the essentially oriental motive in the story of the boy whose blood was to be sprinkled on the foundations of Vortigern's tower did not originate with Nennius. Exactly what is the origin of all the other features we may hardly presume to guess, but that some are Celtic seems not unlikely.

Of one thing, however, we may be certain: the Merlin of the French romances owed nothing directly to the Welsh poems that have come down to us, though floating Celtic legend contributed more than one striking element to the great prose cycle—notably the story of Nymiane. We must not expect perfect unity in the conception of the French romancers. In all probability the romancers had no critical knowledge of the legend, and would not have cared a straw whether their accounts of Merlin were confused or not. They contentedly

jumbled together elements which were perfect strangers to one
another before they were violently incorporated into the original
story.   Throughout the romances we have no hint that more
than one Merlin was known, so that, whether invention played
a large part or not, we find a multitude of incidents bearing
no analogy whatever to the known facts of the life of the Bard
Myrddin.   If, therefore, we assume two Merlins, we must
admit that with one of them the French romances have little
or nothing to do ; if we assume but one Merlin (Myrddin), we
must admit that his features have been altered almost beyond
recognition.   Confused the portrait of Merlin in the romances
certainly is, in the sense that it groups together elements of
very diverse character ; but the portrait is not unharmonious,
and by the very multiplicity of details it seems far more real to
us than the shadowy figure outlined by the Welsh bards.

———

IX.

NOTES ON THE SOURCES.

We are now prepared to look a little farther, and to trace
some of the materials of which the romance is composed.
The ultimate source of many of the incidents is sufficiently
obscure ; but of the romance as a whole we may say that it
is a French superstructure, reared upon a Celtic foundation
according to plans supplied by Geoffrey of Monmouth, but
greatly modified by Robert de Borron and later romancers.

The setting of the story in the French romance is very different from that in Geoffrey of Monmouth; for in Robert de Borron's tale Merlin is the chief character, instead of the subordinate figure that we see in Geoffrey's *Historia*. Hence we find the romancer continually adding traits and incidents of which there is no hint in Nennius or Geoffrey. It is evident, therefore, that we cannot account for every line and paragraph, but that we must regard considerable portions as pure invention. The first six chapters of the French romance contain much material essentially the same as portions of Geoffrey's *Historia*. But this matter Robert probably got at second-hand, for there is no reason to think that he knew any language but his own. Yet we may well suppose that Robert was familiar, at least at second-hand, with floating Celtic tradition, and that he picked up from the lips of wandering singers and story-tellers more than one of the details of his romance. Some legends would unquestionably have come to his ears in that story-telling age; but just which of his materials were so derived is a matter of conjecture. Gaston Paris has argued strongly against Robert's familiarity with Latin,[1] and has urged that he got the leading features of the legend more or less directly from Wace[2] or other French translators of Geoffrey, and modified the outline according to his fading recollection of minor details, piecing out the story with his own inventions.

The following notes on the leading incidents make no pretence to be exhaustive, and they take little account of minor variations from Wace and Geoffrey of Monmouth.[3]

---

[1] *Merlin*, Introd. pp. x.-xviii.

[2] *Cf.* P. Paris, *Romans de la Table Ronde*, i. p. 336.

[3] In tracing the sources I have freely availed myself of the investigations of Villemarqué, Paulin Paris, Gaston Paris, Kölbing, Rhŷs, and others.

THE MERLIN OF ROBERT DE BORRON.

1. *Council of Demons* (*p.* 1).

This was probably suggested by the Gospel of Nicodemus (chap. xvii.), which had been turned into French verse before Robert de Borron wrote.[1]

2. *Begetting of a Child by the agency of a Demon*[2] (*p.* 3).

This incident in its simple form is found in Geoffrey of Monmouth's *Historia Reg. Brit.* vi. 18; Wace, *Brut*, ll. 7623–7644. The belief in the existence of incubi seems to have been very general in the Middle Ages. Geoffrey himself refers to Apuleius, who gives a very singular account of the Demon of Socrates in the *Liber de deo Socratis*, but Apuleius has nothing to say of incubi. St. Augustine, in *De Civitate Dei*, xv. 23, mentions incubi under the name *dusii* or *drusii*—

"Et quoniam creberrima fama est, multique se expertos, vel ab eis qui experti essent, de quorum fide dubitandum non est, audisse confirmant, Silvanos, et Faunos, quos vulgo incubos vocant, improbos saepe exstitisse mulieribus, et earum appetisse ac peregisse concubitum; et quosdam daemones, quos Dusios Galli nuncupant, hanc assidue immunditiam et tentare et efficere, plures talesque asseverant ut hoc negare impudentiae videatur: non hinc aliquid audeo definire, utrum aliqui spiritus elemento aerio corporati (nam hoc elementum etiam cum agitatur flabello, sensu corporis tactuque sentitus) possint etiam hanc pati libidinem, ut quomodo possunt sentientibus feminis misceantur."

[1] G. Paris, *Merlin*, Introd. i. p. xii. *Cf. Trois versions rimées de l'Évangile de Nicodème*, Soc. des Anc. Textes, 1885. The Latin text has been edited by Tischendorf, *Evangelia Apocrypha*, Lipsiae, 1876.

[2] *Cf.* G. Paris, *Merlin*, Introd. p. 13; and Drayton's *Polyolbion*, Works, vol. ii. p. 763 (note by Selden): "I shall not believe that other than true bodies on bodies can generate, except by swiftness of motion in conveying of stolen seed some unclean spirit might arrogate the improper name of generation." *Cf.* also Alf. Maury, *La Magie et l'Astrologie au Moyen Âge*, p. 189, where the *deuce* is discussed. Very curious information on the entire subject of demons may be found in Jean Bodin's *Demonamanie*, Paris, 1580, and in Joh. Wier's *De Praestigiis daemonum et incantationibus ac veneficiis*, Basel, 1563.

When, in the course of the Middle Ages, the belief grew up that Antichrist[1] was to be born of a devil and a virgin, just as Christ was born of the Holy Ghost and a virgin, we see that the essential elements of the story, as we find it in the romance, were already at hand.[2]

Burton, in his *Anatomy of Melancholy*, Part iii. sec. 2, mem. i. subs. 1, gives a considerable discussion of the intercourse of the Devil with women. For several other references see Dunlop's *Hist. of Fiction* (1888), i. p. 146, note; i. p. 156, note; ii. pp. 461, 462; Du Cange, *Glossarium*, art. *Incubi*; Tylor, *Primitive Culture*, i. pp. 189 and 193.

We may incidentally note that when Merlin reaches the age of twelve months he is uttering wise sayings. In the romance of *Kyng Alisaunder* (Morley's *English Writers*, iii. p. 297) we read of women in the East who bear but one child in their lives. "This child is able to begin talking to its mother as soon as it is born."

3. *The Punishment of being Buried Alive*

(*p.* 5) is that to which vestal virgins were condemned if unfaithful to their vows. *Cf.* also Dunlop's *Hist. of Fiction* (1888), i. p. 147, note.

4. *Sprinkling of Foundation with Blood* (*pp.* 23–28).

Nennius, *Hist. Brit.* 40, 42 ; Geoffrey, *Hist. Reg. Brit.* vi. 17. Also in Wace and other translators of Geoffrey. For other references see Dunlop's *Hist. of Fiction* (1888), i. p. 461.

---

[1] Wulfstan, *Homily* xvi., *De temporibus Antichristi* (p. 95), has: "Crist is sōð god and sōð mann, and Antecrist bið sōðlice déofol and mann." See also Ebert *Allgem. Gesch. der Lit. des Mittelalters im Abendlande*, i. p. 97 ; iii. p. 480.

[2] Kölbing (*Altenglische Bibl.* iv. p. lxi.) points out interesting parallels between the mysterious origin of Merlin and that of Richard in the Romance of *Richard Coer de Leon*, l. 207 *sqq.* The mother of Richard was, according to the romance, in league with the Devil, since she could not hear mass; and when compelled to hear it, she flew through the roof with her two children.

5. *The Hermit Blase* (*p.* 23).

Blase may be a mere invention, but Kölbing calls attention [1] to three passages in Laȝamon's *Brut*, where a hermit is mentioned whom Merlin knows and visits. Laȝamon translated (*c.* 1200) Wace, and made some additions, due in part, it may be, to oral tradition. Robert de Borron, of course, knew nothing of Laȝamon, but the two writers might easily have stumbled upon the same popular story, preserved as a local tradition in more detail in one district than in another.[2]

6. *Vortigern and the Sons of Constance* (*p.* 24).

(1) Geoffrey of Monmouth, *Hist.* vi. 5–9.
(2) Wace, *Brut*, ll. 6585–6859.

7. *Vortigern's Tower, and the Boy without a Father* (*pp.* 27–31).

(1) Nennius, *Hist.* 40, 41.
(2) Geoffrey of Monmouth, *Hist.* vi. 17, 19.
(3) Wace, *Brut*, ll. 7491–7710.

M. Gaster has shown that there are curious parallels between the early history of Merlin and several Jewish legends relating to the building of Solomon's Temple, which are told of Ashmedai and Ben Sira, and that these legends are at least as old as the eighth or ninth century.[3]

---

[1] *Altenglische Bibl.* iv. p. cxii.

[2] Mr. Scott F. Surtees, in a short study on *Merlin and Arthur* (E.E.T.S., 1871), identifies Blase with Lupus, but his theory is badly reasoned out. He even identifies Merlin with Germanus (see also p. xc., *ante*). We may admit that certain elements are borrowed from the lives of Lupus and Germanus without assuming identity. Paulin Paris thinks that Blase was introduced as a sort of excuse for the inventions of the romancer, and compares the hermit with the false Dares, Callisthenes, Turpin, etc.—*Romans de la Table Ronde*, ii. 32, 33.

[3] Kölbing, *Altenglische Bibl.* iv. p. cvi. Mr. Ward, of the British Museum, in calling my attention in conversation (April 22, 1890) to this same matter, suggested that the similarity of incident is not due to borrowing, but rather to the fact that the conception had become common property. As early as 1836, F. Michel, *Vita Merlini* (Introd. p. lxxi.) pointed out the oriental element in this

8. *Merlin's bursts of Laughter on going to Vortigern* (*pp.* 33, 34).

Geoffrey of Monmouth, *Vita Merlini*, ll. 490–532.

The setting of these two incidents is, of course, very different in the prose romance and in the *Vita Merlini*. In the poem, Merlin laughs at a beggar who has a concealed treasure, and at a young fellow with a pair of new shoes, who will soon be drowned. The incident of the shoes appears to have been a widely diffused mediaeval legend; and there is good ground for thinking that Robert de Borron did not get it from the *Vita Merlini*.

Without insisting on Robert's ignorance of Latin, we may note that there are in the *Vita Merlini* two instances of Merlin's knowledge, which, as G. Paris remarks,[1] are not less piquant than those here given, and which we might, perhaps, expect Robert to reproduce, but with which he seems not to have been acquainted. The evidence is, however, negative, and should not be pressed too far. Gaston Paris refers to the Hebrew legend of the Talmud, and calls attention to the similarity of the story related of the demon Ashmedai, who was brought before Solomon.[2]

The story of the priest chanting at the head of the funeral procession, in which was borne a dead child that was really the priest's own son, is found in a modified form in Straparola's

incident as found in "The History of the Temple of Jerusalem"—translated from the Arabic MS. of Imam Jalal-Addin al Siúti, with notes and dissertations, by the Rev. James Reynolds, B.A. Lond., 1836, 8vo. Here, too, is a parallel to Merlin's bursts of laughter.

[1] *Merlin*, Introd. i. p. xv.

[2] For a further account of the history of this legend, see M. Gaster's *Jewish Sources of and Parallels to the Early English Metrical Legends of King Arthur and Merlin*, Lond., 1887. Gaster also gives (*Feuilleton-Zeitung*, No. 299, Berlin, March 26, 1890) a Rumanian legend (quoted by Kölbing) of the Archangel Gabriel and a hermit, in which the same motive recurs. Kölbing points out that the Italian version of *Merlin* varies somewhat the account of the churl and the shoes. *Altenglische Bibl.* iv. p. cxi. note.

Tredeci Piacevoli Notte (Venice, 1550). Gaston Paris remarks [1] that the tale probably came to Robert de Borron as one of the floating oral traditions on the *devinailles* of Merlin. [2]

9. *The Fight of the Dragons, and the Interpretation (pp. 38–40).*

    (1) Nennius, *Hist.* 42.
    (2) Geoffrey of Monmouth, *Hist.* vii. 3, 4; viii. 1.
    (3) Wace, *Brut*, ll. 7711–7776.

Wace omits the interpretation by Geoffrey of Monmouth, though he gives the prediction of the death of Vortigern. The interpretation in the prose romance of *Merlin* is different from that in Geoffrey's *Historia*. For instance, in Geoffrey's account the red dragon betokens the British nation, while the white dragon denotes the Saxons. In the romance the red dragon signifies Vortigern, and the white dragon typifies the two sons of Constance. As Robert de Borron cannot have got his interpretation from either Geoffrey or Wace, he must have either invented it or had access to oral or written sources unknown to us. [3]

10. *Death of Vortigern (p. 42).*

    (1) Nennius, *Hist.* 47, 48.
    (2) Geoffrey of Monmouth, *Hist.* viii. 2.
    (3) Wace, *Brut*, ll. 7777–7848.

The *Merlin* strangely confuses the original account. According to Geoffrey of Monmouth, the three sons of *Constantine* were Constance, who became a monk, Aurelius, and Uter-Pendragon; while in the romance we read (p. 24) of a king Constance who

---

[1] *Merlin*, Introd. p. xv.

[2] We may note that the mother of the judge (p. 20) had got her boy with a priest. *Cf.* p. 34 of the English version.

[3] The tale of Llud and Llevelis in the *Mabinogion* (vol. iii.) contains the story of the two dragons—the white and the red—much the same as in Nennius and Geoffrey of Monmouth. *Cf.* p. c., *ante.*

" hadde thre sones, the first highˆt Moyne [that is, a monk], and the tother Pendragoɴ, and the thirde Vter." [1]

11. *Merlin's Prophecy of the Threefold Death of a Baron* (*p.* 51).
Vita Merlini, ll. 310–321 ; ll. 391–417.

In the *Vita* it is a page whose death is prophesied, and it is the queen who disguises him as a woman. G. Paris suggests [2] that Robert de Borron probably got the story indirectly. The different setting seems due to Robert's own invention.

12. *Merlin brings from Ireland the Stones of Stonehenge* (*p.* 58).

(1) Geoffrey of Monmouth, *Hist.* viii. 10, 11, 12.
(2) Wace, *Brut*, ll. 8207–8386.

The circumstances and the purpose are very different in the romance from what is related in the earlier accounts. In Geoffrey's *Historia* the stones are brought over because of their healing properties while Aurelius is living. In the romance Uter sets them up on Salisbury Plain as a monument to his brother Pendragon. [3]

13. *Founding of the Round Table* (*p.* 59).
Wace, *Brut*, ll. 9994–10,005.

As already remarked, no allusion to the Round Table is made by Geoffrey, though there is reason to suppose that the legend is much older than his *Historia*. [4] In the references to the Round Table in the *Merlin* there is some confusion. [5] Wace tells us Arthur founded the Round Table; while the *Merlin* (p. 60)

---

[1] *Cf.* G. Paris, *Merlin*, Introd. p. x.

[2] *Ibid.* p. xvi. *Cf.* P. Paris, *Romans de la Table Ronde*, ii. p. 56; Villemarqué, *Myrdhinn*, p. 125.

[3] *Cf.* P. Paris, *Romans*, ii. 58.

[4] But see P. Paris, *Romans de la Table Ronde*, ii. pp. 64, 65.

[5] *Cf.* G. Paris, *Merlin*, Introd. i. p. xvi.

says that it was founded by Uter-Pendragon.[1] Merlin tells the king the story of the table at which Christ had sat, and of the table which Joseph of Arimathea was commanded to make. The third was to be established by the king in the name of the Trinity, and was to have a void place for the knight yet unborn who should bring to an end the adventures of the Holy Grail. This is one of the not infrequent points of contact in our romance of the Grail legends and those of Merlin, though, of course, originally independent.[2]

14. *Amour of Uter-Pendragon with Ygerne (pp. 63–78).*

(1) Geoffrey of Monmouth, *Hist.* viii. 19, 20.
(2) Wace, *Brut,*[3] ll. 8803–9058.

As we might expect, the variations here introduced by Robert de Borron are considerable, but we cannot take space

[1] For additional references on the Round Table see Dunlop's *Hist. of Fiction* (1888), i. p. 151, note ; ii. p. 456. "It would be interesting to understand the signification of the term Round Table. On the whole, it is the table, probably, and not its roundness that is the fact to which to call attention, as it possibly means that Arthur's court was the first early court where those present sat at a table at all in Britain. No such thing as a common table figures at Conchobar's Court or any other described in the old legends of Ireland, and the same applies, we believe, to those of the old Norsemen. The attribution to Arthur of the first use of a common table would fit in well with the character of a Culture Hero, which we have ventured to ascribe to him, and it derives countenance from the pretended history of the Round Table ; for the Arthurian legend traces it back to Arthur's father, Uthr Bendragon, in whom we have, under one of his many names, the king of Hades, the realm whence all culture was fabled to have been derived. In a wider sense, the Round Table possibly signified plenty or abundance, and might be compared with the Table of the Ethiopians, at which Zeus and the other gods of Greek mythology used to feast from time to time."—J. Rhŷs, *Studies in the Arthurian Legend*, pp. 9, 10.

[2] On the origin of the *Holy Grail* see Rhŷs's *Studies*, ch. xiii., also p. 170 *sqq.* ; and Nutt's *Studies on the Legend of the Holy Grail.*

[3] G. Paris remarks that Wace omits the name Gorlois, and that Robert de Borron does the same. Yet Wace at least once mentions Gorlois under the name—" Gornois un quens Cornvalois," l. 8689 ; " Li quens de Cornuaille," l. 8798 ; " Que li quens a de Cornuaille," l. 8937. Robert of Brunne, translating Wace, does the same :

" Þe Erl of Cornewaille was o þat hyl ;
Gorlens he highte, a man of skyl."
ll. 9207, 9208.

for pointing them out. The ultimate source of this story is difficult to determine. It has been compared with the story of David and Uriah, and with the tale of Amphitryon in Ovid.[1] Possibly Geoffrey's biblical or classical reading helped him to a hint; but not improbably the underlying idea had become common property, and need not be referred to any definite source.

As for the frequent metamorphoses of Merlin throughout the romance, they are not essentially different from the metamorphoses of the old mythologies—Proteus, Vertumnus, etc. We need not, therefore, take especial account of the passages where Merlin appears as a blind cripple (p. 73), etc. But we may note that transformations of all sorts are very common in Celtic stories.[2]

15. *Uter-Pendragon's*[3] *Battles, and his Death* (*pp.* 92-95).

(1) Geoffrey of Monmouth, *Hist.* viii. 18, 21-24.
(2) Wace, *Brut*, ll. 9059-9238.

Of course the details of the battles differ in the romance, and in Geoffrey and Wace; but it is a little remarkable that Robert tells us that Pendragon (who in the romance takes the place of the Aurelius Ambrosius of Geoffrey) was killed in the battle of Salisbury (p. 56), while Geoffrey (viii. 14), as well as Wace, says that Pendragon was poisoned, and that Uter afterwards met a similar fate (viii. 24). Our romance has no account of the poisoning, and agrees with Geoffrey (viii. 22) and Wace only in making Uter suffer a long illness, so that he has to be borne in a horse-litter.

We are not obliged to suppose the dragon standard of Uter

---

[1] *Cf.* P. Paris, *Romans de la Table Ronde*, ii. p. 81.
[2] *Cf. e.g.* the *Mabinogi* of Manawyḍan, Rhŷs, *Studies*, p. 290 ; P. Paris, *Romans*, i. 16.
[3] For the Celtic Uter-Pendragon see Rhŷs, *Studies*, p. 256. *Cf.* also Nutt, *Studies on the Legend of the Holy Grail*, Index I.

the invention of the romancer. Such a standard was used in war by the Dacians and by the Roman emperors after Constantine. A dragon was the standard of Wessex; so, too, in the public processions of the Pope, the image of a dragon under the cross was borne at the end of a lance by *Draconarii*, a name also given to the bearers of the dragon banner of the Roman emperors.[1]

16. *Coronation of Arthur*[2] (*pp.* 95-107).

Geoffrey (*Hist.* ix. 1) and his translator Wace agree in their account of the boy Arthur. The crown is set upon his head by the Archbishop Dubricius[3] at the request of the nobles, because of the increasing numbers of the Saxons. The birth of Arthur (viii. 20) is no mystery. In the romance, on the other hand, the barons know nothing of Arthur till he takes the sword out of the anvil in the presence of the people. This incident of the sword is referred by G. Paris[4] to biblical legends; and it recurs in various forms in the literature of the Middle Ages.

[1] *Cf.* Brockhaus, *Conversations-Lexicon*, Art. *Drache*; Dunlop, *Hist. of Fiction* (1888), i. p. 126, note; ii. pp. 449-456.

[2] For a discussion of "Arthur, historical and mythical," see Rhŷs, *Studies*, ch. i., especially the summary, p. 47.

[3] In the English prose version the name of the archbishop is not given, though in *Arthour and Merlin* (ed. Kölbing), l. 2783, we find "bishop Brice" mentioned, and I have found the name in several of the French MSS. of the prose *Merlin*. In Geoffrey's *Historia* it appears, viii. 12 ; ix. 1, 4, 12, 13, 15.

[4] *Merlin*, Introd. p. xx. *Cf.* also P. Paris, *Romans de la Table Ronde*, i. 234. Essentially the same incident appears in the *Quête du Graal*, where Lancelot refuses to make the attempt to draw it out, "persuaded that this honour was reserved for the most perfect of knights."—P. Paris, *Romans*, v. p. 330. In *Kyng Alisaunder*, l. 2625 *sqq.*, the prince draws out of the ground a spear. *Cf.* Kölbing, *Altenglische Bibl.* p. lxi. In the *Völsunga Saga*, cap. iii., Sigmund, son of King Völsung, pulls out of the Branstock the sword at which all others had vainly tugged, and wins it for himself. This sword was the gift of Odin. For an additional reference see Dunlop's *Hist. of Fiction* (1888), i. p. 153, note. For notes on magic swords and spears see W. A. Clouston's remarks "On the Magical Elements in Chaucer's Squire's Tale," Chaucer Soc., pub. 1889, part ii. pp. 372-381.

The Book of Arthur.

We have seen in our examination of the manuscripts that there are several continuations of the original romance of Robert de Borron. One of these continuations is the basis of the second part (pp. 108–699) of our English translation. It remains to discuss briefly the sources of this continuation— the so-called *Book of Arthur*.[1] The study of the manuscripts has thrown light on the way in which the romance was built up piece by piece, but of the origin of the materials the manuscripts tell us nothing.

The study of the sources belongs rather to French scholars than to English; for the investigation demands a minute comparison of the other French Arthurian romances yet unpublished. A large number of questions, too, must be relegated to the Celtic philologist, who must determine the origin of the various groups of personal and local names. Numerous special investigations, with the help of critical texts, must precede the solution of these and other problems. But we must not overlook the fact that many of the elements of the continuation are invented, or at least selected from the common stock of material that lay ready for any romancer who chose to use it, and can be traced to no definite source. Padding of this sort we may pass by without extended remark. In our discussion we can perhaps best take up the chapters in their order, and bestow a few words on the sources of the leading incidents. The great extent of the romance forbids us to touch any but the more important matters, and those only lightly. In many instances the notes scarcely attempt more than to indicate what the questions are.

---

[1] The author (or authors) of the *Book of Arthur* is unknown. Paulin Paris suggests that he may be the same as the writer of the *Saint-Graal*; but this is a mere conjecture.

The short narrative of Robert de Borron had utilized nearly all that the literature before his time had to tell of the wonder-working Merlin; but the story had quickened the invention of more than one writer. In the recital of Geoffrey of Monmouth, Merlin disappears from view after the adventure of Uter and Ygerne.[1] Robert makes Merlin figure also at the coronation of Arthur.

But after the conception of a diviner and magician was once given, nothing was easier for the romancers who continued Robert's work than to introduce Merlin at all suitable emergencies into the further history of Arthur. This plan involved piecing together in confusing and almost overwhelming detail a congeries of legends and recitals which must have been originally distinct, and in their elements far earlier than the time when the romance was written. Yet out of the confusion stands the outline of a few great events. The rough sketch is furnished by Geoffrey's *Historia*, but in the hands of the romancers this is expanded both by free invention and the insertion of borrowed legends.[2] In the continuation we trace the several narratives running at times side by side, but separate, and at other times tangled together :—

1. The revolt of the seven kings occupies a considerable portion of the romance (pp. 108–599).

2. The wars with the Saxons, which had already begun in the time of Uter, are directed against both Arthur and the kings revolted from him, and ultimately compel the rebels to make common cause with Arthur.

---

[1] There occur later two mere references to him—*Hist.* xii. 17, 18.

[2] Omissions and changes of all sorts occur. In Geoffrey (ix. 1) there is no revolt against Arthur immediately after his coronation. Hoel of Armorica sends help to Arthur against the Saxons (ix. 2). Cheldric is not mentioned in the romance. In Geoffrey (ix. 9) Lot, Urian, and Augusel are brothers. Guanhamara is of Roman descent, and educated under Duke Cador. Arthur's remote conquests (ix. 10, 11) are not reproduced in the romance. Arthur's marriage (ix. 9) occurs in Geoffrey after the defeat of the Saxons, and his coronation after the war with the Romans.

3. The war of King Leodegan with King Rion, and the marriage of Arthur with Gonnore, are more or less of a break in the continuity of the narrative; though, where all is so loosely put together, one may hesitate to determine what is principal and what subordinate.

4. The war with the Romans (p. 639 *sqq.*) is merely supplementary, and not strictly an integral part of the narrative.

5. Along with these larger divisions of the narrative are legends of Merlin, of Nimiane, of Gawain, and others. A slight attempt at unity is made by introducing at intervals the hermit Blase, to whom Merlin relates all that has happened; but this device is crude, and has no advantage further than that it allows Merlin now and then to recapitulate a portion of the story.

CHAPTER VII.

This chapter appears to be for the most part a patchwork of commonplace incidents, though many of the materials are old. The thought of holding a grand court after Arthur's coronation is evidently borrowed, with much modification, from Geoffrey of Monmouth's *Historia*, ix. 12. But Geoffrey says that Arthur held his court at Pentecost, while the romance (p. 108) places it after the middle of August. On the other hand, Robert de Borron [1] agrees with Geoffrey in making the coronation occur at Pentecost. Of the names here introduced, three at least are taken from Geoffrey, viz. Loth, Urien, Aguysas, though with slight changes of form. Prof. Rhŷs points out [2] that these and other names here found are Celtic. Urien is the subject of eight poems in the *Book of Taliessin*. [3] Ventres (Nentre of Garlot), [4] Ydiers

---

[1] *Cf.* p. 107 of the *Merlin*.

[2] *Studies in the Arthurian Legend*, chap xi., " Urien and his Congeners."

[3] *Ibid.* p. 259.

[4] *Ibid.* p. 323.

(Edern, son of Nûd), Carados, Benbras (Brebras),[1] are easily identified in Celtic legend.

In Geoffrey's account there is no revolt, but the rebellion is naturally enough suggested by the circumstances of Arthur's birth as detailed in the *Merlin* of Robert de Borron, and could be easily invented with the attendant features. Apart from the references to King Leodegan and his war with King Rion, to both of whom we shall recur later, the remainder of the chapter is taken up with the commonplace description of a battle of the Middle Ages. The dragon standard has already been commented upon.

CHAPTER VIII.

This chapter is occupied with the mission of Ulfin and Bretel to King Ban and King Bors. We have a résumé (p. 121) of a part of Robert de Borron's *Merlin*, and an account of the children of Ygerne, different from that given on p. 86 of the romance.

On turning to Geoffrey of Monmouth's *Historia*, ix. 2, we learn that ambassadors are sent into Armorica to get the help of King Hoel, Arthur's sister's son, against the Saxons; and he provides 15,000 men. In the romance, Ulfin and Bretel, who had already figured in Robert de Borron's *Merlin*, go to Armorica (or Little Britain) for the help of King Ban of Benoyk[2] and King Bors of Gannes. These are both identified[3] by Prof. Rhŷs with characters in Celtic literature. "The identity of Ban or Pan with Uthr Ben or Uthr Pen-dragon is shown by his name, and the story of his dying immediately after drinking from a certain well (p. 127). This has its counterpart in Geoffrey's account (viii. 24) of Uthr Pendragon's

---

[1] Rhŷs, *Studies in the Arthurian Legend*, p. 172.

[2] On Benoyk (Benoic) see *ibid.* p. 304.

[3] *Ibid.* pp. 161, 162.

death in consequence of his foes having poisoned the well he was wont to drink from. Thus Bors readily falls into his place as Ambrosius or Emrys, brother to Uthr Ben, especially as the two are described by Geoffrey as exiles in France, whence they are invited to come over to take possession of this country against Vortigern and his allies. But under the name Ambrosius or Emrys were confounded the historical Aurelius Ambrosius and the mythic Merlin Ambrosius, in whom we appear to have the Celtic Zeus in one of his many forms." Bors is "the same person called Bort in the Welsh Triads, for, besides the similarity of the name, Bors, like Bort, was one of those who found the Holy Grail."[1] Ban and Bors are warred upon in their own realm by King Claudas de la deserte, in whom Paulin Paris[2] thought he could recognize Clovis, King of the Franks, or Clotaire I., his successor. "Nam Britanni sub Francorum potestate fuerunt post obitum regis Chlodowei, et comites non reges appellati sunt." (Greg. Tur. iv. 3, A.D. 549.)

The other incidents of the chapter relate to the adventures of Ulfin and Bretel, and are plainly invented.

CHAPTER IX.

1. Most of this chapter appears to demand no especial source, as it is largely taken up with the details of Arthur's first great tournament; but there seems little reason to doubt that the original suggestion of this feature came from Geoffrey's *Historia*, ix. 13, 14.

2. The interesting detail with regard to Kay that he was hated because of his surly tongue, and that this was due to his having been nursed by a woman of lower rank than his

---

[1] Rhŷs, p. 161. For the part that Ban and Bors play in the legends of the Grail, see Nutt's *Studies on the Legend of the Holy Grail*, Index I.

[2] *Romans de la Table Ronde*, ii. 109.

mother (p. 135), is shown by Gaston Paris to point to a widespread superstition of the Middle Ages.[1]

3. Towards the end of the chapter, Guynebans, the brother of Ban and Bors, is mentioned (pp. 138–140) as a great clerk whom Merlin teaches many things. What use the young fellow makes of his knowledge we shall see later (*Merlin*, p. 361). Now in Geoffrey's *Historia*, v. 16, a certain Guanius joins with Melga in slaying Ursula and the eleven thousand virgins. According to Rhŷs,[2] "The Welsh versions usually have Melwas and Gwynwas: it is the latter name also, probably, that meets us in Malory's Gwinas, i. 15, and Gwenbaus, brother to Ban and Bors, i. 11."

4. At the end of this chapter we have the words (p. 131)— "But now cesseth the tale of hem, and returneth to speke of kynge Arthur, that is lefte at Logres." This is one of the very numerous instances in the second branch of the *Merlin* of this kind of transition. Paulin Paris finds[3] in these *laisses* an additional proof of the dual authorship of the romance, for nothing of the sort appears in the prose redaction of the *Joseph of Arimathea* or in the first branch of the *Merlin*, although so common in the second branch (pp. 108–699) and in the *Saint-Graal.*

CHAPTER X.

1. The greater portion of the details of the battle of Bredigan is, of course, pure invention, though the legend of the battle itself may have some more substantial basis. This battle parallels the earlier one of Arthur with the rebel kings.[4]

---

[1] *Merlin*, Introd. I. p. xxi.
[2] *Studies*, p. 343, note.
[3] *Romans de la Table Ronde*, ii. 160.
[4] *Cf.* P. Paris, *Romans de la Table Ronde*, ii. 124.

2. The entrusting of a ring to Merlin, which he is to show as a token to Leonces de Paerne (p. 143), is a very familiar motive, much older than the romance.

3. Merlin's account of King Rion and of Leodegan and his daughter Gonnore (p. 114) is repeated (p. 141) in much the same terms, with some additional touches. The discussion of this matter, however, belongs more properly to chap. xiv., and later.

Chapter XI.

For the two chief incidents here detailed I can cite no specific source. The transformations of Merlin may be compared with those recounted by Geoffrey of Monmouth. The poetic glamour in the story of the great churl coming through the meadows, with his bow and arrows, and his coat and hood of russet, seems to suggest some other source than the invention of the French romancer, but I have hit upon nothing precisely the same. Cf. Malory's *Morte Darthur*, book i. chap. xvii.

Chapters XII, XIII.

1. In these chapters we have a prolix account of the return of the Saxons, and of their ravages in Britain. Much of the geography is fantastic, and cannot be explained. But several of the place-names, though strangely disguised, probably represent actual localities.[1]

---

[1] I cannot take space for details, but refer the reader to Prof. Rhŷs's *Studies in the Arthurian Legend*, Index. See also J. S. Stuart Glennie's *Essay on Arthurian Localities* (E.E.T.S. No. 36), and the index of place-names to Malory's *Morte Darthur* (ed. Sommer), vol. ii. The conclusion of P. Paris on this matter is as follows: " Tout ce qu'on peut donc assurer, c'est que la scène des récits qui touchent à la France embrasse la Touraine, l'Anjou, la Poitou, la Marche, la Bretagne, une partie de l'Auverne, et de la basse Bourgogne" (*Romans*, ii. 111). Trebes is Trèves, on the borders of Benoyk and Berry. Benoyk is Vannes. "La terre deserte est le Berry, dont la capitale est Bourges et le roi Claudas" (ii. 110, 111). *Cf.* also Dunlop's *Hist. of Fiction* (1888), i. 198, note.

2. The account of the begetting of Mordred (pp. 180, 181) is variously told in the romances,[1] and in Geoffrey's *Historia*, ix. 9. Geoffrey calls him Arthur's nephew and Lot's son, and seems to know nothing of Arthur's incest with his sister. But the basis of the whole story of Mordred is certainly Celtic, and this ugly feature is doubtless a part of the original myth.[2]

3. The account of Gawain's conversation with his mother (p. 185 *sqq.*) may be compared with that of Ewein and his mother (p. 241), the second being evidently a mere variant of the first. The singular detail with regard to the waxing and waning of Gawain's strength (p. 182) is touched upon by Prof. Rhŷs,[3] who finds in it evidence for regarding Gawain as a solar hero.

4. The enchantress Carnile, who is here mentioned (p. 185) along with Morgain and Nimiane, is evidently to be referred to the same mythical sources with them.

Chapter XIV.

1. The entire story of the relations of Arthur with Gonnore has been greatly embellished by the romancers, with the result that no two accounts precisely agree. In Geoffrey's *Historia* there are but three references to Guanhumara, and of these the first only (ix. 9) is important for our immediate purpose. There she is said to have belonged to a noble Roman family, to have been educated under Duke Cador, and to have excelled in beauty all other women in the island. Geoffrey's whole

---

[1] *Cf.* P. Paris, *Romans de la Table Ronde*, ii. p. 105 *sqq.*; G. Paris, *Merlin*, Introd. i. p. xl. *sqq.*

[2] *Cf.* Rhŷs, *Studies*, p. 20 *sqq.* and the index. Also Dunlop's *Hist. of Fiction* (1888), i. p. 183, note; ii. p. 220, note. On the "black cross" mentioned on p. 181 of the romance, see P. Paris, *Romans*, i. 302.

[3] *Studies in the Arthurian Legend*, p. 14. *Cf.* also Malory's *Morte Darthur*, iv. 18; vii. 15, 17; xviii. 3; xx. 21. For Gawain's part in the story of the Grail, see Nutt's *Studies*, Index I.

account of Guanhumara tallies hardly at all with the account in the *Book of Arthur* and in the other romances, to say nothing of the Celtic sources.[1]

2. As for Leodegan, I can throw no light on the origin of the story of his wars with Rion. Malory touches lightly upon Leodegan (i. 17, 18; iii. 1), but tells us little about the conflicts with Rion. Still, both Leodegan and Rion play too large a part in the romances to allow us to count them as mere figments of the imagination. With Rion is connected the old story of the mantle fringed with beards. The essential outlines of this incident are found in Geoffrey's *Historia*, x. 3, where Arthur, after overcoming the giant of Mt. St. Michel, says that he had found none so strong since he had killed the giant Ritho on Mt. Aravius. In our romance (p. 649) we read that "neuer hadde thei seyn so grete a feende," and on p. 649 we find no mention of Ritho. Malory also omits the name, and makes Arthur say: "This was the fyerst gyaunt that euer I mette with / saue one in the mount of Arabe / whiche I ouercame / but this was gretter and fyerser" (*Le Morte Darthur*, v. 5).

Ritho had made furs for himself of the beards of the kings he had killed, and he offered to give Arthur's beard the most prominent place. We have in our romance two accounts[2] of this mantle, with characteristic differences. In the first (p. 115), we are told that Rion had conquered twenty crowned kings, and made a mantle of their beards, and that he had sworn not to cease till he had conquered thirty kings. According to the second account (pp. 619, 620), he had flayed off the beards of nine kings, and he now wanted Arthur's beard for

---

[1] For some account of the Celtic sources see Rhŷs, *Studies in the Arthurian Legend*, ch. ii., especially p. 38, and the whole of ch. iii., "Gwenhwyvar and her Captors."

[2] At the beginning of the French romance *Li Chevaliers as deus espees* occurs the incident of the demanding of Arthur's beard by King Ris. *Cf.* also *Laȝamon* (ed. Madden), iii. p. 398.

the tassels.   In Geoffrey, Ritho is a giant; and in our romance Rion is called "kynge of the londe of Geauntes and of the londe of pastures" (p. 114).   Later, he is called king of Ireland (pp. 175, 208); king of Denmark and Ireland (p. 228); king of "Denmarke and Islonde" (p. 327); king of the Isles (p. 619); and lord of all the west (p. 620).

In the romance of *Arthur*, as outlined by Dunlop (*Hist. of Fiction*, 1888, vol. i. p. 224), we read that Laodogant "had been attacked by King Ryon, a man of a disposition so malevolent that he had formed to himself a project of possessing a mautle furred with the beards of those kings he should conquer.   He had calculated with the grand-master of his wardrobe that a full royal cloak would require forty beards: he had already vanquished five kings, and reckoned on a sixth beard from the chin of Laodogant.   Arthur and his knights totally deranged this calculation by defeating King Ryon.   Laodogant, in return for the assistance he had received, offered his daughter, the celebrated Geneura, in marriage to Arthur.   Merlin, however, who does not appear to have been a flattering courtier, and who does not seem to have attached to the conservation of Laodogant's beard the importance that it merited, declared that his master must first deserve the princess."

San-Marte pointed out a Celtic legend in which King Rion and his mantle are referred to.[1]

3. Most of the other incidents of the chapter are evident inventions or combinations.   The details of the battles are much the same throughout the romance, and call for no especial attention.   The second Gonnore seems to be a mere variant of the first, and to owe her existence to the ingenuity of the romancer.[2]

---

[1] *Beiträge zur bretonischen . . . . Heldensage*, p. 60.   For the rôle of Rion in the Huth *Merlin* see G. Paris, *Introd.* i. p. lxvi.

[2] *Cf.* also P. Paris, *Romans de la Table Ronde*, ii. 141.

It may, perhaps, be going too far to see in the substitution of the false Gonnore for the queen a recollection of the legend of Charlemagne's mother, Berte, whose place was usurped, as the story goes, by her servant Aliste; but there is considerable similarity in the two accounts. (*Cf.* L. Gautier, *Chanson de Roland*, p. 357; Dunlop's *Hist. of Fiction*, revised edition, ii. p. 446.)

4. By the reference to the Holy Grail (p. 229) we are taken into another cycle of legend; while the introduction of the nephew of the Emperor of Constantinople (p. 230, *cf.* p. 186) is one of several proofs of the influence of oriental material on our romance.[1] This young man figures in many other Arthurian romances.

CHAPTER XV.

For this chapter we can scarcely hope to find a definite source. The actual wars with the Saxons doubtless gave rise to Celtic traditions which were handed on with endless permutations of essentially the same incidents; but the general similarity of the various battles warns us not to look for the source of more than an occasional name or incident.[2]

CHAPTERS XVI., XVII, XVIII.

In these chapters we find a host of easily manufactured incidents, of which I can cite but a few. Seigramor is again brought in (p. 259), but no especially striking motive is introduced. On p. 262 *sqq.* Merlin appears in the guise of an old man. This transformation may be compared with that in Robert de Borron's *Merlin* (p. 72). On p. 263, the old man calls Gawain a coward. The same incident in another

---

[1] For the Saigremors who appears in Chrestien's *Conte du Graal* and in other legends of the *Grail*, see Nutt's *Studies*, Index I.

[2] *Cf.* the conversation of Ewein with that of Gawain in chap. xii.

form reappears a little later (p. 297). Other parallels suggest themselves, as, for example, p. 279, where Merlin appears disguised as a churl, much the same as on p. 167.

Chapter XIX.

1. In this chapter the romancer doubtless makes use of older materials, considerably modified to suit his needs. The prophecies (p. 304 *sqq.*) seem to have been suggested by the similar prophecies of Geoffrey's *Historia*, book vii.

2. The meeting of Merlin and Nimiane is here detailed in a form that does not recur in the other romances. As is well known, Malory (iv. 1) identifies the maiden whom Merlin loved with one of the ladies of the lake. Her name appears in various forms, easily explicable when one takes account of the confusion in the MSS. of the letters *u* and *n* and *m*. The original Celtic character underwent a variety of transformations at the hands of the romancers, who combined and differentiated the original legends with little regard for consistency. We may be somewhat surprised to find Rhŷs identifying Nimiane with Morgain le Fee, but of the justice of this there can be little question.[1]

As for the wonders[2] that Merlin performs before Nimiane,

---

[1] *Cf.* G. Paris, *Merlin*, Introd. p. lxv. Rhŷs, *Studies in the Arthurian Legend*, pp. 284, 348, compares Nimiane with Rhiannon, wife of PwyH. *Cf.* also Nutt's *Studies on the Legend of the Holy Grail*, p. 232, my discussion of the *Vita Merlini*, and Sommer's *Morte Darthur*, vol. iii. p. 117 *sqq.* *Cf.* also Grimm, *Deutsche Mythologie* (4th ed.), pp. 342, 533, 685; n. 117, 128; Dunlop's *Hist. of Fiction* (1888), i. 186, note.

[2] " Manni, in his *Ist. del Decam.* ii. 97, cites an anonymous MS. where it is said that Boccaccio's story [of a garden produced by enchantment: *Decam.* Giorn. x.] is found in a collection much older than his time, and adds that Giovanni Tritemio relates how a Jewish physician, in the year 876, caused by enchantment a splendid garden to appear, with trees and flowers in full bloom, in mid-winter. A similar exploit is credited to Albertus Magnus in the thirteenth century. The notion seems to have been brought to Europe from the East, where stories of saints, dervishes, or jogis performing such wonders have been common time out of mind."—*Originals and Analogues of some of Chaucer's Canterbury Tales*, part iv. (1886), p. 332, note.

they belong to the familiar tricks of the mediaeval 'tregetours,' referred to by Chaucer in the *House of Fame*, book iii., and in the *Frankeleyns Tale*.[1]

CHAPTER XX.

1. This chapter affords scarcely any really new material; for the interminable details of the hand-to-hand conflicts are essentially repetitions, with slight increment, of the details of the preceding battles.

2. Merlin's prophecies here deserve as little attention as the prophecies of the preceding chapter. Guyomar is a disguised form of "Guigemar for Guihomarc[h]us."[2] He is here introduced (p. 316) for the first time, but he reappears later in the story (p. 507 *sqq.*).

3. The account of Nascien (pp. 326, 327) borrows hints from the Grail legend.[3]

4. Merlin's enchantments are of a piece with those in the previous battles. The pretty little scene where Gonnore arms her lover Arthur (pp. 322, 323) is probably the invention of the romancer; as is also the scene where King Leodegan falls on his knee before his steward Cleodalis, and asks pardon for the wrongs he has committed against him.

CHAPTER XXI.

1. The chapter opens with the enchantments of Guynebans (pp. 361–363), which are essentially the same as those of Merlin[4] (p. 309). Here, as elsewhere, the romancer returns several times upon his tracks.

---

[1] *Cf.* also Warton's *Hist. of Eng. Poetry*, sec. xv.

[2] Rhŷs. *Studies*, p. 394.

[3] Cf. *ibid.* pp. 320–322; Nutt, *Studies on the Legend of the Holy Grail*, Index I.

[4] *Cf.* P. Paris, *Romans de la Table Ronde*, ii. 199. These marvels do not differ widely from those which an old man recounts to Lancelot after he has left the Château des Mares and gone to the Forêt Perdue (*ibid.* v. 311).

2. A considerable part of the chapter is devoted to the invented details of battles; but the finding of the treasure (p. 370), and the meeting of Arthur with Gawain and the children (p. 371 *sqq.*), may go back to a somewhat older account. Of course, there is nothing especially striking in any of these incidents; but Gawain is the theme of such a multitude of traditions, some of which are certainly Celtic, that we make no improbable supposition in thinking that the tradition is in this case older than the romance.

Chapter XXII.

This chapter appears to contain little else than mere padding. There is the same familiar fighting, there are the usual enchantments by Merlin, the same fiery dragon (pp. 393, 406), but new motives are conspicuously absent. The introduction of the Romans anticipates the more striking account in chap. xxxii., which follows with considerable variation Geoffrey of Monmouth's story of the battles of Arthur with the Romans.

Chapter XXIII.

This chapter contains three leading incidents—the dreams of King Ban and his wife; Merlin's visit to his love; and, lastly, the dream of Julius Caesar, Emperor of Rome, with the adventures of Grisandol.

1. The motive of the first set of dreams is familiar enough to warrant us in regarding them as inventions of the redactor.

2. Merlin's visit to his love possesses the mysterious charm that appears everywhere in Celtic legend; and I cannot help believing that this incident is essentially of Celtic origin, though I can find no earlier version than in the *Merlin*.

3. The last incident appears to combine a variety of different elements. In the appearance of Merlin as a savage we have, perhaps, a lingering tradition originally relating to Myrddin the Bard. In the repeated laughs of Merlin we have reproduced in varied form motives appearing in chap. ii. Merlin's laugh when brought before the Emperor of Rome (p. 432) [1] parallels the third laugh of Merlin in the romance of *Arthour and Merlin*; only there it is Vortigern who takes the place of the Emperor, and the setting is different. We may compare, too, the somewhat similar incident in the *Vita Merlini* (ll. 253–294). Merlin is taken and bound. Suddenly he laughs as the queen passes through the hall, and the king picks a leaf out of her hair; but the bard refuses to tell why he has laughed unless he is set at liberty. Rodarchus orders it to be done. Then Merlin explains that the king is more faithful to the queen than she to him. [2]

One motive of the incident of the twelve disguised chamberlains appears in a modified form in the *Roman des Sept Sages*, but the hint was probably borrowed from the *Merlin*. [3]

---

[1] It is interesting to find Merlin giving a new account of his birth to the Emperor. His mother lost her way in the forest of "Brocheland," and a savage man came to her. She bore a child, who was baptized (p. 428).

[2] *Cf.* Uhland's ballad on *Merlin der Wilde*, in which a king's daughter is the guilty one, instead of the queen.

[3] M. Gaston Paris (*Roman des Sept Sages de Rome*, Introd. pp. xxxvii., xxxviii.) remarks on this incident—"Quant au dénouement de ce long drame à tiroirs, le traducteur a cru le rendre plus intéressant et plus moral en ajoutant à la faute de l'impératrice envers son beau-fils un autre crime, son adultère habituel avec un *ribaud* habillé en femme. Le fonds de cette addition malencontreuse n'est pas d'ailleurs de son invention : il la prise dans le roman de *Merlin*, en l'adoucissant toutefois un peu ; car ce n'est pas un seul *ribaud* que Merlin sait découvrir parmi les femmes de l'épouse de Jules-César, ce sont les douze chambrières de l'impératrice qui sont des hommes travestis." M. Paris adds in a footnote—"Voyez sur ce recit et les rapprochements auxquels il prête les articles de MM. Liebrecht et Benfey, *Orient und Occident*, t. i. p. 341. etc. Cette histoire a passé, sous forme de nouvelle, dans le recueil de Nicolas de Troyes, le *Grand Parangon des nouvelles nouvelles*, où elle est la cxxiv^e du second volume, le seul conservé. Mabille ne la pas admise dans le choix qu'il a publié dans la Bibliothèque elzévirienne (1869) ; mais

CHAPTER XXIV.

All the incidents of this chapter appear to be invented; but the names recur elsewhere than in the *Merlin*.

CHAPTER XXV.

1. The central incident of this chapter is the marriage of Arthur with Gonnore. There is little to add to what has been already remarked. The original hint is, of course, taken from Geoffrey of Monmouth (ix. 9). In Geoffrey's account Arthur marries Guanhamara after he has subdued the Saxons, and he is not crowned till after all his conquests that occur before the war with the Romans.

2. As an instance of the habit of the romancers to make a motive go as far as possible, we may note that in the tournament at Toraise, after Arthur's marriage, Gawain lays about him with a spar of oak, and stops only when Merlin tells him he has done enough (p. 461). In the tournament at Logres, Gawain repeats the same performance with an apple-tree club (p. 493).[1]

3. The story of the false Gonnore is in its details the invention of the romancer, but some of the material is doubtless not due to him. We find that the trouble which

il l'avait imprimée dans une première publication, parue à Bruxelles et Paris in 1862 ; elle y porte le nº lxii. : c'est un extrait textuel du roman." *Cf.* also P. Paris, *Romans de la Table Ronde*, ii. 44 ; Dunlop's *Hist. of Fiction* (1888), i. 459–461 ; Meyer, *Indogermanische Mythen*, i. 153, 154. A. Vesselovsky has attempted to show that " the whole legend of Merlin is based upon the apocryphal history of Solomon "[a] and Martolf, but the case cannot be said to be made out, although there are undoubted parallels at more than one point.

     [a] See Dunlop's *Hist. of Fiction* (1888), i. p. 457.

[1] *Cf.* P. Paris, *Romans*, ii. 256. *Cf.* also the story of Eldol, Geoffrey's *Hist.* vi. 16, and *Havelok*, ll. 1968, 1969—

         " Havelok grop þe dore-tre,
         And [at] a dint he slow hem þre."

the false Gonnore made for the Queen is related in *Lancelot*,[1] where is recounted the banishment of Gonnore[2] and the story of Bertelak. The putting of Britain under an interdict, as well as the malady of the false Gonnore, is touched upon (iv. 191). How old the story is, may not be easy to determine, but it seems to be in its essentials older than the *Book of Arthur*.

CHAPTER XXVI.

In this chapter there appears to be very little but invention. But at the very beginning (pp. 470, 471) is the banishment of Bertelak, just referred to; and on p. 484 is the admirable portrait of Dagenet the Fool (pp. 483, 484), who seems to be an old type. One may easily suspect that the romancer was drawing this character from life.

CHAPTER XXVII.

1. The references at the beginning of this chapter to the Holy Grail may be left for explanation to those who have traced the origin of that legend.

2. The leading theme of the chapter is the mission of King Loth and his four sons to the rebel kings.[3] In Bib. Nat. MS. fr. 337 the account runs parallel with our version as far as p. 509, l. 7. After that point the French version that is followed by the English translator seems to be almost entirely independent of the version in MS. 337. We may suppose that the later redactor drew freely upon his imagination for details, though he possibly had an older account to

---

[1] For convenient reference see the Analysis by P. Paris, *Romans de la Table Ronde*, iv. p. 97 *sqq.* and pp. 148–175.

[2] *Ibid.* iv. p. 147.

[3] We may note that in our version the message of Loth to King Clarion is delivered through Mynoras. This feature does not appear in some of the French MSS. *Cf.* P. Paris, *Romans*, ii. 275.

guide him in the general course of the story. To follow out the details is quite beyond my purpose.

3. In the references to Pelles and his son (p. 520 *sqq.*) we are again taken into the Grail cycle.[1]

4. For an account of Morgain the reader is referred to chap. xix.

CHAPTERS XXVIII, XXIX.

1. These chapters are filled almost entirely with invented details, playing upon material much older than our romance. Gawain—the Walgan of Geoffrey of Monmouth—here assumes especial prominence, and this he keeps till the close of the romance.

2. The mysterious rubbish uttered by Merlin to Blase (p. 563) affords a not too distant parallel to Merlin's prophecies in Geoffrey's *Historia*, book vii.; while the ideal which Merlin sets up for the knight who is to achieve a great work—that he be chaste and the best knight in the world—is the leading motive of the *Quest of the Holy Grail*.

3. The account of Elizer, son of King Pelles of Lytenoys, and " nevewe to the kynge pellenor and to the kynge Alain " (p. 583), takes us again into the Grail cycle.[2]

CHAPTER XXX.

The adventure of Ban and Bors at the castle of Agravadain (again taken up in chap. xxxiii. pp. 671–675), while hardly fit for a drawing-room story, is certainly related in most decorous style. The exact source is doubtful, though in the mediation of Merlin, in the use of enchantment, and in the innocence of the maiden, there is at least a reminder of

---

[1] *Cf.* Rhŷs, *Studies in the Arthurian Legend*, chap. xii.; Nutt, *Studies on the Legend of the Holy Grail*, Index, i.; P. Paris, *Romans*, iii. 295, 296.

[2] On the confusion of the genealogies see P. Paris, *Romans*, ii. 278.

the amour of Uter with Ygerne. In certain slight particulars there is a parallel to this incident in the *Chevalier au Lyon* of Chrestien de Troyes. Very possibly the incident in the *Book of Arthur* is borrowed from the *Lancelot*, for we read (p. 610, l. 24) that the "maiden hadde conceyved a sone, of whom launcelot after hadde grete ioye and honour for the bounte and Chiualrie that was in him." We may note, too, that in the *Book of Agravain*, towards the end of the *Lancelot*, we have a somewhat similar incident, though with widely different details. Lancelot is overcome by a philtre, and passes the night with Helene, daughter of King Pelles, supposing her to be the queen Guenever. The old Brisane, governess of the princess, is the go-between, and the child afterwards born is Galahad.[1]

CHAPTER XXXI.

Nothing in this chapter calls for especial attention, except the story of King Rion, which has been already discussed (chap. xiv.). Merlin's various disguises really introduce no new motive, though the account of Merlin as a harper (p. 615) is one of the most beautiful bits of description in the entire romance (*cf.* p. 294).

CHAPTER XXXII.

1. On the vision of Flualis, P. Paris remarks[2] that it contains nothing Welsh or Breton. The "arrangers" found the story, he thinks, in some special *lai*, and united it as well as they could with the main recital. There is no evidence

---

[1] *Cf.* also Rhŷs, *Studies in the Arthurian Legend*, p. 146; Malory, xi. 2; and P. Paris, *Romans de la Table Ronde*, v. 309, 324, 325. *Cf.* an article on the Scottish romance of Roswall and Lillian in *Engl. Studien*, xvii. p. 352, where a somewhat similar story is told as a South Slavonic legend.

[2] *Romans*, ii. 329.

that the story was treated in a *lai*, though there can be no question that the vision is not the invention of the romancer.

2. Merlin's visit to Nimiane is another touch of the Celtic legend, which we find reappearing every now and then throughout the romance. What Merlin teaches Nimiane may be compared with what he teaches Morgain le Fee.

3. The interesting story of the maiden and the dwarf is not improbably older than the time of the composition of the *Book of Arthur*, but I cannot point out the original source.

4. The general course of the war with the Romans is evidently suggested by Geoffrey of Monmouth's *Historia* (ix. 15 to x. 13), though there are differences enough. It is not certain, however, that the redactor went directly to the Latin. Wace's *Brut* (l. 10,999) adds to Geoffrey's account the fact that, after the Emperor's letter is read, Arthur protects the messengers from the rage of the Britons. The same incident recurs in the English version (p. 640). On the other hand, the speeches by Hoel and Augusel, though reproduced by Wace, are here omitted, while Cador's is given.

5. Arthur's dream may be compared with that recounted by Geoffrey (x. 2).

6. The fight with the Giant of Mount St. Michel is much the same in Geoffrey (x. 3) and in the romance (pp. 645–649). Bedver accompanies Arthur in each case. The maiden is in each version the niece of Hoel. The romancer, then, borrowed the story more or less directly from Geoffrey, but Geoffrey is hardly to be regarded as the original inventor. Paulin Paris suggests[1] that the exact designation of the locality would seem to make credible a Breton origin for the legend; but that, on the other hand, the outlines of the story are in some respects similar to those of the legend of Cacus,[2] who was killed by Hercules—

---

[1] *Romans*, ii. 350, 351.

[2] *Cf.* Virgil, *Aeneid*, viii. 194-275 ; Ovid, *Fasti*, B. i.

(1) Cacus and the giant (in Geoffrey) both come from Spain.

(2) The flames that Cacus breathes correspond to the fires on the mountain.

(3) The bellowing of cattle shows where Cacus is; the cries of the nurse discover the giant.

(4) Both live at the top of a mountain.

(5) Both are blinded by a stroke of their enemy.

Not impossibly the somewhat forced resemblances just noted indicate a closer relationship of the two legends than appears to me probable. M. Paris also calls attention to M. Breal's study of the mythological origin of Cacus, and the possibility that an analogous tradition could have penetrated into several stories. The Celts, like the Etruscans, could have their giant, the scourge of the country, from which a hero would deliver them.[1]

7. In Geoffrey's *Historia* (x. 11) and in the romance, Walgan (Gawain) performs prodigies of valour, and at last kills the Emperor Lucius (*Merlin*, p. 663). Arthur sends the Emperor's body to Rome, with the taunt that such was the tribute that the Britons paid.[2]

CHAPTER XXXIII.

This final chapter contains a variety of incidents drawn from various sources.

1. The first incident is the very singular fight which King Arthur has with the great cat of the "Lac de Losane." Mr. Phillimore has suggested to me a possible Celtic source, but I must leave the investigation in that field to him and other Celtic specialists.

Through the courtesy of M. Paul Meyer, Director of the École des Chartes in Paris, my attention was directed to a

---

[1] *Cf.* also Rhŷs, *Studies in the Arthurian Legend*, p. 340.
[2] Geoffrey, *Hist.* x. 13 ; *Merlin*, p. 664.

short paper on this incident by Prof. F. Novati, of Milan, who very kindly sent me a copy.[1] The following is a translation :—

" In the *Merlin* we are told how King Arthur, after having conquered the Romans, instead of pushing on as far as Rome and renewing the glory of Berlinus and Brennus, followed the counsel of the prophet, and turned his attention towards freeing Gaul from a monster which spread terror in all the country about Lake Losanne.[2] This monster, this demon, was in fact nothing more than a simple cat, but the battle which the King sustained against him turned out to be more difficult and fierce than the battle with the giant ravisher of the niece of Hoel, Count of Brittany.[3]

" The battle of Arthur against the cat is described not only in the prose *Merlin*, but also in other texts. Thus, as G. Paris[4] has lately shown, it is referred to in a fragment of a German poem of the twelfth century, evidently drawn from a French source, which the editor has called *Manuel und Amande*,[5] from the name of the chief characters. The poet, after eulogizing warmly and in detail the valour of Arthur, apparently goes on to narrate his death, and tells us how the occasion of it had been a monster, which was a fish and at the same time had the form of a cat.[6] I say *apparently*, because the poem is quite obscure, and some verses are lacking.

" This same legend of the death of the valiant British sovereign in consequence of a struggle with a fish-cat (*gatto-pesce*) is

---

[1] Originally printed in the Proceedings of the Reale Accademia dei Lincei (Estratto dal vol. iv. 1º sem., serie 4ª, Rendiconti-Seduta del 20 maggio, 1883).

[2] P. Paris, *Les Romans de la Table Ronde*, ii. p. 358 *sqq.*

[3] *Ibid.* p. 362.

[4] *Les rom. en vers de la T. R.*, Paris, 1887, pp. 219, 220.

[5] Osw. Zingerle, *Manuel und Amande, Bruchstücke eines Artusromans*, in Zeitsch. für deutsch. Alth., N.F., xiv. p. 304, v. 151 *sqq.*

[6] " Daz sie iz fvr war wizzen,
Ein visch wurde vf gerizzen,
Daz der kunic sere engalt,
Als ein katze gestalt."—v. 155 *sqq.*

mentioned secondly by a Norman poet, who, however, animated by strong sympathy for England, is indignant at the story, and repudiates it as a fable invented by the French to throw ridicule on the beloved hero of Britain. The verses of André de Coutances have likewise been referred to by Paris, but they are worthy of being quoted entire—

> 'Il ont dit que riens n'a valu,
> Et donc à Arflet n'a chalu
> Que boté fu par Capalu
> Li reis Artu en la palu ;
>
> Et que le chat l'ocist de guerre,
> Puis passa outre en Engleterre,
> E ne fu pas lenz de conquerre,
> Ainz porta corone en la terre,
>
> E fu sire de la contrée.
> Où ont itel fable trovée ?
> Mençonge est, Dex le sot, provée
> Onc greignor ne fu encontrée.'[1]

"Paris seems inclined to believe that Capalu is the name of the portentous cat. If such be the case, he concludes, we have here the monster of the same name which appears in the *Bataille Loquifer*, and which has precisely the head of a cat, the feet of a dragon, the body of a horse, and the tail of a lion.[2]

"This identification of the cat of Losanne with Capalu, or Chapalu, which, however, Paris does not insist on strongly, raises in my opinion difficulties which are, or which seem to me to be, insurmountable. I believe, indeed, that André de Coutances, in the verses which I have quoted, alludes not

---

[1] A. Jubinal, *Nouv. Rec. de Contes, Dits, Fabliaux*, etc., t. ii. pp. 2, 3. *Le Romanz des Franceis* is the name of this little poem, composed about the beginning of the thirteenth century.

[2] Cf. *Hist. Littér. de la Fr.* t. xxii. p. 537 ; Nyrop-Gorra, *St. dell' Ep. Franc.* p. 143.

to one but to two stories, which if they were not invented by the French, as he seems to believe, were transformed and altered by them so as to ridicule the inhabitants of England by abasing Arthur. We have to do, then, with two adventures of Arthur, entirely independent of each other; with two battles undertaken against two different monsters, battles which had, however, the same disastrous results for the sovereign of Britain, since in the struggle with Chapalu he was worsted and was drowned in a marsh, and in that with the cat he lost his life. And that this is really the state of affairs, will become evident when we come to verify the difference between *Chapalu* and the cat of Losanne.

"If, as Paris saw clearly, the former is to be identified with the Chapalu of the *Bataille Loquifer*, it belongs to the category of fantastic monsters which result from the gathering together of members taken from various animals—to the family, that is, at the head of which is the chimaera. But the Cat of Losanne is something quite different. It is neither more nor less than a cat, but a cat which has attained dimensions far beyond those of ordinary cats, and is endowed with an extraordinary strength and a frightful ferocity. But how and why? We find this how and why described in the most satisfactory manner in a passage of Tristan de Nanteuil, in which the poet is pleased to explain to his hearers the superhuman strength which his hero possessed, and that not less wondrous strength with which the hind was endowed that had nourished him with her milk—

> ' Nourris furent d'un lait qui fut de tel maistrie,
> D'une seraine fut, sy com l'istoire crie.
> . Il est de tel vertu et de tel seignorie
> Que se beste en a beu elle devient fournye,
> Si grande et si poissant, nel tenés [à folye],
> Que nul ne dure à lui, tant ait chevallerie.

> Artus le nous aprouve, qui taut ot baronnye,
> Car au temps qu'i regna, pour voir le vous affie,
> Se combata au chat qu'alecta en sa vie
> Du let d'une seraine qui en mer fut peschie ;
> Mès le chat devint tel, ne vous mentiray mye,
> Que nuls homs ne duroit en la soye partie
> Qu'i ne meist affin, à duel et à hachie.
> Artus le conquesta par sa bachelerie,
> Mais ains l'acheta cher, sy con l'istoire crye.' [1]

"This passage from *Tristan de Nanteuil* is, then, of great interest for the solution of our little problem. It enables us, in fact, to dispel every doubt concerning the nature of the animal under whose claws perished the most valiant of kings, if we believe the legend preserved by the author of *Manuel und Amande* [2] and indignantly repudiated by André de Coutances. The multiform *Chapalu* of the *Bataille Loquifer* has no connection with this monstrous cat, which a fisherman has thoughtlessly nourished with the milk of a siren. In the second place the author of Tristan calls our attention to the fact that the primitive legend of Arthur and the Cat is quite different from that narrated in the *Merlin*, where the appearance of the demon cat is a visitation of the wrath of God, who wishes to punish a fisherman who had failed to

---

[1] P. Meyer, *Notice sur le roman de Tristan de Nanteuil* in Jahrb. für Rom. und Engl. Liter. ix. p. 11 ; and *cf.* p. 8, where the poet narrates at length how a siren suckled Tristan at sea, who on account of this nourishment became great as *un cheval de Chartage*. The idea of making Tristan and the hind drink the milk of the siren must have been suggested to the author by reading a romance of the Arthurian cycle, in which it was told that Arthur had come to blows with the cat, but had been able to conquer him. From this source he must also have drawn what he narrates of the first bloody deeds perpetrated by the hind on the fisherman who had received Tristan and on his family. The diabolical cat does the same thing in the *Merlin*. (P. Paris, *op. cit.* p. 360.)

[2] The ambiguous words of the German poet, who does not know whether the cat is a true cat or a fish resembling a cat, induce us to believe that in his source the event was narrated obscurely or too concisely.

fulfil his vow—a sufficiently heavy penalty for a rather light offence![1]

"That a British or French fisherman should find a siren in his nets will not surprise anyone who remembers how the classic temptresses of Ulysses had preserved their habit of alluring seamen, even in the Middle Ages. Gervase of Tilbury declares that they often appeared in the British Sea.[2] But neither Gervase nor other writers consulted by me say that the milk of the sirens had such prodigious virtue as is attributed to them in the story of the cat and of the hind who nursed Tristan. Perhaps others better versed than I in Bestiaries will succeed in finding some reference to the subject."

2. If we pass over the continuation of the stories of Agravadain and Flualis, we come to the wonderfully poetic legend of the magic imprisonment of Merlin.[3] The ground-work of this legend is probably Celtic, though we cannot

---

[1] "How the idea arose of making Losanne and the Mountain *of the Lake* the hiding-place of the cat, is unknown to me."—F. Novati.

[2] *Cf.* F. Liebrecht, *Des Gervas. von Tilbury Otia Imperialia*, p. 31.

[3] For a discussion of Malory's version see Sommer's *Studies on the Sources of the Morte Darthur*, iii. 127, 128.

As pointed out in the discussion of Malory's *Morte Darthur* (p. lxx., *ante*), the version there given differs from ours. The heading of book iv. chap. 1 reads—"How merlyn was affotted & dooted on one of the ladyes of the lake / and how he was fhytte in a rocke vnder a ftone and there deyed capitulo primo." Malory calls her "Nyneue."

In the romance of *Ysaie le Triste* the fairies "announced that they frequently resorted to the bush which confined the magician Merlin, with whom they had lately enjoyed a full conversation on the merits of different knights, and other important affairs of chivalry."—Dunlop, *Hist. of Fiction* (1888), i. pp. 213, 214.

"We are told in the romance of Lancelot du Lac, that Merlin was confined by his mistress in the forest of Darnant, 'qui marchoit a la mer de Cornouailles et a la mer de Sorelloys.'"—*Ibid.* i. p. 239.

In the *Ancient Scottish Prophecies* we learn that—
  "Meruelous Merling is wasted away
   With a wicked woman, woe might shee be ;
   For shee hath closed him in a Craige on Cornwel cost."
First printed 1503. Reprinted for Ballantyne Club, 1833, and by F. Michel, *Vita Merlini* (p. 80), 1837.

point definitely to an actual Celtic source. We find in a late Triad[1] a story of Merlin entering into the Glass House in Bardsey with his nine bards, bearing with them the thirteen treasures of Britain, and never being heard of afterwards.[2] We may compare, too, the passages in Plutarch (quoted in Rhŷs's *Studies*, p. 368): "Moreover, there is there [around Britain], they said, an island in which Chronus is imprisoned with Briareus, keeping guard over him as he sleeps; for, as they put it, sleep is the bond forged for Chronus." Nimiane's persistent teasing finds its parallel in the story of Samson and Delilah, but we can easily make too much of such resemblances.[3]

3. The remainder of the chapter doubtless rests in part upon older recitals; but in its present form the conclusion is the work of the redactors. As already noted, the conclusion of the romance is differently given in Bib. Nat. MS. fr. 98 (which appends the Prophecies), and in the printed edition of 1498. The material of the romance was very flexible in the hands of the remodellers. Very probably they would have been more puzzled than we to give an account of their sources. No doubt the conclusion was modified by the *Lancelot*, which is frequently placed in the manuscripts directly after the *Merlin*.

---

[1] See p. c., *ante*.

[2] Rhŷs, *Studies*, p. 354.

[3] Brunetto Latino, in his *Li Livres dou Trésor* (pub. by Chabaille, Paris, 1862), mentions prophecies of Merlin, and he evidently knew Geoffrey of Monmouth. Aristotle, he says, was betrayed by woman's wiles, like Merlin. Quoted in *Jahrbücher für Philologie und Paedogogik*, vol. xcii. pp. 283 and 290.

X.

THE LITERARY VALUE OF THE *MERLIN*.

WE have seen that the English *Merlin* is nothing but a close
and almost servile translation of the French *Merlin ordinaire*.
Consequently, the only thing for which the unknown maker
of the English version can be held responsible is the quality
of his translation. The real criticism of the *Merlin* as a work
of literary art must be directed to the French original.

Our investigation of the manuscripts and of the sources has
shown that the French *Merlin* is made up of a variety of
originally unrelated parts, of very unequal merit. To estimate
the *Merlin* accurately, we should, therefore, have to disentangle
out of the congeries of romances the several elements, and look
at them separately. If we deal with the completed romance,
we simply have to consider the work as it left the hands of
the compilers and arrangers. The defects lie on the surface.
The romance is a model of nearly all the faults of construction
so lavishly exhibited in most of the mediaeval prose romances.
According to nineteenth-century notions, the story is intolerably
long and prolix. We are treated to far too many incidents
of the same sort. We yawn in the midst of the confused
and painfully circumstantial battles, as we learn for the
hundredth time that Arthur, or Gawain, or Loth, slit some
one to the teeth, and are credibly assured that there were
shouts "and stour and ffull grete crakke, and noyse ther was
of brekynge of speres, and stif strokes of swerdes vpon helmes."
Of course, elements much the same almost necessarily entered
into all descriptions of mediaeval battles, but that is scarcely
an excuse for spreading the account over scores of pages.
In the *Merlin* as we now have it, perspective and proportion

are entirely disregarded. The story is not an organic whole, in which a germinal motive is developed with logical sequence, and made to control the action of the collective mass : it is rather a loose and inartistic combination of fragments essentially unrelated. Many of the episodes might be dropped altogether, without causing the slightest break in the narrative. Some of these episodes, we must admit, are in themselves interesting, but they stand in no organic relation to the romance as a whole. In other words, there is little or no plot in our sense of that term. The *Merlin* proper—which occupies the first seventh of the romance—is, indeed, simple and reasonably definite in its aim. The beginning is dramatic and impressive, and the conclusion has a poetic beauty felt by every reader. We lose sight of Merlin before the coronation of Arthur ; but we may suppose—if we assume the prose *Perceval* to be based on the work of Robert de Borron—that the author imagined he had given sufficient prominence to Merlin by introducing him again in the *Perceval* immediately after the coronation. What Robert had further to tell he narrated in the modest limits which he assigned to the *Perceval*, the original continuation of the versified romance of *Merlin*. When, however, the original continuation was discarded by the later prose romancers, loose rein was given to invention and unintelligent combination.

The framework borrowed from Geoffrey of Monmouth was itself loose enough to admit of any amount of insertion and omission. Naturally enough, we are puzzled to decide who is really the hero of the last six hundred pages. Merlin is plainly the centre of interest in the first hundred pages ; but after that point we lose sight of Merlin altogether, except at comparatively rare intervals. He is the *deus ex machina* who descends to extricate some one whom the romancer would not willingly let die, but he is by no means the character to whom our attention is steadily directed. Our interest is demanded for Arthur and his friends, for Gawain and his circle, for King Loth and his sons, and numerous other characters.

No principle of subordination or of proportion of parts appears to have guided the romancers. The story runs on according to its own sweet will, or, rather, according to the sweet will of the various literary blunderers who put their hands to the work. As far as we can see, it might run on for ever by the easy process of multiplying the battles and borrowing incidents wherever found unclaimed. There are, of course, passages of rare beauty from the mysterious legend of Merlin, which in a certain nameless charm are scarcely surpassed in the whole range of mediaeval romance. But these are buried under a mass of rubbish as formless and unattractive as rubbish can well be, even in a mediaeval romance. We need not, however, imagine that the romancers were seriously distressed at the thought that their additions to the story might be incongruous. The artistic sense in most of the mediaeval story-tellers was sadly awry. They seem to have regarded it as a literary crime to leave the most trivial detail to the imagination of the reader. We may admit freely the beauty of all the passages that anyone wishes to select, but we shall have to confess that we at last weary a little of the endless and desultory babbling of a story-teller, who, to borrow Trollope's phrase, writes because he has to tell a story rather than because he has a story to tell. The materials of the *Merlin* might have been wrought into a tragedy of wonderful power and beauty; but the lack of artistic grouping allows the fragments to sweep along confusedly, like blocks of drift-ice in a river. All are moving in one general direction, but they are not bound together by any laws of connection.

An almost necessary consequence of this looseness of plot is the abruptness of transition. The favourite formula is—

"But now resteth to speke of hem at this time and telleth of King Arthur," or Gonnore, or Gawain, or anyone else that the whim of the romancer suggests. Paulin Paris commended this feature as indicating progress in the art of narration, but I question whether most readers will share his pleasure.

It follows from what has been urged, that we must lay aside all hope of discovering in the *Merlin* any underlying moral purpose. The story is not made to prove any doctrine of religion, or morals, or politics. All of the characters are assumed to be good Catholics, unless they are specifically mentioned as heathen or Saracens. Their morals are tolerably decent, according to the standards of the time; and occasionally we even get an incidental bit of moral suggestion. But the fact which most strikes a careful reader is, that the character of Merlin has not altogether improved in the slipshod process of development followed in the romance. The dignity of the boy-prophet, as he summons the trembling counsellors and expounds easily what had baffled the clerks, compels a certain sort of admiration. Even when he participates in the plot which results in the birth of Arthur, we look upon him as a grave and judicious adviser. But after the coronation of Arthur, though Merlin still plays the rôle of sage and prophet, and figures in more than one scene full of a strange beauty, we cannot but feel that he is too often degraded to the level of the mountebank and the juggler.

As we read the romance we cannot but be impressed with the fact that most of the characters are unskilfully drawn. The old romancers seem to have been able to imagine but one trait of character at a time, and they display a signal inability to follow out a complicated analysis. The natural result is a remarkable similarity and conventionality in the figures that crowd the page. Instead of delineating the characters by a combination of fine touches, the romancers lay on the colours in broad lines, with little or no attempt at artistic discrimination. The characters are not developed as in Shakspere's plays and in the best modern novels, but are presented about as complete at the beginning of the romance as at the end. Some characters almost appear to have been invented for the express purpose of giving sufficient exercise in the use of the superlative.

That this method of treatment is painfully superficial and external, needs no proof; but it is the method of the *Merlin*. It is, indeed, a striking fact that, although the romance contains much that is mysterious, it contains little that is really profound. The story is a singular mixture of the plain and simple and of the dark and mysterious. The knights and ladies discuss little except love and chivalry and war, and the passing questions of the day. They seem to have troubled themselves scarcely at all with such great problems of life as meet us in the novels of George Eliot, and there is little reason why they should. Theirs was an age of faith, and they did not have to grope in darkness and doubt. Their passions were the simple elementary passions of love, hate, jealousy. Their virtues were the simple virtues of bravery, sincerity, courtesy, generosity. We are almost led to think, therefore, because we are told so much about these men and women, and their characters are apparently so transparent, that we know them; but we never succeed in lifting the veil that hides their inner lives. We catch glimpses now and then of a background of mystery in the strange life of Merlin—most of all when we see the magic spell stealing upon him as gently as music breathes across a bank of violets—but even then we are not allowed to gaze into the depths of the great magician's heart; and we close the book with the feeling that between us and the men and women of the romance is a great gulf fixed, which we must cross before we can know them as they are.

We have sufficiently dealt with the more serious faults in the *Merlin*. We may now bestow a word upon the literary style of the romancers who pieced together the story. Here, too, their work is faulty enough. They have not yet learned how to write a neat and well-balanced prose. Their sentences lack unity; their pronouns have a bewildering vagueness of reference; their paragraphs lack movement and artistic balance. The connection is of the loosest sort, and is helped out by an excessive use of the conjunction *and*. Yet the style at times has a grace and harmony, as well as an air of distinction, not unworthy of the aristocratic circle for which the romance was intended. Even the amorous adventures are related in a tone of high breeding that relieves the artistic conscience, if not the moral sense. Some of the descriptions are charmingly poetic, and are ablaze with light and colour. There is, indeed, a touch of conventionality in many of the descriptions of natural scenery, but even here the mediaeval *naïveté* lends a freshness and beauty that are always engaging. Vivacity is secured by frequent dialogue. Then, too, the air of verisimilitude is almost perfect. Detail is heaped upon detail, until the realistic effect is irresistible. We may feel that the art is defective, but we must admit that art itself cannot make the narrative seem more real.

We may find still other excuses for the *Merlin*. We have been testing the romance by the literary standards of the nineteenth century. If, however, we judge it by the literary standards of seven centuries ago, we ought perhaps to soften our criticism of more than one passage that now seems insufferably tedious. In those days of few books most readers were doubtless glad to have the story drawn out as far as possible. Even the accounts of the battles, which no one now reads except the editor, the printer, and the proof-reader, may have been among the most valued portions of the work. We may thus develop a spirit of charitable judgment otherwise quite beyond us. And yet, in our most charitable moments we may hesitate to believe that the *Merlin* was accepted as a finished specimen of literary art even in the Middle Ages: an age that possessed the work of Chrestien de Troyes and Walter Map was not so devoid of literary sense as to be unaware of the more glaring defects of such a composite romance as the *Merlin*.

Considered as a picture of chivalry the *Merlin* has for us a permanent value. It gives us more than one vivid glimpse of the every-day life of the period to which it belongs. The deeds of Arthur and his knights are transferred to the time of chivalry, and illuminated with all the light and colour of that picturesque age. If we count this of small importance, we can take some satisfaction that in the *Merlin* we have a book of the deepest interest to the Europe of six or seven centuries ago, and that as we read we can imagine more clearly the ideals of an age profoundly important in the development of our modern civilization.

As regards the work of the English translator, we have, perhaps, sufficiently touched upon that in our study of the manuscripts. Most of his translation is a mechanical jog-trot that follows every turn of the original. He freely uses French terms, and transfers French constructions, and even entire French sentences, to the English page. His sentences are in the main the sentences of the original, with all their faults of confusion and overcrowding. Yet the style has numerous distinct excellences. The diction is often direct and vigorous, and invariably escapes the turgid inflation so characteristic of English prose a little more than a century later. The period to which the translation belongs was singularly barren in works of creative imagination, and could not very consistently have made unfavourable reflections upon the unknown scholar who toiled through the heavy task. His achievement is hardly worthy to be placed beside the masterpiece of Malory; but it has an interest all its own, and it may well be valued as a not insignificant monument of old English prose.

XI.

The English manuscript from which the prose romance is printed, is described in the "Advertisement" to Part i. of the *Merlin* (E.E.T.S. Lond. 1865). A fragment of another version is contained in a single folio leaf of a fifteenth-century paper manuscript in the Bodleian Library at Oxford. The passage corresponds to p. 315, l. 15 to p. 317, l. 24. Kölbing gives the variants, and decides that the Oxford fragment cannot be a copy of the Cambridge MS.[1]

I find also in the Catalogue of the Ashmolean MSS. (802 : 4), Oxford, the following notice of a manuscript of *Merlin* contained "In a collection of Apocryphal tracts, genealogical and heraldic collections, astrological observations, and miscellaneous ; by Simon Forman, M.D." : — "The first 32 chapters of a Romance of the life of Merlin, beginning thus: 'The Parliament and consultation of the Devils, and their decree about the begetting of Merlin, about the year of Christ 445.'" (Fo. 66–82.) The last is thus entitled : "Cap. 32. How Merlin told the Hermit who was his father, and entreated him to write this book of his life and others of his works that should follow, and how the Hermit Blase did conjure him by the name of God, being much afeared of him."[2] (Fo. 81 *b*.) "Forman designed to write Cap. 33, but left this copy unfinished, and seven blank leaves follow." (*Catal.* p. 443).

---

[1] *Altenglische Bibl.* iv. p. xxi.

[2] I have modernized the spelling, as I suspect that I did not verify my transcript at the time I made it.

ADDITIONAL NOTES.

It may be proper to observe that pages I to CL have been in print since the summer of 1892. Hence the changes that have been made in those pages are only such as could be made without too great a disturbance of the text. In the remainder of the book, notice has been taken of the more important recent literature on the Merlin legend. This appears chiefly in Section VIII.

I take this opportunity to express my renewed thanks to Mr. H. L. D. Ward for his great kindness in going through the proof-sheets and making several valuable suggestions.

p. XIII. 1893. Zimmer, H.—Nennius Vindicatus, Berlin. A masterly work.

p. XIII. 1893. Ward, H. L. D.—Lailoken (or Merlin Silvester), *Romania*, 1893, pp. 504-526.—This article I have been able to use in Section VIII. as it was passing through the press.

p. XIII. 1894. Richter, G.—Beiträge zur Erklärung und Textkritik des mittelenglischen Prosaromans von Merlin, Erste Hälfte. (Diss.) Altenburg, 1894. Reprinted in *Englische Studien*, xx. pp. 347-377.—The author attempts a critical reconstruction of the English text of our romance by the aid of the French version. The work is so carefully done that one can only regret that it rests for the most part upon a late print of the French text (1528), rather than upon the MSS.

p. XIII. 1894. Sommer, H. O.—Le Roman de Merlin. London.—This edition of the French *Roman de Merlin* is a reproduction in ordinary type of the British Museum MS. Add. 10,292. This book was not accessible to me until after my entire discussion was in print and the "revise" had been returned to the printers. The editor describes the MS. fully, gives its history, and prints a table indicating the relation of the Arthurian MSS. in the British Museum to MSS. Add. 10,292-10,294. His discussion of the text is very brief, and touches only the salient points connected with its development. On p. xxvi., note, he calls attention to a MS. of *Merlin* not mentioned in Ward's *Catalogue of Romances*. This is Add. 32,125 in the British Museum, dating from the beginning of the fourteenth century. It contains the *Saint Graal* ("complete save as to one leaf") and the *Merlin*. Sommer remarks that this MS. "is as valuable and interesting as No. 747 of the Bibliothèque Nationale, but the latter is better written."

p. XIII. 1894. Lloyd, J. E.—Myrddin Wyllt in *Dict. of Nat. Biog.*, vol. xl. pp. 13, 14.

p. XIII. 1894. Maccallum, M. W.—Tennyson's Idylls of the King and Arthurian Story from the Sixteenth Century. New York. A popularly-written book touching on several matters relating to the use of the Merlin legend in literature.

p. xiii. 1894. Kingsford, C. L.—Merlin Ambrosius or Myrddin Emrys in *Dict. of Nat. Biog.*, vol. xxxvii. pp. 285–288.—This article mentions a long life of Merlin in Leland's *Commentarii de Scriptoribus*, pp. 42–48, and a paper by M. Darbois de Jubainville on "Merlin est-il un personnage réel?" in the *Revue des questions historiques*, v. 559–568.

p. xiii. 1895. Wechssler, Edward.—Über die verschiedenen Redaktionen des Robert von Borron zugeschriebenen Graal-Lancelot-Cyclus. Halle a S. pp. 64. —This is an important contribution to the study of the relations of the groups of romances to one another, but it comes too late for me to make use of it. The reader should note the favourable review of this paper by Gaston Paris in the *Romania* for July, 1895, pp. 472–475.

p. xlv. note 1. *For* i. 86 *read* p. xcvi.

p. xlvii. note 3. *For* Völlmöller *read* Vollmöller.

p. li. Lamartine tells a story in his sketch of Jeanne d'Arc (chapter viii.), of her being influenced by a prophecy attributed to Merlin, that the kingdom would he saved by a young, chaste maiden.

p. li. Paul de Musset, in his life of Alfred de Musset, p. 55, tells us of the interest Alfred took in the Merlin story.

p. li. On the Provençal fragments, see also Gröber's *Grundriss der rom. Phil.*, Bd. ii. Abth. 2, p. 68, which refers to the *Revue des l. r.*, 22, 105–115 ; 237–242.

p. lii. For an excellent discussion of the *Conte del Brait*, see Wechssler's paper on the Graal-Lancelot-Cyclus, pp. 37–51.

p. liii. For the Portuguese *Merlin*, see Gröber's *Grundriss der rom. Phil.*, Bd. ii. Abth. 2, pp. 213, 214.

p. liii. note 5. For *to* read *zu*.

p. liii. The best account of *Merlijn* is in W. J. A. Jonckbloet's *Geschiedenis der Nederlandsche Letterkunde*, Groningen, 1884, i. pp. 200–229.

p. liv. In 1892 appeared a novel by Paul Heyse entitled *Merlin*. The story is not a reproduction of the old legend, but is essentially a nineteenth-century novel with here and there a motive, or at least a hint, drawn from the mediaeval romance. Cf. a paper in *The Atlantic Monthly*, March, 1893.

p. liv. note 3. Goldmark's opera appeared in 1886.

p. lxviii. l. 9. As an interesting proof of Merlin's fame as a prophet, we may note that Defoe, in his account of the great plague in London in 1665, says that fortune-tellers and prophets greatly flourished at that time, and that they displayed the head of Merlin as a sign.

p. lxxiii. l. 27. The opinion of Merlin held by the antiquary Leland, who busied himself much with the Arthurian legend, is worth quoting :—" Sunt ibi tamen, si quis penitius inspiciat, talia, qualia magno desidarentur antiquae cognitionis incõmodo, & quae à Gulielmo lecta, potius quàm iutellecta, nullum prae se tulerunt cõmodum. Rursus apponam & aliud eiusdem honorificũ scilicet, non modò de historiae interprete, verũ etiam de Arturio ipso testimonium. Liquet à mendacibus esse conficta, quaecunque de Arturio, & Merlino ad pascendum minus prudentium curiositatem homo ille scribendo vulgauit. Vt sexcenties obganniat: fuit quidem Merlinus vir in rerum naturalium cognitione, & praecipuè in Mathesi vel ad miraculum vsque eruditus: quo nomine Principibus eius aetatis meritò gratissimus erat longèqı alius, quàm vt se putaret subjiciendum iudicio alicuius cucullati, & desidis monachi. Sed Arturiũ, & Merlinum, illum fortiorem, hunc eruditiorem, quàm vt plebis vel dicacitatem, vel importunitatem curent, omittam. Illud, quod monachus monacho etiam mortuo inuidet mihi iniquissimum videtur."—*Assertio inclytissimi Arturij*, p. 35*b*. London, 1544.

p. LXXIV. l. 6. See an interesting page or two on Caermarthen in Prothero's *Life and Letters of Dean Stanley*, ii. pp. 351, 352.

p. LXXVI. l. 9. See the remarks on this play by Halliwell-Phillipps in his *Outlines of the Life of Shakespeare*, p. 193.

p. LXXVII. Blackmore's *King Arthur* (1697) is an enlargement, in twelve books, of the *Prince Arthur*.

p. LXXVIII. Bartlett's concordance to Shakespeare notes several references to Merlin.

In the catalogue of a London bookseller (1894) I note the following title : "Merlinus Anglicus Junior, The English Merlin revived, or his prediction upon the affaires of the English Commonwealth. 1644. 4to."

Maccallum, in his *Tennyson's Idylls and Arthurian Story*, pp. 161–165, calls attention to Fielding's *Tragedy of Tragedies, or the Life and Death of Tom Thumb the Great* (1730), a burlesque piece in which Merlin is introduced here and there.

Among other eighteenth-century references to Merlin may be noted that in Warton's poem on the *Grave of King Arthur* (1777).

p. LXXXIII. Bishop Heber made some use of the Merlin legend in his unfinished *Masque of Guendolen*.

Wordsworth refers briefly to Merlin in one of his sonnets and in his *Artegal and Elidure*.

Bulwer introduces Merlin into his heroic poem *King Arthur* (1849), and remarks in the preface: "Merlin . . . . is here represented less as the wizard of popular legend, than as the seer gifted with miraculous powers for the service and ultimate victory of Christianity."

Emerson wrote two short poems entitled *Merlin*, but they scarcely do more than suggest the name of the hero.

Professor John Veitch has made use of Merlin in his poems entitled, *Merlin and Other Poems*, 1889. These I have not seen.

p. LXXXV. l. 15. My remarks on Nennius were in print before Zimmer's *Nennius Vindicatus* appeared. His book, it is needless to observe, marks a new epoch in the study of Nennius; but for the purpose of our general discussion, the main point is the one which I have emphasized—the priority by a considerable time of the *Hist. Britonum* of Nennius over the *Hist. Reg. Brit.* of Geoffrey of Monmouth. Zimmer assigns the *Historia Britonum* proper to about the close of the eighth century. See p. 66 *seq.*

p. LXXXV. l. 19. Zimmer remarks, p. 282 : "Die sogenannte eigentliche *Historia Brittonum* (7–56) ist als Geschichtsquelle absolut werthlos."

p. LXXXIX. Zimmer's date for Geoffrey's *Hist. Reg. Brit.* is 1132–1135. Cf. *Nennius Vindicatus*, p. 278.

p. XCVIII. l. 8. For the Mabinogion, see Rhŷs's *Studies*, chap. i.

p. CXXV. See F. Lot's *Études sur la Provenance du Cycle Arthurien* in the *Romania*, 1895–96. M. Lot's articles are directed against Zimmer's theory concerning the origin of the Arthurian romances, and conclude as follows : "Après comme avant les travaux du savant celtiste de Greifswald, il paraît évident que l'influence des Celtes insulaires a été beaucoup plus considérable, et même vraiment prépondérante, dans la transmission des éléments du cycle arthurien."

See, on the other hand, Zimmer's article in *Zeitschrift für franz. Sprache und Lit.*, xiii. 230 *seq.* (Beiträge zur Namenforschung in den altfranz. Arthurepen) ; Pütz in *Z. f. f. Spr. u. Lit.*, xiv. 161 *seq.* (Zur Gesch. der Entwicklung der Artursage).

p. CLXXXIII. See a paper by Kellner in *Englische Studien*, xx. 1–24, on "Abwechselung und Tautologie," in which he discusses this marked feature of mediaeval prose style.

p. CLXXXVI. note 3. Rhŷs brings the name Merlin into connection with Moridunum (Caermarthen). He remarks that the form *Merlin* corresponds to the form *Moridûnjos*, i.e. of moridunum or the sea-fort. *Hibbert Lect.*, p. 160.

p. CCVI. l. 1. A poem of 504 lines (Lambeth MS. 853, about 1430 A.D.) is called þe *Develis Parlament*, and describes a scene similar to that in our romance, but with no mention of Merlin.

p. CCVI. l. 12. Leland, in a paper on *Etrusco-Roman Remains*, published in report of Internat. Folk-Lore Congress for 1891, remarks (p. 192) on the widespread recognition of Dusio in Italian country districts.

p. CCVII. l. 2. Skeat has a good note on Antichrist in *Piers Plowman*, vol. iv. sec. 1, p. 442 (E.E.T.S.).

p. CCVII. l. 8. For further references on the intercourse of Devils with women, see the Life of St. Michael in the *Early South Eng. Legendary*, p. 306 (E.E.T.S.), and the *Morte Arthure*, l. 612 (E.E.T.S.). For incubi, see Giraldus Cambrensis, *Itin. Camb.* ch. v. ; Cockayne, *Leechdoms*, I. pp. xxxviii.–xli. ; *Melusine* (E.E.T.S.), p. 383 ; Skeat's *Chaucer*, v. 315. For parallels to Merlin's birth, see Nutt's *Problems of Heroic Legend* in report of Internat. Folk-Lore Congress for 1891 (p. 122), and Child's *Ballads* (large ed.), i. 63, note. *Cf.* also—

> " There ys a gyant of gret Renowne,
> He dystrowythe bothe sete and towyn)
> And aH þat euyr) he may ;
> And as the boke of Rome dothe teH,
> He wase get of the deweH of heH,
> As hys moder on slepe lay."
>
> *Torrent of Portyngale*, 921–926 (E.E.T.S.).

p. CCVII. l. 12. Parallels to Merlin's precocity are found in the story of Hermes in the Homeric Hymns, and in Child's *Ballads* (large ed.), viii. 479, ix. 226.

p. CCVII. l. 18. I might have pointed out the contradiction in the *Merlin*, p. 16, where the boy saves his mother from being *burnt*. On this punishment, Child remarks, *Ballads* (large ed.), iii. 113 : "The regular penalty for incontinence in an unmarried woman, if we are to trust the authority of romances, is burning." See also vi. 508, where C. gives a variety of references from ballads.

p. CCXIV. On the dragon-banner, see also Zimmer's *Nennius Vindicatus*, p. 286, note, where the Roman banner is commented upon, and the significance of *pen dragon* explained.

In the *Chanson de Roland*, l. 3265, there is a dragon-banner in the army of the pagans who are arrayed against Charlemagne. In the romance of *Octavian*, l. 1695 (South Eng. version), the Saracens have one.

p. CCXXIV. Spenser makes use of the story of the beards, F. Q., Bd. vi. c. 1, st. 14 *seq.*, and applies it to Crudor.

In the Norse *Saga Điðriks Konungs af Bern*, c. 12, King Samson orders Elsing, Jarl of Bern, to send him, among other things, a dog-collar of gold and a leash , made of his own beard.

p. ccxxvii. The game of chess (referred to on p. 362 of the *Merlin*) was a common diversion in the Middle Ages. See Child's *Ballads* (large ed.), viii. 454.

p. ccxxix. Meyer, in his *Indogermanische Mythen*, i. 153, 154, urges the Oriental origin of the Merlin legend, or, at least, after mentioning the pranks of that lively little demon Ashmedai, and bringing them into relation to the Gandharve legends of Indian mythology, he passes to discuss " die aus Indien stammende alt-französische Merlinsage . . . . in welcher der wilde Mann Merlin, der erst ungebärdig Speise und Trank umwirft, dann aber nach reichlichem Genuss von Honig, Milch, Warmbier, und Braten einschläft, vom Seneschal des Kaisers gebunden wird und diesem nun die Untreue seiner Frau offenbart, etc." Comparison should also be made with the similar incident in the story of Lailoken, " Part ii. : King Meldred and Lailoken," published in the *Romania* for 1893, pp. 522–525.

p. ccxxx. Gawain's exploits with the club may be compared with those of Gamelyn with the same weapon. *Cf.* Skeat's *Chaucer*, iii. 400. See also Scherer's *Gesch. d. deutschen Lit.* p. 183.

p. ccxxxv. In Rhŷs's Preface to Malory's *Morte Darthur*, pp. xxv., xxviii., xxix., I find the following remarks on a savage cat of Celtic tradition :—" In an obscure ' poem consisting of a dialogue between Arthur and Glewlwyd Gavaelvawr,' occurs at the end of the fragment the following passage, in which Kei is represented as fighting with a great cat :—

> Worthy Kei went to Mona
> To destroy lions.
> His shield was small
> Against Palug's Cat.
> When people shall ask
> ' Who slew Palug's Cat ? '
> Nine score . . . .
> Used to fall for her food.
> Nine score leaders
> Used to . . . .

The manuscript is imperfect, and it breaks off just where one should have heard more about Cath Palug, or ' Palug's Cat,' a monster, said in the Red Book Triads to have been reared by the Sons of Palug, in Anglesey."

INDEX TO OUTLINES OF THE HISTORY OF THE LEGEND OF MERLIN.

COLLATION OF THE PRINTED *MERLIN* OF THE E.E.T.S. WITH THE MS. IN THE UNIVERSITY LIBRARY, CAMBRIDGE, BY ALFRED ROGERS.[1]

Page	Line	*For*	*Read*	Page	Line	*For*	*Read*
1	3	other	othere.	5	20	have	haue.
1	3	plesier	plesiere.	5	25	hir	hire.
1	4	feer	feere.	5	25	wise	wyse.
1	4	to-gedir	to-gedire.	5	32	lyvinge	lyvynge.
1	16	othir	othire.	5	35	doughter	doughtere.
1	17	their [feire?] their semblañt	their sem-blaut [and ignore the note].	6	2	maner	manere.
				6	8	labour	laboure.
				6	22	women	wemen.
				6	30	her	here.
1	17	greved	greued.	6	33	othir	other.
2	5	powre	powre.	6	33	youre	youre.
2	16	suffer	suffere.	6	36	now	neuer.
2	18	power	powere.	7	1	way	wey
2	19	be-raffte	bereffte.	7	14	yet	yet.
2	21	our power	oure powere.	7	14	hir	hire.
2	22	maner	manere.	7	17	sayde	seyde.
2	27	our	oure.	7	18	your	youre.
2	34	ben	bene.	7	27	manere	manere.
3	1	sithe	suche.	7	27	hire	hire.
3	6	have	haue	7	28	hire	hire.
3	7	power	powere.	7	footnote	is repeated twice	is repeated.
3	10	their	theire.				
3	12	euquire	engin.	8	1	hir	hire.
3	16	their	theire.	8	6	have	haue.
3	20	doughters	doughteres.	8	13	oon	oo.
3	22	hir	hire.	8	24	upon	vpon.
3	25	maner	manere.	8	25	which	whiche.
3	27	mannes	mannes.	8	32	her	here.
3	28	their	theire.	9	4	servyse	seruyse.
3	29	their	theire.	9	7	hir	hire.
4	1	gretter	grettere.	9	24	hir	her.
4	1	wrother	wrothere.	9	27	clothed	clethed.
4	18	desier	desiere.	9	30	hir	hire.
4	20	her	here.	10	4	here	bere.
4	21	her	here.	10	8	after	efter.
4	24	manere	manere.	10	10	maner	manere.
4	31	mans werke	maner werkis	10	15	w[orlde]	worlde
5	2	neuer	neuere.	10	28	[haue]	haue
5	8	The man	That man.	10	33, 34	diffoulde	diffouled.
5	10	hir fader	hire fadere.	11	3	[this]	this.
5	14	her	here.	11	7	hir	hire.
5	18	their	theire.	11	27	Jhesu	Ihesu.
5	19	hir	hire.	11	30	slepynge	slepyng.

[1] Kölbing (*Altenglische Bibl.* iv. pp. xix., xx.) gives a collation of the first chapter of the *Merlin* of the E.E.T.S. with the MS. If he had referred to the edition of 1875 he would have found several of his corrections anticipated.—W.E.M.

Page	Line	For	Read	Page	Line	For	Read
12	15	fiendes, and axeden	fiendes axeden ['and' is crossed out].	17	17	son	sone.
				17	20	neuer	neuere.
				17	23	neuer	neuere.
12	27	neuer	neuere.	17	31	[arm]	pue [and ignore the footnote].
12	27	women	wemen.				
12	31	confessour	confessoure.	18	3	examyned	[ignore the note].
12	36	neuer	neuere.				
12	36	after	aftere.	18	18	whom	who.
13	3	syker	sykere.	18	28	shall	shalt.
13	7	feer	feere.	19	10	all	alle.
13	8	for	fore.	19	15	guylte	gylte.
13	13	good	gode.	19	19	claymed	claymed.
13	15	hir	hire.	20	17	layes	layest
13	16	hir	hire.	20	18	Thy[n]ke	thynke.
13	17	after	aftere.	20	24	youre	youre.
13	18	her	here.	22	15	here	here.
13	22	neuer	neuere.	23	2	elayn	Elayn.
13	23	woman	Note the MS. has wonan.	24	14	lyfte hym	lyfte hym in
				24	23	socour	socoure.
13	26	hir	hire.	24	23	returned	returned.
13	30	hir	hire.	24	29	barons	barouns.
13	30	wher	where	24	29	longer	lenger.
13	31	ouer hir	ouere hire.	25	1	youre	youre.
13	31	hir	hire.	25	1	words	wordes.
13	35	hir	hire.	26	18	hym	lym.
14	1	goo	geo.	27	14	straunge	strange.
14	5	tour	toure.	27	19	tour	toure.
14	13	tour	toure.	27	20	maner	manere.
14	17	repentaunce	repentaunce.	28	2	stonde[1] Do me	stonde. it is do me [aud ignore the note].
14	17	modir	modire.				
14	20	ther	there.				
14	21	arte	art.				
14	24	repentaunce	repentaunce.	28	4	sir	sire.
14	24	moder	modere.	28	6	labour	laboure.
14	25	her	here.	28	16	tour	toure.
14	28	were	w[e]re.	28	18	labour	laboure.
14	30	moder	modere.	28	24	anothir	anothire.
14	32	feer	feere.	28	27	mater	matere.
15	3	tour	toure.	29	8	tour	toure.
15	4	after	aftere.	29	22	knew	knewe.
15	4	fader	fadere.	30	2	to-geder	to-gedere.
15	6	moder	modere.	31	9	tour	toure.
15	7	othir	othire.	31	10	hour	houre.
15	10	whan	whane.	31	21	manere	manere.
15	11	lengar	lengare.	31	24	tour	toure.
15	17	hir	hire.	32	11	disease	disese.
15	18	ther	there.	32	17	whiche	whene.
15	19	her	here.	32	19	[s]ef	ef
15	20	suffir	suffire.	32	20	the werke	thi werke
15	20	ther	there.	32	30	Arthur	Arthure.
15	25	neuer	neuere.	33	35	the[1]	tho [and ignore the note].
15	27	hir	hire.				
15	31	neuer	neuere.				
16	16	oughtnotnot	ought not.	34	31	her	here.
16	23	Merlin	Merlyn.	35	9	sir	sire.
17	1	come	comen.	36	16	hier	hiere.

Page	Line	*For*	*Read*	Page	Line	*For*	*Read*
36	17	ther¹ the	ther ther the [and ignore the note].	61	8	when	whan
36	28	no do	ne do.	63	13	had	hadde.
37	7	said	seide.	64	20	theyr	theyre.
37	34	vnder	vndere.	64	27	resceve	receyve
38	3	Vortiger	Vortigere.	66	21	traytour	traytoure.
38	3	dragoñs	dragouns.	66	21	semblaunce	semblaunce.
38	4	other	othere.	67	36	Be-war	Beware.
38	7	other	othere	69	30	baroñs	barouns.
38	9	dragoūs	dragouns.	70	20	barons	barouns.
38	16	other	othere.	70	21	barons	barouns.
38	23	demañdest	demaundest.	72	14	nede	mede.
38	31	greter	gretere.	72	26	told	tolde.
38	35	dragoñs	dragouns.	72	31	este	efte.
39	11	dragoñs	dragouns.	73	9	lawghinge	lawghynge.
39	36	don	don.	73	13	kynge	kinge.
40	3	dragoñs	dragouns.	74	5	oo[n]	oo
40	4	reade	reade.	74	21	performe	pe[n]forme.
40	15	their	theire.	76	9	your baroñs	your barouns
40	32	yeve _	yeue.	77	27	couenaunte²	comenauntis [and ignore the note].
40	34	dragons	dragouns.				
41	3	their	theire.	78	8	baroñs	barouns.
41	10	heir	heire.	78	21	seide he	seide that he.
42	8	their	theire.	78	26	baroñs	barouns.
42	9	power	powere.	78	29	baroñs	barouns.
44	18	say	sey.	79	3	baroñs	barouns.
45	35	kyuge	kynge.	80	2	baroñs	barouns.
46	6	sir	sire.	80	20	heyer.	eyer [corrected from heyer].
46	34	a-queynted	aqueyntid.				
47	21	her	hier.	80	21	hour	houre.
48	24	you	yow.	81	21	baroñs	barouns.
49	19	heir	heire.	81	34	their	theire.
50	25	their	theire.	81	35	seide	seiden.
50	34	great	grete.	82	23	baroñs	barouns.
50	36	bileve to	bileve in [corrected from ' to '].	83	8	baroñs	barouns.
				83	17	come	conne.
				83	33	baroñs	barouns.
52	28	semblaunt	semblaunt.	84	5	somme	somme.
53	8	neke	nekke	84	12	baroñs	barouns.
53	26	other	othere.	84	15	baroñs	barouns.
54	35	be-gynnynge	be-gynnynge	85	20	baroñs	barouns.
55	20	theire	theire.	86	5	o[on]	o
55	22	theire	theire.	86	14	wher-in	where-in
56	11	felishup	feliship.	87	17	a[nd]	a
57	13	quynsyune	[the MS. has quynsyme].	88	14	knight	knyght.
58	9	seden	seiden.	88	22	be a thynge	be thynge.
58	14	couenaunt¹	comenaunt [and ignore the note].	89	7	mannes	mannes.
				90	2	woman	weman.
58	14	labour	laboure.	90	footnote	The words 'soones as' are repeated	The words 'soone as' occur after the words ' sone as.'
58	15	ben	ben.				
59	11	demonstraunce	demonstraunce	91	14	mannes	mannes.
59	34	honour	honoure.	91	35	baroñs	barouns.
60	3	thinge	thynge.	91	36	baroñs	barouns.
61	2	they	thei	93	5	oo[n]	oo

Page	Line	For	Read
94	12	tresour	tresoure.
94	15	advise	advyse
94	32	they	thei
94	33	rede	yede.
95	1	baroñs	barouns.
95	1	heir	heire.
95	19	baroñs	barouns.
95	22	baroñs	barouns.
96	5	gouernoure	gouernoure.
96	15	all	alle.
98	32	reqire	require.
99	16	honour	honoure.
100	31	their	theire.
101	2	other	othere.
101	10	towne	towñ.
102	9	engender	engendere.
102	31	vilenis	vileins.
102	34	performe	pe[r]forme.
104	footnote.	Add after the word ' MS.'	' but crossed through.'
106	7	this	the.
106	20	theire	theire.
107	1	vestementis	vestementz.
107	13	vestymentis rioall.	vestymentz roiall.
108	14	honoure	honoure.
108	18	perveied	purveied.
108	19	presentis	presentz.
109	28	is this that	is that.
110	22	tour	toure.
110	26	a-noynted	a-noyntid.
111	5	engendered	engendred.
111	13	in his kepynge	in kepynge.
113	5	their	theire.
113	11	their	theire.
113	18	seriantis	seriantz.
113	23	out	oute.
115	2	ffro	fro.
116	36	There	ther.
119	13	astonyd	astonyed.
119	26	commons	comouns.
119	31	discounfite[d]	discounfited.
120	12	Neuertheless	neuertbeles.
120	29	castelles	castellis.
122	3	that	thet.
124	2	a[s]	as.
124	26	a[t]	at.
125	2	both	bothe.
126	30	youre	your.
126	32	imprisonment	inprisonment
127	1	vylenis	vyleins.
127	6	Sir	Sire.
134	16	boteler	botelere.
134	17	encourtir	encourtire.
134	32	stour	stoure.
136	17	socour	socoure.
136	23	delyuer	delyuere.

Page	Line	For	Read
137	10	shorte	short.
137	11	woued	wued.
138	18	sholder	sholdere.
138	11	boteller	bottelere.
138	24	deliuer	deliuere.
138	26	their	theire.
140	8	archebissbop	archebishop.
141	11	their	theire.
141	18	doughter	doughtere.
141	19	valour	valoure.
143	6	lenger	lengere.
143	8	that they	that ther.
143	20	o[on] worde	o worde.
145	32	his	hys.
146	10	their	theire.
146	17	through	thourgh.
148	12	be-war of the ¹	bewar of them of the [and ignore the note].
149	10	I-comē	I-comen.
149	31	soper	sopere.
151	9	baner	banere.
153	19	ther	there.
154	16	baner	banere.
156	20	cleped the roy	cleped roy
158	19	vigerousely	vigerously.
160	17	us	vs.
162	26	kynge	kynge.
165	1	ther was	ther nas.
167	11	a[nd]	a
169	32	times	tymes.
170	27	embraced	enbraced.
171	4	heyr	heyre.
174	3	lond	londe.
174	11	That beste	The beste.
174	15	socour	socoure.
176	35	socour	socoure.
177	17	bacheler	bachelere.
179	12	a[nd]	a
179	21	myster	mystere.
179	22	and ther the kynge	and the kynge.
179	31	wife	wif.
180	4	barouns	barouns.
180	17	squyer	squyere.
180	19	coretted	coveited.
181	11	y[e] be	v be.
185	8	City	Cite.
186	3, 4	Emperour	Emperoure.
187	20	the xj	tho xj
191	13	Gaharet	Gaheret.
193	13	soone as that	soone at that.
195	14	ther was	ther nas.
195	31	of Jeshu criste	to Ihesu criste
196	28	lost	loste.
197	13	theire	theire.

Page	Line	For	Read	Page	Line	For	Read
197	16	forayoures	forrayoures.	252	21	alle the	alle tho.
198	22	asonder	asonder*e*.	253	30	vengeaunce	vengaunce.
200	29	stour	stour*e*.	254	11	Br[angu]e	Bra[ugu]e.
200	30	socoure	socour*e*.	256	19	a[t]	a
201	14	powder	powder*e*.	258	12	oo[n]	oo.
201	15	a-nother	another*e*.	260	6	gon to	gon into.
201	18	made	made*n*.	260	28	silueir	siluir.
202	4	thei hym	thei in hym.	260	29	theire	their*e*.
202	20	discounfited	discoumfited.	262	19	ansuered	ansuerde.
203	19	maner	maner*e*.	263	note	fellowles	felowles.
204	12	nothyng*e*	nothyng.	264	14	mischief	m[i]schief.
204	27	feire and welle	feire and wel be.	269	21	come	conne
				269	31	repress	repreff.
206	20	com Geauntes	com the Geauntes.	270	17	and well	and we.
				270	32	that thei were	that were.
210	30	euer	euer*e*.	271	8	othere	other*e*.
212	8	forest	forrest.	271	10	a[nd]	a
212	11	blois	blios.	272	16	fier	fier*e*.
212	13	leonpadys	lampadys.	274	28	ther*e*	ther.
212	14	*Christoier*	*Christoiere*.	276	5	were	were*n*.
217	17	Chalis	Clialis.	278	6	Arundell	Arondell.
212	22	xxxix	the xxxix.	282	10	castell Randoll	castell of Randoll.
212	22	xl	the xl.				
212	31	troweth	trowth.	283	18	hundre	hundr*e*.
213	23	had	hadde.	284	28	*J*eshu	*I*hesu.
214	18	fellowes	felowes.	287	33	lig*rans*	li g*rans*.
215	34	stour	stour*e*.	288	6	socour	socour*e*.
217	20	this	thise.	290	22	socour	socour*e*.
219	12	socour	socour*e*.	291	31	socour	socour*e*.
219	30	marveilouse	merveilouse.	292	22	Estranis	Estrains.
219	35	douhter*e*	doughter*e*.	293	2	squyers	squyres.
221	22	helpe neuer	helpe me neuer.	293	26	comyng*e*	comyng.
				294	14	slaughter*e*	slaughter.
221	34	*ɟoure*	*ɟour*.	295	33	life	lif.
225	29	hir	hir*e*.	296	4	tha[n]	tha.
227	6	precious	preciouse.	296	20	receyued	resceyued.
228	27	Ieshu	Ihesu.	296	27	snewen	snewen.
229	33	an	fin.	299	9	smote	*Note.* The MS. has somte.
231	13	of the saisnes	of saisnes.				
236	10	Tradilyuant	Tradilyuau*n*t	299	18	hire	hir*e*.
236	21	fier	fier*e*.	301	25	swore	swor.
239	16	alle	all.	301	28	thei dide	thei seide.
241	21	Ffeire	feire.	303	10	his	hys.
242	21	ther voys	clier voys.	303	25	mighty	myghty.
243	23	a[nd]	a	305	25	is the trouthe	is trouthe.
243	26	be gode	be a gode.	306	5	puyssant	puyssaunt.
244	14	nexte to the	nexte the.	309	31	acerne	acerue.
244	22	lette	lete.	309	34	briogne	brioque.
244	34	lose	losse.	310	2	cerne	cerue.
245	33	plente	pleinte.	310	33	coueuaunt [1]	comenaunt [and ignore the note].
246	14	were [1]	were [and ignore the note].				
				311	11	sechyng*e*	sechinge.
248	10	spred	sprad.	313	32	Bregnehan	Breqnehan.
248	12	kyngnenans	kynquenans.	313	34	their	their*e*.
248	22	gret	grete.	314	1	Nimiame	Nimiane.
250	17	kyng*e*	kyng.	314	2	Briogne	Brioque.

Page	Line	*For*	*Read*		Page	Line	*For*	*Read*
315	4	Antoneyes	Antonyes.		378	30	her-after	here after.
317	12	the fyve	tho fyve		381	10	briogne	brioque.
317	16	honour	honoure.		381	17	Briogne	brioque.
317	31	soch	soche.		381	21	garnyyshed	garnysshed.
317	33	shull	shall.		381	25	Briogne	brioque.
318	2	out me	out mo.		381	31	Then	Than.
318	19	tentely	tentefly.		382	15	shull	shall.
319	20	appareiled	apparailed.		382	22	dissevered	disseuered.
319	31	courtesie	courteise.		382	29	delyver	delyuer.
325	3	prowese	prowesse.		382	31	vouchesafe	vouchesaf.
325	27	the shafte	tho shafte.		382	32	dissevered	disseuered.
326	29	wher-of	where-of.		383	11	dissevered	disseuered.
326	30	here-after	here-after.		383	21	have	haue.
326	35	nd seide	and seide.		383	23	succour	succoure.
327	36	the v	tho v.		383	29	tecche	teche.
328	27	smyte	smyten.		383	29	shall	shull.
328	36	com	come.		384	8	got	gost.
331	5	vengeaunce	vengaunce.		384	19	stiwarde	stiward.
332	33	gret	grete.		384	19	dissevered	disseuered.
334	9	Ieshu	Ihesu.		384	30	banere	baner.
336	6	ne myster	no myster.		385	16, 17	embrowded	enbrowded.
337	8	othere	other.		385	17	dyvers	dyuers
339	1	hym-selfe	hymself.		385	32	dissevered	disseuered.
339	26	bounte	bountee.		387	24	p[ep]le	pe[p]le.
340	4	Vlcan I-forged	Vlcanus forged.		388	4	Seigramor	Siegramor.
					390	5	there	there.
342	11	Brauremes	Biauremes.		390	23	[deed or]	[deed] or
344	20	the xiij	tho xiij.		391	7	[and at the last it]	[and at the laste] it.
345	20	despite	dispite.					
346	27	strife	strif.		392	4	manere	maner.
347	21	skaberke	ska[be]rke.		392	20	ffor	ffore.
347	26	a-uenture	aventure.		393	6	beire	beire.
348	35	and a-noon	but a-noon.		393	29	sangh	saugh.
349	3	norisshed	norisshid.		393	31	upon	vpon.
352	20	hem so arayed	hem arayed.		394	20	king	kinge.
354	4	of the two	of two.		396	24	hym	hem.
354	7	longere	lengere.		397	35	full	ffull.
354	31	forfeited	forfeted.		398	18	thei	thai.
355	34	assailed	assailled.		399	22, 23	vnderstode	vndirstode.
357	4	let	lete.		399	32	him	hym.
362	9	couenaunts[2]	comenauntes [and ignore the note].		400	5	a[nd]	a
					400	7	brioke	brioske.
					400	20	my baners	iiij baners.
362	27	Guynebans	Gynebans.		401	17	mortall	and mortall.
362	34	coniursion	coniurison.		402	4	Antonye	Antony.
363	6	sones	sone.		402	19	dicounfite[2] theym	discounfite the theym [and ignore the note].
366	36	Amaunt	Amaunt.					
367	11	astoyned	astonyed.					
367	17	her-after	here-after.					
367	32	yef he hadde	yef it hadde.		402	22	were	wer.
372	3	somme	somme.		402	31	Antonye	Antony.
372	4	deffended	diffended.		403	14, 15	some-what	somwhat.
373	29	segramor	segramore.		405	18	valoure	valour.
376	5	hem	ham.		406	30	dide	did.
377	27	enter	entere.		408	10	maistres	maistries.
377	32	a[nd]	a		408	14	sharpe	sharp.
378	28	he gan	began.		408	21	way	wey.

Page	Line	For	Read	Page	Line	For	Read
409	14	maistres	maistries.	455	1	life	lif.
413	22	lordshippe	lordship̄.	455	18	next	nexte.
413	33	upon	vpon.	456	8	alle	all.
414	1	lordshippe	lordship̄.	458	15	how well it	how it.
415	17	prayour	prayoure.	459	20	overthrewe	ouerthrewe.
416	7	shull	shall.	463	12	wife	wif.
416	10	comfort	counfort.	463	28	a-perceyued	aparceyved.
416	17	shall reste	shull reste.	466	10	disceyued	disceyved.
416	27	seid	seide.	466	19	enderdited	enterdited.
417	7	mighty	myghty.	467	2	for the	fro the.
417	12	shall	shull.	467	33	a-baisshed	abaissed.
418	30	vilonye	vylonye.	468	4	worshippe	worship̄.
420	18	Emperour	Eemperour.	468	11	manere	manere.
420	28	most	moste.	468	25	iourneyes	iourneyes.
420	29	the dredde	she dredde.	469	4	to hande	in hande.
421	4	semblannce	semblaunce.	470	28	wher-as	whereas.
422	3	sholde he do	sholde be do.	471	12	necessarie	nessessarie.
422	11	come	comen.	471	23	hundre	hundre.
422	31	gate	yate.	472	5	worshippe	worship̄.
423	14	noon sey	noon cowde sey.	472	17	Amnistian	Annistian.
				473	14	hundre	hundre.
424	11	grett	grete.	473	17	hundre	hundre.
424	13	theire	their.	473	32	hundre	hundre.
424	29	be-heilde	behielde.	475	2	hundre	hundre.
426	26	seruise	servise.	475	15	hadde	had.
428	6	I telle	I well telle.	477	4	caitife	caitif.
429	32	Emperour	Emperoure.	478	5	come	comen.
429	34	come	conne.	478	11	shippe	ship̄.
432	6	Emperour	Emperoure.	479	15	on	in.
433	17	thowe	thow.	479	26	and in this	and [in] this.
434	31	eny	ony.	479	36	recouered	recovered.
435	15	seide Emperour	seide the Emperour.	480	3	every	euery.
				480	23	archebisshoppe	archebisshop̄.
435	32	shall	shull.	480	24	wife	wif.
435	34	us	vs.	482	10	life	lif.
438	18	book	booke.	482	28	worshippe	worship̄.
438	25	nyght	nygh[t].	482	30	us	vs.
438	27	knyght	knygh[t].	485	6	qui	qui.
439	4	brenbas	brenbras.	489	22	us	vs.
439	32	myght	nyght.	491	14	Galiscowde	Galascowde.
440	22	hedde	heede.	494	11	suerde	swerde.
441	4	surprised	supprised.	494	27	come	com.
441	5	Hardogabrans	Hardogra-brans.	495	6	com	come.
				496	16	ther [1] the knyghtes	ther ther the knyghtes [and ignore the note].
442	22	theire	theire.				
442	33	puyssant	puyssaunt.				
444	7	and toke	and to toke.				
444	16	departed	departen.	498	20	felowes	felewes.
445	31	Scotlonde	Scotlond.	499	23	dyuerse	dyuerse. [*]
449	33	wele	well	499	28	send	sende.
452	6	shippe	ship̄.	500	5	have	haue.
452	10	shippe	ship̄.	501	18	com	come.
452	22	ther	thei.	501	33	a[nd]	a
452	26	shippe	shipp.	502	21	Ieshu	Ihesu.
453	31	Archebisshoppe	Archebisshop̄	502	25	Bisshoppe	Bisshop̄.
453	35	Archebisshoppe	Archebisshop̄	502	26	Ieshu	Ihesu.
453	36	Amnistan	Annistan.				

[*] Spelt dyuerese in MS.

Page	Line	*For*	*Read*	Page	Line	*For*	*Read*
503	32	that the best	that×the best	551	14	enemyes	enmyes.
504	15	col[d]e	cole.	555	1	moche	moche.
505	30	performe	parforme.	556	1	valoure	valour.
505	35	welwellinge	welwillinge.	556	20	Northumbir-	Northumbir-
506	36	done	don.			londe	lond.
507	6	netther	neither.	556	32	shall	shull.
507	9	somme	somme.	557	29	sette	sente.
507	27	went	wente.	558	14	iocunde	iocounde.
508	31	aperceyued	aparceyved.	560	6	manere	maner.
509	26	Careuges	Caranges.	562	5	felowes	felowes.
511	13	upon	vpon.	564	7	houre	hour.
512	16	resceve	resceyve.	564	27	there	ther.
513	28	sire	sire.	565	11	hir	hire.
514	3	weepe	wepe.	566	24	the	the.
515	13	go we	gowe.	567	34	kyng	kynge.
515	35	the other	the tother.	568	18	returne to	returne for to.
516	11	kutte the	kutte of the.	568	23	our	oure.
516	16	Agrauain	Agravain.	569	3	they thought	they that
516	18	doun	down.				thought.
516	29	harme thei	harme that	569	17	Segramore	Segramor.
			thei.	569	20	sharpe	sharp̄.
517	17	gate	yate.	569	26	appareiled	apparailed.
518	30	doucrenefar	doutrenefar.	570	17	sharpe	sharp.
520	1	Alcon	Alain.	571	12	bledde	bledden.
521	2	discorde	discourde.	572	25	Segramore	Segramor.
521	4	hool	hooll.	573	7	tothere	tother.
521	33	Monagins	Monaquins.	574	9	surprised	supprised.
522	24	under	vnder.	574	15	own	owne.
523	2	a[t]	a	575	18, 19	hardogabran	hardogobran.
513	21	kute	kitte.	575	24	surprised	supprised.
524	36	wife	wif.	578	24	Jhesu	Ihesu.
526	30	brothere	brother.	578	32	hede [how]	hede how.
527	10	worshippe	worship̄.	579	6	worshippe	worship̄.
527	34	matter	mater.	579	10	many goode	many of
528	10	socoure	socour.				goode.
528	18	asscilled	assailled.	580	27	good	goode.
528	19	socoure	socour.	580	36	oquarell	o quarell.
529	13	swore	swor.	581	10	with these	with the these.
532	35	ground	grounde.	582	14	surprised	supprised.
533	23	stroke yeve	stroke cowde	583	9	renomee	renome.
			yeve.	583	14	destroye	distroye.
533	30	handes	hondes.	583	24	the yonge	this yonge.
534	6	bridell	bridill.	584	23	savioure	saviour.
535	9	the tweyne	tho tweyne.	584	24	honoure	honour.
537	7	thou	thow.	584	31	Elizer	Elyzer.
538	25	wele	well.	585	18	alle	all.
539	24	nether	nother.	586	36	shall	shull.
541	17	and he bowed	that he bowed.	587	6	batailes	bateiles.
541	35	vnderstode	vndirstode.	587	31	there	ther.
543	32	hede of	hede to.	587	32	and thei	that thei.
545	8	morowe to	morowe till.	588	14	sharpe	sharp.
547	30	seruauntes	seruauntis.	589	20	Pignoras	Pignores.
548	27	Go we a-geins	Go ageins.	591	16	nevewe	nevew.
549	26	wh[ich]e	we.	592	4	hardogabrant	hardogobrant.
549	27	ouertoke	overtoke.	592	20	honoure	honour.
549	28	euere	euer.	593	33	halfe	half.
549	29	houre	hour.	594	20	*that*	þat.

Page	Line	For	Read	Page	Line	For	Read
594	24	through	thourgh.	620	3	archebisshoppe	archebisshop.
596	11	wonder	worder.	621	17	harpoure	harpour.
596	21	dede	dide.	621	24	othere	other.
597	9	there	ther.	621	25	up	vp.
597	13	there	ther.	622	18	harpoure	harpour.
598	27	shull haue	shull have.	623	35	here	here.
599	18	sharpe	sharp.	624	14	othere	other.
600	9	stoure	stour.	625	4	comynge	comyng.
600	23	remountede	remounted.	625	9	resceyued	resceyved.
600	30	bateile	bataile.	626	31	well	wele.
601	13	Gosenges	Gosengos.	627	9	kyng	kynge.
601	34	that herde	that hadde herde.	628	6	come	com.
				628	11	seith	seth.
602	5	wonderfull	worderfull.	628	26	which	whiche.
602	28	went	wente.	628	33	hondes	handes.
603	26	resceyued	resceyved.	629	26	vailante	vailaunt.
604	6, 7	departynge	departinge.	630	18	godde	god.
605	24	noire	noir.	630	32	grete	gret.
606	5	powere	power.	631	last	swyfte	swifte.
606	33	gates	yates.	632	9	all	alle.
607	3	othere	other.	633	7	life	lif.
607	4	dide helpe	dide hem helpe.	633	27	serpentes	serpentes.
				635	20	sharpe	sharp.
608	21	of hym	on hym.	636	12	leife	leif.
608	31	honoure	honour.	636	16	spekere	speker.
609	23	surprised	supprised.	637	13	awmenere	awmener.
609	24	acheive	acheiue.	638	6	coloure	colour.
610	8	surprised	supprised.	638	29	knowe	knewe.
610	14	semblaunt	semblant.	639	17	Archebisshoppe	Archebisshop.
610	15	for	ffor.	639	26	formednesse	fonnedness.
610	17	manere	maner.	639	34	dost	doist.
611	18	euer I	euer that I.	640	18	archebisshoppe	archebisshop.
612	last	all	alle.	640	36	bettere	better.
613	21	wife	wif.	641	16	Emperoure	Emperour.
613	26	honoure	honour.	641	17	manere	maner.
613	29	honoure	honour.	642	16	that he hadde	that hadde.
613	35	worshippe	worship.	642	27	honoure	honour.
613	36	curtesie	curteisie.	642	32	Emperoure	Emperour.
614	1	life	lif.	643	35	iijml	iiijml.
614	6	Stephene	Stephene.	645	35	com	come.
614	11	iogeloure	iogelour.	646	13	brennynge	brennynge.
614	14	Arthure	Arthur.	646	19	life	lif.
614	16	Arthure	Arthur.	646	last	svffre	suffre.
615	18	streight	strieght.	648	3	up	vp.
616	13	clamoure	clamour.	648	12	tho	the.
616	28	youre	your.	648	33	atame	[?] ataine.
617	5	cam	com.	649	10	chyne, than	chyne and than.
617	7	drofe	drof.				
617	21	thus	this.	649	21	grete was that	grete that.
617	34	swor	swer.	649	27	mounteyne	mounteyn.
618	1	lettere	letter.	650	3	when she	whens he.
618	6	houre	hour.	650	32	come	comen.
618	8	therefore	therfore.	651	16	vs manased	vs so manased
618	27	blu-sht	blusht.	651	24	Emperoure	Emperour.
619	7	harpoure	harpour.	652	24	and passed	that passed.
619	31	honoure	honour.	652	28	it werse	it the werse.
619	32	as my	as is my.	652	29	swifte	swyfte.

Page	Line	For	Read	Page	Line	For	Read
653	8	that	than.	671	17	frendes	frendes.
653	12	swyfte	swifte.	676	11	Ieshuralem	Iherusalem.
655	18	grete	gret.	676	16	renoome	renooun.
659	28	honoure	houour.	676	26	had	hadde.
660	22	powestee	powstee.	677	15	un-ethe	vn-ethe.
660	25	cristein	cristin.	678	7	messagere	messnger.
660	29	and thei ride	and ride.	679	3	time	tyme.
662	15	softely	softly.	679	12	duerfe	duerf.
662	19	powere	power.	680	1	disturue	disturne.
662	34	thousande	thowsande.	681	9	bussh	bush.
663	33	to my	of my.	681	14	cerne	cerue.
664	5	montaigne	mountaigne.	681	14	wymple	wynple.
664	7	manere	maner.	681	16	cerne	cerue.
665	6	I telle	I wele telle.	685	16	litere	liter.
665	25	there	ther.	685	35	youre	your.
666	2	undirstode	vndirstode.	686	17	othere	other.
666	4	vengeaunce	vengaunce.	687	27	honoure	honour.
666	last	in the cattes	in cattes.	689	3	seid Ewein	seide Sir Ewein.
667	19	hym	hy[m].	689	17	that	þat.
668	20	my-self	mysilf.	690	7	most	moste.
668	23	ye haue	[these words are repeated in MS.]	691	21	sleeves	sleves.
				693	28	be	by.
669	28	sergeauntes	sergauntes.	694	21	be-teche	be-teche.
670	3	yet sholde	yet thei sholde.	695	12	lordshippe	lordship.
670	6	sharpe	sharp.	695	17	socoure	socour.
670	last	douhter	doughter.	696	19	and countirfet	that couutirfet.

ABBEY of the Royall Mynster, 416.
ABIGANS, king, 159.
ACALAS, Acolas, a Saxon, 355, 357.
ACES, Aces de Bemonde, Aces of Campercorentin, Acon, Acon de Bemonde, 284—287, 294, 375, 481.
ADAX, 276.
ADRAGAIN, Adragain des vaux de gailore, Adragain li bruns, Adragains, Adragayn, Adragayn li bruns, Adragayns li bruns, Adragein le noir, Adrageins. *See* Agravadain.
ADRASTUS, king of Greece, 340.
ADRIAN, Adryan, emperor of Constantinople, 186, 373, 374, 437, 449; his daughters, 186; son-in-law Brangore, 186.
AGLONALL, a knight of Arthur, 480.
AGRAVADAIN, Agrauadain, Agrauadain des vals de gailore, Agravadain des vaus de gailore, Agrauadain ly noire, Agravadayns, Agrauadins, Agrauandain, Agragayns, 257, 327, 329, 330, 331, 337, 342, 343, 345, 351, 356, 383, 407, 410, 456, 458, 470, 484, 490, 496, 561, 562, 566—574, 604—609, 611, 670, 672—675; his wife, 607; his daughter, 607, 608, 670, 671, 672, 674, 675; his daughter's son, *see* Estor; his brother Belynans, 561; his brother Madagot, 345; his nieces, 607, 608; his castle, 257, 604, 672, 673; best knight destramars, 561, cf. 345.
AGRAVAIN, Agrauuayn the prowde, 147; his mother, 86, 372; father, 179, 285, 526, 555; second son of Lot, 555; his aunt Basyne, 373; resolves to join Arthur, 183, 240, 251, 260, 439, 557; accompanies Galeshyn, 190, 191; battle with the Saxons, 193, 194, 230; rescues Gaheries, 196; upset by a Saxon, 198; rescued by Gawein, 199; upset by Guynebans, 199; rescued by Galeshyn and Gaheries, 199; slays the nephew of Guynebans, 199; sojourns at Logres,

201, 202; Arthur is told of his coming, 230; slays Orienx's nephew, 265; upset by Orienx, 265; horsed afresh, 265; goes to Camelot, 267; fells Guynebant, 268; Merlin calls him coward, 269; Gawein goes to help Ewein, 280; leads the first ward of the army, 280, 282; charges the Saxons, 283, 284; retreats, 285; a reverse, 287; keeps the bridge, 282; at Arondell, 290—293; prowess, 294; a strange quest, 297—301, 314; cuts Taurus in pieces, 299, 300; returns to Arondell, 301; at Logres, 301; makes a vow, 301, 314, 449, 450; Arthur is coming, 370; goes to meet him, 370, 371; salutes Arthur on his knees, 371; Gawein tells Arthur they are come to be knighted, 371, 372; Arthur promises, 372; presented to Arthur, 372; Arthur makes great joy of him, 373; goes to Logres with Arthur, 374; the vigil in the minster, 374; dubbed knight, 374, 449; Arthur gives him a treasure sword, 374; goes with Gawein's host to Dover, 377, 378; has part command, 378; his prowess at Trebes, 388, 407, 410; falls under his horse, 396; rescued by Ban and Gawein, 396; horsed again, 396, 397; at Carmelide, 447, 448; at the marriage of Arthur and Gonnore, 453, 454; in the tournament at Toraise, 459; at Arthur's court Royal at Logres, 481; tournament at Logres, 485; jousts with Pynodas, 485; his deeds, 487, 488, 489; the reconciliation of the Round Table and Queen's knights, 500; is to go with his father and brethren with a flag of truce to the princes, 505, 506, 507; they start at midnight, 509, 510; encounter with Saxons, 510, 511, 512; can't find Gawein, 513, 514; Gawein comes, 514, 515; butchery of Saxons, 515; rescues Gueheret, 516; arrives at a forester's house and lodges there,

517, 518; on the journey again, 524, 525, 526; his foul-mindedness, 526, 527, 528; his foulness duly punished, 527; cured of his sickness by Gawein and Launcelot du Lak, 527; the rescue of Elizer and Lydonus his squire, 528, 529, 531; taunted about his foulness, and gets angry, 528, 529; quarrels with Gaheries, 529, 530; unhorsed, 531; sore bestead, 532; horsed by Gawein, 533; quarrels with Gaheries, 535, smites him, 536; but is knocked down by Gawein for his pains, 536, 537, 538; a general squabble, 537, 538; horsed by Elizer, 538; is turned out of the company, 538; with them again at the hermitage, 544; jealous of Gawein, 544, 545; at Roestok castle, 545, 546; battle with Saxons before Cambenyk, 547—551; unhorsed, rescued, 552; slays Dodalus, 552; rout of the Saxons, 554; in Cambenyk, 555; Gaheries chaffs him about the maidens again, 555; goes to North Wales and then to Arestuell, 557, 558; in the battle of Garlot, 525; vows to find Merlin, 682.

AGRESIANX, one of the forty-two fellows, 212.

AGUYGNERON, Aguygueron, Aguyneron, seneschal to Clameden, 577, 578, 594.

AGUYSALE de desirouse, one of the forty-two fellows, 212.

AGUYSANS, Aguysant, Aguysanx, the Roy de Cent Chiualiers, 235, 313; with the twelve kings, 152; a sudden attack by Arthur, 153; unhorses Kay, 156; horses Ventres, 156; attacks Arthur, 157; felled by Arthur, 158; his steward Margnam unhorsed, 158; goes with his men to the strait near the river, 160; Bors comes, 161, 162; succours Carados, 163; his prowess, 163; attacks Ban, 163, 164, who unhorses him, 164; fights on foot, 164; is worsted, 165; leaves Sorhant, 184; goes to his lady at Malonant, 184; his high position, 184, 185; the reason of his name, 185; goes to succour Tradilyuant, 233; his deeds, 233, 234; the Saxons worsted, 234, 242; counsels Tradilyuant, 235, 312; rides to Arundell, 236; goes to Malohaut, 236; his messengers see the princes, 312; at Leicester, 312; counsels war at once, 313; his cousin Calchous, 173; the expedition to Clarence against the Saisnes, 438, 439; leads the first ward of 7,000 men, 438; a night attack, 439, 440, 441; his courage, 443; discomfited by the Saisnes, 444; makes a fresh night attack, 444, 445; totally beaten, 446, 449; goes home, 447, 449; hears of Arthur's arrival at Logres,

449, 450; wishes for peace with Arthur, 450, 451; a messenger of peace on his way from Arthur, 546; his joy on seeing him, 546, 556; a conference agreed to, 556; the conference with Lot at Arestuell, 558, 559; a truce, 560; the assembly of the hosts at Salisbury, 565, 575, 585; leads the second ward in the battle of Garlot, 594; in battle before Clarence, 601; in the battle between Arthur and Rion's hosts, 626; aids Arthur against Luce, 643; in the second division, 659.

AGUYSAS, Aguysans, of Scotland, 108, 439, 558; a fresh young knight, 108; goes to Arthur's court at Logres, 108; disdains Arthur and his gifts, 108; threatens Arthur's life, 108; son of Briadas and Ygerne's daughter, 121; unhorsed in the battle against Arthur at Bredigan, 156; felled by Lucas, 158; leads his men to the strait between the wood and the river, 160; his host aids Ydiers, 161; leaves Sorhant, 187; at Corengers in Scotland, 236; the Saxons come, 236; tells his barons to arm, 236; in the forefront of his host, 237; his cousin-german Gaudius, 237; has great loss, 237; Urien and Baudemagn come to the rescue, 238, 239, 242; discomfited, 239, 242; leads the tenth ward to Clarence against the Saisnes, 438, 439; a night attack, 439, 440, 441; discomfited, 444; a fresh onset on the Saisnes, 444, 445; his nephew Gaudin, 445; is totally beaten, 446, 447, 449; goes home, 447, 449; hears Arthur is at Logres, 449, 450; wishes for peace with Arthur, 450, 451; a conference with Arthur's envoy, 557, 558, 559; the host assembles at Salisbury, 565, 575; in battle before Clarence, 601; aids Arthur against Luce, 644; leads the first division against the Romans, 659.

AGUYUAS LI BLOIS, 151.

AIGLINS des vaus, Ayglin de vans, one of the forty-two fellows, 212, 682.

ALADAN the crespes, one of the forty-two fellows, 212.

ALAIN, Alechin, Ales, 286, 294; dubbed knight by Arthur, 375, 449.

ALAIN, Alein, Aleon, de Lille in Lytenoys king, 173, 229, 520, 583, 539, 577; called Mehaignyes, 229; kin to king Pelles, 173, 520, 539, 577; of the forain londes, 539, 577; uncle to Elizer, 539; kin to king Pellynor, 173, 520, 539, 577.

ALECHIN, Ales. See Alain.

ALI PATIN, Alipatin, Alipantius, king, 349; of the londe des pastures, 616, 662.

ALIAUME, steward to Ban of Benoyk, 152.
ALIBOS, a young knight, 442.
ALIERS, a knight, 441.
ALMAYNE, 303, 306, 379, 380, 386, 394, 398, 402, 411, 419, 421, 450.
ALMAYNE, duke of. *See* Matan *and* Frolle.
ALMAYNES, 402, 408, 438.
AMADAS, Amynadus, the rich king of Ostrich, 252; his brother Maglaas, 252; king of Danes, 152.
AMADAS DE LA CRESPE, knight, 682.
AMANT, Amaunt, Amaunte, king, 350, 351, 358, 359, 364—370, 375, 382, 563, 565, 567; his son Gosenges, q.v.
AMNISTAN, Sir, chaplain to Leodogan, 453, 472.
AMORET LE BRUN, one of the forty-two fellows, 212.
AMYNADUS. *See* Amadas.
ANABLE, Auenable, Avenable, Avenables. *See* Grisandoll.
ANADONAIN, king, 173.
ANGIER, Angiers, Aunger, Aungier, Aungiers, Aungis, Aungys, a Saxon, 27; his daughter, 27, 42, 43, 44, 45, 46, 49, 50, 54; his uncle, 152, 243, 585; his kin, 172, 248, 600.
ANMADIUS, the proude, one of the forty-two fellows, 212.
ANTICOLAS LE ROUS, one of the forty-two fellows, 212.
ANTIDOLUS, steward to king Brandon, 587.
ANTONY, Antoneyes, Antonye, Antonyes, 303, 306, 315, 375, 379, 380, 387, 390, 392, 393, 398, 402, 406, 408, 409, 411, 416, 419, 449, 450. *See* Antoynes.
ANTONY and Pounce, 303. *See* Pounce.
ANTOR, Arntor, Merlin tells Uter Pendragon he is a good man, 88; his wife good and wise, 88; poor, 88; his wife in child-bed, 88; goes to Uter Pendragon, who makes great feast to him, 88; swears to keep counsel, 88; Uter Pendragon asks him to send his son Kay (who is six months old, 112) out to nurse and adopt Arthur in his place, 88, 91; hesitates, 88, 89; he promises, 89; has great gifts from Uter Pendragon, 89; tells his wife all, 89; his wife demurs, 89; they find a nurse for their son Kay, 89; Arthur is brought by Merlin, 90, 91, 111; asks if he is christened, 91; the messenger says No, 91; christens him Arthur, 91; puts out his son Kay to nurse, 91, 97, 102; nourishes Arthur until he is fifteen, 97, 112, 347; he has nourished him well, 97; always calls Arthur "son," 97; and Arthur calls him

"father," 91; makes his son his knight, 97; goes to Logres withwno two sons (? Kay and Arthur), 97; Kay brings him Calibourne, 101; Kay says he drew it, 101; he tells Kay he lies, 101, 102; tells Arthur to replace the sword, 101; he does so, 101, and Kay cannot draw it, 101; tells Arthur he is not his father, 102; Arthur cries, 102; tells Arthur how he got him to nourish, 102; asks Arthur that when king he will make Kay his steward, 102; Arthur swears to do it, 102; tells Arthur to draw the sword, 103; he and his friends side with Arthur against the rebel barons, 103; the archbishop in council with him, 104; Kay made steward, 102, 104, 109, 136, 405, 453; Merlin tells the barons Arthur is not his son, 109; Bretell comes to fetch him, 109, 110; goes to the barons, 110; confirms the story of Arthur's youth, 112; in council, 114; strikes down king Carados in battle, 119; watches the tourney at Logres, 133; in council, 138; knows Arthur's parentage, 139, 178; Merlin leads him to Bredigan, 150; horsed by Kay, 158; upsets Margnam, 158; horses Bretell, 158; fights with Escam, 159; Arthur's incest, 180; one of Arthur's forty-two fellows, 212; felled by Sorfarin, 220; unwounded, 224; at Toraise, 224; in the fights with Rion, 337; the fight with the Saxons, 349; on foot, 352; Arthur sees him thus and gets fierce, 352; Arthur aids him, 353; tries to dissuade Bors from fighting Amaunt, 366; lodged in Trebes castle, 412; at the marriage of Arthur and Gonnore, 453, 454; the tournament, 455.
ANTORILAS, knight, ally of Claudas, 394.
ANTOYNES, Antony, 130; steward of Benoyk, 146, 163.
ANTYAUME, 381, 384, 400, 401, 564; steward of Trebes; seneschal of Benoyk.
ARADE DE GALOIRE, king, an ally of Rion, 616.
ARANS, Aroans, Aroant, king, son of Brangue, 291, 292, 293, 295, 296, 329, 330.
ARCHBISHOP? of Toraise, 453, 454, 620. ? of Logres, 639, 640.
ARESTOBOLUS, knight of the Round Table, 598.
ARESTUELL, in Scotlande, 509, 519, 525, 546, 548, 556, 557, 558, 562.
ARGANS, king, an ally of Rion, 616.
ARIDOLUS, knight, 321.
ARNTOR. *See* Antor.
AROAISE, a little river, 386.
AROANS. *See* Arans.

151; [Danish kings assemble and ravage Cornwall and lay siege to Vandelers, but are driven out by him again, 152;] king Lot's dream, 153; attacks the sentries, 153; throws the enemy into confusion, 153; chases the fugitives, 153; takes them in the rear, 157; upsets Tradilyvaunt, 157; severe battle, 157; is attacked by Aguysans, 158; issue doubtful, 159, 160; ruse of the enemy, 160, 161; rescues and horses Ban, 164, 165; slays a knight, 165; routs the seven kings, 165; chases them over the bridge, 165; wants to follow, 165; but Merlin forbids him, 165; to go back to Logres, 166; divides the spoil, 167; at Bredigan, 167; the "great churl," 167; sees the churl is Merlin, 170; intrigue with Lysanor, 171; their son Hoot, 171; goes to Tarsaide in Tamelide, 171, 202, 240, 260, 294, 303, 307; to succour Leodogan, 175, 202, 203; barons afraid, 175; his sister's sorrow for him, 182; his fame spreads, 183, 184, 186, 190; his sister Morgein, 185, 507, 508; worsts the Saxons, 185; who have ravaged his lands, 186, 188; fame reaches Constantinople, 186; his nephews Galaishin and Gawein, and his brethren are coming to aid him, 191, 192, 197, 240, 251, 260, 285, 290; has a band of forty knights to aid Leodogan, 203, 396, 454; they are all in disguise, 203, 204; Merlin bears the great dragon-banner, 206; description of it, 206; dashes at the Saxons, 206, 207; does marvels with Calibourne, 210, 220; Gonnore wonders who he is, 210; the name of his forty fellows, 212; [marries Gonnore, 213, 451;] slays Margalyvaunt, 217, 224; laughs at Merlin, 219; his prowess, 219; Gonnore watches his deeds, 220; dashes at Sorfarin, 221; Ban dissuades him, 221; Merlin calls him a coward, 221; attacks Sorfarin, 221, 222; is wounded, 222; overthrows Sorfarin, 222; Gonnore watching, 222; slays Malore, 222, 223; slays Ffreelent, 223; puts the Saxons to flight, 223; Rion prepares revenge, 223; Leodogan gives him the spoil, 225; his largess, 225, 257; Gonnore serves him at the feast, 225, 257; Leodogan thinks he might marry Gonnore, 226; she brings him wine, 227; he falls in love with her, 227, 229; she praises him, 227, 228; Ban asks Leodogan why she is not married, 228; the answer, 228; Merlin smiles at Ban, 228; Leodogan wonders at the respect they all show Arthur, 229; is told by Merlin of Gawein's and Galeshyn s

deeds, 230; Arthur's castle of Arondell, 232; his men help Tradilyvaunt, 233; his sister's son Ewein the grete, 238, 285; of Dodynell the savage, 247; of Kay Destranx, 249; Seigramor lands at Dover, 259, 262, 270; Merlin comes disguised to Camelot, 261—271; repentance of Ydiers, 282; a band of young nobles coming to him, 292, 293; Lot's repentance, 295; Logres his capital, 301, 316; the obstinacy of the barons, 304; the quest of the St. Grail in his time foretold, 304; his cousin Leonces, 307; Merlin comes, 312, 314; Merlin's counsel, 314; Merlin tells him of his nephews, 314; and of their vow, 314; sorrow for Ban and Bors, 315; Merlin's dark saying, 315; is to go to Forest Denoyable and knight his nephews with the twelve good swords there, 316; Guyomar comes to fetch him to Leodogan, 316, 317; goes, 317; Leodogan wonders who he can be, 318; Merlin tells Leodogan that they seek a wife for Arthur, 319; Leodogan at once offers Gonnore, 319; betrothal to Gonnore, 319, 320, 341, 357; discovers his name and estate to Leodogan, 320; Leodogan's joy, 320; Leodogan, Bors, Ban, and the barons do homage, 320, 341; leads the first ward, 321; [the fair adventure of the rings and Ydiers of Norway, 321;] Leodogan's court royal, 322; sits at the head of the dais, 322; Gonnore arms him, 322; Merlin laughs at this, 322; Merlin says she must make him a real knight, 322; he asks how, 322; she must let him kiss her, 322; kisses her, 323; she gives him a wondrous helm, 323; sets on Rion's host, 323, 324, 325; Merlin tells him to think of Gonnore's kiss and be brave, 325; attacks and unhorses Jonap, 325; is unhorsed, 325; Nascien, 326; [counselled by him, 327;] his prowess, 327; follows the dragon-banner, 327, 332, 334, 335; follows Merlin to rescue Nascien and Bors, 331, 332, 333; the marvel of the banner, 332; one against four, 332, 334; slits a Sarazin, 333; Saydoynes comes to the rescue, 334, 335; Merlin says he has forgotten the kiss, 335; he becomes furious at this, 335; slays Clarell, 336; upsets Rion, 336; giants in revenge bear him down, 336; Merlin comes to the rescue, 336; horsed by Ban, 336; throws down Rion's standard, 337; defeat and retreat of Rion, 337; dashes alone after Rion, 338; overtakes him, 338; Rion fourteen feet high, 339; overthrows Rion, 339; Arthur twenty and Rion forty-two years old, 339; grips

Calibourne, which gives out a great light, 339, 340; Rion slips and drops his club, 339; Rion draws his sword Marmadoyse, 340; Arthur covets it, for it flames like his, 340; Rion offers to let him go if he will give up his arms, 340; answers disdainfully, tells Rion to submit, 340; tells Rion he is Arthur, 341; hears Rion's name and estate, 341; Rion swears not to eat till he has killed him, 341; tells him it will be a long fast, 341; gives Rion a great wound, 341, 342; Rion rushes at him madly, 342; hits him a great stroke, but can't "attain" him, 342; Nascien, Adragains, and Hervy come, 342; Rion flies, 342; chases him, 342; six kings attack Arthur, and Rion escapes, 342, 343; king Kehenyns attacks him, 343; maims him, 343; the other five attack him, 343; slits Ffernicans and fells Heroas, 343; the rest fly, 343; chases them, 345; comes to Ban and Bors, 345; [slays a nephew of Madagot, 345; Madagot in revenge captures Galeshyn, 345; Galeshyn rescued by Gawein, 345;] three of Rion's kin slain, 346; Rion in a rage comes to Arthur, 346; his shield slit by Rion, 346; smites Rion on the arm, 346; Rion's sword sticks fast in the shield, 346; throws down the shield, 346; Rion seizes him by the shoulders, 346; throws down Calibourne lest Rion should get it, 346; and holds on to his horse's neck, 346; Ban comes and Rion lets go, 346, 347; Ban wounds Rion, 346; Rion flies, vowing future vengeance, 346, 347, 450; unwounded, 347; tells Ban he has won a jewel, 347; shows him Marmadoyse, 347; is proud of it, 347, 648, 351, 352; his fellows follow the Saxons, 348; goes to Toraise, 349; some of his knights lose him, 349; goes to Danablaise, 351, 450; finds Guyomar, Ydiers, and Synados fighting with Saxons, 351; dashes at the Saxons, 352; does well with Marmadoyse, 352; is pleased with the sword, 352, 353; the knights say he will be a noble knight when old enough, 351; meets some of his knights fighting Saxons, 352; finds Antor fighting on foot, 352; dashes down the Saxons, 352, 353; likes Marmadoyse better than Calibourne, 353; beats off the Saxons, 353, 615; meets Merlin and the dragon-banner, 353; goes to help Leodogan, 353; the banner sheds light, 353; does marvels on the Saxons, 355, 356; the bright dragon, 356; Merlin leads him to the three Saxon kings, 356, 357, 359; slays Ysdras, 357; the day breaks and they rest, 357; returns to

Leodogan's tents, 357; collects the spoil, 357; distributes it as Merlin tells him, 357, 358; raises a company of twenty thousand bachelors, 358, 382; goes with Bors and Leodogan to Toraise, 358, 359, 360; Bors goes to Charroye, 358, 359; Leodogan asks him to marry Gonnore, 360; Merlin says they must wait a bit, and tells him to meet Bors at Bredigan, 360; leaves Leodogan, 360; Gonnore says "be quick back," and he says he wishes he was back already, 360; at Bredigan, 363; Ban comes, and tells him of Guyneban's magic, 363; hears of the fair lady, and says he would marry her but for Merlin, 363; waits at Bredigan for Bors, 363, 364, 365; Amaunt refuses allegiance, 365; Bors fights and slays him, 365—370; Amaunt's men split, some go away, others come with Bors to do homage, 368, 369; praises Bors, 370; digs for the treasure Merlin told of, 370; carries it to Logres, 370; finds twelve good swords in the Forest Denoyable, 370; his nephews hear he is coming, and come out to meet him, 370; waits for them, 370; Gawein is their spokesman, and says Arthur's renown has made them come to be knighted by him, 371, 372; commends Gawein, and promises to knight them all, and to make them lords in his court, 372; asks their names, 372, 373 [i.e. Gawein, Agravain, Gaheret, and Gaheryes, sons of king Lot; Galaishin, son of Ventres; the two Eweins, sons of Urien; Dodynell the sauage, the son (?sons) of Belinans; Alain and Acon, nephews of king (? Brangore) of Strangore; Kay Destranx and Kehedin; Ewein white hand; Ewein Esclins; Ewein Cyvell; Ewein de lyonell; Seigramor]; puts his arms round Gawein's neck and kisses him, 373; makes great joy of Seigramor, 373; makes Gawein constable of his household, 373, 374; Gawein thanks him, 374; all go to Logres, 374; his sister, Lot's wife, comes to meet him, 374; and Morgne le fee, 374; goes to the palace, 374; his welcome, 374; the "children" go to keep their vigil in the minster, 374; Ban and Bors wait on them, 374; before high mass next day takes Calibourne, 374; girds Gawein with it, 374; dubs him, 374, 449; gives him a treasure sword, 374; dubs Gaheret, Gaheries, and Agravain, Ewein and Ewein Avoutres, Galaishin, Kay Destranx, Kehedin, and gives them treasure swords, 374, 449; dubs Dodynell, 374, 449; dubs Seigramor, and puts on his spurs, 374, 375, 449;

dubs Ewein white hand, Ewein Esclyn, Ewein Cyuell, Ewein de Lyonell, Alain, Acon, and gives them treasure swords, 375, 449 ; all go to mass, and then to a banquet in the palace, 375 ; forbids quintain because of the Saxons, 375 ; his largess, 375 ; Merlin tells him to prepare to go to Benoyk, 375 ; tells Gawein to get the host of forty thousand men ready to move at midnight, 376 ; Doo is to guard Logres with twenty thousand men, 376 ; remains at Logres, 378 ; Merlin tells him to wait for him at Rochell, 378 ; Merlin goes to Blase, 378 ; goes from Logres to Dover, 379 ; arrives at The Rochell, 379 ; meets Merlin there, 379 ; Merlin tells him to start for Trebes, 381, 382, 400 ; leads the fourth division with the knights of the Round Table, 382, 383 ; Kay is to bear the dragon-banner, 383, 385, 386, 393 ; Blioberis is to lead the host, 383, 384 ; Merlin's departure for Briogue, 383, 384 ; the start for Trebes, 384, 385, 386, 399 ; the army waits for Merlin's signal, 386 ; Claudas on the alert, 386 ; the signal given, 386, 387 ; the battle begins, 387 ; attacks Randolf, 387 ; Claudas loses ten thousand men and is wroth, 387 ; routs the French under Randolf, 392 ; helped by the Knights of the Round Table, 392 ; attacks Pounce and Antoyne, 392, 393 ; succours Bohors, 392, 393 ; Kay's dragon-banner terrifies the enemy into confusion, 393 ; the meaning of the banner, 393 ; the dragon signifies his power, 393 ; the flame the slaughter of his time, 393 ; the tortuous tail the treason of Mordred and his band, 393 ; [passes over sea to fight the emperor of Rome, and to take the realm of Gannes and Benoyk, because of the false love of Launcelot, who had seduced Gonnore, Arthur's wife, 393 ;] the battle is fierce, 393 ; Gawein succours Ban, 394, 395 ; and unhorses Claudas, 394 ; Claudas discomfited, 397, 398 ; the prowess of the company of the Round Table, 398 ; the field covered with the dead, 398 ; the Trebes folk come on the wall to see what is amiss, 398 ; the two queens, Helayn and her sister, come on the tower, and see the dragon-banner, 398, 399 ; they wonder at it, 399 ; they send a messenger, 399 ; Bretell tells him that it is Arthur, and the two kings come to raise the siege of Trebes, 399 ; joy in Trebes, 399 ; the joy of the besieged queens at his rescuing them, 400 ; lays an ambush with three hundred chosen knights, 401, 402, 404 ; [after his death, and Ban's and Launce-

lot's guardianship of Logres, Bors slays Claudas, 401 ;] the battle begins again ; he has twenty-eight thousand, and Claudas has thirty-five thousand men in the field, 402 ; the three hundred knights withdraw to repair their armour, 402 ; Claudas is getting on better, and drives Pharien and his men back a little, 402 ; but Leonce succours Pharien, 403 ; people of Logres are getting worsted, 404 ; Merlin scolds him for his idleness, 404, 407 ; and asks him what Gonnore will think of his cowardice, 404 ; ashamed, 40 ; hangs his shield on his back, and does wonders with his two-handed sword, 406, 408 ; slays more than two hundred, 406 ; attacks Frolle, Pounce, and Antony, 408 ; Frolle makes him bend over the saddle with his spear, 408 ; Gawein is furious at this, and unhorses Frolle, 408, 409 ; asks Gawein to stay by his side, 409 ; enemy confused 409 ; meets Bans and Bors, 409, 410 ; and Adragain, Nascien, and Hervy de Rivell, 410 ; it is past noon, 410 ; Kay finds Arthur's shield on the ground, fears he is dead, and searches for him, 410 ; Kay finds him, and is glad he is alive, 410 ; his shield round his neck again, 410 ; Merlin comes with the dragon, 410 ; Merlin's signal for onset, 410 ; Gawein upsets Claudas, 410 ; Claudas routed, and half his army destroyed, 411, 412, 438, 449, 450 ; the pursuit lasts till dark, 411, 412 ; many prisoners, 412 ; finds great spoil in the tent, 412 ; Pharien and Grascien keep watch the night, 412 ; Ban and Bors lead him into Trebes castle, 412 ; Ban's queen Helayn and her sister the queen of Bors welcome him, 412 ; well housed, 412 ; Helayn's marvellous dream, 413, 414, 415 ; is tired with the day's work, 415 ; sojourns there a month, 416, 417, 418 ; makes daily inroads into Claudas' land, 416 ; [succours Ban and Bors' heirs, who are reduced to straits by Claudas, 416, 699 ; troubles at home, 416 ; death of Ban and Bors, 416, 699 ;] Merlin tells him of Helayn's dream, 416 ; and partly explains it, 416, 417 ; Merlin's return, 419 ; Gawein ravages Claudas' lands, 419 ; Gawein returns with much plunder, 419 ; all go to Gannes, 419 ; stays there two days, 419 ; goes to the Rochell, and thence to the sea, 419, 420, 447 ; Merlin tells him to make haste to Carmelide with three thousand men, 420 ; asks Merlin to come now so as to be at his marriage, 420 ; Merlin says he will follow soon, 420 ; Merlin goes to Rome, 420 ; [defies Julyus

Cesar, who invades Logres, 420; battle with Julyus at Logres, and Julyus slain by Gawein, 420;] Merlin his master counsellor, 436, 437; [the fight at Trebes was with the Almaynes, Romaynes, and the Frenchmen of Gaule and la Deserte, 438;] arrives at Bloy Bretayne, 447; at Logres, 447; all ride to Carmelide, 447, 448, 468, 471; welcomed to Toraise by Leodogan, 448; Gonnore's joy at seeing him, 448; a day set for his marriage with Gonnore, 448, 449, 450, 561, 635; awaits Merlin's arrival, 449, 451; the barons begin to repent of their enmity, 450; Lot schemes to get back his own wife, and to capture Gonnore, 450, 472; a plot to substitute the step-daughter of Cleodalis for Gonnore, 451, 452, 463, 562; Merlin is counter-plotting, 452; the marriage procession, 453; married to Gonnore, 213, 451, 453, 482; Gonnore's extreme beauty, 453; wedded at the minster door, 453, 467, 562; the tournament at Toraise, 454, 461, 562; Leodogan hears of the plot to kidnap Gonnore, 465; Merlin and Leodogan lead him to Gonnore, 466; [his wife leaves him and is three years with Galehaut, 323, 466, 470; her love for Launcelot, 466; his adultery with Gonnore, step-daughter of Cleodalis, 466; the realm is accursed on account of Bertelak, 466, 470;] the false Gonnore is banished, 468, 469, 562; the trial and banishment of Bertelak, 469, 470, 562; Bertelak vows revenge, 470; prepares to return to Logres, 471; tells Gawein to go to Logres, and get all ready for the court royal, 471, 562; Gawein goes, 470; is left with only five hundred men, 471; Gawein anxious for Arthur's safety, 471; three days afterwards he starts with Gonnore and Ban and Bors for Bredigan, 472, 473; Merlin goes to Blase, but says he will be at the court royal, 472, 473, 562; Lot lays an ambush to capture him, 472, 473, 562; Lot has seven hundred men, 473; meets the enemy, 473; unhorses Lot, 474; his horse killed by Lot, 474; his horse falls over him, and pins him down, 474; Lot essays to cut his head off, 474; rescued by his knights, 474; Gawein and Kay come to help with eighty fellows, 475, 562; Kay is a true knight to him, 475, 476; [his son Lohoot (*see* Hoot) slayn in treason by Kay, 475; Percevale ly Galoys is wrongly accused of the deed, 475;] asks Gawein how he knew he was in trouble, 477, 478; Lot and his knight do homage to him, 478, 479, 480, 518, 557; returns to

Logres with Lot, 479; great joy in Logres, 479; he and his wife give great gifts, 479, 480; the court royal assembles, 480, 481; establishes his court royal, 481; vows that he and his knights will redress all wrongs brought before them, 481, 484, 562; the knights of the Round Table vow to aid distressed maidens, 481, 484, 562; Gawein and his fellows vow to be the queen's knights, and do her pleasure, 482, 483, 484, 562; gives his queen charge of his treasure, 483; sends for Gawein, 485; tells Gawein to prevent strife and disorder in the lists, 485; the tournament, 485, 500, 562; Gawein won't promise, 485; he and Gonnore watch the jousting, 485; ordains a band of men to keep order, 486; foul play by the Round Table knights, 489, 490, 492; a messenger from Gawein, 491, 495, 498; stops the fight, 495; upbraids Gawein for his conduct, 498; cessation of the tourney, 499; reconciliation of the Queen's knights and Round Table knights, 499—502; the quest of the St. Grail, 502; in council, 504; Ban says don't let the knights tourney unless with strangers, 504, 562; Lot says, drive out the Saxons, 505; the queen commends Ban's advice, 505; Lot proposes a truce with the princes, and a confederation against the Saxons, 505, 562; agrees to send Lot as an ambassador to the princes, 505, 519, 559; Lot agrees to go, and will take his four sons with him, 506, 510, 546, 559, 561; sorry to spare Gawein, 506; but the queen persuades him to let him go, 506; the embassy getting ready, 507; it meets with the Saxons, 510, 562; Elizer setting out for his court, 520, 521, 528, 539; the eldest son of Pellynor of the sauage fountain comes to take arms of him, 539; his castle of Roestok, 545; a truce made with the barons, 560, 562, 576; land is released from the excommunication, 560, 577; a day of meeting on Salisbury plain, 560; great preparations for attacking the Saxons, 560; glad of the truce, 561; Merlin is busy collecting forces, 565; Merlin comes, 566; is told by Merlin to hasten the preparations for attacking the Saxons, 566, 567, 574; hears that Nabulall de Camadayse and a young lord, son of Amaunt, and Cleodalis, are coming to the assembly, but Leodogan does not intend to come, 567; Merlin tells him the treason of the three Round Table knights, 567, 568; sends Ewein, Kay, and Gifflet to stop the three traitors,

568; their return, 573; pacifies the knights, 573; upbraids the three Round Table knights, 574; bad blood between the Queen's and the Round Table knights, 574; goes to Salisbury, 575, 578; the Saxons on their guard, 575, 576; talks with Merlin, 578, 579; Merlin's prophecy that the father and the son shall slay each other, and of the crowned and uncrowned lions, 579; visits each of the lords in their tents, 579, 580; consultation with the twelve princes, 581, 582; a start for Clarence agreed to, 582, 585; Elizer is to be knighted, 583, 584; offers Elizer arms and sword, 584; departure with the host to Clarence, 585; his banner borne by Merlin, 585; slays Magloras, 591; the rescue of Morgeins, 591, 592; Gonnore in Garlot, 592; start of the host for Clarence, 592; the battle before Garlot, 594; takes the Saxons in the rear, 596; rout of the Saxons, 597, 617; his losses, 598; advance to Clarence, 598; the barons do him homage, 599; the battle before Clarence, 599, 601, 602; utter rout of Saxons, 602; division of the spoil, and five days' revel in Clarence, 603; return to Gonnore at Camelot, 603; Merlin tells Ban and Bors to return home, 603; their stay at Agravadain's castle, 606; ordains a court royal at Camelot, 613, 614, 615, 617; Merlin enters disguised as a blind harper, 615; receives a letter of defiance from Rion, 617, 618; Rion wants his beard to add to the eleven he has flayed already, 619; laughs at Rion's request and defiance, 620, 621; the blind harper wants to be banner-bearer, 621, 622; refuses, and the harper vanishes, 622; knows it is Merlin, 622; a little naked child comes in, and asks to be banner-bearer, 622, 623; and tells him to prepare to fight Rion, 622; he thinks it is Merlin, and grants his request, 623; Merlin resumes his form, 623; preparations for battle, 623, 624; starts for Carmelide, 624; arrival at Toraise, 624; battle with Rion's host, 624, 630; Rion offers to settle the question by a personal encounter, 627; Arthur consents, 627, 628; Gawein wants to go instead, but he won't allow him, 628; the combat, 628; vanquishes Rion, who, however, will not yield, 630; cuts his head off, 630; his joyful entry into Toraise, 630; his wounds healed, 630; Rion's barons pay their homage, 630; leaves Toraise, 630; joins Gonnore at Cameloth, 630; returns to Logres, 630; Merlin talks of leaving him now that his work is done, 630; is much

disturbed by Merlin's dark saying that a lion, son of a bear and leopard, shall aid him, 631; departure of Merlin, 631; Merlin's return, 635; the advent of the maiden and dwarf, 635, 679, 698; the maiden asks a boon, 635; he grants it, 635, 636; she wants him to knight her lover the dwarf, 636; Kay scorns her, 636; two squires appear with shield and horse for the new knight, 636, 637; dubs the dwarf knight, 637, 679, 682; the two strange lovers depart, 638; Gonnore and the knights ridicule the dwarf, but Merlin tells them he is of royal blood, 638; an embassy from Luce, emperor of Rome, 639; ordering him to do homage to Luce, 640, 644; he answers that he will take Rome, not Rome him, and claims Rome by right of his ancestors, 642, 643; invasion preparing, 643; his princes assemble, 644; his host take ship to Gannes, 644; has a vision of a bear and a dragon, which Merlin interprets, 644, 645; hears of a great dragon which is the terror of the country, 645; goes with Kay and Bedyuer to attack the giant, 645, 649; the sorrow of the woman whom the giant has enthralled, 646; attacks the giant single-handed, 647; slays the giant with his sword Marmadoise, 648, 668, 679; returns victorious with the giant's head, 649, 650; advance to Burgoyne, 650; joined by Ban and Bors, 650; sends defiance to Luce, 650, 651, 653; the adventures of his embassy, 650, 653; sends succour to his ambassadors, 653, 657, 669; erects a castle, 650, 653, 676; return of Gawein from the embassy with prisoners, 655; an attempt at rescue of the Roman prisoners, 656; return of the succourers, 657; goes to Oston, 658; prepares for battle with Luce, 658; his dragon-banner is set up, 658; appoints leaders of his divisions, 659; the battle, 660, 664; the great gonfanon of the Gold Eagle of Luce, 662; Luce is slain by Gawein, 663, 699; the battle is critical, 663; dashes into the fight and slays Gestoire and Polibetes, 663; rout of the Romans, 664, 676, 679; sends the body of Luce on a bier to Rome as his trewage, and asks Merlin what to do next, 664; Merlin says, go on your way, as some people want your help, 664; the devil cat at Lak de losane, 664; goes against the cat, 666; fights with the devil cat, and slays it, 667, 676, 679; fight between some of his and Claudas' knights, 669, 670; kinsmen of Fflualis come to serve him; his battle with Mordred, 676; goes to the

castle on the Aube and to Benoyk, 676;
sends Gawein to destroy the castle of
the Marche, 677, 678 ; Gawein returns
successful, 678 ; hears that Leodogan
is dead, 678; goes to Logres and
comforts Gonnore, 678 ; Merlin's farewell, 678, 681 ; sends his knights in
search of Merlin, 682, 694, 697 ; the
further adventures of the maiden and
dwarf, 684 ; at Cardoell, 685, 694 ; the
maiden and dwarf bring a captured
knight, 685, 687, 690 ; the adventures,
in quest of Merlin, of Seigramor, 687 ;
Ewein, 689 ; Gawein, 692 ; Gawein
finds Merlin's prison, 693 ; Gawein's
coming back, 695, 697 ; the dwarf
returns in his own shape as Evadeam,
697, 698 ; the story becomes silent about
king Arthur, 698.

ARUNDELL. *See* Arondell.

ATALAS LAMNACHOUR, 348.

AUADAIN, Evadeam ; turned dwarf by
sorcery of his love the Feire Beaune,
635—638, 679, 682—691, 697, 698 ;
knighted by Arthur, 637, 638, 682 ;
son to king Brangore, 638, 688.

AUBE, river in Burgoyne, a castle there,
650, 676.

AUENABLE. *See* Grisandoll.

AUNGIER, AUNGIS. *See* Angier.

AUNGIS, 243.

AURELIUS AMBROSE, 42.

AYGLYNS DES VAUX, Ayglin des
Vaux, Aglins des Vaus, brother to Ke-
bedins le petit, 480 ; kin to Meranges
de Porlesgues, 518 ; nephew to Belynans, 577.

BAHARANS, king, 248.

BALAN, a giant slain by Ulfin, 217.

BALFINNE, Balfinnes, 345 ; kin to
Rion, 346.

BAN OF BENOYK (brother of Bors,
472, etc.); parentage, 122 ; his enemy,
122, 124 ; dispute with Claudas, 124 ;
lands ravaged, 124, 382 ; his castle
holds out, 124 ; goes against Claudas,
124, 125 ; puts him to flight, 125 ; his
wife Elein, 125, 144, 380, 381, 603 ;
goes to Arthur, 125 ; Arthur's messengers, 128 ; they tell him of Merlin and
of Arthur, 129 ; fears to leave because
of Claudas, is assured by Merlin of
safety, 130 ; agrees to go, and enter-
tains the messengers, 130 ; entrusts his
lands to Leonces and Pharien, 130,
131 ; goes by ship, 131 ; his magnificent reception by Arthur, 132 ; the
revels, 133, 138 ; the tourney, 133,
137 ; his brother Guynebande, 133, 139 ;
praises Kay, 136 ; conference in the
chamber, 138 ; asks about Merlin, 138 ;
Merlin comes and questions him, 139 ;
confronts him with his brother, 139 ;

does homage to Arthur as his lord,
140, 173 ; in council with Arthur,
141, 557 ; withstands Merlin's advice
at first, but agrees to it, 142, 146 ;
collects reinforcements for Arthur, 142,
143 ; Merlin his messenger, 142, 143 ;
his godson Bawdewyn, 144 ; his son
Launcelot, 147 ; Merlin comes, 149 ;
Merlin leads him to Arthur, 150, 173 ;
arranges his forces, 151, 152 ; leads
the fourth division and is the "best
knight in the host," 151 ; Aliaume bears
his banner, 152 ; takes the enemy in
the rear, 154 ; rescues Arthur, 160 ;
assails Ydiers, 161 ; his banner borne
by Anthony his steward, 163 ; routs his
foes, 163, 164 ; attacked by Loot, 164 ;
upsets Roy de Cent Chevaliers, 164 ;
attacked by Brangore, 164 ; upsets
Brangore, 164 ; Arthur comes to the
rescue, 164 ; on foot, 164 ; horsed by
Arthur, 165 ; with Arthur at Brede-
gan, 167 ; the great churl, 168 ; goes
to Tarsaide, 202 ; to Tamelide, 171,
175, 303, 307 ; worsts the Saxons, 185 ;
his age, 203 ; incog. at Tamelide, 203,
204 ; the battle with the Saxons, 206,
207, 212 ; he gives great strokes with
Carchense, 210 ; slays Clarion with it,
210, 211 ; Merlin's counsel, 216 ; puts
Sonygreux to flight, 216 ; his prowess,
220 ; wants to fight Sorfarin, 221 ;
follows Arthur, 221 ; slays Sortebran,
222 ; assailed by Malore and Freelent,
222, 223 ; rescued by Arthur, 223 ;
cuts off Randoul's arm, 223 ; served
by Gonnore, 225 ; asks Leodogan why
Gonnore is not married, 228 ; his
answer, 228 ; Merlin goes to Logres,
258 ; Merlin's fears for him, 303 ; his
cousin Leonces, 305 ; half Brioke
forest his, 308 ; his vassal Dionas, 308 ;
gives Dionas half Brioke forest, 308 ;
Merlin comes, 312, 314 ; Merlin's
counsel, 314—316 ; hears of Claudas,
314, 315 ; Merlin's dark saying, 315 ;
goes to Leodogan, 317, 318, 382 ;
Arthur's betrothal, 319, 320 ; discovers
his name, 320 ; does homage to
Arthur, 320 ; in the first ward, 321 ;
Leodogan's court royal, 322 ; sits
at the head of the dais, 322 ; praises
Gonnore's love for Arthur, 322 ;
follows the dragon-banner, 327 ; goes
to the rescue of Nascien and Bors,
331, 332 ; does marvels, 332, 333 ;
slays Minap, 333 ; help comes, 335 ;
horses Arthur, 336 ; throws down
Rion's standard, 337 ; pursues Glorienx,
Mynados, and Colufer, 338, 343 ; they
are reinforced, 343 ; slays three of
their fellows, 343 ; fells Pignoras,
344 ; kills Sinagrex, 344 ; Bors comes,
344 ; in a strait, 344 ; Rion comes,

first believe her innocence, 11 ; gives her a penance and absolution, 11, 12 ; she is great with child, and comes to him, 12, 13 ; promises to aid her when accused, 13 ; questioned by the judges, 13 ; tells the judge to wait till the child is born before burning her, 13 ; and to put her in a strong tower, 13 ; they act on his advice, 14 ; the birth of Merlin, 14, 16 ; the trial, 16, 23, 121 ; Merlin devises the book for him to write, 23 ; Merlin tells him he will go where the holy Grail is, 23 ; messengers from Vortiger, 30, 31, 32 ; is told by Merlin to follow him to Northumberland, 32, 33 ; and that he shall be supplied with all the matter for the book there, 32 ; the book shall be called the Boke of the St. Grail, 32 ; goes to Northumberland, 33 ; Merlin comes with news for the book, 41, 42, 46, 47, 53, 56, 81, 88, 97, 143, 166, 259, 260, 261, 303, 305, 327, 378, 635 ; Merlin's book of prophecies, 53, 54 ; Merlin tells him of the Round Table, 61, 62 ; Merlin's love for him, 123 ; Merlin's dark sayings, 303, 304, 305 ; another visit from Merlin, 438, 450, 451 ; more news for his book, 438, 451, 472, 562, 563, 679 ; another visit from Merlin, 472 ; asks Merlin whether the Saxons will be driven out, and about the dark prophecy of his, 563 ; Merlin's answer, 563 ; writes letters which Merlin sticks up in the highways, 563, 564 ; Merlin's departure, 564 ; Merlin again comes, 612, 635, 679 ; Merlin's farewell, 679, 688.

BLEORIS, Blaaris, Bloaris, knight, 162, 212, 487 ; godson of Bors, 162 ; son of Bors, 212.

BLIOBERIS, Blioberes, Bliobleris, Blyoberis, one of the forty-two fellows, 136, 137, 151, 212, 349, 352, 383, 384, 385, 459, 480.

BLIOS, lord of Cloadas castle, 321.

BLIOS, Blioc de Cassell, Blios del Cassett, Blyos de la Casse, 682, one of the forty-two fellows, 135, 136, 212.

BLOY BRETAIGNE. See Bretayne.

BLOY MOUNTAYNE, 307.

BLOYS of PLAISSHIE, 442.

BOCLUS, king of Mede, 661, 662.

BOHORT, son of Bors, 698 ; brother of Lyonel, 698.

BOORS of BENOYK, 125. See Ban.

BORELL, 655. See Bretel.

BORS of GANNES, Bohort of Gannes, 698 ; brother of Ban, 472, etc. ; parentage, 122 ; his enemy, 122, 124 ; ravages Claudas' land and subdues Claudas, 125 ; marries Elein's sister, 125, 144, 380, 603 ; messengers from Arthur, 125 ; they are attacked, 126 ; fears to

go to Arthur because of Claudas, 130 ; is reassured by Merlin, and goes by ship, 130 ; grand reception, 132 ; revels, 133, 138 ; the tourney, 133, 137 ; his brother Guynebande, 133, 139 ; praises Kay, 136 ; the conference in the chamber, 138 ; does homage to Arthur as liege lord, 140, 173 ; in council with Arthur, 141, 146, 557 ; his castle Mouloir, 144 ; Merlin comes, 149 ; Merlin leads him to Arthur, 150, 173 ; his forces set in battle order, 151, 152 ; his ensign borne by Pharien, 151 ; leads the third division, 151 ; takes the enemy in the rear, 154 ; rescues Arthur, 160 ; assails Ydiers, 161 ; "the grete baner," 161 ; dashes into the fight, and attacks Carados, 162 ; his godson Blaaris bears his banner, 162, 212 ; prowess, 163 ; with Arthur at Bredigan, 167, 168 ; goes to Tarsaide, 202 ; to Tamelide, 171, 175, 303, 307 ; worsts the Saxons, 185 ; his age, 203 ; the battle with the Saxons, 206, 207, 212 ; his prowess, 210 ; smites Sarmedon, 211 ; upsets Seleuaunt, 217 ; his prowess, 220 ; follows Arthur, 221 ; slays Clariel, 222 ; served by Gonnore, 225 ; Merlin goes to Logres, 258 ; Merlin's fears for him, 303 ; his cousin Leonces, 305 ; his vassal Dionas, 308 ; gives him a town, 308 ; Merlin comes, 312, 314 ; Merlin's counsel, 314—316 ; bears of Claudas, 315 ; Merlin's dark saying, 315 ; goes to Leodogan, 317, 318 ; Arthur's betrothal, 319 ; name discovered, 320 ; does homage to Arthur, 320 ; in the first ward, 321 ; Leodogan's court royal, 322 ; sits at the head of the dais, 322 ; praises Gonnore, 322 ; follows the banner in the fight, 327 ; chases king Saron, 328 ; gets a great stroke, 328 ; is surrounded, 328 ; attacked by Rion, 328 ; unhorses Saron, 328 ; despairs of his life, 329 ; hits Rion, 329 ; rescues Hervy the Rivell, 329 ; upsets Aroans, 329 ; upset by Rion, 330 ; rescued by Hervy, 330 ; and by Nascien, 331 ; Ban and others come, 332, 333 ; fighting on foot, 330, 333 ; help comes, 335 ; overthrows Rion's standard, 337 ; meets Ban, 344 ; his great deeds, 344 ; he and his brother hard bestead, 344 ; Rion comes against them, 344 ; overthrown by Rion, 344, 345 ; surrounded by Saxons, 345 ; can't rise, his horse has fallen upon him, 345 ; wounded, 345 ; rescued, 345 ; rises again, 345 ; slays Maltailliet, 345 ; slits Rion's helm, 345, 346 ; Rion cleaves his shield, 346 ; Uter Pendragon gives him Carroie castle, 350 ; gives it to Guynebant his brother, 350 ;

DODRILAS, an Amyrall, slain by Bors, 357

DODYNELL the SAVAGE, son of Belynans, 247, 373, 449, 576; his mother Esclence, 247; cousin of Galeshyn, 247, 373; hears Lot's sons are going to join Arthur and resolves to go too, 251; goes with Kay Destranx and Kehedin to Logres, 251, 252, 258, 377; battle with the Saxons, 294; meets Arthur, 373; dubbed knight by Arthur after the usual vigil, 374, 449; who gives him a treasure sword, 374; the banquet, 375; goes with Gawein, 377; in command under Gawein, 378; his prowess at Trebes, 396; unhorsed, 407, 408; succoured by Gawein, 407, 408; lodged in Trebes castle, 412; at the marriage of Arthur and Gonnore, 453, 454; in the tournament of Toraise, 456, 458, 459; at Arthur's Logres court royal, 480, 481; his deeds in the Logres tournament, 489; his comeliness, 499; goes seeking adventures with Seigramor and Galaishin, 561, 562, 566; the treason of Three Round Table knights who attack them, 561, 562, 566, 573; overthrows Monevall, one of them, 571; the fight stopped by knights sent by Arthur, 571, 572.

DOLEROUSE GARDE, 273. See Ladris, Lord.

DOO of CARDOEL, his son Gifflet, 133, 135, 138, 571; castelein of Cardoell, 197; a noble man and a true, 197; hears the banner, and aids Gawein, 200; overthrown by Madelen, 200; capture of Logres, 200, 376; divides the spoil, 201; makes great joy of Gawein and his fellows, 301; asks Gawein about Merlin, 302; master forester to Uter Pendragon, 133; vows to find Merlin, 682.

DORILAS, Dodalis, Dodalus, a Saxon leader, slain by Agravain, 348, 549—552

DORILAS, Doriax, a Round Table knight, kin to Ventres, 243—246, 441, 443, 491, 587, 588.

DOUCRENEFAR, a castle, 518; castelein. see Grandilus, 518.

DOULAS, a Saxon, slain by Gosenaym, 217.

DOVE, Doue, Dione, river and bridge, 281, 282, 286, 287, 288.

DOVER, 250, 259, 377, 378, 379, 678.

DRIANT the REDE, a Saxon, slain by Seigramor, 268.

DRIAS DE LA FOREST SAUAGE, Drias de la foreste sauge, Diras, one of the forty-two fellows, 135, 151, 157, 159, 212.

DRIAS LE GAIS of the forest Perilouse, 250, 441.

DRIAS, the lord of Salerne, 441.

EASTRANGORE, the chief city of Carados, 187; of Brangore, 247, 250, 685.

EBRON, husband of Enhyngnes, 326.

ELEIN, see Helayne.

ELEINE, Elein, wife of Ban of Benoyk, 125.

ELIZER, son of Pelles of Lytenoys, 521—524, 528—535, 538, 540, 542—546, 550, 553—556, 584, 585, 587—590, 596, 602; Pellynor his uncle, 520, 539, 583; his cousin germain, 539; his uncle king Alain, 583.

ELUNADAS, a young lord, and nephew to the wise lady of the foreste saunz retour, 321, 361, 362, 363.

EMPRESSE of ROME, wife to Julius Cezar, 420, 421, 429, 430, 431, 434; burnt for her untruth, 432, 433.

ENGELONDE, kings of, 53.

ENHYNGNES, sister to Joseph (Abaramathie), wife to Ebron, 326.

ENTRE of ROME, 422.

ESCALIBOURE, see Calibourne.

ESCAM, duke of Cambenyk, comes to help the seven kings against Arthur, 145; in the battle of Bredigan, 157, 159, 160, 161; arms Cambenyk his city against the Saxons, 188; a messenger from Clarion, 255; leads his men to aid Clarion against the Saxons, 256; a battle, 256, 257, 258, 271—277; his castle Suret, 313; leads the sixth ward in the expedition against the Saisnes before Clarence, 438, 439; a night attack, 439, 440, 441; discomfited, 444; but makes another attack, 444; is totally beaten, 446, 449; goes home, 447, 449; hears Arthur is at Logres, 449, 450; wishes for peace with Arthur, 450, 451; Lot and his sons come to aid him just as he is driven in by a Saxon host, 547—551; unhorsed, 551; horsed and rescued by Gawein and Gaheries, 551; unhorsed again, 553; horsed by Lot, 553; complete rout of the Saxons, 554; finds who Lot is and his company, 554, 555; entry into Cambenyk, 555; praises Elizer, 555, 556; Lot proposes peace with Arthur, 556; agrees, 556, 557; sends messengers to the other barons to come to the conference, 557, 558; Lot and his sons go to Arestuell, 557, 558; the conference, 558, 559; the assembly of the host at Salisbury, 565, 575, 576, 582, 584, 585; the battle before Garlot, 588; leads the first division, 593, 594; slays Salubrun, 594; in battle before Clarence, 601; aids Arthur against Luce, 644; in Arthur's first division, 659.

ESCLENCE, wife of Belynans, daughter of king Natan, sister to Ventres, and her son Dodynell, 247.

words, 376; says it was one called Merlin, 376; Arthur laughs and tells him all, 376, 377; says he is at Merlin's service, and wants to see him, 377; his eyes are opened, 377; Merlin tells him to take leave of his mother, 377; and then lead the host to Dover, 377; and to assemble ships there, 377; takes leave of his mother, 377; Sir Ewein, Galaishin, Dodynell, Seigramore, Ewein Avoutres, the four Eweins, and his brethren lead the host under his command, 377, 378, 395; Keheden and ˚Kay Destranx with him, 377, 378, 395; arrives at Dover, 378; assembles a great navy, 378; at the Rochell, 379; makes great joy on meeting Merlin, 379; the expedition to Trebes preparing, 381, 382; is to lead the first division of ten thousand knights, 382, 384, 385, 395; Ulfyn to bear his banner, 382; the start, 384, 385; the battle begins, 387; falls upon Frolle's host, 387, 394; slays five thousand of his men, 387; a fresh onset, 388; rescues Seigramore, 388; his prowess, 388, 394; sees Claudas fighting Ban and fells him, 394; slays Mysteres and Antorilas and two thousand others, 394; Ban's gratitude, 394, 395; their friendly feelings, 395; Ban wants his company, but Gawein says he must go to see if his cousins and brethren are safe, 395; dashes after Claudas, 395, 396; as he goes he sees his brethren and cousins in distress, goes to succour them, leaving Claudas to escape, 396; Agravain unhorsed, Gaheret also, and Galaishin in the hands of Frolle, 396; Ban and he succour their fellows, 396; fells Frolle and releases Galaishin, 397; applauds Galaishin's bravery, 397; busy in the fight, 398; defeat of Claudas, 398, 399; Ban's own men appear on the field, 400; suggests an ambush, 400; taunted with cowardice by Merlin, 404, 405; prowess, 407; slays Randolf, the seneschal of Gawle, 407; meets with Dodynell the savage and Kehedin the litill, unhorsed and in trouble, 407, 408; aids them, 408; the enemy shun his onset, 408; wounds Frolle because he smote Arthur, 408, 409; at Arthur's side, 409; fells Pounce Antony and wounds Randolf, 409; Arthur asks him to keep by his side, 409; meets Ban and Bors, 410; Merlin gives the signal for another onset, 410; wounds, upsets, and rides over Claudas, 410; is admired for his valour, 410; Claudas loses half his army and is routed, but escapes, 411; led by Ban and Bors into Trebes castle, 412; well housed,

412; Queen Helayn's dream explained by Merlin, 416, 417; ravages Claudas' lands, 419; returns to Benoyk, 419; Merlin is waiting for him, 419; goes to Gannes the Rochell and to sea, 419, 420; starts for Carmelide, 420, 447, 448; slays Julyus Cesar in battle at Logres, 420; in Toraise, 448, 449; at Arthur's marriage with Gonnore, 453, 454; the tournament at Toraise, 454, 461; always wears a habergeon of double mail for safety, 454; his victory in the tournament at Logres, 455, 462; ever true to God and to his lord, 455; gets furious, seizes a beam of oak and rushes again into the tornament, 460; the knights of the Round Table are angry at his victory, and swear revenge, 461; becomes a knight of the Round Table, 462; trial and banishment of Bertelak, 469, 470; starts for Logres with all Arthur's host but five hundred men, 471, 562; anxious for Arthur's safety, 471; makes great preparations for the court royal at Logres in August, 471, 472; his character detailed, 472; goes with forty fellows to aid Arthur who is hard bestead by Lot, 475, 476, 562; overthrows Lot, and rides over him, 476; is about to slay Lot, 476; but finds who it is, 476, 477; Lot tries to embrace him, 477; will not know him until he has done homage to Arthur, 477, 560; takes Lot to do homage to Arthur, 477, 478, 562; at the court royal at Logres, 480, 481; he and twenty-four of his fellows vow to be Queen Gonnore's knights, 482, 483, 484, 518, 562; the details of the vow, 482, 483; the queen appoints four clerks to write his and his fellows adventures, 483; they are called the Queen's knights, 483; Dagenet's cowardice, 484; makes ready the tournament at Logres, 484; the tournament, 484, 500; Arthur sends to speak with him, 485; Arthur asks him to keep order in the tournament, 485; would not promise, 485, 486; a band of squires and sergeants to keep order, 486; drives back the Round Table knights, 487; sends ten of them captured to the queen, 488, 502; again worsts the Round Table knights, 488; the Round Table knights are wroth, and in felony use war spears and drive in the Queen's knights, 488; remonstrates with them, 489; they will not cease their foul play, 489; arms himself and his fellows in complete armour, 489, 490; returns to the tournament, 490; Lot's knights offer help, 490; accepts it, 491; sends Galescowde to tell Arthur of the state of the tourney, 491, 495, 498; the Round Table knights

465; baptism, 114, parentage, 114, 115, 141, 208, 222, 404, 448, 472, 623, 678; of royal blood, 141, 213, 465; her beauty, 141, 227; Merlin counsels Arthur to marry her, 141, 177; an heiress, 141; the battle at Tamelide, 208; sees her father taken prisoner, 208, 209; sees him rescued by Arthur, and Merlin, 210; her joy, 210; her anxiety for Arthur, 219; sees him upset Sorfarin, 222; serves Arthur at the feast, 225, 257; the three kings, 225; pleased with Arthur, 225; brings him wine, 227; praises him, 227, 228; loves him, 229; her wisdom, 229; injures Guyomar, 316; Arthur comes, 317, 318, 319; her father offers her to Arthur, 319; Arthur and she are betrothed, 319, 320, 341, 357; "is glad of her new lord," 320; at the court royal, 322; her likeness to Cleodalis' daughter, 322; arms Arthur, 322; kisses him, 323, 325, 335; gives him a wondrous helm, 323; her father is anxious for the marriage, 360; Merlin postpones it, 360; Arthur goes to Bredigan, 360; asks him to come back soon, 360; the love treason of Launcelot, 393; Merlin taunts Arthur with cowardice, 404; Arthur comes back again, 448; makes great joy of him, 448; the wedding day fixed, 448—451; Lot's scheme to capture her, 456, 472; a plot to kidnap her and to substitute Gonnore, the step-daughter of Cleodalis, 451, 452, 463; her mistress, 452, 463; the marriage, 452, 453, 562, 213, 451; her extreme beauty, 453, 562; led up to the ceremony by Ban and Bors, 453, 562; seized by the plotters, 463, 464; rescued by Ulfyn and Bretel, 463, 464, 465; leaves Arthur and dwells with Galehaut for the love of Launcelot for three years, 466, 323, 470; Arthur's adultery with Gonnore, step-daughter of Cleodalis, 466; the false Gonnore banished, 468, 469; Gawein goes to Logres, 471; Arthur is left with only five hundred men, 471; sets out with Arthur for Bredigan, 472, 473; begs Sir Annestan as chaplain, 472; her cousin and her brother Sodoyne accompany her, 472; has an escort of forty knights, 473; Kay is a true knight to her, 475; in Logres with Arthur, 479, 480; the court royal, 480, 481; accepts the vow of Gawein and his fellows to be her knights, 482, 483; Arthur gives her the charge of his treasures, 483; chooses four clerks to write the adventures of Gawein and his band, 483, 503; watches the tournament of Logres, 485; Gawein sends her ten captured knights, 488, 502; foul play in the tournament, 492; grants her knight a chamber in his palace, 499; makes great joy of Ewein and Gawein, 499; reconciliation of her knights with the Round Table knights, 499—502; claims the ten captive knights as her own, 502; the quest of the Holy Grail, 502, 503; commends Ban's counsel, 505; and Lot's, 506; persuades Arthur to let Gawein go with Lot, 506; Gawein asks her to see that the knights of the Round Table and her knights don't quarrel again, 507; she promises, 507; Arthur's sister, Morgain, shames her, 508; because she discovered the amour between Morgain and Guyomar, 509; glad of the truce with the barons, 561; is loved by Amaunt's son, but her father and his are at strife, so cannot marry him, 565; constant intercourse with him, 565; Merlin comes, 566; the treason of the three Round Table knights, 468; the three knights brought in by Ewein, 573; discord between her knights and the Round Table knights, 574; goes with Arthur to Salisbury, 575; in Garlot, 592; valour of her knights at Garlot, 596; return of Arthur and his men to Camelot, 603; court royal at Camelot, 613, 614, 615; Merlin disguised as a harper enters and sings a lay in her honour, 615; victorious return of Arthur from Toraise, 630; goes with him to Logres, 630; Merlin's return, 635; a strange maiden brings a dwarf, her lover, to be knighted by Arthur, 638; she loathes the dwarf, 638; but Merlin says he is of royal blood, 638; death of her father Leodogan, 678; Arthur's return, 678; the maiden and dwarf come again, 685; Merlin's imprisonment, 694; the fair Beaune dwells with her, 698.

GORGAIN, fellow of Merangis, 349.

GORRE, 108, 145, 146, 176, 623.

GOSENAIN, hardy body, 481.

GOSENGES, Gosengos, son of King Amaunt, 563, 601, 565, 566, 567; his seneschal Nabunal, 644.

GOSNAYN DE STRANGOT, Grosenayne, 220, 292, 294.

GOSNAYNS CADRUS, 212, 217, 220, 352.

GRAAL, the, 32, 59, 173, 229, 304, 326, 341, 502, 520.

GRAALANT, 442.

GRANDILUS, his son Ewein Lionell, 518; castelein of Doucrenefar, 518.

GRANDOYNES, a knight of Round Table, 487.

GRASCIEN, 124, 135; of Trebes, 136, 144, 167, 306, 380, 381, 384, 400, 401, 406, 412, 564, 565, 587, 588, 589, 650, 699; death, 699.

JULIUS CEZAR, Julyus Cesar, Emperor of Rome, killed by Gawein, 420, 423, 426—431, 435, 436, 438 ; his daughter Ffoldate, 423, 434, 437 ; his wife Avenable, q.v. ; his first empress, q.v., empress of Rome.

JURDAN, 76. *See* Jordan.

KAHADINS, king, ally of Rion, 616.

KARISMANX, a knight of the Round Table, 487.

KARLION, 108, 109, 120.

KAY, second son of Antor, 88, 453 ; his mother, 88, 135 ; born, 89 ; sent away, 89, 90, 112, 135 ; knighted, 97 ; Arthur brings him Escalibur, 101 ; thinks by it to be king, 101 ; says he drew it, 101 ; his father incredulous, 101 ; confesses his ruse, 101 ; gives it to his father, 101 ; Arthur replaces it, 101 ; he can't draw it, 101 ; Arthur's steward, 102, 104, 109 ; chief banner-bearer, 116, 136, 405, 453, 475, 480, 484, 488, 489, 596, 614, 645, 649, 575, 571, 504, 661, 475, 596 ; rescues Arthur, 119 ; chases the rebel kings, 119 ; serves at the banquet to Ban and Bors, 133 ; rushes into the tourney, 135 ; his character, 135 ; he is a japing, reviling man, 136, 636 ; unhorses Lydonas and Grascien, 136 ; cries "Clarence!" 136 ; praised by Arthur, Ban, and Bors, 136 ; attacked by Blioberes, 136 ; Gifflet comes to the rescue, 136 ; attacked by Placidus, 136 ; rescued by Gifflet, 137 ; his followers join in the melée, 137 ; honours awarded him, 138 ; in council, 141 ; leads Arthur's first battalion, 151 ; the banner, 151, 155, 596 ; Ulfyn comes to the rescue, 155 ; goes himself to the rescue, 156 ; is unhorsed, 156 ; helped by Gifflet, 156 ; helps Antor, 158 ; helped by Arthur, 159 ; meets Merlin, 169 ; an incident of his youth, 180 ; aids Arthur at Tamelide, 212 ; overthrows Sonygrenx, 214 ; fights a giant, 216 ; upsets Dandevart, 217 ; is whole and sound, 224 ; in the battle with Arthur against Rion, 337, 349 ; tries to dissuade Bors from a single combat with Amaunt, 366 ; bears the great dragon banner in the battle before Trebes, 383, 393, 398, 399 ; people of Trebes scared by the fiery banner, 399 ; Merlin snatches the banner from him, 405, 406 ; finds Arthur's shield on the field of battle, 410 ; fears Arthur is dead, and searches for him, 410 ; finds him with Ban and Bors, and restores the shield, 410 ; lodged in Trebes castle, 412 ; at the marriage of Arthur and Gonnore, 453, 454 ; in the tournament at Toraise, 459 ; goes to help Arthur, 475 ; his character detailed, 475 ; slays by treason Lohoot, the son of Arthur, 475 ; Percival by Galoys is accused of the deed, 475 ; at Arthur's court royal at Logres, 480, 481 ; the tournament at Logres proposed by him, 484 ; his deeds in it, 488, 489 ; serves at the high dais, 504 ; sent by Arthur to stop the treason of the Round Table knights, 468—473 ; takes the great banner to Salisbury, 575 ; it has a red cross under the dragon on it, 575 ; at Salisbury, 579 ; in the battle before Garlot, 596 ; also that before Clarence, 601 ; banner-bearer again, 601 ; at the court royal at Camelot, 614, 615, 619 ; the unknown maiden and her dwarf lover, 636 ; scorns the dwarf, 636 ; when Arthur agrees to knight the dwarf he wants to set his spur on, but the maiden stops him, 637 ; the adventure of the giant, 645, 649 ; the giant slain by Arthur, 649 ; in the battle between Arthur's host and the Romans, 661 ; succours Bediuer, 661 ; overthrown, 651.

KAY-DESTRANX, his nephew Kehedin, 251, 293 ; squire to Carados, 249 ; Carados wants to knight him, 249 ; but he says he will only be knighted by Arthur, 249 ; meets Dodynell, 251 ; goes with Dodynell to Logres, 252, 258 ; leads a band of squires against the Saxons, 291, 292, 377 ; his prowess, 294 ; meets Arthur at Logres, 373 ; vigil, 374 ; dubbed knight, 374, 449 ; given a treasure sword, 374 ; the banquet, 375 ; in command under Gawein, 378 ; his prowess at Trebes, 396 ; nephew of Carados, 449 ; at Arthur's Logres court royal, 480, 481 ; at the Salisbury conference, 577.

KEHEDIN DE BELLY, 212 (251).

KEHEDIN LE BEL, 349.

KEHEDIN LE BENS, Kehedin li bens, 251 ; nephew of Kay Destranx, 251, 252, 377, 378 ; goes with Kay Destranx to Logres, 252, 258 ; he and Kay Destranx lead the squires against the Saxons, 291, 377 ; meets Arthur, 373 ; nephew of the King of Strangore, 373 ; dubbed knight after a vigil, 374, 449 ; is given a treasure sword, 374 ; the banquet, 374 ; in command under Gawein, 378 ; at Arthur's Logres court royal, 480, 481 ; vows to find Merlin, 682.

KEHEDIN THE LITILL, 294, 396, 407.

KEHEDINS LE PETIT, 480, 518, 577 ; his brother, 400, 518, 577.

KEHENYNS, knight, 342, 343.

KINGS, four mighty Saxon, 585, 586, 588.

says they need go no further, for Arthur shall have Gonnore, 319; brings Gonnore in, 319; gives her to Arthur, 319, 341, 357; Merlin tells him who Arthur is, 320; his joy, 320; does homage to Arthur, 320; prepares his army, 321, 330; he and Cleodalis lead the tenth division, 321; holds court royal, 322; slain by Bertelanx the traitor, 322; the two lovers kiss, 322, 323; a fierce onset, 332; his nephew Saydoynes comes to the rescue, 334; they smite in fiercely, 335; chases Rion, 337; he and Cleodalis get separated from their men in the dark, 347; the giants see they are but two, and turn on them, 348; overthrown, 348; Cleodalis gives him his horse, 348; he repents his foul deed to Cleodalis, 348; his knights think he is lost, 349; Amaunt takes advantage of his troubles, 350, 351, 365; is in great peril, 353; the noble truth of Cleodalis, 353, 354; asks Cleodalis to forgive his foul deed, 354; fight together against their foes till midnight, 355, 615; Merlin comes to the rescue, 355; horsed again, 355; they all return to their tents at dawn, 357; gives all the spoil to Arthur, 357; goes to Toraise, 358; asks Arthur to marry Gonnore, 360; Merlin says they must wait a little, 360; Arthur's departure, 360, 404; Arthur's return, 448; at Toraise, 448, 471; Arthur's wedding day fixed, 448, 449, 451; Merlin comes, 451; the marriage of Arthur and Gonnore, 213, 451, 452, 453; his chaplain Sir Annistan, 453, 472; the tournament afterwards, 455; hears of the plot to kidnap his daughter, 465, 466, 468; leads Arthur to Gonnore, 466; his knight Bertelak, 466; Bertelak's complaint, 466, 467; banishes the false Gonnore, 468, 469; Bertelak has slain a knight in revenge, 467, 469; brings Bertelak to judgment, 469, 470; banishes him, 470; Bertelak vows revenge, 470; Gawein takes leave and goes to Logres, 471; Ban and Bors, and Arthur and Gonnore take their leave, 472; Merlin leaves, 472, 473; does not go to the Salisbury assembly, 567; Rion prepares to re-attack him, 616; besieged by Rion in Toraise, 616, 617, 624; makes a stout defence, 618; in the battle between Arthur and Rion outside Toraise, 626, 627; Arthur slays Rion, 630; departure of Arthur from Toraise, 630; his death, 678.

LEODOBRON, king, 191.

LEONCES DE PAERNE, a knight of Ban and Bors, 129; is left in charge of their lands, 130; cousin of Ban and of Bors, 143, 307, 381; gathers his people together before Benoyk, 144; Merlin comes, 144; goes with Merlin to the Rochell, 146; arrives at Great Britain, 147; leads Ban's second ward at the battle of Bredigan, 151; the battle, 152, 161; his prowess, 161; keeps watch, 166 ; returns to guard the lands, 167; Merlin comes, 305, 308; Merlin prophesies, 305, 306; counselled by Merlin, 306, 315, 381; is to lie in ambush, 306; Merlin goes away, 307, 379; cousin to Ban and Bors, 305, 315; prepares to resist the invaders, 379; at Benoyk, 380; nigh cousin to Banyn, 381; goes to the forest of Briogne, 381; his nephew, 381; Merlin comes, 384; his host gets ready for battle, 384; before Trebes, 400; goes to aid Pharien, 403, 409; his valour, 403; Merlin comes, 564; is told by Merlin to get the host ready and go to Salisbury Plain, 564; is to carry a red cross banner, 564; agrees to follow Merlin's advice, 565; goes to the rescue of Morgeins, Ventres' wife, 587, 588, 589; Merlin tells him to start for Camelot with his host, 623; keeps the land against Claudas, 650; succours some of Arthur's knights, 670; his valour, 699.

LEONELL, wife of Blaires, 204.

LEONES DE PAERNE, Leonces, 129, 130, 143, 144, 146, 151, 161, 166, 167; cousin to Ban and Bors, 305—308, 315.

LEONOYS, Leoneys, 254, 285, 291, 295, 372, 477.

LEONPADYS OF THE PLAYN, 212.

LERIADOR, 671, 673, 674.

LESPINE, castle de, 562.

LESPINOYE, a plain, 509.

LEYCESTRE, 312.

LILLE, Caues de, 682.

LITTLE BRITAIN, 121, 124, 146, 147, 166, 173, 402, 563, 564, 662, 690, 692.

LOGRES, see New Troy and Bloy Bretaigne, 57, 67, 97, 104, 106, 107, 110, 120, 121, 123, 124, 131, 132, 134, 135; fellowship of the Table of, 136, 141, 149, 180, 186, 191, 192, 194, 196, 200, 201, 230, 240, 252, 258, 262, 283, 301, 303, 314, 316, 341, 374, 376, 378, 379, 401—404, 406, 420, 447, 449, 450, 455, 462, 471, 472, 473, 479, 484, 502, 550, 562, 566, 573, 579, 598, 630, 631, 635, 643, 644, 658, 674, 676, 678, 682, 690, 692.

LOGRYN, Logryns, 147.

LOHOOT, son of Arthur, and slayn by Kay, 475.

LONDE DES PASTURES, Londe of pastures, 114, 616.

LONDE of GEAUNTES, 114.

LONDON, i.e. Logres, Arthur's chief city, 95, 120.

King Rion, 114, 115 ; of the daughter Gonnore, 115 ; promises his help to Arthur for ever, 115 ; the dragon banner, 115 ; sets the barons' tents on fire, 116, 120, 129 ; counsels Arthur, 121 ; explains his nature, 123 ; makes Arthur swear secrecy, 133 ; counsels Arthur, 131 ; goes to Arthur, 131 ; arranges the reception of Ban and Bors, 132 ; accounted the greatest astronomer, 133 ; tells Arthur of the messengers, 138 ; Ban wants to see him, 138 ; sent for by Arthur, 139 ; he goes, 139 ; is questioned by Guyne-bande, 139 ; tells Ban the history of Arthur, 139 ; and that Arthur is his liege lord, 139 ; instructs Guynebande, 143 ; swears that Arthur is the son of Uter Pendragon, 140 ; Ulfyn corrobo-rates him, 140 ; in council, 141 ; tells Arthur to marry Gonnore, 141 ; to go to Carmelide for a year or two, 141 ; Ban withstands this, 142 ; foretells that Arthur will gain Leodogan's kingdom, 142 ; and the battle with the barons, 142 ; goes to collect reinforcements, 142, 143, 144 ; and to Blase, 143 ; to Little Britain, 143 ; to Gannes, 143 ; delivers the ring taken to Leonces, 144 ; leads the reinforcements by ship to Arthur, 144, 146 ; the seven kings vow revenge on Merlin, 145, 148 ; the ships arrive at Bloy Bretaigne, 146 ; Arthur's death, 147 ; his precautions, 147 ; joins Arthur with the army, 148 ; goes to the three kings, 148 ; arrives at Logres same day, 149 ; says that Arthur will lose only twenty-four men in the battle, but the three kings, thousands, 149 ; leads them to Bredi-gan, 150 ; shows Arthur a great treasure in the ground, 150 ; prepares for the battle, 151 ; rides in front of the army, 151 ; attacks the sentries, 153 ; appears to Arthur, 165 ; tells him to return to his kingdom, 166 ; goes to Blase, 166 ; Arthur sojourns at Bredi-gan, 167 ; the great churl, 167 ; is recognised by Ulfyn, 168 ; resumes his usual form, 170 ; helps Arthur's amour, 171 ; his counsel, 173, 175 ; barons fear his power, 173, 175 ; love for Nimiane, 185, 607 ; goes with Arthur to Leodo-gan, 202, 203, 212, 257 ; sojourns with Blaire, 204 ; bears Arthur's dragon-banner, 206, 209 ; town gate flies open at his bidding, 206 ; the great battle with the Saxons, 206, 207 ; raises a storm of wind, 209 ; rescues Leodogan, 209 ; and the knights of the Round Table, 210 ; the marvel of the dragon banner, 210, 219 ; aids Cleodalis, 211, 215 ; his advice, 216, 224 ; rests his men, 218 ; is joined by the Round

Table knights, 218 ; charges the Saxons, 218, 219, 221 ; calls Arthur coward, 221 ; king Leodogan gives them the spoil, 224, 225 ; his advice, 225 ; Gon-nore serves Arthur, 225 ; sees Leodo-gan, wants Arthur to marry Gonnore, 228 ; tells Arthur of his nephews, 230 ; says he must go to Logres, 258 ; goes to Blase, 259, 260, 261 ; in disguise to Camelot, 261 ; questioned by Gawein, 262, 263 ; tells him of Seigramor, 263, 302 ; battle with Orienx, 265, 266 ; again disguised, 269, 270, 279 ; goes to Bredigan, 279 ; his crafty letter, 279, 280, 290 ; disguised, 294 ; goes to Leoneys in Orcanye, 295 ; disguised as a knight, 296, 302 ; sends Gawein and his company to the rescue of Mordred and his mother, 296, 301, 302 ; discovered, 302 ; Blase's books ordered by Merlin, 327 ; goes to Blase, 303 ; tells him he is going to Benoyk, 303 ; his fears for Ban and Bors, 303 ; the wolf that shall bind the leopard, 304, 563 ; foretells his own fate, 304 ; the quest of the St. Grail, 304 ; goes to Leonces at Benoyk, 305, 308, 315 ; takes him into confidence, 305, 315, 381 ; the serpent shall over-come the leopard, 305 ; tells Leonces to victual and arm his castles, 306 ; foretells an incursion into Benoyk, 306 ; foretells the great battle with the Saxons and giants, 307 ; goes to the forest of Briok to meet Nimiane, 307, 308 ; his love has been foretold by Diana, 307 ; disguises himself as a young squire, 308 ; temptation, 308, 309 ; sees Nimiane, 308 ; her beauty, 307, 308 ; her prudent answer, 309 ; tells her of his power in magic, 309 ; she promises her love, 309 ; he grants her powers, 309, 310, 314 ; raises a magic bower and company, 309, 310, 311 ; the fatal pledge, 310, 311 ; converses with her, 311 ; teaches her some magic, 312 ; agrees to see her again on St. John's Eve, 312 ; goes to Toraise in Tamelide, 312, 314 ; his welcome, 312, 314 ; counsels the three kings, 314 ; tells Arthur of his nephew's doings, 314 ; and Ban and Bors of Claudas, 314, 315 ; counsels them, 315 ; great dragon shall overcome the lion, 315 ; but a leopard shall aid the lion, 315, 316 ; the kings wonder at his dark saying, 315, 316 ; tells Arthur he is concerned in it, 315 ; tells him of the swords in the forest, 316 ; goes to Leodogan and counsels him, 317, 318 ; Leodogan wonders who he is, 318 ; his craft, 319 ; tells Leodogan that they seek a fit wife for Arthur, 319 ; Arthur's be-trothal, 319, 320 ; discovers Arthur's name and estate to Leodogan, 320; discovers himself to the Round Table knights, 320; Leodogan's court royal, 322; sits at the head of the daïs, 322; laughs at Arthur and his love Gonnore, 322; tells them to kiss each other, 322, 323; leads the first ward, 323; the dragon-banner borne by him, 323, 324, 327, 332, 336; sets on Rion, 324; makes a storm, 324; disguises himself and encourages Arthur, 325; leads Arthur to the rescue of Nascien and Boors, 331, 332, 333; raises a tempest, 332; the dragon-banner throws out fire and flame, 332; help comes, 335; collects the fellowship of the Round Table, 335; encourages Arthur, 335; dashes into the fight again, 336; Arthur overthrown, 336; goes to the rescue, 336; follows a band of Saxons, 349, 350; raises a storm over them, 350; and a river in their front, 350, 351; causes friends to take each other for foes, 351; fetches Arthur to aid Leodogan, 353; the dragon-banner lightens the darkness, 353; goes to Leodogan, 353, 354; finds Leodogan on foot and weary, 354; fetches reinforcements, 356; in the thick of the fight, 356; bears the dragon, which lights up the darkness, 356; leads Arthur to the three Saxon kings, 356, 357; they rest at dawn, 357; returns to Leodogan, who is glad, 357; tells Arthur how to divide the spoil, 357, 358; Leodogan wants Arthur's marriage to come off, 360; says it must wait until he has been to Benoyk, 360; at Bredigan, 363; Ban comes, 363; asks Ban about Guynebans, 363; Bors comes, 369; the treasure, 370; the twelve swords, 370, 374; Galeshyn, Seigramor, Gawein, and his brethren come to meet Arthur, 370, 371; they all enter Logres, 374; counsels Arthur to gird Gawein with Calibourne, 374; tells Arthur not to let the knights joust in the meadows, because of the Saxons, 375; teaches Morgne le fee astronomye and egremauncye, 375, 508; tells Arthur to get ready to move to Benoyk, 375, 376; asks Gawein about the mysterious knight, 376, 377; tells Gawein to take leave of his mother and to lead the host to Dover, 377; remains at Logres and tells Arthur to move to the Rochelle, and not to move until he sees him again, 378; goes to Blase in Northumberland, who is joyful at seeing him, 378; tells Blase of Nimiane, 378; Blase chides him, and tells him of prophecies, 378; goes to Arthur at the Rochelle, 379; arranges the expedition to Trebes with Arthur and the others, 381, 382,

383; Blioberis is to lead the host, 383; goes off to Leonce, 384; vanishing powers, 384; the hosts encompass Claudas, but wait for Merlin's signal, 386; gives the signal, 386, 387; the battle begins, 387; his miraculous powers, 386, 387; the wonder-working banner, 393; sends Arthur and the two kings to help the people of Logres, who are being worsted, 404; scolds and taunts Arthur, 404, 407; taunts Gawein, 404; taunts Ban and Bors, 405; takes the banner from Kay, 405, 406; his marvellous deeds, 405, 406; rides into the thick of the battle, 405, 406; Merlin's personal appearance described, 405, 406; on a black horse, 406; never known to slay any man unless by riding down, 406; his company counts a thousand, 406; dragon vomits fire, 406; leads on Arthur and his knights to the attack, 410; utter rout of Claudas, 411, 412; many prisoners, 412; lodged in Trebes castle, 412, 413; Helayn's marvellous dream, 413, 414, 415; relates and explains the dream, 416, 417; on St. John's day departs and goes to his love Nimiane, 416, 417, 418; she meets him at the well, 417; she conducts him secretly into a chamber, 418; tells her how to make people sleep at will, 418; tells her three names which will guard her chastity from violence, 418; stays there eight days, 418; he is quite chaste, 418; teaches her the past and future, 418; she puts them in writing, 418; leaves her and goes to Arthur at Benoyk, 418, 419; waits for Gawein and goes to Gannes, 419; welcomed by Bors and stays two days, 419; goes to la Rochelle and to the sea, 419, 420; tells Arthur, Gawein, and the two kings to sail for Carmelide, 420; Arthur wants him to come too so as to be at the marriage, 420; says he will follow soon to Carmelide, 420; leaves Arthur, 420; goes to the forests of Rome, 420, 422; this was in the time of Julius Cesar that Gawein slew, 420; Julius has a beautiful but lecherous wife, 420; her devices, 420; she disguised a dozen squires as women to serve her will, 420; the arrival of Grisandoll, 421; the dream of Julyus Cesar, 421, 422; Julyus is pensive, 422; arrives at the entry of Rome, 422; casts an enchantment and becomes a large hart, 422, 435, 436, 437; is chased through Rome, 422; rushes into the Emperor's palace, upsetting the dinner tables, 422, 423; tells the Emperor he will never understand the dream until a savage man explains it, 423, 436, 437; enchants the doors of the palace and

into his secret, 452 ; the tournament, 455, 461 ; stops the tournament, 460, 462 ; tells Leodogan of the plot to kidnap Gonnore, 465, 468 ; leads Arthur to Gonnore, 466 ; consults with Leodogan, 467; the false Gonnore banished, 468, 469 ; the trial of Bertelak, 469, 470 ; takes leave of Arthur, but promises to be at the court royal, 472, 473, 562 ; goes to Blase, 472, 473, 562 ; tells Blase everything, how Lot lies in wait for Arthur, 473, 562 ; Blase asks about the chance of driving out the Saxons, 563 ; is going to fetch Ban and Bors' people to the gathering at Salisbury, 563 ; says the Saxons will not be driven out until peace between Arthur and barons, 563 ; makes Blase write letters, and sticks them up in highways, 563, 564 ; goes to little Britain, 564 ; instructs Leonce and Pharien to go to Salisbury with their host, 564, 565 ; goes to Nimiane and teaches her some of his cunning, 565 ; goes into Lamball, into Carmelide, 565 ; with Nabulall and Bandemagn, 566 ; goes to Logres, 566 ; Arthur makes great joy of him, 566 ; tells Arthur of the assembly collecting, 566, 567 ; tells Arthur of the treason of the three Round Table knights, 567, 568 ; the three knights are brought back, 573, 574 ; Arthur's great dragon-banner has a red cross put on it, 575 ; others like it, 576, 585, 586, 601 ; talks with Arthur at Salisbury, 578, 579 ; his prophecy that the father and the son shall slay each other, and of the crowned and uncrowned lions, 579 ; visits the lords with Arthur, 579, 580 ; consultation with the twelve princes, 580, 581, 612 ; urges them to do homage to Arthur, and they demur, 581 ; advises a start for Clarence, 582 ; the start, 585 ; bears Arthur's great banner, 585 ; meets squires who say the Saxons have taken Ventres' wife, 586 ; goes to the rescue, 587, 588, 590, 612 ; Elizer's prowess, 587, 589 ; meets the Saxon host, 593 ; the disposition of his host, 593, 594 ; the attack, 595, 596 ; tells Arthur to take the Saxons in the rear, 596 ; defeat of Saxons, 597 ; Arthur advances to Clarence, 598 ; tells the barons they must make peace with Arthur, 598, 599 ; they do homage, 599 ; the battle before Clarence, 599 ; carries the great banner, 599 ; harangues the host, 601 ; rout of Saxons, 602 ; tells Ban and Bors to return to their homes, 603 ; goes with Ban and Bors, 605 ; at Agravadain's castle, 605—608, 612 ; causes Ban to lie with Agravadain's daughter, 607, 612 ; is transformed into a young knight, 608, 622 ; goes to Benoyk, to Nimiane,

and to Blase, 612 ; goes disguised to Arthur's court royal at Camelot, 615, 621 ; and asks to be banner-bearer, 621, 622 ; recognized by Ban, 622 ; Arthur refuses his request, and he vanishes, 622 ; makes the request again, disguised as a naked child, 622 ; Arthur grants it, and he throws off his disguise, 623 ; beats up reinforcements in Gannes, Paerne, Benoyk, Gorre, and Orcanye, and returns to Camelot, 623 ; the battle with Rion, 624 ; rescues Bors and Loth, 625 ; Arthur slays Rion in personal combat, 630 ; at Logres, 630 ; tells Arthur he must go now that his work is done, 630, 631 ; another dark saying of his of the lion that was son of the bear and leopard, 631 ; departure from Arthur, 631 ; goes to Flualis, king of Jerusalem, 632 ; explains Flualis's marvellous dream, 633, 634, 675 ; is invisible while he does it, 623 ; goes to Benoyk to Nimiane, 634 ; he never loses his chastity, 634 ; goes to Blase, 634, 635 ; goes again to Arthur at Logres, 635 ; the dwarf and maiden adventure, 638 ; a message from Luce, Emperor of Rome, to Arthur, 639 ; preparations for war with Luce, 643 ; warns Arthur's princes to get ready, 643, 644 ; Arthur's host at Gannes, 644 ; Arthur's vision, which he interprets, 644, 645 ; an embassy to Luce, 650, 653, 657 ; defeat of the Romans and death of Luce, 664 ; tells Arthur to go on his way still, 664, 665 ; to tackle the devil-cat, 664, 665 ; goes against the devil-cat, 666, 669 ; with Arthur at Logres and takes farewell of Arthur and Gonnore, 678 ; and sets out for Blase and Nimiane, 678, 679 ; farewell to Blase, 679, 680 ; with Nimiane, who gets power over him, 680 ; is shut up by her through enchantment, and never returns, 681, 693 ; Arthur's quest for him, 682, 687, 689, 690, 692 ; speaks to Gawein, 692 ; Gawein recognises his voice, though he can't see him, 693, 694 ; calls himself a fool, 694 ; tells Gawein to tell Arthur the quest is useless, as none will see or hear him again, 694.

MINAP, king, 333.

MOLAIT, 411.

MOLEHAUT, castelein of, 442 ; cite of, 546.

MONACLYNS [Saxon], 510, 511.

MONAGINS, Monaquyn, Saxon king, 521, 524 ; brother of Pygnoras, 524 ; cousin-german to Hardogabran, 535.

MONEVALL, a knight of the Round Table, 561, 562, 566, 567, 568, 573, 574.

MONGIN, 640 ; mountains of, 643.

MONPELLIER, a riche town in Province, 435, 436.

the fight between them, 338, 343, 346, 347 ; flies, 347, 450 ; his sword Marmadoise, q. v., captured by Arthur, 346, 347, 352, 353, 615, 648 ; his friends' rage and sorrow, 349 ; prepares for revenge on Arthur and Leodogan, 615, 616 ; besieges Torayse, 616, 617, 619, 620, 624 ; hears that Arthur has beaten the Saxons, 617 ; sends defiance to Arthur, 617—620 ; wants Arthur's beard, 619 ; Arthur laughs at his request and defiance, 620, 621 ; battle with Arthur's host, 624, 630 ; offers to settle the matter by a personal combat with Arthur, and Arthur agrees, 627, 628 ; the combat, 628, 629, 630 ; vanquished but will not yield, so Arthur kills him ; his body taken home and buried, 630.

RIVER at Cambenyk, 550. See Saverne.

ROCHE FLODOMER, 564.

ROCHE MAGOT, 256, 274.

ROCHE OF SAXONS, castle, 176, 185, 188, 242, 247, 250, 252, 341, 521.

ROCHELL, the, 378, 379, 419.

ROCHES, Duke, 561.

ROESTOK, 538.

ROMANS, 303, 306, 391, 392, 400, 402, 438, 639—642, 651—661, 663, 664, 669, 676, 679, 699.

ROME, 303, 305, 306, 393, 419 ; forests, 420, 422, 423, 426, 427, 433, 436, 437, 438, 639, 641, 642, 650, 653, 655, 660, 664, 665, 678, 699.

RORESTOK, valey of, 535.

ROSTOCK, 250, 256 ; a plain or plains, 509, 510, 521, 528 ; valley, 535, 538, 539, 543 ; lord of, 545, 546.

ROUND TABLE, founded by Uter Pendragon, 60 ; empty seat, 61, 108, 114, 141 ; members and governors, 205, 208 —211, 215, 217, 218, 224, 247, 316, 319 —322, 325, 327, 331, 332, 335, 336, 337, 345, 348, 349, 358, 360, 371, 374, 378, 382, 383, 392, 398, 401, 407, 408, 410, 412, 413, 453, 454, 455, 458—462, 471, 474, 477, 481—484, 486—499, 500—504, 507, 561, 562, 566, 567, 568, 570, 572, 573, 577, 584, 585, 594, 596, 597, 624, 626, 630, 678, 698.

ROY DE CENT CHIUALIERS, reason of the name, 185. See Aguysans.

RYOLENT, king of Ireland, 205.

SACREN of the STREITE MARCHE, knight of Arthur, 682.

SADOYNE, Sadoynes, nephew of Leodogan, 334, 337 ; the castelein of Daneblaise and brother of Gonnore, 472, 566.

SADUC, 217.

ST. BARTHOLOMEW'S DAY, 519.

ST. JOHN, feast of, 381, 417, 421.

SAISNES (Saxons), 173—176, 179, 182, 185, 187, 188, 191, 192, 193, 195—199,

201, 213, 214, 217, 219, 221, 223, 224, 225, 230—240, 242—250, 252, 253 ; siege of, 254, 256, 257—260, 262—267, 271, 277, 278, 302, 312, 313, 314, 316, 332, 348, 349, 350, 352—355, 356, 357, 359, 371, 377, 438—444, 447, 450, 479, 500, 505, 506, 509, 510, 511, 513—516, 518—525, 528, 534, 535, 539, 547—554, 556, 559, 562, 568, 573, 575, 576, 579, 580, 582, 585—592, 594, 595, 598, 599, 602, 603.

SALEBRUN, Salubruns, Saxon, 510, 593 ; slain, 594.

SALERNE, lord of, 256, 273, 274, 441, 445.

SALISBERI, 147 ; Salisbury, 565, 585 ; Salesberye, Salisburye playne, 54, 55 ; the battle, 56, 57, 121, 560, 564—567, 574, 575, 576, 580, 585, 612.

SALUBRIUS, 236.

SAPERNYE, forest, 472, 473.

SAPHIRUS, king, 255.

SAPINE CASTELL, 509.

SARAZINS [Saracens, heathens], 49, 50, 54, 55, 94, 172, 174, 194, 209, 210, 307, 325, 327, 330, 333, 335, 336, 342, 351, 664.

SARMEDON, the gonfanoned, 211.

SARNAGUT, king, 194.

SARON, king, 328, 329.

SARRAS, city, 502.

SATHANYE, gulf, 341.

SAVARNE, river of, 256, 257, 271, 272, 277.

SAXOYNE, Saxoynie, king of, 172, 250, 292, 510, 592, 603.

SCOTLONDE, 108, 145, 121, 158, 160, 161, 187, 236, 237, 439, 445, 509, 519, 546, 548, 558, 601.

SEGAGAN, king, 191.

SEGARS, Segras, nephew of Bediuer, 661, 662.

SEGURADES [on barons side], 441.

SEGURADES de la forest perilouse, 682.

SEIGRAMORE, son of a king of Blagne and Hungary ; a knight, 186 ; goes when fifteen to Great Britain to Arthur, 186, 271 ; heir to Adrian, emperour of Constantinople, 86, 230, 262, 270, 280, 373, 449 ; Arthur is told of him, 230 ; his prowess foretold, 230 ; goes with knights to Dover, 259 ; his adventures, 260—263 ; Gawein comes to aid him, 264 ; welcomed by Gawein, 266, 302 ; goes to Camelot, 266, 267 ; smites Driant, 268 ; tries to take Orienx, 268, 279 ; revels at Camelot, 271 ; leads Gawein's fourth ward, 280, 281 ; charges the Saxons, 287 ; a reverse, 287 ; at Arondell, 290—293 ; prowess, 294 ; a strange quest, 297—301 ; return to Arondell, 301 ; at Logres, 301 ; Arthur is coming, 370 ; meets him, 370, 371 ; salutes him kneeling, 371 ; Gawein tells

GLOSSARY.

a, conj. and, 523, 6 ; 524, 12.

a, interj. ab. 8, 7.

Aatine, s. quarrel, 497, 30.

abaisshed, v. abashed, defeated, 12, 25 ; 232, 4.

a-bakke, adv. aback, 40, 16.

a-bandoned, v. risked, sacrificed, 354, 29.

abide, v. to wait for, endure, 44, 24 ; 50, 12.

a-bidinge, s. waiting, stay, delay, 45, 18 ; 256, 17.

abode, v. waited for, 205, 17 ; 379, 8.

a-boode, v. remained, 297, 15 ; 432, 25.

a-bouten, adv. about, 7, 30.

a-bouen, prep. above, over, 134, 4.

abreedeed, pp., 275, 14.

a-brethe, v. to give time to recover breath, 335, 17.

a-brode, adv. open, abroad, 396, 28.

absoyle, v. to absolve, 11, 88.

a-coled, v. embraced, 501, 35.

acolee, s. embrace around the neck of the newly dubbed knight, 374, 25.

a-complysshen, v. to accomplish, 61, 17.

a-coole, s. same as acolee, 520, 9 ; 570, 4.

acooley, s. 267, 3.

a-corded, v. agreed, 380, 13.

a-dongon, s. dungeon, 389, 33.

a-dubbe, v. to dub, furnish with arms, 122, 20 ; 183, 14 ; 637, 7.

afeerde, 14, 29 ; afeirde, adj. afraid, frightened, 16, 32 ; a-ferde, 221, 28.

aferid, v. feared, took fright, 15, 26.

affiaunce, s. trust, 103, 22.

afficched, v. fixed, fastened, 117, 21.

affiered, belonged, 225, 36.

affraied, pp. frightened, 8, 2.

aflayed, pp. frightened, alarmed, 296, 5.

after, prep. until, for, 50, 12.

after that, according as, 167, 8.

again, 1, 7 ; ageyn, 26, 28 ; prep. against.

a-geins, conj. by the time, 55, 15.

a-geyn, prep. towards, 94, 19.

ageyn, adv. again, 12, 1.

a-guylte, pp. guilty of, sinned, 19, 15.

aissh, s. ash, 390, 12.

aisshen, adj. of ash, 117, 18.

a-kele, v. to cool, 590, 21.

alle, gen. pl. of all, adj., 3, 10.

almesse, s. alms, benefit, 12, 7 ; 505, 17.

a-lowe, v. praise, approve, 355, 35.

als, conj. as, 48, 14.

alther, gen. pl. of all, 138, 6.

alther, firste, *i.e.* first of all, 401, 3.

ambeler, s. ambler, 521, 24.

amenuse, v. get less. 657, 4.

a-merveyled, adj. surprised, 30, 20.

50

amoneste, v. advise, 559, 20.
amyrall, adj. admiral, 281, 28.
an, conj. and, 92, 24.
and, conj. if, 45, 1 ; 46, 31.
and, adj. an, 221, 20.
a-newe, s. another one, 399, 8.
anguyshous, adj. sad, painful, 257, 15.
angwisshouse, adj. anxious, 262, 10.
annoye, s. annoyance, injury, 154, 22 ; 156, 27.
a-noon, adv. anon, 47, 33.
a-noyed, pp. hurt, affected, 300, 14.
ant, conj. and, 263, 19.
a-pair, v. injure, 397, 35.
a-paraile, v. apparel, 241, 31.
a-peche, v. accuse, 492, 17.
a-peire, v. to impair; a-peired, pp. impaired, 110, 30 ; 355, 23.
apele, v. challenge, 469, 15.
aperceyvaunte, pres. p. understanding, 73, 36.
a perceyve, v. to perceive, 29, 10 ; aparceyved, pt. 64, 28 ; aperceyved, pt. 12, 14.
a-pert, adj. free, open, 507, 34.
aperteneth, appertaineth, 106, 2.
aperteliche, 76, 23 ; apertly, 35, 22 ; adv. openly, clearly.
appareile, v. prepare, furnish, 357, 26.
appareilleden, v. prepared, got ready, 360, 17.
apperly, adv. dexterously, 155, 12.
a-putayn, adj. 496, 1.
a-putein, adj. 542, 10, same as a-putayn.
a-quyt, a-quytte, pp. acquitted, 87, 27.
a-race, v. remove, 346, 26.
arached, v. pulled off, 134, 19.
a-rafte, v. struck, smote, 210, 22.
araide, pp. beaten, thrashed, 343, 18.
araied, v. 571, 21 ; same as araide.
a-raught, v. reached, 264, 26.

a-rayment, s. dress, 507, 4.
arblast, s. cross-bow, 196, 4 ; 254, 30.
arblaste, s. bow-shot, 194, 31.
arblastiers, 659, 21 ; arblasters, 143, 7 ; arblastis, 113, 18 ; s. cross-bowmen.
a-reche, v. reach, come at, 154, 8 ; pt. a-raught, 193, 19.
a-reised, v. raised, 57, 4.
a-resoned, v. 508, 25 ; a-resoned, v. 17, 10 ; a-resonde, pp. 18, 33 ; questioned, examined.
aried, pp. arrayed, 107, 13.
a-rivage, s. 54, 29 ; aryvage, s. arrival, landing, 56, 1.
a-rived, pp. arrived, 42, 13.
aryve, v. to arrive, land, 54, 27.
armure, s. armour, 242, 9.
a-rome, adv. aloof, off, 477, 13.
a-rowme, 627, 20 ; same as a-rome.
arson, s. the bow of a saddle, 119, 17.
artrye, s. artillery, 115, 21.
as armes, to arms ! Fr. aux armes ! 192, 34.
a-say, v. try, prove, 51, 2.
ascaped, v. escaped, aschaped, 56, 33 ; 240, 15.
aschape, v. to escape, 154, 12.
a-scride, a-scryed, v. cried out upon, 343, 1 ; 464, 13 ; 473, 35.
ascry, s. shout, outcry, 160, 4.
a-sege, v. besiege, 258, 18.
asked, v. asked for, 317, 7.
assaie, s. trial, test, 100, 11 (assay, 219, 24).
assaien, v. to try, prove, 99, 4.
assaute, 71, 1 ; a-saute, 157, 6 ; a-sawte, 217, 17 ; s. assault.
assawte, v. to assault, 69, 27.
asseles, s. shoulders, cf. N. E. D., 116, 30.
assels, s. ; same as asseles, 473, 33.
assoiled, v. pardoned, 11, 35 ; 560, 26.
asspie, s. spy, 306, 30.
assured, v. agreed, 362, 16.

astoned, 48, 12; astonyed, 21, 22;
  astonyd, 8, 4; pp. astonished.
at, prep. on, 265, 27.
atame, v. penetrate, 648, 33.
atise, v. brag of, 404, 31.
atised, v. challenged, provoked,
  366, 12.
attones, adv. at once, 118, 31.
attonys, 551, 3; same as attones.
atynes, s. hatred, wrath, 490, 14.
auctorite, s. authority, power,
  21, 3.
auenaunt, adj. becoming, graceful,
  507, 34; 607, 35.
auerouse, adj. avaricious, 106, 13.
auenture, 5, 18; a-uenture, 188,
  29; aventure, s. adventure,
  danger, chance, 35, 35.
auer, s. horse, 167, 20; 272, 11.
auers, s. possession, property, 92,
  31; 106, 22; 176, 20; Fr. avoir.
auncyent, adj. ancient, 305, 27.
auoir, s. property, goods, 173, 28;
  357, 31.
aust, s. august, 132, 33.
auter, 102, 34; awter, 98, 29;
  s. altar.
a-valed, v. let down, lowered,
  476, 24; 571, 13.
a-vaunte, v. boast, 263, 9; 275, 28.
a-vaunter, s. a boaster, braggart,
  126, 36.
avauntour, s., 398, 17; same as
  a-vaunter.
a-vented, pp. lowered the aventaile, 335, 20; 459, 6.
aventeed, v. opened the aventaile
  for the purpose of breathing,
  371, 9.
avise, 79, 21; a-visement, 78, 28;
  s. advice, counsel; v. look at,
  308, 31.
a-vised, pp. advised, assured, 45, 36.
avoure, s. possessions, 433, 35.
avouterye, s. adultery, 17, 34.
a-voy, v. away, leave, 486, 31.
a-vye, v. advise, ask, 284, 25.
a-wayte, s. trouble, mischief, 478,
  1; 653, 36.

awmenere, s. purse, 637, 13.
axed, v. asked, 3, 23.
axeden, v. 12, 15.
ayre, s. air, 56, 5.

baas, adj. low, whispering, 611, 23.
baile, 113, 22, 248, 28; baill, 113,
  14; s. an enclosure by the keep
  of a castle.
baile, 350, 15; baille, 350, 26,
  518, 18; s. power, custody.
bailly, 111, 13; baillye, 185, 20;
  s. custody, government.
baisyers, s. kisses, 323, 7.
bakke, s. back, 101, 8.
bapteme, s. baptism, 214, 2.
bar, v. 16, 36, bore, carried.
bar hir on-hande, 9, 18; to keep
  a person in play, to pretend for
  a sinister purpose, to deceive.
barbe, s. beard, 117, 14.
barbican, s. an outwork, a watch
  tower, 618, 23.
barnysshed, pp. made, propor-
  tioned, 520, 5.
baronye, s. baronage, 106, 34.
baste, s. bastardy, 86, 12.
bataille, s. army, 56, 33.
bawdrike, s. belt, 608, 3; 615, 3.
be, pp. been, 1, 13; 263, 28.
be, prep. by, about, 3, 3; 14, 2.
be-come, pp. gone, 259, 6.
beerdes, s. beards, 619, 29.
beere, s. bier, 674, 2.
be-fill, adj. suitable, 546, 29.
be-fill, v. happened, 12, 35; 153, 1.
be-heilde, v. looked, beheld, 7, 8;
  158, 16.
be-hielde, v. 514, 8.
be-hote, v. to promise, 59, 33.
be-hoved, v. were compelled,
  forced, 479, 9.
beilde, v. to build, 63, 27.
be-knowe, v. to confess, acknowledge, 20, 22.
be-lefte, pp. remained, left, 202,
  32.
beleve, 27, 11; bileve, 50, 36;
  s. belief.

be-leve, 48, 13; bileve, 17, 23; v.
 believe.
ben, v. to be, 2, 3.
beudes, s. bands, stripes, border,
 279, 26; 161, 32.
be-raffte, pp. bereft, 2, 19.
be-raften, v. carried away, seized,
 396, 19.
berde, s. beard, 43, 1; 279, 28.
bere, v. bear, 176, 16.
be-reve, v. to bereave, deprive of,
 145, 32.
be-seged, 42, 22; besieged.
be-seke, v. to beseech, 37, 9.
bestes, s. beasts, 3, 27.
be-taught, v. committed, handed
 over, 12, 6; 162, 13.
bete, v. covered, overlaid, 608, 5.
betell, s. mallet, 329, 17.
beth, imper. be, 16, 13.
betid, pp. happened, 53, 16.
betyden, v. to happen, come to
 pass, 69, 23.
bewte, 12, 29; 177, 18; bewtee,
 347, 27; s. beauty.
beyes, s. horses, 117, 36.
beyeth, v. buys, purchases, 93, 7.
biried, v. buried, 95, 22.
birthon, s. burthen, 648, 6.
bith, v. be, 556, 14.
blenche, v. to start, deviate, 159,
 31.
blisse, v. bless, 8, 23; 170, 7.
blissynge, s. blessing, 11, 35.
blody, adj. bloody, 193, 18.
bloy, adj. sad, unhappy, 147, 16.
blusht, 265, 22; blusshet, 120, 3;
 494, 5; v. fell, dropped.
blusshed, v. came upon, 259, 32.
bobaunce, s. boasting, bombast,
 116, 23.
bode, v. waited for, 329, 15.
bokill, s. buckle, 339, 31; bocle,
 395, 22.
bole, s. bull, 343, 17.
bon, s. bone, 338, 24.
bonche, s. bunch, 635, 18.
boorde, v. to tourney, jest, sport,
 100, 28.

bordclothes, s. tablecloths, 240, 8.
bordes, s. tables, 454, 7.
bore, pp. born, 1, 9.
borough, v. borrow, 434, 8.
botiller, s. butler, 349, 4.
boton, s. button, 486, 34.
bounte, s. goodness, favour, 102,
 16; 122, 18.
bourde, s. table, game, feast, 67, 32.
bourded, v. tilted, 133, 16.
bourdeyse, s. sport, play, 455, 24.
bourdinge, part. pres. 31, 29;
 311, 14; playing, sporting.
bourdise, s. tournament, play,
 sport, 100, 29.
boustouse, adj. rough, clumsy,
 42, 36.
bowes, s. boughs, 349, 11.
boysteis, adj. rough, 168, 7.
braied, v. started, 464, 19.
braied, 298, 33; brayed, 343, 17;
 v. shouted.
brakke, v. broke, 53, 8.
brasen, adj. of brass, 339, 33.
braste, v. broke, burst, 200, 21.
braundon, s. flame, 386, 7.
brayt, s. a cry, 216, 36.
breche, s. breeches, 536, 4.
bregge, 53, 6; brigge, 53, 9; 165,
 31; s. bridge.
breke, v. to break, 52, 31.
brenne, v. to burn, 18, 27.
brennynge, part. burning, 18, 25.
brent, pp. burnt, 16, 26.
breres, s. briars, 517, 13.
brestes, s. breasts, 268, 18.
bretesches, s. brattices, bartizans,
 ramparts (Fr. les bretesces),
 677, 33.
briaunt, adv. brilliant, well, 117, 20.
briddes, s. birds, 168, 14; 169,
 2; bridde, 183, 35.
briste, adj. breast, 194, 10.
bristelis, s. bristles, 421, 30.
broder, s. brother, 8, 35; brothern,
 122, 13.
brondes, s. swords, 246, 25.
brosed, all to, i.e. very much
 bruised, 157, 17.

brosed, pp. bruised, 391, 26.
brosten, v. broken, burst, 649, 10.
brunt, s. ? leap, 282, 34; at a brunt=suddenly.
brut, s. tumult, 574, 36.
bruyt, s. report, noise, rumour, 211, 32.
burgeys, s. burgesses, 453, 28.
but, conj. save, except, unless, 43, 31; 56, 7; 104, 11.
butte, s. *butte length*, *i.e.* the distauce between two butts or targets, 385, 22.
by, prep. on, 278, 2.
by, v. be, let me be, 183, 22.
bye, v. buy, pay for, 299, 26.
by-fore, prep. before, 24, 8.
by-leve, s. belief, 578, 20.
by-sette, v. allotted, 369, 13.

cacchynge, adj. catching, 106, 10.
caliouns, s. flint stones, 281, 15; 329, 4; 677, 28.
carfowgh, s. junction of four roads, 273, 35.
cariage, s. baggage, 658, 20.
carl, 33, 22; karll, 261, 30; s. rustic.
carnell, adj. related by blood, 117, 8.
casteleyn, s. 545, 35; castelleynes, s. 320, 21; same as castellein.
castell, s. castle, 49, 30.
castellein, s. constable or keeper of a castle, 247, 30.
cauchie, 278, 13; cawchie, 380, 17; chauchie, 604, 28; s. path or road.
cerne, s. circle, 309, 31; 310, 2; 681, 14.
cesse, v. to cease, 5, 2; 116, 19.
chacche, v. to go, 424, 25.
chacche, v. to catch, 640, 6.
chaffed, pp. excited by anger, 460, 13; chauffed, 460, 36.
champ, s. field of the shield, 636, 29.
chaple, 134, 34; 389, 29: chaplee, 326, 11; s. battle, fight.

charge, v. to weigh, carry, 57, 35.
chauchie, s. on the road or highway, 493, 22.
chede, s. child, 15, 23.
chekier, s. chess-board, 362, 28.
chere, s. countenance, look, 44, 7; 227, 19.
cherl, s. churl, 43, 26.
ches, v. saw, 336, 7.
chese, v. to choose, 60, 21.
cheyer, s. chair, seat, 362, 11.
chielde, s. person, 264, 25.
childeren, s. knights, 259, 31.
chiualrie, s. cavalry, 256, 25.
chyne, s. backbone, 118, 21.
chyne, v. to split, 265, 22.
chyne, s. chin, 635, 20.
chyuachie, s. contest, war, expedition, 145, 13; 173, 2; 174, 13; 274, 30; 370, 32.
Clarance, cried a Clarance, *i.e.* "the word and sign of King Arthur," 287, 16.
claretee, s. brightness, 340, 15.
clatered, v. noised abroad, 12, 29.
clayned, pp. justified, cleaned, 19, 19.
clepe, v. to call, 45, 16.
clepid, 13, 20; cleped, 29, 27; clepeden, 16, 18; called.
cler, adj. clear, 338, 9.
clerenesse, s. brightness, light, 8, 28.
clergesse, s. female clerk, 374, 6.
clergie, s. learning, science, 634, 32; 27, 33.
cleymed, v. claimed, see *quyte cleymed*, 502, 2.
clier, adj. clear, 191, 8.
clipt, v. embraced, 143, 4; 149, 6.
clobbe, 648, 4; clubbe, 649, 2; s. club, weapon.
clowte, adj. "clowte leather," *i.e.* leather for mending, 33, 26.
clowte, v. to mend or patch shoes, 33, 23.
coffin, s. cover for a letter, 279, 20.
cofres, s. coffers.
cole, s. cool, 191, 16.

com, v. came, 5, 16.
comaunde, v. to commend, 8, 1 ; 33, 13.
comberaunce, s. trouble, 8, 21.
comen, adj. common, 104, 7.
comounte, s. mass, quantity, 574, 33.
complayned, v. bewailed, lamented, 24, 25.
complysshe, 61, 20; complesshen, 62, 1 ; v. to accomplish, fulfil.
comynyally, adv. in assembly, 96, 19.
condite, v. to conduct, 50, 2, used passively, 50, 30.
condite, s. conduct, 82, 28.
conditour, s. conductor, 392, 14.
coniorison, 607, 20 ; coniurison, 362, 34; 608, 14; s. conjuring, sorcery.
conne, v. to know, 22, 16.
conne, v. give, render, 73, 8 ; 123, 9.
conuynge, s. knowledge, science, 2, 29.
connynge, adj. knowing, acquainted with, 17, 4 ; 122, 1.
couseille, conseill, s. council, 3, 12 ; 2, 22.
constabilrie, s. management, care of, 373, 32.
contene, v. defend, preserve, 77, 6 ; 264, 18.
contened, v. continued, 355, 13.
contirfet, adj. counterfeit, 635, 13.
coutre, s. country, 5, 12 ; 153, 17.
contrey, s. 153, 19.
couvenable, adj. like, fitting, 59, 29.
couveye, v. to show, put in the way, 538, 33.
conveyed, v. showed, 525, 4.
conysshaunce, s. badge, crest, 510, 12.
corage, s. inclination, intention, heart, 228, 30 ; 309, 3.
cordewan, s. Spanish leather, 615, 7.
corse, s. corpse, 34, 9.

corsure, s. horseman, 328, 4.
cosin, cousin, 117, 28.
cote, s. coat, 261, 5.
coton, s. cotton, 294, 27.
couctyse, 13, 8 ; covetise, 106, 22 ; s. covetousness, desire.
counfort, s. comfort, 7, 16.
counscile, v. used intransitively, 95, 25.
counterfeited, pp. ill-shapen ; Fr. contrefais.
counterynge, s. encounter, meeting, 200, 21.
courbe, adj. bent, curved, 635, 17.
courbed, pp. bent, 261, 6.
covered, v. recovered ? hid his feelings ? 213, 6.
covyne, s. secret contrivance, 306, 31 ; 465, 12.
cowde, v. knew, 28, 8 ; 482, 7.
cowde, 9, 7; cowden, 2, 14; could.
cowpe, s. cup, 67, 7.
coy, adv. shyly, 125, 16.
cracchinges, s. scratchings, 668, 30.
crasinge, s. 200, 26; same as crassinge.
craspe, v. grasp, seize, 649, 10.
crassinge, s. crashing, noise, 155, 17.
crature, s. creature, 11, 30.
creaunce, s. belief, 5, 29; 340, 36; 662, 13.
crepell, s. cripple, 73, 5.
crewell, 39, 1 ; cruewell, 281, 28 ; adj. cruel.
cride, 161, 24; cryde, 215, 7 ; v. proclaimed, exposed.
cristen, s. christians, 57, 3.
cristendom, s. christianity, 55, 11.
christynte, s. christianity, 226, 12.
croupe, 117, 25 ; crowpe, 128, 5 ; s. the buttocks of a horse.
crull, adj. curled, 508, 24.
crysten, adj. christian, 23, 31.
cure, s. care, desire, 229, 1.
curroure, sb. courier, runner, 279, 19.
curroyes, couriers ? runners ? 485, 12.
curteys, adj. courteous, 266, 9.

daisght, pp. spoilt, 246, 23.

damage, s. injury, defeat, 349, 13.

dampned, pp. condemned, punished, 11, 32.

daunger, 2, 27; daungier, 434, 14; s. power, dominion.

dawe, v. to dawn, 98, 9.

dawenynge, s. daybreak, 297, 35.

day, s. time, 82, 25.

deboner, adj. courteous, gentle, 266, 9.

debonerly, adv. courteously, 105, 21; 140, 31.

debonertee, s. gentleness, courtesy, 123, 7.

dede, s. deed, 5, 24.

dede, v. caused, made, 37, 29.

deduyt, s. pleasure, delight, 307, 34; 437. 8; 640, 31.

deed, adj. dead, 34, 8.

deffence, s. prohibition, defence, 54, 27.

deffende, v. to forbid, 54, 23.

deffende, v. to preserve, defend, 39, 26; 121, 17.

defensable, adj. able to defend, 54, 18.

delicatys, s. delicacies, 6, 26.

delyte, s. delight, 6, 25.

delyuer, adj. active, nimble, 267, 34; deliuere, 136, 23; adj. free, 692, 20.

delyuerly, adv. actively, nimbly, 158, 36.

demaundes, s. questions, 16, 12.

demened, pp. treated, 465, 13; 656, 35.

demened, pp. conducted, directed, 75, 33; 79, 9.

demonstraunce, s. demonstration, sign, 59, 11.

departe, v. to separate, divide, distribute, 61, 8; 92, 29; ended, 90, 13.

dere, adj. dear, 49, 27.

derenged, v. attacked, fought, 549, 1.

derke, adj. dark, 348, 2.

derkly, adv. darkly, obscurely, 53, 22.

deserue, v. serve for, do work for, 660, 25.

desese, s. inconvenience, hardship, trouble, 260, 2.

desesse, s. decease, 228, 25.

desier, s. desire, wish, 4, 18.

desseuered, pp. divided, separated, 259, 33.

deth, s. death, 45, 6.

dever, s. duty, 162, 13.

devise, s. at all points, 278, 32; 508, 10; 519, 2.

devised, v. directed, 659, 23.

devynour, s. deviner, 45, 19.

deyen, v. to die, 3, 29.

deynteis, s. dainties, 471, 12.

deyse, s. high table in hall, 480, 28.

dierly, adv. dearly, eagerly, 302, 12; 631, 4.

diffence, s. gainsaying, 686, 17.

diffende, v. to prohibit, prevent, resist, 29, 10; 428, 14.

diffoulde, pp. 10, 33; defiled; diffoiled, 276, 35.

dight, pp. arrayed, dressed, 113, 13.

disavaunce, v. forestall (Fr. desauanchier), 658, 15.

disavaunced, pp. thrown or driven back, 250, 22.

discendir, v. to fall, drop, 118, 19.

discesed, pp. deprived, 229, 31.

disceytis, s. deceits, 8, 7.

disceyve, 3, 23; disseyve, 87, 29; v. to deceive.

discheueled, pp. dishevelled, 453, 16; 646, 15.

discheuelee, s. entanglement of hair, 298, 31.

disconfited, pp. discomforted, defeated, 24, 24.

discouert, adj. uncovered, 628, 34.

discounfit, v. to discomfort, defeat.

discounfited, discomfited, 120, 14.

discure, v. to discover, make plain, 58, 19.

disered, v. desired, 27, 7.

diserte, s. desert, 59, 8.

disese, v. to trouble, discomfort, 2, 26; 115, 31; 649, 29.

disese, s. harm, injury, 1, 20; 30, 25.

disgarnysshed, pp. deprived of, go without, 440, 17.

disherit, v. to disinherit, 42, 7.

disparble, v. to disperse, 208, 5; disparbled, pt. dispersed, 196, 19; 214, 18.

dispeire, s. despair, 4, 17.

dispitously, adv. pitifully, 355, 6.

disporte, v. engage, practise, 352, 15.

dispyte, s. pity, regret, 70, 23.

disray, s. clamour, commotion, 407, 11; 460, 10.

dissese, s. discomfort, trouble, 54, 30.

distraught, pp. distracted, 20, 21.

distreined, v. vexed, upset, 71, 3.

distreyned, v. constrained, 193, 4.

distrif, s. strife, 536, 9.

distrowed, 26, 19; distrued, 184, 29; distrowied, 40, 28; pp. destroyed.

distroyne, 174, 31; distrye, 191, 22; v. to destroy.

distrubier, s. disturber, 240, 22.

distrubinge, s. disturbance, upset, 296, 4.

distrubled, v. disturbed, troubled, 154, 5.

distruxion, s. destruction, 172, 6.

disturbier, s. hindrance, 509, 36.

disturdison, s. moaning, suffering, 266, 35.

disturue, v. dispute, question, 680, 1.

distyne, distynes, s. destiny, 166, 3; 582, 30.

do, v. execute, fulfil, 5, 13.

do, v. caused, 25, 25; 57, 16.

doctryne, s. doctrine, teaching, 5, 30.

doel, 34, 9; doell, 4, 25; s. grief, sorrow, mourning.

dolent, adj. sad, sorrowful, 331, 1; 572, 20.

dolven, pp. buried, 5, 14.

don, prep. down, 53, 8.

dought, v. ought, should, 47, 17.

dought, v. thought, 3, 36; seemed, 106, 14; feared, doubted, 6, 9; 248, 36.

dought, s. thought, 555, 18.

dought, s. fear, 226, 29.

doute, v. to fear, 62, 7; 171, 7.

doute, 70, 15; 94, 22; dowte, s. fear, 117, 32.

douted, v. feared, dreaded, 265, 17; 343, 7.

draweth, v. resembles, 434, 35.

drede, s. fear, dread, 16, 27.

dressed, v. reared, prepared, set in order, 58, 11; 110, 25; went, addressed, 255, 2.

drof, v. drove, 26, 36.

drough, 17, 22; drowgh, 28, 28; drow, 47, 31; v. drew.

druweries, s. love, esteem, 641, 2.

dubbe, v. dub, 316, 7.

duelled, v. dwelled, remained, 645, 16.

duerf, s. dwarf, 638, 13.

dure, v. to endure, last, 116, 8.

duresse, s. constraint, confinement, 19, 10.

dureth, v. extends, 260, 18.

dyed, v. died, 4, 25.

dyen, 65, 26; dye, 3, 34; v. to dye.

ech, eche, adj. each, 110, 32.

efte-sones, adv. afterwards, presently, 226, 31.

egramauncye, 375, 30; 508, 4; egremauncye, 176, 6; s. magic, divination.

eiled, v. ailed, 3, 33.

eleccion, s. election, choice, 96, 25.

ellis, 76, 15; elles, 54, 2; adv. else.

elther, adj. older, 5, 29; 529, 6.

empeire, v. hurt, 606, 27.

empere, s. empire, 105, 36.

emprise, s. enterprise, 263, 9.

en, conj. and, 14, 27.

cnarmynge, s. handle of a shield, 667. 25.

enbelynk, 584, 9.

enbrace, v. puts on his arm, 516, 5.

enbuschemcnt, 161, 5; enbusshe-ment, 135, 5; s. ambush.

cnbusshed, pp. amassed, ambushed, 246, 12.

enchase, v. to pursue, 218, 6.

encombraunce, s. encumbrance, 5, 23.

cncrese, v. to increase, 223, 31.

cnderdited, pp. interdicted, 466, 19.

enffeffe, v. infeof, 373, 32.

enforce, v. increase, 443, 3.

engender, 102, 8; cngendre, 62, 1; v. to beget.

engyn, 20, 33; engyne, 14, 14; s. craft, subtlety, deceit.

enmy, 20, 32; enmye, 55, 9; s. enemy.

ennoisies, adj. gay, lively ["mis-reading for *envoisies*." N.E.D.], 106, 12.

cnprise, s. enterprise, 242, 30.

enquere, v. to enquire, ask for, 44, 3; 49, 22.

enquesitif, adj. inquisitive, 292, 34.

enquest, s. search, 687, 10.

cnquire, s. enquiry, 3, 12.

ensele, v. seal, 617, 32.

entailled, v. carved, shaped, 362, 31.

entassed, pp. incumbercd, heaped, 337, 29.

entassement, s. accumulation, heaping, 398, 7.

entende, v. learn, pay attention, 310, 11.

entended, v. heard, attended, 23, 18; 266, 34.

entcnte, s. intent, intention, 97, 25.

entententifly, adv. attentively, 567, 25.

entered, v. buried, 647, 9.

cntermedled, intermixed, 227, 7.

entermete, v. to meddle with, interfere, 19, 31; 39, 33.

enterpassaunt, v. returning, pas-sing back, 329, 10.

enterpendaunt, adj. independent, enterprising, 475, 7.

entiere, v. buried, interred, 369, 13.

entirpassinge, v. passing back, 407, 32.

entrauerse, adj. crossed, 163, 12.

entre, s. entry, 55, 23; beginning, 191, 7; entreynge, s. begin-ning, 205, 12.

entysement, s. enticement, 5, 1.

enuay, envaie, s.; Fr. envahie, an assault, an onset, 318, 15; 352, 18.

enuoysed, v. 463, 2.

cnviron, prep. about, around, 113, 22; 153, 17.

er, adv. before, 190, 19.

errour, s. chagrin, vexation, 318, 25.

erthe, s. earth, 128, 5.

ese, s. ease, 257, 23.

espleyted, pp. fulfilled, complcted, 10, 16.

cspyes, 146, 10; esspies, 575, 15; s. spies.

este, adv. first, 72, 31.

estres, s. ins and outs, 242, 13.

euell, adv. ill, mis-, 5, 22.

eure, s. luck, fortune, 320, 32.

evereche, 31, 36; everich, 63, 32; adj. each one, every.

evesonge, s. evensong, vespers, 102, 36.

expowned, pp. expounded, ex-plained, 42, 26.

eyder, pron. either, 148, 6.

facion, s. appearance, 427, 27.

fader, 5, 10; ffader, 102, 5; fadir, 5, 18; s. father.

fadome, s. fathom, 430, 11.

falle, pp. fell out, happened, 5, 11.

false, v. betray, deceive, 608, 28.

falsed, v. falsified, 666, 7.

fantasie, s. desire, liking, 213, 5.

faste, adj. near, close, 213, 22.

fauced, 628, 22 ; faused, 456, 25 ; v. pierced, cut.

faucouns, s. falcons, 135, 9.

faugh, v. fought, 159, 8.

faute, n. want, 568, 27.

fecche, v. to fetch, 100, 35.

feed, adj. paid, 472, 16.

feende, 3, 35 ; fende, 1, 11 ; s. fiend.

feffed, v. infeofed, 374, 2.

feire, 8, 8 ; fere, 114, 19 ; s. fear.

feire, 4, 13 ; feyre, 6, 31 ; adj. fair.

felen, v. to feel, perceive, 38, 3.

felischep, 28, 10 ; felschip, 6, 9 ; felishep, 34, 31 ; 56, 11 ; s. fellowship, company.

fell, adj. fierce, strong, cruel, 30, 8 ; 102, 30.

fellenouse, adj. fierce, wicked, 118, 7 ; 352, 25.

felliche, adv. cruelly, felly, 571, 11.

felly, adv. fiercely, 215, 31.

felon, adj. dangerous, 548, 9.

felonously, adv. fiercely, cruelly, 216, 1.

felt, s. hat, 279, 23.

fenisshe, v. to finish, end, stop, 54, 12.

fer, adj. far, distant, 6, 3.

fercely, adv. fiercely, 119, 35.

ferde, v. acted, conducted, 4, 15 ; went, 211, 22.

ferde, adj. afraid, frightened, terrible, 27, 4 ; 346, 23.

feriage, s. passing over water, 606, 20.

ferly, adj. strange, 93, 30.

ferther, adj. foreign, distant, 103, 36.

feste, s. feast, 63, 22.

fewtee, s. fealty, 121, 3.

fewtre, s. the rest for a spear, 127, 9.

ficched, v. moved uncomfortably, 335, 30.

ficchid, pp. fixed, fastened, 98, 14 ; 164, 9.

fieraunt, adj. becoming, suitable, 583, 26.

fiers, adj. fierce, 193, 19.

fill, v. fell, went, 4, 17.

fill, pt. fell out, happened, 44, 5 ; 59, 6.

fin, s. end, conclusion, 229, 33.

fin, 249, 16 ; 287, 6 ; fyn, 156, 16 ; adj. sheer, entire.

fitz, s. sons, 496, 1 ; 542, 10.

flain, 268, 34 ; flayn, 347, 9 ; pp. flayed, skinned.

flat, v. ? extend, 275, 30.

flawme, s. flame, 332, 17.

flayle, s. portion of a gate, the bar, 206, 29.

fle, v. to fly, 199, 28.

flekered, v. fluttered, waved, 324, 30.

fleynge, part. pres. flying, 56, 5.

florte, adj. ? flowered, decorated, 395, 14.

flos of the see, high tide, 646, 5.

flote, s. mass, company, 198, 3.

flour, s. flower, i.e. best, 401, 8.

fly, v. flew, 199, 25 ; 216, 34.

fole, s. fool, 53, 14 ; 357, 15.

folily, adv. foolishly, 7, 18 ; 650, 32.

fonde, v. found, 11, 1 ; 36, 29.

foorde, s. ford, 606, 17.

for, adv. because, inasmuch as, 108, 17.

for, prep. from, 260, 4.

for-swellen, very much swollen, 172, 19.

for-swette, i.e. covered with sweat, 296, 19.

fore, prep. of, 300, 25.

forewarde, s. first portion, van, 276, 16.

forfet, s. offence, 69, 8 ; 109, 2.

forfet, v. prepared, 84, 20.

forfete, v. to injure, offend, misdo, 115, 18.

forgeven, v. to forgive, 55, 31.

for-juged, pp. wrongfully judged, 470, 19.

for-leyn, v. lain with, 544, 3.

formednesse, s. silly action, conceit, 639, 26.

formeste, adj. foremost, 46, 12.

forrears, 146, 17; forryoars, 230, 13; s. scouts, foragers.

forry, v. forage, 272, 7.

forse, s. force, number, 126, 19.

for-swollen, adj. 538, 6.

fort, adv. forth, 361, 12.

for-thought, pp. repented, grieved, 40, 28.

forthynke, v. to repent, 25, 15.

foryete, v. to forget, 71, 33.

foryete, pp. forgotten, 9, 33.

for-yeten, pp. forgotten, 138, 18; 545, 6.

foryevenesse, s. forgiveness, 10, 28.

foundement, s. foundation, 31, 24.

founden, pp. found, 4, 15.

fowled, v. trampled, 494, 36.

fowrtithe, 40th? 171, 19.

foyson, s. plenty, 150, 31; 176, 34.

frayen, v. rubbed, dashed, 594, 34.

frayinge, s. collision, struggle, 339, 14.

frayned, 6, 13; freyned, 50, 7; v. asked, questioned, enquired.

freissh, adj. fresh, gay, 203, 10.

fremyssh, v. tremble, shake, 284, 9; 336, 18.

fremysshed, v. trembled, shook, 162, 28; 648, 32.

frende, s. friend, 49, 27.

fres, adj. vigorous, 156, 10.

fro, prep. from, 4, 22.

frote, v. rub, 76, 20; 424, 25.

frotinge, v. rubbing, 649, 7.

frusht, 207, 2; frussht, 164, 14; ffrushed, 219, 18; 661, 5; v. dashed, smashed, rushed, violently.

fulfilde, v. filled, 59, 28.

full, adv. very, quite, 41, 17.

fullich, adv. fully, 275, 14.

fyngres, s. fingers, 635, 19.

fynyshment, s. end, conclusion, 23, 3.

gabbe, v. to lie, talk idly, 31, 4.

gabbynge, s. lying, 13, 5.

ganfanon, s. standard, 205, 35; 323, 18.

ganfanoner, s. standard-bearer, 211, 7.

garcion, s. stripling, boy, 103, 32.

garnement, s. garment, 384, 29.

garnyson, s. garrison, 174, 29.

garnysshed, v. garrisoned, 381, 21.

garnysshe, 115, 19; 55, 22; 176, 14; garnyssh, 174, 23; v. to furnish, prepare, guard?

gate, v. got, 333, 29.

gavelokkes, s. spears or javelins, 300, 34; 662, 33.

geauntes, s. giants, 209, 15.

gete, v. to get, beget, 3, 5; 3, 9; 67, 34.

geve, v. to give, 95, 26.

gige, s. handle of a shield, 344, 36; 496, 31.

gipser, s. pouch or purse, 608, 5.

girde, v. smite, strike, 408, 33; 596, 8.

glenched, v. glanced, slipped aside, 158, 6; 329, 6.

gleves, 660, 34; glevis, 275, 23; gleyves, 264, 1; 331, 26; s. a weapon composed of a long cutting blade at the end of a lance.

glode, v. glided, 594, 29.

glood, do., 595, 23.

glose, v. flatter, cajole, 680, 9.

go, pp. gone, 267, 6.

gode, s. goods, property, 4, 4.

gode, adj. good, 3, 27.

gome, s. man, 594, 29.

gonne, v. began, commenced, 369, 30.

goolde, s. gold, 57, 15.

goste, s. ghost, 12, 3.

gotere, s. gutter, 38, 1.

goth, imper. go, 13, 12.

goules, 205, 35; gowles, 395, 15; s. gules.

gowe = go we, let us go, 68, 4.

gramercy, interj. great thanks, many thanks, 115, 32.

graunted, v. promised, 557, 13.

gre, s. favour, pleasure; to take in gre = take kindly, 204, 13.

greces, 279, 30; 427, 30; greeces, 555, 8; s. ? steps, entrance.

grees, s. same as greces (279, 30), 639, 3.

grennynge, v. roaring, crying, 209, 9.

gret, adj. great, 50, 26.

gretinge, s. greeting, 47, 24.

gretnesse, s. pregnancy, 86, 19.

grette, adj. great, 648, 4.

greve, v. to vex, injure, 154, 24.

greves, s. shores, beach? 649, 29.

grewe, 436, 20; griewe, 437, 15; s. Greek.

griped, v. seized, 9, 21; 119, 14.

growe, adj. grown, 390, 12.

grucched, 355, 24; 392, 26; grucchid, 206, 32; v. opposed, resisted.

grucchynge, s. opposition, 73, 19.

grym, adj. rough, dirty, 43, 1; 196, 18.

grysly, adj. horrible, terrible, 15, 8.

guerdon, v. reward, 102, 22.

gyde, s. guide, 280, 26.

gyge, same as gige.

gynneth, v. begins, commences, 313, 8.

gynnynge, s. beginning, 10, 30.

gysarmes, s. bills or battle axes, 281, 31.

habergon, s. breast-plate, armour for the neck and breast, 110, 21.

halowmasse, s. the feast of All Saints, 97, 12.

halsed, v. embraced, 74, 26.

haluendell, s. half, 157, 25.

haly, adj. holy, 12, 2.

happed, v. happened, 7, 11.

harde, adv. hard, terribly, strongly, 214, 19.

hardely, adv. boldly, 35, 7.

hardy, adj. bold, brave, 113, 23.

hardynesse, s. boldness, 103, 18; 169, 3.

harlotis, s. harlots, followers, scouts, base men, 9, 12; 276, 14; 404, 16.

harneyse, s. weapons, armour, 120, 26.

haten, v. to hate, 5, 22.

hau, have, 111, 21.

haubrek, 118, 35; hauberkes, 628, 21; s. a coat of mail.

hedylyche, adv. ? heavily, strongly, 119, 4.

heer, s. hair, 261, 6.

heirdes, s. herdsmen, 3, 28.

heire, adv. here, 23, 30.

heire, s. air, 393, 6.

heiren, v. to hear, 32, 33.

heir-to, adv. hereto, 24, 8.

hele, s. health, 71, 27.

helue, s. helve, handle, 339, 28.

hem, pron. them, 3, 28; 5, 17.

henge, v. hung, 4, 22.

hens, adv. hence, 15, 14.

hente, v. seize, take hold of, 30, 8; 101, 8.

her, pron. their, 34, 6.

herbegage, s. quarters, lodgings, 154, 25.

herberewe, 30, 31; herberowe, 204, 20; s. lodging, shelter, harbour.

herberough, s. hauberk, 387, 5.

herberowed, pp. lodged, 546, 34.

here, pron. her, 3, 17.

here, v. to hear, 23, 23; heren, 171, 16.

herken, v. to listen, herkened, pt., 23, 17.

hertely, adv. heartily, 48, 26; 81, 31.

hertys, s. ? persons, 22, 9.

hevied, v. made heavy, depressed, 182, 19.

hevy, adj. heavy, dull, 53, 25.

heryeth, v. hesitate, 368, 13.

heyer, s. heir, 80, 20.

hider, adv. hither, 25, 16.

hidouse, adj. hideous, frightful, 40, 36.

hidously, adv. 207, 22.

hier, adj. higher, upper, 175, 17.

hierdes, s. shepherds, 252, 20.

hiest, adj. highest, most renowned, 55, 1.

hight, 24, 2; 59, 25; highte, 129, 3; pp. called.

hilde, v. held, 14, 18.

hir, pro. their, 33, 33.

hire, v. to hear, 102, 36.

hit, pro. it, 91, 22.

hoilde, v. to hold, side, 42, 9.

hoill, adj. whole, entire, 52, 28; 57, 2; hool, 224, 23.

holicherche=holy church, 14, 18.

holtes, s. woods, groves, 274, 1.

holy, adv. wholly, 86, 4.

hom, s. home, 250, 35.

horse, s. horses, a company of horse, 4, 3; 50, 17; 117, 1; 193, 14; 335, 17.

hosebonde, s. husband, 19, 27.

hoseled, pp. comforted, 415, 35; was hoseled, i.e. received.

houe, pp. brought up, reared? 124, 28.

houeth, v. behoves, 33, 9.

hovid, v. stopped, 200, 4.

howsolde, s. household, family, 49, 10.

howsynge, s. housing, houses, 63, 27.

huch, s. hutch, 4, 20.

hurdeysed, v. hurdled, 604, 21.

hurtelid, v. rushed, dashed, 117, 35.

hym, pron. he, 250, 30.

iape, v. to jest, mock, 66, 28; 113, 31.

iapes, s. jests, mockery, 113, 32.

I-be, pp. been, 258, 16; 363, 28.

i-come, pp. come, 25, 16.

i-don, pp. done, 76, 23.

i-douted, pp. feared, dreaded, 163, 34.

iepardye, s. jeopardy, 69, 28.

i-gon, pp. gone, 68, 35.

I-loste, pp. lost, 312, 33.

[I have heard a gamekeeper say to his retriever, when he had shot some game, and wished the dog to go and get it, "I-lost, I-lost."—W. A. D.]

in-countre, s. encounter, 134, 6.

indure, v. to last, 24, 27.

Inngendure, s. ? charge of guilt, 18, 23.

I-nowgh, 213, 29; i-nough, 68, 18; i-nowe, 77, 5; adj. enough.

inteript, pp. interrupted, 105, 28?

intermete, v. to interfere, meddle with, 24, 21.

in-to, prep. until, 30, 1; 105, 27.

ioly, adj. pretty, 106, 12.

iolye, adj. pleasant, joyful, 47, 18.

iour, s. day, 67, 5.

iourne, s. journey, 251, 15.

Iowes, s. jaws, 273, 22; 496, 34.

iren, s. iron, 98, 13.

irouse, adj. angry, enraged, 71, 3.

I-spredde, pp. spread, 240, 7.

isse, v. issue, sally forth, 255, 22; 334, 31.

issed, 111, 6; isseden, 42, 13; v. issued forth.

issu, issue, s. doorway, outlet, 90, 3; 357, 21.

I-teyed, v. moored, 464, 3.

iustice, v. to judge, 122, 35.

iustynge, s. jousting, 127, 21.

iuwelles, 64, 8; juwels, 65, 29; s. jewels.

Iuyse, s. judgment, 35, 4; properly imoyse fin judicium.

iyen, s. eyes, 172, 18.

kach, v. to catch, 9, 23.

keeled, v. cooled, 371, 9.

keen, s. kine, 274, 12.

keled, pp. cooled, 214, 4.

kenne, v. to know, recognize, 45, 22.

kenrede, s. kindred, 79, 35.

kilde, pt. killed, 209, 21.

kirchires, s. covering for the head of a woman, 689, 33.

knowe, pp. 11, 16; knoweth, pres. pl. 2, 3.

knowleche, s. knowledge, 2, 29.

knowliche, v. to acknowledge, 26, 12.

knowynge, s. knowledge, wisdom, 3, 11; 13, 22; 58, 23.

knyghthode, s. chivalry, warlike deed, 56, 29.

kowde, 21, 22; kowthe, 100, 5; v. could.

koye, adj. quiet, coy, shy, 78, 11.

krowne, s. crown, 24, 13.

kutte, v. cut, 339, 28.

kyngeles, adj. kingless, 24, 30.

kyton, s. kitten, 665, 28.

kyttynge, v. cutting, 118, 15.

kyutte, 195, 4; kutte, 195, 2; kytte, 137, 16; v. cut, cut off.

laden, v. to dip or bale water, 37, 29.

lakke, s. lack, 54, 30.

lappe, s. skirt, 101, 10.

lardre, 336, 28; lardure, 337, 27; 655, 18; s. slaughter.

lasted, v. extended in space, 274, 15; 350, 23.

laught, v. caught, 199, 29.

launchant, part. leaning forward, 288, 33.

launde, s. bit of open country, 298, 6; Fr. lande, 683, 4.

laweers, s. lawyers, 434, 14.

layners, s. cords, 697, 6.

leche, s. doctor, 336, 7.

lechours, s. lustful men, 434, 29.

leder, s. leather, 168, 7.

leed, s. lead, 63, 5.

leff, v. leave, 299, 24.

lefte, v. remained, 70, 25; 95, 20.

lefte, pp. broken, 85, 15.

leged, v. laid, fixed, 166, 29.

leide to the deef ere, i.e. turned a deaf ear, 261, 34.

leife, s. lover, 636, 12.

leiser, s. chance, opportunity, 346, 21.

leneth, v. lendeth, 434, 9.

lenger, adj. longer, 110, 11.

lenton, s. the season of Lent, 142, 24.

lenynge, part. pres., leaving, resting, 168, 1.

leopart, 304, 11; lupart, 304, 6; s. leopard.

lepe, v. leapt, 68, 32; 195, 13.

lerned, v. taught, 5, 31; pp. 9, 7.

lese, v. to lose, 6, 8.

lessed, v. deprived, 401, 18.

leste, v. to please, desire, 48, 32.

lesynge, s. lye, lying, 31, 6; 62, 9.

let, v. to hinder, 7, 24; prevent, 12, 19.

lete, 12, 19 (to cause, ?13, 17; 18, 31; 27, 18).

lette, v. prevent, to hinder, 188, 29.

letted, pp. hindered, 228, 18.

lettynge, s. hindrance, 6, 36; 131, 10.

leve, v. to believe, 11, 21; 29, 5; 62, 28.

leve, v. to live, 24, 34.

leve, v. accept, follow, 365, 11; 507, 21.

leven, v. leave, forsake, 202, 20.

lever, adv. rather, sooner, 35, 33.

leyser, s. leisure, 7, 2; 32, 26.

leysere, s. chance, 100, 20; all be leysere.

lifly, adv. lively, 355, 5.

lifte, adj. left, 211, 5.

liggynge, 58, 11; 155, 6; lyggynge, 196, 10; part. pres. lying down.

lightly, adv. quickly, 241, 17; 634, 32.

litere, 93, 31; letere, 94, 6; lytier, 92, 25; litier, 301, 14; s. litter.

logged, pp. lodged, encamped, 277, 25.

logges, s. tents, lodges, 116, 23.

loigge, v. to lodge, stay, 127, 18.

loigges, s. tents, camp, 387, 1.

loigginge, 43, 34; loigynge, 68, 8; s. lodging, abode.

loiginge, s. tent, lodging, 387, 8.

londe, s. land, 26, 26.

louged, v. belonged, 42, 4; 470, 15.

longes, s. lungs, 357, 8.

longinge, pres. part. belonging, 605, 21.

loose, v. to lose, 6, 30.

lordinges, s. Sirs, masters, 172, 30.

lordship, s. estate, 350, 23.

lorn, pp, forsaken, 58, 27.

lose, s. honour, fame, praise, 176, 18.

losenges, s. [in heraldry], 205, 35.

lothly, adj. loathsome, 262, 16.

lotly, adj. ugly, 265, 32.

lough, v. laughed, 33, 25.

lowed, v. lowered, 397, 8.

lower, s. hire, reward, 59, 5.

lowted, v. bent, bowed, made obeisance, 98, 19.

lurdeyn, s. lazy person, 537, 7; 538, 2.

luste, s. will, desire, 7, 23; 268, 25.

lusty, adj. vigorous, merry, 191, 12.

lyen, v. to lie, 86, 27.

lyfte, adj. left, 128, 4.

lyfte, v. lifted, raised, 24, 14.

lym, s. limb, 321, 33.

lynage, 59, 8; lyngnage, 105, 6; s. lineage.

lyntell, s. lintell, s. lintel, 436, 19.

lyonsewes, s. young lions; Fr. lionçeaux, 413, 22; 417, 10.

lysted, pp. edged or bordered, 163, 12.

maat, adj. stupefied, overpowered, 125, 16.

magre, s. 40, 7; 83, 17; misfortune, displeasure, s.; in spite of, prep. 206, 31; 214, 23.

maister, s. master, 3, 30.

maister, adj. chief, 110, 6.

maistries, 78, 17; mastryes, 134, 14; s. feats, deeds.

maistris, s. leaders, 549, 35.

make, v. used passively, 38 1; 57, 16; to cause, ? 6, 17; 29, 25.

males, s. wallets, budgets, 147, 34.

maletalentif, adv. with ill-will, 338, 27.

malle, s. club, mallet, 339, 9.

maltalente, maltelente, s. anger, evil disposition, 500, 27.

manased, v. menaced, 651, 16.

manasynge, s. threats, 26, 22.

manece, 652, 10; manese, 26, 25; v. threaten.

maners, s. ways, 2, 13.

mantelent, s. anger, ill-will, 339, 2.

maras, 254, 27; 380, 16; s. marsh.

marasse, s. bog, 604, 28.

marche, s. border, boundary, limit, 167, 23.

maroners, s. mariners, 379, 5.

marteleise, 211, 26; martileys, 334, 23; s. hammering.

martirdom, s. slaughter, 163, 29.

martire, s. torment, martyrdom, 17, 7; slaughter, 193, 25.

maryne, s. sea-coast, 230, 6.

marysse, s. marsh, 254, 19.

mased, pp. confounded, 201, 12.

massage, s. message, command, 29, 28.

massagiers, 33, 20; massanger, 31, 7; massenger, 33, 18; s. messenger.

mat, adj., same as maat, 145, 24.

mate, adj. dejected, exhausted, 269, 33; 355, 8; 396, 20.

matelentif, adj. angry, 219, 30.

mater, s. ? matter, 503, 25.

matere, 114, 7; matire, 50, 34; s. matter, business.

maundement, s. demand, 643, 15.

mayden, s.: "He was a preste . . . and also a mayden," i.e. unmarried, 326, 36.

mayme, s. injury, 527, 9.

maymen, v. to maim, 208, 13.

mayne, meyne, s. retinue, household, 42, 15; 46, 26.

mayntene, meyntene, v. to main-
tain, uphold, 97, 22 ; 112, 33.
me, s. men, 244, 13.
meddelynge, 199, 32 ; medelinge,
207, 28 ; 352, 12 ; s. fighting.
medle, 100, 33 ; 118, 7 ; 156,
15 ; medlee, 163, 29 ; s. fray,
tourney, fight.
mees, s. mice, 665, 30.
mene, adj. many? mean? common? 243, 28.
mene, s. means, way, 20, 14.
mennes, s. men's, 262, 33.
ment, v. meant, 25, 2.
mervelle, 3, 30 ; merveyle, 5, 15 ;
merveile, 42, 2 ; s. wonder.
merveloise, adj. marvellous, 56,
29.
merveyled, v. marvelled, wondered,
3, 29.
mese, s. mess, meal, 614, 36.
messagers, s. messengers, 29, 36.
messe, s. mass, service, 52, 11.
mete, s. food, 240, 6.
mevable, adj. movable, 116, 5.
meve, v. to move, 38, 15 ; start,
go, 130, 11.
meyne, s. (chess) men, 362, 30.
mo, pron. me, 431, 19.
mo, 56, 7 ; moo, 258, 10 ; adj.
more.
moche, adj. broad, great, 97, 7 ; 117,
13 ; 351, 20 ; many, 262, 35.
moche, adv. much, 4, 1.
modir, 5, 18 ; moder, 8, 35 ;
modre, 15, 5 ; s. mother.
monestede, v. admonished, 530, 18.
monge, prep. amongst, 244, 4.
morderid, pp. murdered, 46, 10.
moreyn, s. murrain, 3, 30.
morowe, s. morning, 204, 30 ;
545, 8.
morownynge, s. morning, 273, 36.
mortalite, s. mortality, 56, 27.
mortalite, s. mortality, 337, 10.
mortall, adj. deadly, 214, 16.
morthered, v. murdered, 401, 29.
mossell, s. morsel, 6, 24 ; mossel
brede, a morsel of bread.

moste, adj. greatest, 210, 36.
mouncels, s. portions, 413, 36.
moustred, v. mustered, 560, 26.
mowe, v. may, 22, 29.
musardes, s. dull persons, fools,
183, 34 ; 582, 15.
mustre, s. muster, 658, 22.
myddill, s. middle, 108, 3.
mynistre, s. minster, 98, 26.
myri, adj. merry, 384, 31.
myrily, adv. pleasantly, joyously,
77, 7.
mysaventure, s. misadventure,
mishap, 68, 1.
mysbelevynge, adj. unbelieving,
191, 23.
myschaunce, s. misfortune, 78, 27.
myschef, s. danger, injury, 4, 5 ;
356, 18.
myscheved, pp. injured, 8, 36.
myschief, s. odds, 265, 1.
mysdon, pp. done wrongly, 500,
20.
mysese, s. discomfort, 64, 33.
mysese, adj. injured, troubled, 94,
13.
myshevouse, adj. unfortunate, in-
jurious, 5, 28.
myslyvinge, s. evil life, 2, 10.
myssese, s. trouble, discomfort,
331, 21.
myssey, v. to slander, revile, 30,
10.
myster, s. need, necessity, 44, 31 ;
65, 33 ; 93, 28.
mystere, s. skill, occupation, 14,
6 ; 156, 34.
mystered, s. needed, 22, 35.
mystily, adv. obscurely, darkly,
54, 6.
mystrowe, v. to mistrust, 21, 12 ;
48, 33.

namly, adv. especially, 8, 20.
nas, was not, 267, 25.
nat, adv. not, 4, 30.
natht, s. naught, 18, 23.
navie, s. ships, navy, 50, 31.
nay, adv. no, 3, 34 ; 5, 26.

ne, adv. not, 264, 12.
ne a-bide not, double negative, 258, 31.
ne, conj. nor, 2, 20.
nece, s. niece, 63, 33.
neethe, s. needs, wants, 505, 28.
neke, 53, 8; nekke, 51, 17; s. neck.
nempned, pp. named, 143, 9.
ner, adv. near, 277, 30.
netherdeles, adv. nevertheless, 43, 30.
nevew, 171, 34; nevewe, 152, 11; s. nephew.
nyegh, 215, 1; nyghe, 684, 25; v. to near, approach.
neighed, 207, 31; neyhed, 263, 21; v. neared, approached.
no, adv. not, 302, 8.
noon, adv. no, not, 6, 17; 33, 14.
norice, s. nurse, 135, 34.
norished, v. brought up, 26, 1.
norisshe, v. to nourish, nurse, bring up, 88, 10.
not, v.=ne wot, know not, 20, 5.
not, s. naught, nothing, 54, 2.
nother, adv. 102, 5; adj. 109, 2, neither.
nought, adv. not, 1, 7.
noye, v. annoy, 368, 17.
noysaunce, s. injury, 456, 2.
nurture, s. training, cultivation, 227, 13.
ny, adv. nigh, nearly, 199, 1.
nys = neys, is not, 87, 10.

o, adj. one, 318, 20.
obbeye, v. to obey, 66, 18.
occision, s. killing, slaying, 118, 24; 159, 15.
of, adv. off, 53, 8; 220, 5.
of, prep. from, 33, 8; 59, 7; for, 210, 1; by, 265, 30; concerning, about, 47, 16; during, 171, 29.
olyfauntes, s. elephants, 327, 29.
olyvere, s. olive-tree, 541, 29.
on, prep. in, 86, 12; on baste = in bastardy.

on, 2, 32; 167, 7; oo, 220, 16; 316, 26; oon, 3, 1; 4, 34; adj. one.
ones, adv. once, 11, 20.
only, adj. alone, 264, 8.
ordenaunce, s. ordinance, plan, 3, 11.
ordeyned, v. provided, 301, 14; prepared, 473, 24.
orfraied, adj. gold-embroidered, 615, 7.
orped, adj. valorous, bold, 439, 22.
orphenyn, s. orphan, 212, 18.
oste, s. host, army, 24, 16; 43, 22.
osteill, s. hostel, lodging, 130, 13.
osteye, v. to make warlike incursions, 70, 5.
other, adv. either, 217, 24.
ouer-gate, v. overtake, 276, 28.
ouerlede, v. to oppress ?, 122, 35.
ought, adv. very . . . he shall come er ought long, 449, 8.
ought, s. anything, 269, 6.
ought, v. owed, 302, 11.
oughten, v. owed, 138, 25.
oure, s. hour, 13, 2; 151, 4.
outerage, s. outrage, violence, 69, 6; 81, 35.
outerly, adv. entirely, 340, 33; 571, 15.
outraied, 629, 20; 630, 8; outreyed, 458, 6; outrayed, 458, 11; pp. beaten, ruined.
ouerene, prep. over, 18, 29.
overthrewe, v. fell down, fell over, 27, 22.
owe, 83, 13; 369, 23; owen, 60, 11; oweth, 54, 36; 449, 7; v. ought.
owther, adv. either, 357, 12.
owzht, v. ought, 14, 7.

paas, 127, 24; pas, pase, 162, 15; s. pace.
pailet, s. pallet, couch, 95, 5.
paleis, 105, 2; paleise, 202, 21; s. palace.
pament, s. pavement, 496, 7.
panes, s. skirts, 501, 27.

pantoneres, 323, 21 ; s. spies.

paramours, (Fr. par amour), with love, tenderly, 9, 19.

paraunt, adj. marked, conspicuous, 356, 1.

par-a-venture, adv. haply, 204, 11.

parde, adv. an oath, *par Dieu*, 652, 25.

pareile, like, 584, 15.

parentes, s. relatives, 463, 10.

parformed, v. completed, finished, 629, 22.

parlament, 99, 25 ; parlement, 311, 13 ; s. conversation, a meeting for consultation.

partie (grete partie, 48, 26; a grete partye, 21, 5 = in great part); partye, 32, 34 (?) ; 139, 11 ; 195, 11 ; s. part, portion.

parties, s. districts, 321, 3.

party, s. a body of men for military work, 54, 16.

Pasch, 63, 30 ; Passh, 104, 11 ; Phasche, 178, 35 ; Easter.

passe, v. to pass away, die, 55, 14.

pavelouns, s. pavilions, 116, 11.

pawtener, s. rascal, vagabond, 268, 36.

paynymes, s. pagans, 446, 18 ; 594, 15.

paytrell, s. the breastplate of a horse's armour, 330, 34.

peas, 175, 33 ; pees, 27, 6 ; pes, 16, 13 ; s. peace.

pelow, s. pillow, 634, 23.

penon, s. skin that covers the shield, 570, 9.

pepill, 26, 32 ; peple, 32, 33 ; s. people.

perage, s. lineage (Fr. parage), 655, 36.

perche, s. pole, 4, 21.

perchemyn, s. parchment, 312, 5.

perdurable, adj. everlasting, 93, 4.

pereyle, s. peril, 142, 11.

peringall 394, 1 ; peryngall, 163, 4 ; adj. equal.

persch, 155, 13 ; persh, 327, 25 ; pershe, 293, 16 ; v. to pierce.

pervcied, pp. provided, 108, 20.

pesaunt, adj. heavy, weighty, 119, 12.

peses, s. pieces, 136, 26.

petaile, s. infantry, followers, 253, 20.

peyne, s. pain, torment, 122, 34.

peyned, v. strived, desired, took pains, 5, 31 ; 119, 21 ; 412, 20.

picche, v. to pitch, strike, 116, 11.

pight, pp. pitched, erected, 150, 30 ; 239, 32 ; 476, 19 ; 672, 30.

pilche, s. outer garment, 424, 22.

piled, pp. pilfered, robbed, 191, 33 ; 207, 8.

pite, s. pity, sorrow, 5, 9 ; 208, 35.

pitosly, 17, 12 ; pitously, 54, 8 ; adv. piteously, pitifully.

plaisshes, s. pools of water, 337, 28.

plants of an oke, s. pike, 600, 6.

playnynge, v. lamenting, 171, 28.

pleet, s. ? pleading, 366, 33.

plegge, s. pledge, 11, 31.

plegge, v. become surety for, 571, 32.

plegged, pp. pledged, 35, 33.

pleide, v. played, 529, 19.

plenteuouse, 191, 23 ; plentevouse, 202, 26 ; adj. plenteous.

plesier, 1, 3 ; 39, 27 ; plesire, 74, 18 ; s. pleasure.

pletere, s. pleading, 18, 29.

pletours, s. pleaders, 434, 11.

plite, s. condition, 354, 14.

plites, v. folds, 265, 11 ; 338, 33.

plukkynge, s. drawing, pulling, 339, 31.

poste, s. power, 610, 9.

pouke, v. poke, 367, 24.

powestee, s. power, might, 660, 22.

pownes, s. pawns, 362, 30.

powste, s. power, 639, 20.

poynt, s. dawn, 585, 13.

pray, s. cattle driven off, 192, 20 ; 196, 35.

prayes, s. raids, plunder, 26, 34;
272, 8; 276, 16.
preced, v. pierced, 117, 23; 155,
9; pressed, went, 156, 7.
preche, v. to preach, 110, 35.
preiden, v. prayed, 450, 12.
preised, v. valued, 464, 13.
prese, s. press, multitude, 61, 11.
prevy, adj. privy, secret, 47, 21.
prewe, v. to prove, 18, 26.
preyse, v. prize? praise? 6, 22.
priked, v. rode hard, spurred on,
73, 33.
prikinge, adv. galloping, 329, 15.
pris, s. enterprise, hazardous under-
taking, 176, 18.
prise, v. to take, 670, 16.
privees, s. trusted persons, 377,
13.
processe, s. progress, 255, 28.
provertee, s. poverty, 59, 1.
pryme, s. six o'clock a.m., 132,
7; 182, 3.
purchased, v. gained, acquired,
obtained, 190, 28.
putaile, s. populace, common
people, rabble, 192, 9.
puyssaunce, s. power, 202, 28.
pyne, s. pine-tree, 605, 10.
pytaile, s. foot-soldiers, 256, 25.

quarelles, s. arrows, cross-bow
bolts, 196, 4; 271, 33.
quat, 463, 26; quatte, 463, 22;
pp. hidden, squat, out of sight.
queche, s. thicket, 540, 9.
queynte, adj. artful, cunning,
113, 28.
quod, quo, v. quoth, said, 3, 25;
33, 36.
quyk, adj. alive, living, 12, 33;
29, 11; 347, 9.
quynsyme, 374, 16; quynsynne,
57, 11; quynsyne, 62, 22 (s.
Fr. quinzième), fifteen days, or
fifteenth day.
quyntayne, s. a board set up to
be tilted at, 133, 16; 375, 17;
584, 33.

quyte, v. requite, reward, 173,
20; 377, 8.
quyte, pp. acquitted, 19, 12; 37, 21.
quytely, adv. freely, 651, 28.

raced, v. took, pulled away, 424,
31; 633, 27.
radde, v. read, 280, 3.
raile, v. run, 342, 2.
randon, 401, 10; ranndon, 118,
34; raundon, 210, 3; 219, 5;
s. force, impetuosity; pace, 652,
21.
rasour, s. razor, 427, 18.
rattes, s. rats, 665, 30.
raught, v. lifted, 697, 11.
raught, v. reached, 159, 25.
ravayn, s. force, rage, 127, 12;
raveyn, 444, 27; ravyn, 549,
32; swiftness, 600, 15.
reade, adj. red, 37, 16; 635, 15.
reame, 40, 19; reeme, 84, 32;
reme, 259, 10; s. realm, kingdom.
recche, v. care for, reck, 93, 35.
recete, s. place of refuge, 684, 26.
recouer, s. remedy, stratagem, 332,
27.
recouerer, s. recovery, 4, 19.
reddure, s. violence, punishment,
538, 9.
rede, v. to advise, counsel, 25, 14.
rede, s. advice, counsel, 60, 7.
reden, v. rode, 30, 3.
redy, adj. assembled together,
243, 24.
refraite, 615, 19; refreite, 310,
12; s. refrain, burden of a
song.
refroide, v. restrain, cool, 500, 27.
refte, v. took from, deprived,
27, 3.
regrated, v. sorrowed for, 646, 24.
regrater, s. huckster, 168, 12.
rehete, v. cheer, encourage, 549, 19.
reinde, ? [f]reinde = freineth
(imp.), ask, inquire, 18, 2.
reine, lete reine, v. urge, 243, 36.
relented, v. remained, 323, 28.

releve, v. get up, 397, 22.
relied, v. to rally, relead, 196, 31;
    relye, 281, 2.
relikes, s. relics, 75, 26.
reme, s. realm, 610, 10.
remeve, v. to remove, 58, 10;
    397, 33.
renge, s. rank, row, course, 133,
    30; 162, 28.
renged, 127, 27; v. set in order,
    arranged.
renne, v. run, 347, 2.
renomede, 431, 35; renomee, 186,
    17; s. renown.
renomede, pp. renowned, 124, 29.
renon, s. renown, 106, 21.
repair, 20, 33; repaire, 43, 8;
    repeire, 311, 19; 669, 6; s.
    abode, place of resort.
repeyred, v. resorted, 132, 25.
repress, v. reprove, 269, 31.
requere, v. require, request, 49, 29.
requereth, pp. required, 65, 27.
rerewarde, 276, 17; 194, 7; s.
    after portion of an army, rear-
    guard.
rescewe, 214, 20; rescouse, 586,
    14; rescowe, 119, 18; s. rescue,
    deliverance.
rescettes, s. places of refuge, 568,
    27.
resceve, 224, 32; resceyve, 54,
    36; 32, 1; v. to receive.
rescowed, pp. rescued, 119, 18.
resorte, v. fall back, 391, 32.
resovned, v. resounded, 274, 4.
reuerse, v. fall, overturn, 157, 33.
rewarde, s., precaution, regard,
    599, 26.
reynes, s. body, 465, 33.
reynes, s. kidneys, 53, 10; loins,
    213, 33.
riall, adj. royal, 320, 27.
ribaudes, 277, 1; 278, 7; 317,
    34; s. base men, the lowest
    sort of retainers of the nobility.
richesse, s. property, riches, 3, 20;
    92, 36.
right, v. put in order, 209, 35.

rimpled, pp. wrinkled, puckered,
    168, 10.
rivelid, pp. wrinkled, 262, 16.
roche, s. coast, 250, 13.
roches, s. rocks, 125, 14.
rody, 335, 29; rody, 181, 21;
    adj. red, ruddy.
roiall, 108, 4; rioall, 107, 1; adj.
    royal.
ronne, v. run, 243, 22.
rought, v. cared, 654, 21.
rounge to messe, 97, 26; rang for
    mass?
rounsies, s. horses, 636, 27.
rowe, adj. rough, 168, 10; 635, 15.
rowned, v. whispered, 95, 6.
roynouse, adj. mangy, scabby,
    eaten up with itch, 527, 27.
rudely, adv. furiously, 350, 6.
ruse, v. give way, retire, 494, 26.
rused, 333, 34; rused, 155, 9;
    330, 15; rused, 288, 9; ruseden,
    409, 20; rusen, 550, 14; 662,
    20; v. rushed.
ryiche, adj. rich, 3, 17.
rympled, adj. curled, 424, 21.
ryvage, s. shore, beach, 377, 25;
    378, 12.

sacred, pp. consecrated, 26, 4; 57, 9.
sacred, v. consecrated, 502, 33.
sacringe, consecration, 105, 13.
sadde, adj. staid, solemn, 106, 14.
sadly, adv. seriously, 226, 18.
saf, adv. safe, 266, 12.
safe, 5, 19; saf, 273, 18; conj.
    save, but.
safte, s. safety, 471, 28.
saisnes, 176, 28; sasnes, 172, 31;
    s. Saxons.
salew, s. salutation, 506, 32.
salude, v. saluted, 266, 9.
salue, s. salve, 193, 20.
salued, saluted, hailed, 36, 3.
samyte, s. a kind of rich silk,
    608, 5.
sanourly, adv. heavily, soundly,
    415, 13.
sarazin, s. ? infidel, 193, 16.

sarazins, s. Saxons (saisnes), 260, 16.

sauacion, 96, 3; sauacion, 580, 28; s. salvation.

saunz-faile, without fail, 91, 11.

savete, s. safety, 542, 1.

sawter, s. psalter, 213, 22.

sayned, v. 14, 31; 66, 20; 304, 16; crossed himself? blessed himself?

scade, s. pity, misfortune, 678, 12.

scarmyshe, v. skirmish, flourish arms, 648, 19; Fr. escrimer.

scawberk, s. scabbard, 460, 14; scauberke, 367, 34.

schoved, v. shoved, pushed in, 218, 34.

scirmyssh, v. skirmish, 570, 26.

se, v. to see, 29, 1; pt. sien, 1, 3; sye, 3, 35; sygh, 18, 6; sigh, 64, 7; pt. sedd, 18, 5; saugh, 17, 21; pp. seyen, 21, 16; seyn, 108, 29; seye, 26, 7.

seche, v. to seek, 10, 24; 23, 22; used passively, 41, 27.

see, s. sea, 263, 28; 313, 31.

seel, s. seal, 617, 32.

sef, adv. only, 63, 35.

sege, 63, 19; 152, 19; scege, 254, 31; s. seat, encampment, siege.

seilden, adv. seldom, 6, 16.

seinge, part. pres. of verb to see, 86, 36.

seintewaries, s. holy things, 75, 25.

seke, 51, 25; sike, 52, 5; adj. sick.

sekenesse, s. sickness, 52, 28.

seleres, s. cellars, 125, 14.

self, 26, 12; seluc, 32, 23; adj. same.

semblant, 1, 17; semblaunt, 25, 12; 204, 3; s. semblance, pretence, appearance.

semblaunce, s. likeness, appearance, 45, 25; 57, 15; 170, 16.

sendall, s. thin silk, 281, 8.

seneschall, s. steward, 169, 13.

sercle, s. circle, 531, 1.

serkeles, s. circles, 220, 8.

sesed, v. seized, 649, 2.

sesid, v. ceased, 49, 23.

seth, 12, 30; sethe, 71, 22; conj. since.

sethen, adv. afterwards, 209, 35.

sette, v. to send, grant, 114, 17.

sewed, v. followed, 33, 30; 349, 35.

sewen, v. pursue, follow, 274, 18.

sey, v. to say, tell, 7, 22; 5, 21; 172, 1; pt. seyde, 7, 12; sede, 7, 17; seide, 1, 12; pp. seyde, 7, 5.

shalbe, shall be, 14, 34.

shamefest, adj. full of shame, 269, 33; shamefaste, 426, 11.

shapte, s. shape, form, 43, 30.

sheltron, s. division of soldiers, troop, company, 151, 13; 326, 6; 660, 24.

shet, pt. 9, 25; 14, 5; pp. 10, 10; shett, pp. 29, 26; shut.

shette, adj. shut, 545, 15.

shetynge, v. shooting, 170, 29.

shewde, 56, 22; sewde, 57, 17; v. appeared.

shof, v. shoved, 199, 18.

shofte, 208, 12; shoffe, 219, 19; s. shove, push.

shold, sholde, 1, 9; 6, 30; shulde, 1, 14; v. should.

sholdres, s. shoulders, 635, 17.

shone, 33, 22; shoon, 279, 25; s. shoes.

shour, 336, 24; 353, 14; shour, 663, 17; s. fight, encounter.

shrewdely, adv. in bits, 313, 5.

shrewe, s. giant, enemy, 347, 16.

shrewe, s. pity, sin, 568, 26.

shulder, s. shoulder, 211, 5.

shull, v. shall, 5, 34.

sibbe, s. relation, 373, 9.

siche, adj. such, 3, 1.

sigh, v. saw, 361, 8; 605, 27.

siker, adj. secure, safe, 32, 16.

sith, conj. since, 10, 5; 25, 25.

sithes, 24, 11; sythes, 7, 6; s. times.

sithes, s. sides, parties, 244, 31.

sitteth, v. becometh, 537, 9.

skaberke, 347, 21; skabrek, 118, 10; skawlerke, 340, 15 scabbard.

skirmerie, s. fencing, fighting with
the sword, 368, 20 ; 571, 5.
sklender, adj. slender, 279, 24.
skole, s. school, 86, 13.
skyle, s. skill, 27, 33.
slade, s. a valley, 256, 33.
slakede, v. slacken, 293, 13.
sle, 21, 23 ; slen, 15, 30 ; v. to
slay, kill.
slode, v. did slide, 570, 12.
slouthe, s. sloth, 640, 30.
slowe, 4, 3 ; slow, 217, 8 ; v.
slew.
snewen, v. follow, 296, 27.
soche, adj. such, 4, 7.
socour, s. succour, 50, 12.
soell, 4, 11 ; soill, 75, 5 ; sole, 9,
29 ; soole, 128, 33 ; sool, 297,
3 ; adj. alone.
sogect, 6, 30 ; soget, 627, 26 ; s.
subject.
soiour, s. sojourn, 311, 25.
somdell, s. somewhat, 135, 4.
someres, 192, 1 ; sommers, 378,
5 ; s. sumpter horses.
somowne, v. to summon, 41, 20 ;
249, 6.
somte, misprint, perhaps for smote,
299, 9.
sone, adv. soon, 3, 26.
sooll, adv. sole, 634, 1.
sop, 260, 33 ; soppe, 218, 29 ; s.
body, company.
soper, s. supper, 59, 22 ; 545, 26.
sopores, s. spurs, 299, 21.
sore, adv. very, sorely, 52, 13 ;
much, 169, 11.
sore, sorrow, 126, 35.
sore-holdynge, adj. very tenacious,
222, 8.
sorte, s. chance, lot, destiny, 36,
29.
soth, true, truth, 7, 12 ; 37, 35 ;
51, 16.
sotilly, adv. artfully, knowingly,
21, 36.
souercine, adj. sovereign, 48, 11.
souke, s. suck, 646, 31.
sowke, v. to suck, 112, 4.

sowderes, 120, 25 ; 174, 16 ;
sowdiours, 175, 28 ; s. soldiers.
sowowne, s. swoon, 134, 5.
sowowned, v. swooned, 208, 23.
sparble, v. to scatter, 396, 28.
sparbled, v. ran away, 274, 30 ;
scattered, 411, 6.
sparre, s. spar, 460, 16.
spayne, 615, 15 ; spaynell, 615,
17 ; s. spaniel.
splyndered, v. broke, splintered,
244, 24 ; 338, 36.
sporered, v. spurred, 282, 34.
spores, s. spurs, 101, 1 ; "at the
spore," 282, 27 ; 531, 33.
stablie, s. stand, 386, 26.
stablisshement, s. establishment,
61, 29.
stale, v. make water, 526, 12.
stall, kept at, i.e. kept back, with-
stood, 286, 9.
stalled, v. met in confusion, 324,
26.
stalleden, v. fixed, placed, 161, 28.
starke, adj. long, 214, 31.
startelinge, adj. spirited, 257, 3.
steill, 118, 16 ; stiel, 98, 20 ; s.
steel.
steirne, adj. stern, fierce, 43, 1.
stelen, adj. of steel, 119, 5.
stent, v. to cease, 145, 14.
stered, v. guided, directed, 4, 33.
sterten, v. started, leaped, 214, 34.
stightlynge, s. fear, dread, 408, 3.
still, s. steel, armour, 618, 21.
stilliche, adv. stilly, silently, 180,
36.
stinte, 253, 22 ; stinte, 548, 34 ;
v. remain, cease.
stynte, pt. stopped, 127, 11 ; 217, 33.
stodye, s. condition of mind, 243, 2.
stonyed, pp. stunned, 265, 30.
stounde, s. short time, 594, 29.
stoupe, v. to stoop, 119, 16.
stour, stoure, s. tumult, battle,
passion, 119, 20 ; 161, 16 ;
125, 2.
straitely, adv. strictly, closely,
221, 6.

stranght, v. stretched, handed, gave, 639, 15.

straungeled, pt. 4, 14; strangelid, pp. 4, 23; strangled.

streite, s. strait, 256, 1.

streite, adj. narrow, 558, 32.

streite, 126, 2; streyte, 205, 2; adj. strict.

streugthes, s. pl. form of strength, 1, 6.

stroied, pp. ruined, 5, 4.

stronge, adv. very, 52, 5.

strongeleche, adv. strongly, greatly, 13, 1.

stronke, adj strong, 380, 7.

stuffed, v. filled, garrisoned, 70, 16; 120, 30.

sturopes, s. stirrups, 117, 21.

stwarde, s. steward, 24, 9.

styghtled, pp. fought, struggled, 333, 3.

styth, 98, 12; stithi, 98, 14; stith, 98, 19; s. anvil.

sue, v. to follow, 206, 10.

suerdes, s. swords, 388, 14.

suffraite, s. suffering, 59, 1.

suffretouse, sufferers, 201, 35.

surbated, v. rushed, 531, 5.

sured, v. plighted, 628, 2.

surmounte, v. excel, 602, 3.

surnoun, s. surname, 57, 13.

sustene, v. stand, 354, 11.

suster, sustres, syster, s. sister, 4, 34; 5, 18; 7, 18; 399, 26.

suweth, v. follow, 210, 3; 331, 36.

swarned, pp. turned aside, 341, 36.

swenene, s. dream, 430, 25.

swerde, s. sword, 100, 17.

swight, adj. swift, 324, 35.

swote, adj. sweet, 133, 1.

swowne, s. swoon, 119, 6.

swyfht, adj. swift, 209, 36.

sye, v. see, 248, 15.

sye, v. saw, 597, 1.

sympilliche, adv. simply, 140, 32.

sympilly, adv. weakly, 78, 20.

symple, adj. weak, 116, 36.

tacched, pp. taken, 88, 4.

talent, s. disposition, desire, 32, 6; 573, 3.

talentif, adj. desirous, 352, 10.

targe, s. a small shield, 338, 24.

tarie, v. to wait, stay, 47, 35.

tarien, v. tarry, 259, 5.

taste, v. feel, touch, 681, 12.

tasted, v. tried, groped, 649, 6.

tastinge, pr. part. trying, 648, 26.

taught, v. (1) led, 316, 26; (2) told, 550, 3.

tecche, s. fault, peculiarity, 135, 34; 182, 1.

tecches, s. devices, 462, 33.

teche, v. teach, take or intrust to, 72, 18.

techynge, s. teaching, instruction, 7, 21.

teinte, 46, 10-12; teynte, 116, 11; s. tent.

tentefly, adv. steadfastly, 506, 16.

teyed, v. tied, 413, 30.

teysed, v. drawn, 590, 3.

thaire, pr. their, 5, 22.

tham, 2, 2; theym, 1, 15; 141, 36; pron. them.

than, 4, 12; thanne, 4, 13; adv. then.

tharchebisshop, the Archbishop, 104, 21.

tharldom, s. thraldom, 1, 20.

that, pro.=that which, 2, 34; 3, 2.

þat, conj. that, 73, 16.

thaugh conj. though, 103, 19.

the, pro. (1) thee, 44, 28; (2) they, 256, 4.

þe, adj. the, 63, 21: 352, 32.

theder, 36, 15; thider, 32, 20; adv. thither.

thei, pr. they, 3, 3.

þei, pron. they, 197, 33.

their, adv. there, 3, 16.

thencheson, s. the reason, cause, 28, 11.

thens, adv. thence, 25, 16.

thens-forth, adv. thenceforth, 121, 5.

ther, conj. where, 263, 18.

ther, adv. where, 25, 8.

ther-as, adv. where, 3, 15.

þer-inne, adv. therein, 188, 28.

thirthe, adj. third, 121, 34.

this, adj. these, 363, 14.

this, adv. thus, 14, 28.

thise,' pro. these, 3, 33.

thiside, n.=? this side, 562, 15.

tho, adv. then, thereupon, 7, 11; 44, 33; thoo, 273, 31.

tho, pro. those, 2, 22; thoo=those who? 162, 34.

thonkeden, v. thanked, 210, 1.

thourgh, prep. through, 4, 34; 34, 7.

thove, v.=thave, permit, allow, 18, 22.

thowz, conj. though, 2, 8.

thre, adj. three, 50, 4.

thunder, s. lightning, 387, 1.

þus, adv. thus, 79, 32.

tierce, s. the third hour of the artificial day, 182, 4; 274, 29.

tierme, s. time, 41, 20.

to, adv. too, 258, 7.

to-brosed, pp. bruised, battered, 268, 24; 548, 29.

to foren, adv. before, 201, 18.

to-geder, adv. together, 29, 36.

to hewen, hewn to pieces, 135, 23.

tokenynge, s. sign, token, 60, 32; 98, 3.

tole, v. told, 50, 19.

to-morou, s. to-morrow, 60, 22.

ton, the ton=the one, 216, 9.

tortue, adj. twisted, 206, 17.

tother, adj. the tother=that other, 34, 16.

tow, adj. two, 5, 16; towe, 214, 33.

towaile, s. towel, 225, 21.

towarde, adv. near at hand, 353, 25.

towon, s. town, 379, 8.

traied, pp. betrayed, 463, 10.

trauayle, 32, 25; traucill, 32, 28; traucile, 32, 30; 128, 23; traucyle, 122, 34; s. toil, injury, labour, pain.

trauers, in trauers, adv. contrarily, 262, 14; 429, 19.

trauerse, "on traverse," 425, 31; "a trauerse," 427, 17; adv. leeringly, with side glance.

trayned, pp. dragged, 299, 11.

tresour, s. treasure, 167, 6.

trewage, s. pledge, hostage, 50, 17; 126, 28.

trewis, s. truce, 505, 13.

troath, 18, 11; trouth, 107, 21; s. truth.

trobellion, s. ? storm, tempest, 324, 10.

tronchon, s. fragment, 248, 25.

tronchown, s. truncheon, staff, 156, 19.

trouble, adj. dense, thick, dark, 248, 5; troble, 248, 34.

trowe, v. think, suppose, 2, 34; 22, 22.

trumpes, s. trumpets, 276, 9.

trusse, v. pack up, 378, 5.

trussed, v. fastened, 259, 27.

trymbled, v. trembled, 27, 26.

tukked, pp. ? dressed, 279, 23; tucked up?

turment, s. tournament, 102, 36.

turmente, s. torment, 5, 20.

turney, s. tourney, 404, 33.

tweyn, 49, 1; tweyne, 129, 4; twey, 225, 22; two.

tymbres, s. spears, 117, 34.

tymbres, s. bells, 276, 12.

tysed, v. enticed, 418, 25.

un-ethe, adv. scarcely, 677, 15.

unpossible, adj. impossible.

untrouthe, s. untruth, falsehood, 69, 21.

valed, v. let down, 478, 13.

vauasour, s. a sort of inferior gentry, 204, 19; 307, 15.

vaunt garde, s. van guard, 151, 3; from French avant?

venged, pp. avenged, revenged, 119, 32.

venquysshed, v. gained, 56, 33.

vergier, s. orchard, 310, 6.

very, adj. true, 11, 27.

very, v. ferry, 605, 31.
viage, s. journey, voyage, 130, 7.
vilenis, 102, 31; vylenis, 127, 1;
vileyns, 26, 21; adj. disgraceful,
shameful.
viliche, adv. basely, 477, 12.
vitaile, s. provisions, 50, 12.
vn-couthe, adj. unknown, 190,
30; un-cowthe, 381, 22.
vnethe, 19, 7; vn-ethe, 154, 4;
vn-nethe, 172, 19; adv. scarcely.
vnther, adj. under 169, 5.
vn-to, prep. until, 160, 23.
vn-trewe, adj. untrue, 276, 34.
vntterly, adv. utterly, entirely,
181, 22.
voide, v. to leave, depart (make
empty), 108, 28–30.
volage, adj. ? light, giddy, 436, 1.
volente, volunte, 22, 30; 29, 21;
58, 29: voluntee, 201, 32; s.
will, pleasure.
vowarde, s. the vanguard, 285, 25.
voyde, adj. empty, vacant, 59, 21.
voyded, adj. 279, 25; open-worked.
Cf. Fr. *percé à jour.*
vp-right, adv. perpendicularly,
58, 11; 542, 7.
vp-right, adv. flat on the back,
128, 3; 476, 21.
vtas, s. that day week, 449, 12.
vyces, s. practices, deeds, 51, 6.
vyuier, s. ? fish pond, pool, vivary ?
308, 6.

wacche, 76, 9; 656, 25; waicche,
46, 14; s. watch, guard.
waisshe, 301, 11; wosh, 225, 20;
wossh, 301, 13; v. wash.
waisshen, 2, 3; waisch, 225, 25;
pp. washed.
wake, v. watch, 584, 29.
walop, s. gallop; a grete walop =
in full gallop, 209, 11.
walshe myle, s. 247, 36.
wape, v. to weep, 30, 10.
war, adj. aware, 274, 34; 654, 25.
warant, 29, 5; waraute, 162, 30;
v. save, preserve.

warantise, v. keep harmless, 269, 3.
warde, s. army, division, 286, 7.
wardeyns, s. guards, watchmen,
220, 8.
ware, adj. cautious, wary, 5, 26;
113, 2.
warishen, v. cure, 696, 24.
warne, v. to proclaim, command,
60, 15; used passively, 62, 16.
warrisshed, v. pp. recovered from
sickness, 173, 11.
waymentacion, 513, 33; weymen-
tacion, 347, 10; s. lamentation.
waymented, pp. lamented, 262, 2.
wedde, s. pledge, 477, 18.
weder, s. weather, 150, 33.
wedowe, s. widow, 596, 33.
wele, adv. well, 44, 27.
wele, v. to will, wish, intend, 54,
14.
well, v. 243, 26; to will, desire.
welwellinge, s. welfare, interests,
505, 35.
wende, v. ? would, 246, 6.
wende, v. intended, thought, 1,
12; 156, 7.
wene, v. to think, deem, 52, 19.
wepnes, s. weapons, 264, 2.
werre, s. war, 26, 27; 49, 21.
werre, v. to make war, 115, 6.
werreden, v. made war, 24, 10.
werrye, v. dwell, 318, 16.
werryen, v. 320, 15; make war on.
werse, adj. worse, 56, 28.
wery, adj. weary, 128, 23.
wete, v. to know, 10, 28; 28, 2;
wethet, 34, 17.
wetynge, s. knowledge, 14, 12.
weymente, v. lament, 513, 31.
what, adv. partly, in part, 205, 7.
whens, adv. whence, 44, 7.
where-as, conj. where, at which
place, 242, 22.
where-as = where were, 635, 9.
wherthourgh, adv. whereby, 17, 22.
whider, adv. whither, 61, 25.
whowle, v. to cry as a cat, 668, 9.
whowpe, v. to whoop, 358, 23;
whowped, 168, 3.

wiesshe, v. to wish, 113, 36.
wight, adj. active, swift, 136, 22; 350, 28.
wight, s. weight, 57, 35.
wiste, v. knew, perceived, 4, 12.
wite, 45, 4; 13, 11; witen, 82, 20; v. to know, perceive; wyte, 5, 23; I do the to wite, 93, 21=make to know.
with-holde, v. receive, retain, 372, 21.
with-outen, prep. without, 69, 18.
with-sey, v. to deny, 204, 4.
wode, s. wood, 199, 10; 337, 22.
wode, adj. mad, 165, 5; 196, 19.
woke, s. week, 82, 33.
wolde, would, 2, 12; 4, 1.
woned, v. dwelt, 687, 13.
wordynesse, s. worthiness, 203, 32.
worschipe, v. to honour, 166, 2.
worship, 20, 29; 134, 2; wurship, 54, 9; 132, 13; s. dignity, honour, worth-ship.
worthen, v. be, go, 58, 13.
woste, v. knowest, 19, 36.
wote, v. knew, 101, 28; wote, pres. know, 162, 9, 11.
woued, v. wooed, loved, 137, 11.
woxen, v. waxed, grown. 228, 14.
wrathe, 18, 16; 41, 8; wratthe, 3, 31; 639, 30; v. to be angry, enraged.
wreche, s. wrath, anger, vengeance, 113, 27.
wrenne, s. wren, 573, 2.
wreten, pp. written, 53, 32.
wroken, pp. revenged, 451, 22.
wrothe, adj. angry, 3, 26.
wrother, adj. more angry, 4, 1.

wurship, s. dignity, honour, 54, 9.
wurshipfullest, adj. most honoured, 5, 12.
wymple, s. covering for the neck, 361, 14; 681, 14.
wynnynge, s. spoil, 224, 25.
wyssher, s. miser? 168, 12.
wytinge, 190, 3; wityuge, 12, 19; 45, 9; s. knowledge.

yaf, pt. gave, 3, 16; pp. yove, yoven, 22, 12; 4, 7.
yat, s. gate, 509, 13.
yates, s. gates, 125, 10.
ye, adv. yea, 12, 34; 32, 9.
yed, 167, 27; yede, 2, 13; yeden, 1, 15; went.
yef, conj. if, 2, 9; but yef=unless, 2, 5; 5, 6; 182, 32.
yefte, s. gift, 4, 8; 55, 21.
yelde, v. to yield, 33, 9.
yelde, pp. yielded, 8, 21.
yen, s. eyes, 85, 33; 648, 17.
yesse, adv. yes, 54, 11; 85, 21; 169, 27.
yeste, s. ? feasts, 55, 28.
yeve, v. to give, 47, 26.
yie, s. eye, 304, 36.
ylles, s. isles, 316, 13.
ympe, s. part of a tree, 418, 16.
ynde bende or *undé bendé*, ? 161, 32.
ynge, adj. young, 198, 4.
yole, 63, 30; yoole, 96, 13; s. Christmas.
yoven, pp. given, 106, 17; 241, 8.
ys, v. is, 103, 32.
ysse, v. to issue forth, 113, 23; yssed, pt. 207, 19.